by Angela Wren

For permission requests, contact the publisher below:

Cayélle Publishing/Celest Teen Imprint
Lancaster, California USA
www.CayellePublishing.com

Cayélle® is a registered trademark of Cayélle Corporation

Orders by U.S. trade bookstores and wholesalers, please contact:
Freadom@Cayelle.com

Categories: 1. Fantasy 2. Young Adult 3. Supernatural/Contemporary Fantasy
Printed in the United States of America

Cover Art by Ljiljana Romanovic
Interior Design & Typesetting by Ampersand Bookery
Edited by Dr. Mekhala Spencer

ISBN: 978-1-952404-73-3 [paperback]
ISBN: 978-1-952404-72-6 [ebook]
LCCN 2021951280

A CAYÉLLE IMPRINT

Firekind

DEDICATION

For the ones who dream of more...

Chapter One

The magic of the Fagradalsfjall volcano system was on display, and Poppy wasn't about to miss the fireworks. Scattering gravel, she pulled into her driveway, rushed inside, and jogged upstairs. Her fingers flew over the keyboard as she searched for the webcam trained on the new series of fissures opening near the young Icelandic volcano.

Biting into an apple, she opened the sushi she'd grabbed at the end of her shift. Because of work – at the lone Target in Riverston, Missouri – Poppy had missed the beginning coverage of the newest eruption. Now, she had all of Friday night to witness the fiery plumes of lava and glowing lava fields. But catching sight of the screen, she dropped the apple. The live stream of the eruption was replaced with, *Webcam Offline*.

No! No! No! Searching for another webcam, she clicked link after link. A camera trained on the north side of the mountain showed only grayish fog, and another wasn't much better. On the shelves above, her collection of gemstones, geodes, and rock specimens glared along with her, blue in the glow of the laptop.

Ever since increased seismic activity had indicated magma intrusion, she'd been waiting for the eruption – her first opportunity to study a major volcanic event. Her fists clenched. *This is just typical.* Disappointment curdling in her stomach, Poppy spun, grabbed her bag, and hopped up. She needed to move, to get some air. Maybe the view would improve by the time she returned. It wasn't like she could hop on a plane to Iceland. Not with work, the cell phone bill due, Deidre's medicine to pay for…

In the living room, her mother huddled on the sofa, chin on her chest, asleep in front of *Renovation Ruination*. A glass of Chardonnay tilted in her lap, barely upright. If hope-deferred was typical for Poppy, passed out on the couch was a typical Friday night for Deidre.

Poppy sighed, her chest tightening with an ambivalent mixture of tenderness and irritation. Paired with her purple garage sale dress, the gray streaks in Deidre's auburn hair looked peak flower-child. Wrinkles surrounded her elegantly curved cheekbones, as perfect as if a renaissance sculptor had shaped them. Some days Poppy wished she'd taken after her mom. Some days she didn't. Today was one of those days. But Deidre was the only mom she had, and Poppy had decided a long time ago to make the best of it.

Intentionally, Poppy stepped on a loose floorboard, squeaking the wood like a crypt hinge. With a snort, Deidre startled awake. Dropping the sushi on the coffee table, Poppy plucked the wine glass from Deidre's fingers, took a swig, and wrinkled her nose. "That's awful."

Reclaiming it, Deidre finished it in one gulp. "Barefoot does the job." Yawning, she focused on the Geico commercial parading across the television. "Oh! I've missed my show." She pawed around for the remote. "I thought you were watching volcano death and destruction somewhere in Russia."

"Iceland." Poppy had given up trying to explain her interest in volcanos. "Going for a walk."

Happy wrinkles deepened around Deidre's mouth. "Oh good! Normal behavior. Tell me you're going to pick up some guys. Or go clubbing. Something like that."

"I'm going to pick up some guys and go clubbing."

Deidre tilted her head. "You're joking."

"Of course I'm joking, Mom."

Rolling her eyes, Deidre handed her the glass. "I need a refill."

Poppy slid the sushi to her. "Promise to eat something."

Deidre muttered under her breath, poking at the sticky rice.

In the kitchen, Poppy tilted the bottle of Deidre's Risperidone. Four pills left. She scribbled a note to pick up the refill. Over the past six months, Deidre's worst crisis had been a persistent fear of bats getting into the house; best keep a good thing going. The grin lines frequenting her mom's face, hearing her snappy retorts, made it easier to breathe somehow. It made everything easier.

Shrugging into her anorak, Poppy slung her bag over her shoulder. "See you later."

"Hold on." Deidre shuffled toward her, moving like a drunken bumblebee.

Rotating the wine glass on the counter, Deidre cleared her throat. "So, your Dad's coming home for a visit. Sooner than I expected. Maybe in the next month." Her eyes darted around, and her toes curled. "He's really looking forward to seeing you."

Do we have to talk about this now? Tonight? This very moment? Poppy struggled with the zipper of her anorak. *No, we don't.*

Finding her hand, Deidre gripped it, the little bones in her fingers sharp. "Look, Treefrog, I'm sorry about all this. He—"

"Yeah, I know how it is." Poppy extracted her hand. "Call if you need me, alright?"

Poppy escaped to the front porch, sucker-punch nausea joining the burning in her stomach. Even after four months, Felix Paquin's failure to show at her high school graduation still stung. Poppy had tried feigning indifference, parroting the explanation that his work was important enough to justify his absence, but her heart still felt bruised. She didn't want to be excited about the possibility of his visit, but a part of her still leapt for it, like a crow hopping to a carcass on the road.

Hugging her elbows in against the chilly air, she set out, knowing where her feet would take her. The spice of dried leaves mingled with the smell of grass, as if their neighbor had just mowed their lawn. The scent coalesced with the earthiness of the Twin River, which stretched north below the bluffs where her neighborhood perched. Rain was coming. Maybe soon, maybe in the middle of the night.

Jogging to warm herself up, she descended the hill out of her neighborhood, passing cape cods with peeling paint and squat bungalows. On the High Street, the cigarette smoke from Paddy's corner pub tickled her throat. She hurried past the chink of dishes and the raucous harmony of the Irish trio. If Katherine were here instead of at college, she would suggest they slip inside and sneak a pint of Guinness.

As she approached the defunct city park overlooking the river – known as Olive Street landing – Poppy's legs dragged. Without Kat's friendship, she wouldn't have survived Riverston High. They'd often while away Friday nights here, munching on onion rings from Bobo's diner and dreaming about the future. Lately, when Poppy visited the landing, it felt as if Kat lingered right around the corner, her red Civic idling as she applied lipstick in the mirror. Poppy could almost hear her laugh echo off the river.

Now, eight hours away at Vanderbilt University, Kat was only as close as Snapchat, and that sucked worse than a glitching webcam. Poppy wanted to message her, but it was Friday night. Hopefully, Kat would be hanging out with new friends. Besides, she would inquire if Poppy had asked anyone from work to hang out (ahem, the new guy), and Poppy didn't feel like explaining herself tonight.

She sank onto a bench facing the river. Above, skeletal branches of locust trees stretched into the darkness, a few stubborn leaves fluttering down to join the piles gathered on the floor. Iron railing shielded a north-facing overlook, where rows of train tracks lay below, lining the wide, fast-flowing expanse of the Twin. If she couldn't study the volcano, the delicious gloominess of the night was the next best thing; it felt as though she'd stepped into a gothic novel. It lessened the sting of her disappointment, of Kat's absence, if only a little.

A train thundered by, the locomotives growling like mechanical tigers, shaking the concrete under her feet. The draft tossed her hair, stirring the mist drifting around the landing. A horn blast wailed over the river, echoing between the bluffs. As the train disappeared, the scent of coal lingered in the air, the taste dirty in her mouth.

Mist swarmed the rails and curled around the landing lights; animalistic in the way it crept. Poppy clutched her bag in her lap, twisting the worn leather straps, scanning the darkness over the river, then the foggy street. Goosebumps flooded her neck and she pulled the anorak tighter around her body.

The mist rolled and crept until it obscured the lights from Paddy's back patio. It sweated in slimy beads on her fingers and face. Involuntarily, the muscles of her shoulders tensed; someone was leering at her, hidden by the misty shadows. She scoffed at the suspicion. It was only a little fog. She'd been here a million times at night and never felt threatened.

But not without Kat. Glancing around, Poppy's mouth went dry.

Like silent storm clouds, the fog crowded the landing, con-cealing the curb and the street beyond, as thick as a blanket thrown over the park. As though it had been muted, the clamor from Paddy's faded and the silence pressed into her ears, like being underwater. Instinctively, she pawed through her bag for the metal cylinder of pepper spray.

From behind, a slimy touch on her neck, a *shusshhh*. Flying to her feet, she whirled around, her heart pounding in her ears. Mist congregated around her, stepping on her toes, crowding her into a corner. Nothing explained the phantom touch. At least nothing visible.

With a crunching of glass, the landing lights went out. Something snatched the phone out of her hand and it clattered to the concrete. Spindly shadows surrounded her – apparitions of trees, growing out of the mist, stretching higher than the streetlights. As if she'd been transported from the landing into an ancient forest, malignant and rotten to its roots.

No. She felt around for the phone. *This isn't real. I'm just tired.* Her hands shook. Was this what it felt like when Deidre had an episode? *No!* Poppy gritted her teeth. *That's not what this is.*

But the dense weight of the mist crippled her movements, her sense of direction. *Forget the phone.* Heart thundering, she lunged for the street. But the mist slowed her flight, wrapping around her ankles like she'd stumbled into a bog. A shadowy tree loomed in her path, and she yelped.

It's not real. This can't be real.

From all directions, mist-hands pawed at her, surrounding her like weeds in an overgrown field. Breath ragged, she broke into a faltering run, searching for the curb, but finding grass instead. She tripped and pain radiated through her shins. Scrambling up, she fought for each step, feeling the way with her hands, but the location of the street – the way out – evaded her.

The pressure in the atmosphere intensified and her ears popped. Gravel underfoot. Train tracks and ballast. How had she ended up so far from the landing, across the tracks, at the bank of the river? Her bag slipped out of her grasp. She cried out, but the mist shoved her voice back into her mouth, like a gag.

Something squishy and strangling surrounded her ankles, yanking her off balance and down the muddy bank into the river. Gasping at the frigid water, she paddled as the river climbed up her body, wrapping around her neck, assisting the fog with creeping, arm-like eddies. Water lapped at her chin and she tilted her face, fighting to stay above the surface. From the depths of the river, a ghostly glow began to spread, illuminating the weeds covering the riverbed, rippling like an underwater forest.

She tried to scream, but again the sensation of being gagged stopped her.

A powerful whirlpool pulled her toward the glow. She thrashed and kicked, fighting to stay close to the bank. Mud sucked at her feet and one of her sneakers slipped off. Reeds scraped her ankles. A sharp pain stabbed the ball of her foot.

She dragged in a breath and forced out, "Help! I'm in the riv—"

A tug at her ankle plunged her underwater. Scissoring her legs, she broke the surface, gasping, sputtering through her hair, but again the mist forced her head below the water. A grip slithered up her legs.

Holding her breath, her heart thundered, and the water frothed and bubbled in her ears. Her fingers raked over a branch, and she gripped it with both hands, but it broke free from the bank, sending her deeper into the river, rotated by the currents, nearing the eerie light.

In the depths of the Twin, a pale creature hovered, its sickly luminescence penetrating the river's murkiness. With a terrifying stillness, it locked onto her, like a spider feeling a tug on its web. Despite the sting of the water, Poppy's eyes widened with horror. The creature's formless limbs merged and disappeared like currents in the mist-illuminated water, gripping her legs, pulling her toward it. White eyes with long slit pupils took up most of its doughy face, above a puckered mouth, wrinkled like water-soaked skin. Dizzy with fear, she struck at its limbs, her heart thudding fast, her lungs aching.

Stars peppered her vision. *Oh God, no. Not like this. They'll never find my body. Who will take care of Mom?*

The water bubbled as something solid slammed into her shoulder, clasped her around the ribs, and flung her away from the creature, toward the riverbank. The creature's expression sharpened, its pupils widening and writhing from within – a maggot cartoon of anger. A flash of light – brighter than the unnatural glow – split the water like lightning. Then the water clouded, distorting her view.

Adrenaline threaded her veins and she kicked for the surface, almost free. But as she broke out of the water, filling her lungs, a stinging grip at her ankles dragged her under again. The water frothed with the struggle, growing murky, disorienting her.

Ribbons of light flashed through the murkiness. The creature shrunk its limbs close to its body, like a dying spider. Through the haze, a person's silhouette appeared and struck the creature's gut, causing an eruption of dark liquid. The grip on her ankles loosened and vanished. Abruptly, the light dimmed, and the water went black. Warm, unpleasant currents slithered by her cheek.

Move! Taxed by the burning in her lungs, Poppy thrashed, but her limbs only flapped weakly, disconnected from her body. Worse, she didn't know what direction to swim.

Arms hooked her waist and dragged her through the water, so quickly her hair covered her face. The impact at the surface jolted her and she gasped, choking. Mud pulled and sucked at her legs, and her head dipped under the surface again. Water invaded her lungs, burning and rasping. She shuddered and surrendered to the stinging darkness.

Chapter Two

T he purple of the deep night clouded the sky through Poppy's window. Sprawled on her bed, her lungs seared, and her hair hung in dank clumps, soaking her cold, crumpled pillow. A soggy pile of clothes next to her bed tinged the air with a swampy scent.

On her nightstand, her inhaler and phone lay next to her bag. Snatching up the medicine, she took a hit. Delusions stampeded into her consciousness – the mist, the horrible white creature, the water stinging her lungs. Her temples throbbed. *That can't be what happened. That's impossible.*

Scrabbling for her phone, she knocked her bag to the floor. The screen revealed the time: Saturday, 4:34 a.m. In a couple hours, she had to be at work. Her hands shook so violently she dropped the phone. *It's not real. It can't be real.*

What happened between ten o'clock and now? How did I escape the water? How did I get home? With my phone? And what was – her stomach clenched. *that thing? And who was in the water with me?*

Since returning to sleep was impossible, she stumbled to the bathroom and showered, scrubbing the mud and the smell of the river off her skin until it stung. The ragged gash on the bottom of her foot had been cleaned and bandaged, the laceration held together with surgical tape. But by whom?

Under the streams of hot water, she gripped the tiled walls, fighting dizzy spells. *There has to be a reasonable explanation for this. Think.*

No reassuring explanations came to mind. Thinking only rattled the cage where she'd stuffed her panic, feeding it, and that wouldn't do. Mindlessly, she dressed for work and whiled away the time before she had to leave rotating through the meager webcam views of Fagradalsfjall, chugging coffee and fabricating plausible explanations. It wasn't like she'd never experienced *weird* before.

The *weird* thing was; she had very little memory of her life before age twelve. In fact, 'very little' was wishful thinking. That year, her body had been ravaged by a strange flu causing her to spike a fever of 103 F for a straight week, frying the memories stored in her hippocampus. Her convalescence had taken two months. The first time she'd tried to walk across the room, she'd passed out cold.

In the months after, her hair shed its crimson pigment for mottled silver, a grannie-like hue that resisted all but the most expensive hair dyes, which they couldn't afford. Sure, silver hair was a thing now, but the trend had shown up too little, too late for her. Poppy had spent much of her early adolescence in an awkward, don't-look-at-me crouch, her hair braided or swept up into a bun, less of a target for ridicule.

During her recovery, her family had moved to Riverston. Eternally confused by computers, Deidre had failed to back up their files, so when the hard drive ended up in pieces in their driveway, they lost most of their family photos. Sometimes it felt as though she'd never had a childhood – no Christmases, lemonade stands, bike rides, or playdates. Her parents' vague explanations anchored her history, insufficiently, and as they'd never broached the foreign world of social media, Poppy often felt like a ghost. Her father's increasing absences had exacerbated that feeling.

But there was probably a more obvious reason for last night's weirdness. Her mom's medicine cabinet was packed with drugs like Risperidone, Olanzapine, and Xanax. Even on a good day Deidre was nutballs. And such afflictions tend to run in families. *No.* She wouldn't – she couldn't think about it.

Refilling her coffee mug, she paused in front of the painting mounted above the fireplace, a ritual reserved for her worst days. The painting was of her and her Dad – a moment of unremembered happiness. Felix was reclined in a wood framed chair, his grin accenting his square jaw. His eyes shone ghostly gray and his powerful hands rested on his knees. On his lapel gleamed a detailed emblem of a compass star. Maybe seven years of age, she stood next to the chair, her arm draped about his shoulders, a wide smile crinkling her face, her red hair as brilliant as a poppy. The window behind them was thrown open, revealing grassy hills and pine forests.

Ambivalent warmth spread in her chest. The explanation of her father's absences was simple; he had an important job he couldn't talk about. A job protecting thousands of people. The kind of job which required sacrifice on the part of his family. She'd heard the explanation so often she could mime it along with Deidre.

But he would visit soon. And maybe things would change. Even the government must know people can't sustain that kind of life forever. Maybe he would have good news. Maybe he would finally be there for her, for Deidre. And she could go to college, actually visit volcanos like Fagradalsfjall. Like Eyjafjallajokull. Someday.

Where are you when I really need you, Dad? When Mom needs you? When I'm afraid of what might be happening to me?

By the time she claimed a parking space at Target, Poppy mustered enough composure to function, muting her fear and confusion about the night before. Glancing at her reflection in the visor mirror, she groaned. Somehow, fuzzy strands of her silver hair had slipped out of the fishtail braid she'd labored over. Shadows camped out under her eyes, mingling with the freckles sprinkled across her nose, casting her eyes into a colorless hue that was almost creepy.

Jogging into work, her thoughts lingered on the new guy. Scanning the store for his tall form, she greeted coworkers Bella and Cheri, logged in at her checkout station, and clipped on her nametag. *Relax,* she told herself. *Stay cool.* But her thoughts argued, spiraling. *What's wrong with you? Acting like nothing happened last night? That isn't normal.*

But I don't know what happened last night. What else can I do? She asked herself.

Thom Magnusson glided out of the break room with easy, long-legged strides, paperwork under his arm. He'd started about a month ago and her tongue still malfunctioned around him – even on normal days. Today was anything but routine.

His footsteps approached. "Morning, Poppy."

She swallowed hard, mustering a smile. "Hey."

Meeting his eyes required her to look up, unusual considering she was five feet, nine inches tall herself. He handed her a Target-branded document. Ungluing her gaze from the riot of colorful tattoos creeping up both his forearms, she scanned it.

"Policy updates," His mouth twitched with a grin. "Everyone's favorite. Let's just pretend we had a meeting about this and go on with the day."

"Really?" Her mouth melted into a smile. "No meeting?"

"Just kidding. I wish that was an option." He glanced toward the Starbucks. "Better get your coffee."

He distributed the papers, and slipped away, his red polo tucked neatly into his belted jeans. Poppy caught herself staring. Looking away, she retreated to the Starbucks counter to dose up.

Coffee in hand, flipping through the papers, she tried – unsuccessfully – to not watch him as he fetched his own coffee and chatted with one of the other managers. Anything to distract herself. She couldn't tell his age, but she wouldn't have been surprised if he was pushing twenty-three or twenty-four. *Probably a little old for you, Pops.*

If she was honest, she didn't care.

Thom was an enigma in man form, a truly interesting – and surprisingly kind – person. All the chain-smoking hags loved him, and they *never* loved managers. Sharing cigarettes, he sat outside during break and listened to their stories. He went out of his way to make schedules that helped Cheri, the single mom with three kids. When he discovered Rose's hip hurt after standing too long at her checkout station, he found her a chair. Unlike past managers, if he had a moment, he didn't shirk menial tasks like bathroom checks. And he could tame troublesome customers with a mere eyebrow raise.

Before the end of Thom's first week, Poppy came to the inconvenient conclusion that he was irresistibly attractive. To make matters worse, when his face crinkled with amusement, shedding his usual stoicism, a compelling sense of familiarity gripped her brain. On good days, the feeling made her feel awkward and desperate. On worse days, creepy.

In all but thought, she'd repressed her attraction. And thus far, being privately smitten with her manager hadn't resulted in any royal screw-ups, so there was hope for her yet. If she could just keep it together today.

The meeting passed without a hitch. She even resisted gazing at Thom's hazel eyes as if they were labradorites in a geology lab. Eying her hair, Bella complimented her fishtail braid, and she managed to respond with a normal, "Thanks." Things were looking up. Miraculously, she'd kept her shit together.

During a lull in customers, Poppy slumped against the counter at her station – her body leaden with exhaustion, her lungs sore. Outside, the sunlight reflected off the parking lot, blazing golden through the mechanical doors. The doors opened and closed, revealing a strange mirage-like energy field, shot with hot, gold light. The ground seemed to tremble beneath her feet.

Memory of the murky depths of the river ambushed her; the eerie glow, the cold squishy arms as they tugged her beneath the surface.

Don't think about it. Don't. Think. About. It. Her heart rose into her throat like it wanted to escape. Rubbing her forehead, she shut her eyes. The white-creature-thing appeared in her mind; the widening pupils, the long formless limbs reaching for her. Her hands trembled. *This isn't real. Not here, not now, not at work!*

Merchandise thumped onto the conveyer belt. A couple quarts of motor oil and a twelve pack of Guinness trundled toward her.

If it had been next month, she'd have been old enough to ring up the alcohol. As it was, three weeks shy of nineteen, she needed a manager, and none were in sight. It was near lunchtime. She flipped her station light to blinking and grabbed one of the jugs of Amsoil.

The customer-guy wore a denim jacket. A vintage-ish canvas backpack hung over one shoulder below a shiny black undercut. Across his neck crept a white-silver tattoo of a web, scarred on his skin in places. Dark brown eyes traveled over her, stopping on her nametag.

"Hello, Poppy," he said, a grin oiling his mouth.

Poppy couldn't say exactly why, but her body tensed with wariness. "Did you find everything you need today?"

A row of immaculate teeth flashed behind his lips. "Naw. But that's okay."

Looking around, she stopped, hovering over the Guinness. He leaned against the counter, his eyes fixed on her with a suffocating gaze – like crude oil on waterfowl – so close she smelled wintergreen on his breath.

"You look like you could use some of that," he said.

"Sorry. I need a manager for this."

"S'okay." His grin twitched again. "I don't mind."

Well I do, she thought, zipping up her jacket and hugging her elbows. Why did this guy creep her out so much? After all, he was only a customer. Just a guy. No reason to be afraid of him.

Shoulders back, she met his eyes, as if to reassure herself this was true. His brown irises appeared darker now, like masses of soil, an avalanche of earth, squeezing the air from her lungs…*No, Poppy. There's always a reason to be afraid.*

Footsteps approached. Abruptly, the customer-guy straightened up, like he'd been poked with a cactus. The fear gripping her snapped and air flooded her lungs. Thom Magnusson glanced from her, to the guy, the beer, and back to the guy. His eyebrows drove into a frown, lines deepening around his mouth, visible even through his short beard.

The guy slid his sunglasses back on and smirked, but it lacked the bite of his earlier arrogance. "Can I get my beer now or what?"

In icy silence, Thom completed the transaction. Fidgeting in his jacket pocket, the guy dropped some cash on the counter – the jingle of the coin startled her. Thom dumped the bag of motor oil on the end of the station and shoved the beer into the guy's arms. The venom in his expression made her step back involuntarily.

"Have a nice day." The scowl on Thom's face would've intimidated a felon.

A tense silence filtered around the checkout lanes.

Posturing, sunglasses-guy grinned, his gaze flickering to her before he swaggered out of the store. Thom observed him until he reached a parked motorcycle. Not even sure what she was going to say, Poppy started to stammer.

But Thom was already across the lobby and through the doors, marching toward the guy, who was strapping on a helmet.

"Whoa," Bella said. "What did he do?"

Poppy just shook her head. Outside, Thom halted next to the bike, blocking her view of the customer. His back was to her, making it impossible to read what sort of chat they were having. Turning back to the register she tried to reset herself, but after a moment, ended up facing the doors again, watching nervously.

Returning to the entrance, Thom glided through the mechanical doors, his expression mild, like nothing had happened. Their eyes met, and he headed in her direction.

Fidgeting with her braid, she swallowed hard. He paused next to the register, regarding her for the space of three heartbeats, his expression as readable as a faded receipt.

He turned off her station light. "Are you okay?" His voice was throaty, like he'd overused it.

"Uh. That guy, I couldn't ring up…the alcohol. So I—" She trailed off. *You're babbling in front of Thom Magnusson. Keep it together, girl.*

"You did what you were supposed to do." Except for a tiny lift of his eyebrows, his expression remained as emotional as a bag of rocks. "No worries."

The motorcycle roared as it sped by the entrance. A frown dented the space between his eyebrows as he tracked it. "Let me know if you see that guy again, okay?"

Poppy frowned. What did he know about this guy? "Was he just released from Calgoa or something?" she asked.

He turned back to her. "Calgoa?"

Seeing the concern in his hazel eyes, Poppy felt silly. She was making a bigger issue out of the situation than it warranted. She didn't want Thom to think she was fragile, or something worse. "Forget it."

"The medium security prison east of town." Cheri said from a register nearby. "They release on Saturdays."

"No. He wasn't." Thom's voice stayed flat and unconcerned, but the wrinkles across his forehead deepened.

Begging the universe for a customer with a loaded cart, she glanced around, fidgeting with the end of her braid. Why did she have to make everything so awkward? Thom didn't move.

Leaning toward her, Thom lowered his voice. "Why don't you take five minutes? Get a drink. Some fresh air." He smelled like fresh air, like morning in the forest.

Poppy swallowed. "No, it's okay. I'm okay."

"Of course, you are." He glanced around. "But we're not busy. No harm in taking a moment."

Before she could rattle off another excuse, he walked off. Poppy stared after him, her cheeks burning. Facing the register again, her vision pitched, and she grabbed the counter. Maybe a short break wouldn't be such a bad idea.

When she was certain she could make it to the Starbucks without face-planting in the middle of the lobby, she bought a cold brew and settled on the bench outside. Was this weirdness connected to last night? Even worse, was whatever illness afflicted her mom activating in her DNA?

Googling *'symptoms of fugue states'*, her shoulders tensing up as she scrolled through the results. Could her coworkers – Thom Magnusson – see her cracking? She stiff-armed the thoughts. Did it really matter what Thom Magnusson thought of her when she had bills to pay? No, it didn't.

Chapter Three

By the end of her shift, angry, purple clouds unloaded a torrent of rain, flooding the parking lot, shaking the store with growling peals of thunder. Poppy plodded to the breakroom to fetch her bag, eager to escape back home to volcano webcams. But, at the side door exit, Thom held his bike helmet, surveying the storm with a frown. The rain splashed on his shoes and beaded on his tattooed arms.

He. Needs. A. Ride. Poppy. Ask him. Her eyes combed his broad shoulders and panicked warmth slithered through her body. *After today?* Zipping up her bag, she slung it over her shoulder and pivoted. *Screw it. Why not?*

"Hey. Do you want a ride?" she asked. "Or would you rather swim?"

His expression softened, like he was coming out of faraway thoughts. "Yeah." He smiled, crinkling the skin around his eyes. "That'd be great. Thanks."

They exited out the side door, rain pelting their shoulders. She jogged ahead, suddenly worried that her mom might've left a pile of garage sale crap in the passenger seat.

Whew. Just newspapers. Tossing them in the back, she slid into the driver's seat. Thom folded himself into the passenger seat, adjusting it so his knees weren't crammed against the glovebox.

She fidgeted with the stereo and left *Ben Howard* playing. *Screw him if he doesn't like it.* Her face flushed. A white-knuckled grip on the steering wheel, she pulled out of the parking space. "So, where am I going?"

"Take a right," he said. "Go up to Laclede and then east to Sonnet."

The windshield wipers squeaked and flew. He rubbed a tattoo on his forearm, his forehead scrunching as he surveyed the water pooling in the intersection. "Biking in this would be awful. You really saved my ass."

"Sure. Happy to." She adjusted her hold on the steering wheel, painfully aware of every move of her body.

"So, do you like working at Target so far?" She almost cringed. Now that she had her chance, now that she was alone with him and they could talk non-work stuff, she was choking.

He shrugged. "It's okay. Nice change of pace."

"What did you do before this?"

"I'm a veteran."

A grisly pink scar started at the back of his forearm, grazed his elbow, and then cut deeply into his bicep, disappearing underneath his red shirt sleeve, marring the cobalt waves that covered that part of his arm. It wasn't the first time she'd noticed it. Veins crawled over his muscles like rivers on a map, almost concealed by the artwork. Muscles. Lots of them. The kind of muscles a life drawing instructor might dream of. Her face grew hot.

"Oh. Where were you stationed?"

"A lot of places." He glanced at her, a corner of his mouth twitching in a smile. "I can't talk about it."

She blinked. There it was again, the interesting lilt she'd noticed in his speech, an emphasis on the *R*s and *W*s, especially when he was amused.

He nudged her. "I'm just kidding, Poppy."

"Yeah. Hilarious. I've never heard that one before."

They passed an overflowing storm drain. She swerved into the turn lane to avoid the water. The interior of the car grew stuffy with humidity and she tapped the defrost.

He pointed. "Go right at Seventh."

"You're brave to bike this route," she said. "Even on a good day."

"It's not too bad. I enjoy it."

The car surged onward through the rain. Ahead, the traffic light turned yellow. The Taurus shuddered and purred, coming to a stop. *Ben Howard* crooned.

"So, where are you from?" she asked.

The gray flecks rimming his green irises stood out, the color of an overcast sky through a canopy of trees. A coppery-colored patch dominated his left iris, the hue of fall leaves. Again, the sense of familiarity ambushed her, so powerful she had to look away. *I've seen those eyes before. Other than at work. But how could that be?*

"Hmm. How to answer that." He swept his hair away from his forehead. "I guess I'm not…really from anywhere. I've lived in a lot of places." He fidgeted with the leather cuff on his wrist and then rested his elbow on the car door, rubbing his neck. "My father's Icelandic. My mother's American."

She gaped. "Iceland!"

His expression sparked with amusement. "I usually don't get that kind of response. I think I like it."

A honk from behind startled her. Unnoticed, the light had turned green. Biting her lip, she accelerated. "There are a lot of – volcanos. There."

"Yes, there are. You must like volcanos."

"I want to study them. At the university in Reykjavik. And other…things."

He tilted his head, regarding her with sincere interest. "Fascinating."

She couldn't suppress her goofy smile. *He said fascinating. Fascinating!* "So, how did you end up here?"

"Long story. Maybe I'll tell you over lunch break sometime."

Over lunch break? Her heart did a little leap. *Yes, please.* "Have you ever visited?" she asked, fascinated. "Iceland?"

"I lived there until I was fourteen."

"So you speak Icelandic?"

"Yfirleitt ekki, en ég get talað hana ef ég þarf þess."

That explains the lilt.

"What did you say?" she asked.

"Not usually, but I can if I need to."

"But your name? Don't Icelandic people have to pick from specific names?"

His grin faded, replaced by a look Poppy didn't recognize. She focused on the road again, "Sorry, that was nosy—"

"No." His smile reappeared. "Most people here don't know that much. But I guess you're not most people."

Poppy bit the side of her cheek. Was her face flaming?

"My full name is Valur Thomas Magnusson. It was a compromise between my parents, but my mom always called me Thom, so it stuck."

Hearing the accent when he said his full name, she blushed harder, scrambling for another question, a distraction. "How do you handle living here, in the Midwest? It's so boring."

"It's not too bad. Change of pace, remember?"

Again that smile. *Keep your eyes on the road, girl.*

"Where are you from?" he asked.

This was one of those moments when she would've given a year of her life to have a more interesting answer. "I don't remember anything about the city where I was born. So, I guess I'm from Riverston."

Serious lines deepened across his forehead. Again, there was a prick deep in her brain, an acute sense of familiarity. But it was elusive, like something too afraid to come out of hiding.

Rain splattered across the windshield, obscuring the road. She leaned forward, concentrating on the lanes. A stoplight gleamed ahead. "What was the deal with that guy today?"

Lines deepened between his eyebrows. "There's been complaints about him. And he's been warned. Thought I'd jog his memory."

She didn't remember seeing the guy before. Of course, he might've visited another station, so that didn't necessarily mean anything. But still, she wagered there was more to the story.

"That's all?"

"That's all," he repeated. "Why?"

The stoplight flickered to red, and she braked, stopping at the intersection. "I don't know. He was just – unsettling."

"What did he say to you?"

Feeling his gaze, she glanced at him. "Nothing. Really."

Her attention swerved. Thom's sleeve had rucked up against the door, revealing the tattoo on the inside of his bicep; a multi-faceted compass star, colored green, gray, and white with strange symbols at the poles.

Like lightning, realization stabbed at her mind. The star was identical to the one on her father's coat, in the painting. *How is that possible?*

A weird tension grew in her skull, burgeoning like storm clouds.

The light turned green and she accelerated automatically, focusing on the wet road, her fingers clamped on the steering wheel. Even as she fought it, her consciousness began to float from her body, metaphysically cleaving her in two. A jolt in her brain gave way to a rapid succession of images – beginning with the compass star – overpowering her mind, like she was experiencing a dream she had no power to wake from.

"Poppy."

Thom's voice barely cut through the mind-coup of images: a speckled red fish, a night sky with pink and green and blue stars, a pile of dusty hay, a lantern glowing with a lavender-orange light, a compass star carved in stone, a rock-strewn waterfall surrounded with towering spruce trees. Her brain buzzed painfully, and she shook her head, trying to snap out of it.

"Poppy!"

His hand fell onto her shoulder. An explosion of flame encompassed her vision, spreading like a pyroclastic blast, blotting out the world around her, until only the pictures remained in her mind. She struggled to breathe, her hands petrified on the steering wheel, her eyes unseeing.

The wheel turned in her fingers, and her body collided with the door. The car shuddered to a stop. A hand fell on her shoulder – the shock of the contact a relief. Again, she became aware of the springy seat beneath her, the humidity of the air.

"Poppy!" Warmth cupped her chin and she found herself looking into Thom's hazel eyes – wide with concern. "Poppy! Can you hear me?"

The car had stopped in the left turn lane. A passing car gunned its engine and honked, the occupants flipping her off. Her breath came in wheezes and her eyes watered. He snatched up her bag, which had tumbled to the floor, and found her inhaler. Shakily, she took a hit.

The world outside the car pitched. Her vision blurred at the edges. Mortification seeped into her, like the needle of a syringe slipping into muscle. *What just happened?*

He studied her. "Are you okay?"

"I'm—sorry—I— don't know what happened."

"It's alright. Take your time."

She clenched her hands in her lap, trying to stop them from shaking.

"Something caused your asthma, just now. What was it?" he asked.

"I don't know."

She didn't. The realization made her so scared she felt sick. Was it another episode, like last night? *What's happening to me?*

He nudged her shoulder. "I've been in worse situations, Poppy."

Another weird black-out. Only this time it happened in front of Thom Magnusson. Sweat broke out at her temples. Gripping the steering wheel, she traced the logo with her eyes. How was she ever going to live this down? Checking the lane, she put the car into drive, squirming under his gaze.

The streetlamps came to life in the rain-darkened evening. After passing a handful of streets he indicated a left turn. *Thom Magnusson lives in my neighborhood.* She was too mortified to be happy about the discovery.

"Stop at the corner." he pointed. "This street is narrow with dead ends. I'll walk the rest of the way."

He can't wait to get out of the car. Humiliation prickling her skull, she stopped next to the curb.

"How far do you have to go to get home?" he asked.

"A couple streets."

He scrutinized her, like a cop assessing an impaired driver.

"Are you going to be okay?" he asked.

She nodded, watching raindrops scuttle down the windshield.

"Poppy?" He waited.

She dragged her eyes to his.

"Get some rest, okay?" The dim light shadowed his expression, but his voice was unbearably gentle.

Gritting her teeth, she nodded, refocusing on the dashboard.

"Thanks for the ride." The door thumped shut.

He slid down the street, past the dilapidated Victorian houses crowding the bluff overlooking the river. The sky flashed with lightning, making her blink. By the time she'd refocused, he'd disappeared.

It didn't matter where he lived. She'd had her chance alone with Thom Magnusson. And it had turned out worse than even she could've imagined.

In less than a minute, she came to a stop in her driveway. Leaning against the steering wheel, she listened to the rain patter on the roof, dashing away humiliated tears with her sleeve.

Chapter Four

From the shadows, Thom watched Poppy's car lurch into gear and continue up the street, its taillights disappearing into the twilight. Staying hidden, he jogged after it, the rain making him squint, keeping to the cover of the neighborhood's overgrown hedges and tulip poplars. *I've got to make sure she's safe,* he thought.

He'd seen that look on Poppy's face before; a look like she was seeing the dead walk again. It had happened on his first day of work, when their eyes had briefly met, and a couple of times since – an agonized expression like she was trying to remember, to relive moments that seemed impossible. At least for someone who hadn't been told the truth.

How much longer could he witness Poppy's confusion, stand by and do nothing? After the near-catastrophe at the river last night, and now today? He had to make Ayden understand the danger. Even if he couldn't produce the evidence Ayden asked for.

Crouching by a yew hedge one-hundred yards away, he surveyed Poppy's house. The car had stopped in the driveway. Except for the patter of rain and the hoot of owls calling across the street, the neighborhood was silent. Her form motionless, she stayed in the driver's seat. Thinking of her pale face on the drive home, he clenched his jaw – if only they'd told her! All of this could've been avoided. Poppy was suffering in a dumpster fire of another's making, and he had to stand by and watch it burn.

Members of the guard's cohort – Alan and Neil – lived next door to the Paquin's little bungalow, strategically stationed in case of trouble. Thom considered texting them, to make sure she arrived inside safely, but after the screw-up at the river, he felt responsible. Besides, Dane might be there, and he didn't want his attention pricked. Not after his mischief today.

Remembering, Thom scowled, an expression black enough to wilt the wet grass at his feet. Showing up at Poppy's work like that? Dane was gunning for a fight, prodding him, wanting to get under his skin. And if he'd been behind the attack at the river, like Thom believed he was, Dane was scouting for vulnerabilities, looking for another opportunity.

Both of them were *Offysfyn* veterans, with years of service. By now, Dane had probably guessed Thom was keeping tabs on him. If the man believed he had a target on his back, Dane might throw caution to the wind – endanger Poppy and Deidre even more. It was on him to walk this tightrope

— outfox Dane's evolving scheme, obtain proof of the man's treachery, and protect the Paquins as Ayden had entrusted him. If only he had more time.

Why hasn't she gone inside? He adjusted the hood of his raincoat and crept closer. Within the car, just illuminated by the porch light, she leaned against the steering wheel. Her silver hair had slipped from its braid, highlighting her shoulders, which tremored.

Andskotans helvítis djöfull. For a tenuous moment, he fought the urge to march up to the car, open the door, and tell her everything. But orders. Poppy's brother's orders. As much as he hated them, disagreed with them, he didn't want to interfere in family matters. Ayden would make things right. Poppy would recover, eventually. He scowled. *Would she?*

But she thinks you're her manager, remember? Suddenly showing up at her house would earn him a creepy-guy-from-work badge, probably rattling her even more. Not the end goal.

What if you're not around the next time a Gren elemental decides to snatch her? What then, Magnusson? What if her memories return like an avalanche? Will you stay silent? Let her think she's cracked? Like Deidre did in those first months?

He could always dose up Poppy and Deidre, and take them through the well with Alan and Neil's help. But, considering how the transition had affected them the last time, that course of action would undoubtedly be traumatic, for both of them, especially Poppy. And to pass through safely, he needed elemental assistance, which he didn't have.

Besides, the thought of doing something like that made his stomach sick. Even if it was the most expedient way to deal with the problem, it felt like something Felix Paquin would do, and he would never walk in that man's footsteps. Both the Paquin men, Ayden to a lesser degree, had a blind spot for power, a hubris that steamrolled anything that didn't serve the greater good of the homeland.

No, however much he wanted to intervene, to make things right for Poppy, it was up to Ayden to decide how to take care of his mother and sister. No matter how much he cared, sticking his nose in places it didn't belong would only make things worse. But that didn't mean he couldn't push Ayden.

Heat threaded his veins, humming along with his pulse. This had gone on long enough. If the last twenty-four hours didn't convince Ayden, Thom would give him a thrashing, even if it landed his ass in a cell.

The car door squeaked as Poppy exited, jumping over the puddles in the gravel drive. As she disappeared in a flood of light from inside the house, Thom jogged away, unaware of the rain drenching his work shoes. At his apartment, he shed his wet clothes, texted Alan and Neil directions to follow in his absence, and dragged a large trunk from the coat closet, unlocking it with a brass key.

By the time he had packed for the journey, the rain outside had intensified into heavy cold drops, mingling with a wind that hinted at winter. His boots impervious to the rainwater running along the curb, Thom set out toward the Twin. Maybe it was the pressure of the storm, or the dank chill, but his left hip protested with each stride, aching deep in his bone marrow, the still-healing muscles feeling like they'd been dried and cracked open. Undaunted, he maintained his pace, relishing the movement, snubbing the pain. After all, a year ago, he hadn't been able to walk three steps.

As he glimpsed the dark expanse of the Twin, he wondered if he was risking too much, leaving the Paquins with only Alan and Neil to watch over them. Depending on conditions in the well, the trip could take him all night. And when he returned, how compromised would he be, reentering? Maybe it was the strain from his recovery, but the journey through this well took a brutal toll, as though it slurped the life out of his mitochondria.

No. He didn't see any other way.

His boots sinking into the bank, he studied the murky river. The deadly waters melded into the blackness of the night, glinting like oil in the lights of the massive steel bridge a quarter mile west. Twigs, candy wrappers, and plastic bottles bobbed among the eddies, alongside rubbish that would make most humans think twice about touching the water. The pungent, oily smell reminded him of the enzyme-treated privies home-side.

Hidden in the shadow of a sycamore near the bank, he listened, scanning the darkness with trained eyes, looking for any hint that Dane might be lurking nearby. For all he knew, those watching the well – he was certain Dane was using elemental spies – would report the moment he disappeared. He would have to shoulder the risk, relying on Alan and Neil to fill in the gaps earth-side.

Breathing deeply, he let oxygen saturate his body, slowing his heart with practiced care. Gripping the cuff on his wrist, he stepped into the water, feeling it slide around him, leaving a space the width of a knife blade between the oily river water and his body. Like a blanket woven of ice, the cold surrounded him, and he clenched his jaw to keep his teeth from chattering.

Concentrating, he switched to the internal hum of elemental speech, bartering with the murky water like a snake charmer taming a cobra, until it relented, allowing him to pass unmolested. The eerie red luminescence of the well appeared, reminding him of a crack in a cave wall. Just as the river grew ambivalent about cooperating, he slipped through into the current of the well, breathing in its selcouth, tart air, glad to be rid of the heavy stench of the Twin, of *Uther-Erai* – of earth.

Chapter Five

Wiping her eyes, Poppy trudged up the porch stairs and unlocked the door. Warmth and quiet washed over her as it clicked shut behind her. From the kitchen, amber light streamed across the foyer's wooden floor. Tiptoeing around it, Poppy made for the stairs.

"Poppy?" Came her mother's voice.

"Not here."

Deidre chortled. "Nice try."

Before Poppy could escape up the stairs, Deidre appeared in the foyer, wiping her bony knuckles with a towel, her face shadowed by the light from the kitchen. "Aren't you hungry?"

Still facing the stairs, Poppy shook her head.

"I got a fryer at a garage sale. Thought I'd make funnel cakes." Deidre tossed the towel back into the kitchen, her mouth twitching with a grin. "Bet you're hungry now."

Mounting the stairs, Poppy grimaced. "I'm not in the mood."

Glimpsing her tear swollen face, Deidre's grin lines disappeared. "Oh, sweetie. What happened?" She tried to steer her toward the kitchen. "You should eat something."

"I don't want funnel cakes made in a garage sale fryer, Mom."

"I'll make you a sandwich then. I've got bread and butter pickles. And that multigrain bread you like."

Poppy didn't want to think about the ride home with Thom Magnusson, much less talk about it. The urge to be alone was as strong as the sleepiness tugging at her eyelids. But the thought of pickles made her mouth water. Dropping her bag, she trudged into the kitchen.

Poppy expected a barrage of questions as she ate, but her mom was strangely quiet, scanning a funnel cake recipe in a yellowed cookbook. Deidre's eyes kept darting from the page, to the window, to the side door, as she fidgeted with her beaded earrings, and Poppy guessed she had more than funnel cakes on her mind. As Poppy swallowed the last of her sandwich, Deidre shoved the cookbook aside, and, with a deliberate gesture bordering on awkward, placed a blue rock the size of a deck of cards next to Poppy's plate.

The stone was oval in shape, wider at one end, and smooth – as though it had been palmed for centuries in a river in some distant place. The narrow end had a natural hole. *A hag stone!* Poppy thought, fascinated. Flecks of mica glimmered across its surface. An orange sunset hue bordered the brilliant cobalt of the middle – so saturated it almost appeared luminescent, like a firefly.

Angling it in the light, Poppy examined it, curiosity overcoming her angst. "This is beautiful. Where did you get it?" *Maybe garage sales are good for something after all.*

Deidre's mouth crinkled in a half-smile. "It's special. But, not for your collection."

Lost in thought, Poppy turned it over. "I'm not even sure what kind of rock this is. I've never seen anything like it. What do you mean, special?"

Her smile turned stiff and anxious. "Poppy, I want you to know…your father and I, we've not always been on the same page about things. We've made some bad decisions. Some of them, most of them, I didn't have a choice in. But still, they happened." Lines deepened around her eyes, competing with a sorrowful divot on her forehead. "Oh, it feels bad tonight." She clutched her temple. "The atmosphere feels so… heavy. Like in a story. Like something bad is going to happen. What's the word?"

"Foreboding."

Deidre snapped her fingers. "That's the one."

Poppy twisted her fingers in her lap. "He's not coming to visit then."

Her hand flattened on the table. "No, that's not what I'm trying to say."

Waiting, Poppy examined the stone. She was tired of bad news.

"That stone," Deidre's bony shoulders lifted with an exaggerated shrug. "I didn't even know I had this. It was buried in a trunk, from our home. From long ago. A time you don't remember."

Not this again. Poppy's fingers tightened around the stone. *Did she forget her meds?*

"I had this feeling." Deidre's forehead scrunched into tight wrinkles. "I was outside tonight, and suddenly there were sparks, all over the sky, like at home. Like the stars. And I remembered. This rock. Sparks inside. It has..." she tapped it, "sparks inside."

Poppy's stomach rebelled against the food she'd just eaten. Her delight over the new stone disappeared, replaced with gut-clenching worry.

Deidre hit the table with the flat of her hand. "This isn't coming out right. It's all crazy sounding." She covered her eyes. "Lord, I have a headache."

"Why don't you lie down? Maybe it'll be clearer when your headache's gone."

Deidre's eyes widened with realization. "No. No. I know how this sounds. But I've taken my pills. It's just – there's so much you don't know. I shouldn't have waited so long to tell you. And now it's so difficult. To know where to start." Holding her head, she squeezed her eyes shut. "You're different. Do you know that? Different. In a good way. A strong way. A way you should be proud of."

What did the therapist say to do? Keep her calm. Distract. Don't feed the delusions. Leaning forward, Poppy put her hand over her mom's, almost shrinking away from the thin, cold skin. "I'm off Monday. Why don't we have breakfast at Bobo's? Then, if it's still bothering you, we can talk. Deal?"

Blinking hard, Deidre bit her lip. "Okay. But this," she tapped the stone, "it's important. Keep it with you. It's a Poppy-specific talisman." Her voice trailed off, as though hiding in the shadows in the kitchen. "Yes. It will be clearer, later. It can wait. Just keep this with you. Please."

It's happening again. Poppy's temples throbbed.

But also, her mom meant well. She knew how much Poppy adored rocks, and she was just trying to love her – in her own, batty, messed-up way. That was more than some kids ever got. Tucking the blue stone into her anorak pocket, she patted it. "A Poppy-specific talisman. Got it."

Smoothing Poppy's hair, Deidre tucked a stray lock behind one of her ears. "You look so much like my mother. Like your gran. Even without your red hair." Her green eyes teared up. "So much more than I. I wish you could've known her."

"Yeah, me too." Poppy stood. "Thanks, Mom." Leaning down, she kissed Deidre's forehead. "Get some rest, okay?"

That night, Poppy's sleep overflowed with unsettling dreams. Sparks rattled her window, swirling on the wind, calling her name – thousands of sparks, like fiery dust, or jeweled flecks of lava. On a draft, they trickled inside her bedroom, coaxing her out of the bed, toward the blue stone.

As she cradled the smooth surface, flames emanated from its edges, like the stone was a tiny twin to the Grand Prismatic Spring. Opening her mouth, she tasted the flames, inhaling them like opium smoke. Sparks flooded her insides, filling her lungs, her stomach, her muscles – tingling her body like she'd guzzled wine.

Startling awake, her brain churned, reliving a tangle of dream-images; spiked black hair, a glowing jawline, muscular legs emerging out of smoke, skin the color of copper, an oversized stone necklace resting on a massive chest. Eyes the color of scotch, radiant as though wildfire burned within.

Was this more evidence that her mind was slipping away to some scary, phantasmic place, just like her mother's? It felt as though a wildfire loomed on her horizon, and she had nowhere to run, no path to escape.

Maybe I'll just stop running. She thought. *Let it burn right through me.*

Chapter Six

After the disastrous car ride with Thom, Poppy was dreading work, so much so that she'd prepared a mantra to get her through the day – *you need this job, so hold your head high, work your ass off, and pretend you give zero fucks.*

But Thom didn't show up. And, other than an elderly woman wrecking a motorized cart, the day was so normal it was practically boring. By the time her shift ended, Poppy was elated. Maybe her luck was turning. Maybe Deidre would be back to normal. Maybe she'd read too much into things.

Outside the store, the October air turned in her nostrils, smoky and frostbitten. Goosebumps flooded her arms and legs. Against the hulking shadow of the building, the sun dipped below a cloud bank in dazzling beams of peach and magenta. Yellow leaves clustered around her feet, slippery with the remnants of yesterday's rain. Shoulders hunched against the chill, she rushed toward the car.

In her jacket pocket, her fingers brushed against a smooth, dense object. *The blue stone.* She extracted it, and a glitter of copper flickered across its glossy surface. The orange hue on the edges shone so vibrantly it might've been reflecting the sunset. Seeing it made her feel as if she'd been turned inside out. Shoving the stone back into her pocket, she set her chin.

"Hey, Poppy."

She stumbled on the curb before pinpointing the source of the voice. A man in a hooded coat leaned against the side of a building, shadowed by one of the ash trees lining the front of the store. Shoving his hood back, he flicked a glowing cigarette into the grass. Poppy scrutinized his swagger, square jawline, and black hair, highlighted pink from the sunset.

An icy knot of panic tightened in her stomach. *It's the guy from yesterday.* The guy that Thom told her to watch out for. The guy that had creeped her out way beyond normal creepiness.

That hadn't changed. In the shadowy light he appeared taller than she remembered, his shoulders wider. *Keep walking.* Closing the distance between them, his mouth tilted in a confident, blasé smirk, sending shudders of warning down her back.

"Hey. It's Poppy, isn't it?"

Narrowing her eyes, she picked up her pace. "What do you want?"

His smirk stretched into a grin. "Just saying hi, sweetheart. That's all."

"You don't know me well enough to say hi."

As she reached the corner of the building, her body jolted, like she'd walked into an invisible electric fence. The ground shuddered. Inside her pocket, the stone trembled and grew warm against her palm, sending a tingling buzz up her arm. She hissed, her heart kicking like a jump-started engine. *Strange.*

As the man stepped onto the sidewalk, the trees nearby cringed, as though straining to get away from him. Was it the wind? Next to her thrumming heart, a grating rumble resonated in her chest, like the grind of tectonic plates.

"Hold on." He moved as though he'd never tripped a day in his life. "Maybe we can fix that."

"No." She broke into a jog. "We can't."

He materialized in front of her, so quickly she almost ran into him.

"I'm Dane. Pleased to meet you." A faceted geometric tattoo emblazoned his palm.

Forced to halt, anger flickered in her throat. "Look, dickhead. I'm not interested in, hello? I'm not interested in shaking hands. I just want to go home. So. Leave. Me. Alone."

Elbows stiff, she tried to pass him, but he side-stepped, blocking her escape. All pretense of charm had vanished from his features.

"Felix Paquin's little girl should have better manners."

Poppy froze, her eyes widening. *How could he know that?*

His expression remained cold, but a sneer lifted his mouth, pleased with her reaction.

"Leave me alone." She shoved past him.

Liquid as a striking snake, he seized her wrist. Grabbing her other arm, he spun her, crushing her against his chest, dragging her around the corner of the building, out of sight of the parking lot. It happened so fast, and now she couldn't breathe, think, scream.

His acrid, smoky breath washed over her ear, and she shuddered. "Nice and easy, Poppy-dear. One foot in front of the other." He frog-marched her toward the back of the building.

Her breath came in tight wheezes, her mind trapped in a thick, white void. As her body slumped into dead weight, his hold tightened with bone-snapping strength.

"Move, bitch." He shook her. "You might want to consider who your friends are, Pops. Because you have no idea what's happening here, what kind of monsters I'm protecting you from. Remember the river?"

She went rigid. *The river. He knows about the river.*

He continued, "I can take you. Or they can. You choose."

But just as fight surged in her muscles, a jolt of black-hole energy grated inside her chest, steamrolling her resistance. A vision oozed into her consciousness; masses of black dirt, pouring over her body, driving the breath from her lungs. The force of an avalanche, crushing her chest, driving debris into her gut, pounding her with stones, trapping her as cold pink worms and wriggling centipedes forced their way into her mouth, her nose, her ears. Her knees wobbled with fear and whiteness peppered her vision.

"That's more like it." His voice sounded far away.

Still clutched in her fingers, the stone pulsed. A surge of icy heat punched through her veins. Like she'd been given a shot of epinephrine, her lungs cleared. Inside her chest cavity – the space around her heart – a voice split her consciousness: *Poppy! Fight!*

As she clutched the stone, lava-hot strength flooded her limbs, injecting her muscles with an outlandish power. With a yell, she threw her arms back, sending his body flying, crashing into the cement block building. From the impact, cracks shot out in a starburst across the concrete. With a surprised grunt, he thumped to the ground, face-first, coughing up blood.

In the fray, the stone slid from her grasp to the ground. As it fell, a detonation of multi-colored flame expanded around it like a nebula, as bright as the sunbeams pouring through the clouds. Prostrate, Dane's eyes followed its path, his jaw dropping. Warmth spread from her chest, into her neck, through her limbs, and into the base of her skull. Her vision grew startlingly clear, tinged with color.

Dane's expression went sour and his jaw snapped shut. Just as he lunged for the stone, she grabbed it, her hand closing around the core of flames. She'd expected first-degree burns, but multi-hued sparks swirled around her hand and snaked up her arm, tingling her skin like fireflies. *Sparks.* Gasping in surprise, she braced herself against the ground, trying to regain her footing. Beneath her touch, the ground trembled as though awaking from slumber.

A tremor shot across the earth and flames licked up Dane's pantlegs, charring the gray fabric. In dazed panic, he thrashed in the dewy grass, snuffing them out.

What the hell? Looking between the flaming stone and the thrashing man, Poppy backed away. The smell of smoke and something like burnt orange filled her nose.

Mingled awe and fury crossed Dane's face. Leaping up, he backed away, hands lifted as though she had a gun trained on him. When she didn't move, he broke into a sprint, and disappeared around the corner. The roar of a motorcycle echoed from behind the building.

Poppy stared down at the stone clutched in her palm, the multi-colored flames fading as she watched. *Talisman.* That's what her mom had called it. What could this be? *A hallucination? No. Not this.*

Sparks, her mom had said about the stone. *Sparks, all over the sky, like at home. Sparks inside. It has sparks inside.*

But this time, she'd seen it, felt it. And someone else had too.

Chapter Seven

By the time Poppy skidded to a stop into the driveway, the sun had dipped below the horizon. Questions for her mom buzzed on her tongue; the stone, the sparks, the multi-colored light – Poppy was almost excited to tell her she'd thrown a guy the size of a rugby player with enough force to crack a concrete wall. Poppy wanted, needed, to spill everything that had happened to her. Deidre sounded like she had important, difficult things to say last night. And now she was ready to listen.

There's so much you don't know. Deidre had said. *I shouldn't have waited so long to tell you.* Could there be an explanation waiting for her that wasn't heartbreaking? Could it be that her differences were actually good, like her mom had said?

Tell me about the time I don't remember, Mom. Tell me every- thing. Clutching the stone in her jacket pocket, she jogged up the stairs to the front porch.

As she opened the door, an odor hit her like a gut punch. The smell was as rancid as if a rat had peed all over the place and then decayed in its own waste. Covering her mouth with her shirt, she peered inside. The curtains were drawn, hiding the room in murky twilight. She swiped at the light switch, but the pendant in the foyer stayed dark. Flipping it on and off had no effect. *Strange.*

"Mom?" she called, and immediately regretted opening her mouth.

A bitter, sharp tang invaded her throat, and the veins in her temples began to throb. The room shuddered and tipped. As she dropped her bag on the table in the foyer, she stum- bled, knocking a milk glass vase to the floor. Glass shattered and spun across the wood planks. Clutching at the table, she staggered. *What's happening to me?* Her vision blurred and her knees collided with the floor, her cheek meeting the rug inches from the white shards.

From the kitchen, the flooring creaked, and quivering scratches were dragged across the wooden floor. Trying to glimpse what made the noise, she craned her neck, but only managed to half-roll on her back before her limbs froze, as though they had been injected with cement. *I can't move. What's happening to me?* Thick waves of fear shuddered through her body.

The floor shuddered, and the shadows in the kitchen seemed to ripple with movement, breathing in a rhythmic, sucking rattle. The smell intensified. Choking, she tried to crawl, to hide, but could only twitch.

A dark shape crept out of the opening, predator-slow. Faint light illuminated a black oval abdomen surrounded by long hairy legs; a spider the size of a Labrador, creeping closer, ready to strike the paralyzed flesh of her face, her arms, her chest. The smell intensified, and panicked gorge snaked up her esophagus.

The spider's muscular legs gripped the wood floor with claw-like appendages, circling her body, hovering inches from her face, scraping her cheek with short, prickly hairs. A scream caught in her throat. Short, craggy appendages began to prod and massage at her, rasping at her neck, her collarbone, her breast, the wiry hairs scratching her bare skin, snagging on her clothes. Her vision blurred and a sob leaked out of her lips. She didn't want to die wrapped up in spider silks, feeling the blood drain from her body. She didn't want her mom to find her like this.

The spider's hairy limbs paused, sliding into her anorak pocket and pawing around. The odor of piss and decay assaulted her nostrils. She wheezed, her eyes wide, afraid to look away from the glossy cluster of black eyes, inches from hers. Would she suffocate even before the spider slashed at her flesh? Inject her with poison?

With an easy leap that made the floor tremble, the spider disappeared into the shadows. Her breath came in strangled gasps. *Where did it go?* An agonizing minute passed before the back door rattled and squeaked, and the house settled into a sickening silence, worse than a cemetery at midnight. *Why didn't it kill me?*

Fear thrummed inside of her. *MOM! Where is she? Did it hurt her?*

Fighting to move, Poppy imagined the spider plucking at the crepe skin of Deidre's body, disappointed at how little juice she contained. Still, her limbs only jerked, like broken machinery.

Men's voices echoed from the backyard garden. Listening, she went still. Deidre's raspy alto responded, raised and harsh, followed by muffled thumps and crashes. *Mom!* Poppy's voice thundered, its rhythm going wild and awry. Deidre cried out, ragged, and metal pinged on concrete, as if she'd kicked over the watering can, but the sound faded. A sickening silence spread through the house, until all Poppy heard was her heart-beat, and the kitchen sink dripping.

Just when she thought she might die from fear, her body shivered and came unstuck. Her hand scuttled to her face, and she was able to roll onto her side. She scrabbled for balance, but her legs crumpled and she face-planted on the rug. Using the sofa, she dragged herself up and wobbled into the kitchen, clutching the walls for support. Her head throbbed and her mouth tasted as bitter as acid.

Her thoughts drummed, persisting through the pain. *Mom – I have to help mom!* Stomach lurching, she pivoted, vomiting in the trashcan. Wiping her mouth, she glimpsed a person-shaped lump sprawled on the threshold of the laundry room.

The light in the breakfast nook didn't work. Hands shaking, she scrabbled in her pocket for her phone, but it wasn't there. In the streetlight through the window, she knelt by the person. The boots covering the limp feet were at least a size twelve, caked with mud that smelled of the river. She felt for a pulse, recognizing the blonde buzzcut. The guy next door, Alan – the towhead. His light, amber eyes were open, unmoving. A pool of blood was spreading from a dent in his skull the size of an apple. Nausea spiked in her stomach and her horror returned, as piercing and real as the smell in her nostrils.

Poppy shrank away, stumbling back to land on her backside in the living room. Why was their neighbor lying dead in their house? She rubbed her forehead, trying to think; it felt like her brain had been diced up and shoved back into her skull in a jumble. She had to find her phone. No, she had to call the police. No! She had to find her mom!

Curling her fingers around the fireplace poker, she rushed back into the kitchen, stepped over the body, waded through a pile of laundry, and flung open the back door. From the direction of the river, an eerie creaking sound echoed, followed by a muffled cry. Mom!

An earthquake-like rumble rippled through the ground, making the house shudder and pop. As fast as she could move her feet, Poppy staggered down the driveway, her weapon ready to strike.

Chapter Eight

Weller Street lay deserted and quiet in the falling dark. A crescent moon had risen, glowing weakly in the dusky sky, not enough to see by. Poppy's breath fogged in quick bursts as she turned down the Meadows, ears perked for distant cries. Leaves blew across the pavement, the dry rasping startling her.

Call the cops at Paddy's. She thought, picking up her pace. *Hurry!*

The street leading to the landing resonated with the staccato of distant voices, tremoring with strange rumbling, as though a wild college party raged somewhere nearby. Maybe one did. Maybe she was having another episode. Still dazed, her temples throbbed with each step. Another tremor rocked the ground, making the boxwood hedge at her right shiver from east to west. She stared. College parties didn't cause earthquakes.

Her stomach sickened as the memory of Alan's bashed-in, bloody head leapt into her mind, transforming to Deidre's broken body...*No. I'll find her. She'll be okay...*

Past the hedge, shadows moved underneath the poplar trees lining both sides of the street. Her fingers tightened around the poker. But it was only low handing boughs, tossed by the wind. Seeing Paddy's ahead, she rushed toward the corner of the Meadows.

A hand surrounded her bicep, yanking her to a stop. Yelping, she swung the poker, but the man grabbed the wrist that held the weapon and squeezed. It clanged on the road, disappearing in a grassy drainage ditch. She cringed at the shooting pain up her wrist, and the man's teeth flashed behind a grin. *Dane!*

With her other hand, she scrabbled in the pocket of her anorak for the blue stone, but it was empty. *Oh no!* Realization prodded her. *The spider...* She tried to wrench her arm away, but it was stuck as fast as a tire locked in a boot.

A snigger. "Not so dangerous without your little relic, are you?" Dane gave her an experimental shake. "What a fool you made me. But not this time."

"Where's my mom? Why are you doing this?"

"I promised to deliver the Paquin crone, you, and a certain artifact. And I always deliver on my promises." His voice purred, self-satisfied.

Howling, Poppy struck for his eyes with her knuckles. Lazily, he blocked her hand, the strike rattling the bones of her wrist. Adrenaline flooding in her veins, she thrashed, a whirlwind of elbows and knees. Sunburn pain seared her cheek as he slapped her with enough force that her head flew back – she would've fallen, but his fingers clamped around her bicep. A nauseating ache spread in her temples. Stunned, she hung for a moment, unable to think.

"Give me another reason to hit you. Please."

The second blow rattled her teeth and she tasted copper. She crumpled, his grip still pinching her arm.

"That's right." His voice, almost cheerful. "I don't need a reason. Remember that, Pops."

As he dragged her past Paddy's, she risked a yell. It came out hoarse, a torn-paper sound.

"No. No. Hush." His hand clapped over her mouth and nose, squeezing, cutting off her air.

He smelled of wet earth and a familiar, sour tang – the spider! As if she were a piece of luggage, he dragged her down Olive Street, toward the landing, still preventing her from breathing. Her lungs throbbed and mewled in her throat, begging for air.

"Will you behave in the river? Huh?" Pulling her up, he grabbed her chin, bringing her level to his eyes.

NO! Not the river! White stars crowded her vision.

"You will if you're unconscious." His hand tightened, pinching her nose.

The world dissolved into pieces of sand-fine glass, fading into shadow. *I'm sorry, Mom.*

Her shoulder slammed into concrete. Air rushed into her lungs and she shuddered, her body folding with coughing and gasping. Movement caught her eye.

Dane tumbled across the sidewalk bordering the landing, kicked in the gut by another man. In their wake, a knife clattered to the pavement. The man took a fistful of Dane's hair and banged his forehead against the concrete. Dane thrust an elbow into the man's face. Blocking it, the man struck him with a flat palm. Recovering, Dane spun as they traded blows with rapid, action-movie precision. Chests heaving, they broke apart, circling each other.

Streetlights glinted off of bright red hair. "Thom!" the man roared. "Get her out of here!"

A hooded figure materialized next to her. Startled, she scrambled away, her back hitting the retaining wall next to the landing.

"Ayden Paquin." Dane growled, fixated on the red-haired man.

Paquin? Did he say Paquin? Shocked, her gaze darted between them, snapping to the nearest threat; the hooded person crouching in front of her.

"Poppy." The man pushed back the hood of his jacket.

She blinked at Thom Magnusson's bearded face. Her heart felt like it had been unplugged. *What the hell?*

"Poppy," His voice stayed low and calm. "You're not safe here. You need to come with me."

A mocking laugh erupted from Dane, meant for the man – for Ayden Paquin. "Does Daddy know you're here?" Blood ran down his face from a laceration across his forehead and he smeared it like war paint.

Ayden scowled. "Where have you taken Deidre?"

Paquin? Ayden Paquin? Poppy found her voice. "Thom? What?" Her hand shaking, she pointed. "Who is that?"

"Wouldn't you like to know?" Dane side-stepped, his back hunched like a wolf's. "Maybe we can come to an arrangement? I'm on the side with the highest bidder."

Thom nudged her arm. "Later, Poppy. Come on."

Hissing, she recoiled from him.

"It's okay." Disarming, Thom held up his hands.

Eyes darting between him and the fight, she stuttered, "No. Not okay. Nothing is…okay."

Behind Thom, the two men circled each other. "Governor Paquin will give you to Asa." Ayden spat. "He's good with the liars. Then we'll see how much you're smiling."

Anxiety flickered across Dane's face. Brandishing a staff-like weapon, he charged. A similar weapon appeared in Ayden's hands. More traded blows, too fast to track. Blood flecked the concrete.

"Poppy." Coaxed by the calmness of his voice, she looked at Thom. "I don't want to toss you over my shoulder," he said. "But I will."

She shrank against the stone at her back, her fists clenched. *Mom? Where's my mom?*

Dane feigned. Dodged. Flipped over a bench. Leapt on Ayden's back. Choked him with the staff. Ayden head-butted him. Dane recoiled, grunting. In seconds, their momentum carried them on a crash course with Thom and the knife on the pavement. Spinning, Thom put himself between her and the fight.

Close enough that she smelled their sweat, Ayden slammed Dane to the pavers. Dane's breath came with an *oof*! Ayden rolled, struck Dane's chest. Dane blocked another blow, spun his legs, and lunged for the knife, but Thom snatched the blade and flung it toward the river. It clanged on the tracks beyond the landing.

With a snarl, Dane charged Thom. Ducking, Thom crouched like a boxer on one knee, delivering a rib-crushing punch to the man's gut, leaving him staggering. Swinging his staff-weapon like a baseball bat, Ayden lunged between them and pummeled Dane across the kidneys. The man crumpled face-first onto the pavement, groaning. Ayden landed a swift kick to the side of Dane's face before whirling on Thom. "I said to get her out of here!"

"Now we can go together."

Chest heaving, her back still against the wall, she glanced between them and Dane's unconscious body, ten feet away.

"Poppy," Ayden knelt.

The purr of a diesel locomotive vibrated the ground. The train thundered by the landing, its brakes screeching.

"Who are you?" she shouted over the din.

His face twisted into an expression she recognized. "I don't have time to explain. But you need to come with us! Now!"

Chapter Nine

Poppy studied Ayden, dumbfounded. *Could he be?…No. It's impossible.* She tore her eyes away, finding Thom. *What about him? Who?…*

Her fists clenching, she stood, baring her teeth, looking between them. "No! I'm not going anywhere until I know my mom is safe!"

Deep within the earth next to the landing, a rumbling began, the vibration as powerful as the train. The hill west of the landing shuddered and broke open. A dark shape extracted itself from the weeds, straightening like a small mountain. Dirt and gravel tumbled down the incline and scattered across the concrete. The ground bucked and she lost her footing. The men faced the shadow, their posture ready to spring.

Involuntarily, Poppy's chest clenched, and her insides ground with sudden strain – it felt the same when Dane attacked her outside Target, like an alien was trying to mind-meld with her, but instead of her mind, it aimed for her soul.

Scowling, Ayden forced a breath through his nose. "I thought you killed it."

Thom grimaced. "It's difficult to tell with *ullis*. They always look half dead."

Ullis? Poppy stared.

The sulfur glow of the streetlights revealed a hideous horned visage. Dark brindled skin, bulging with angular muscles, covering a frame the size of a water tank. Above a meaty, protruding jaw, a cluster of milky eyes blinked in the middle of its forehead, blending with primitive sand-colored dashes and swirls. Beneath spikes, more eyes dotted its shoulders and arms, reminding her of grub worms in soil. A musty smell, like an old basement, crowded the air. A choking noise escaped her throat as she jumped to her feet. *What. The. Hell.*

"Piss and Ire." Ayden spun his staff-weapon. "Dane likes his ugly, doesn't he?"

Eyes trained on the creature, Thom straightened, fisting a staff-weapon-thing like Ayden's. Sidestepping, he glided away from them.

He's giving it two targets. Dividing its attention.

Shielding her, Ayden readied his staff in front of them like a spear.

The creature's eyes darted around, surveying her, the two men, Dane's prostrate body, the landing, and the speeding train. Except for a large eye on its forehead, the milky eyes disappeared into its spiked flesh. Mirroring Ayden, Thom spun his staff and crouched, tense as a loaded crossbow.

Leaping up, Dane sprinted toward the creature.

Aiming for him, Ayden launched his weapon. Before it found its mark, the creature deflected it with a *crack*, the blow notching its flinty skin. Another ear-splitting *pop* as the creature blocked Thom's weapon. Spinning, it bounced off a tree and returned to Thom's hand.

"Yellow-blooded *gortaug!*" Ayden roared, giving chase.

Before they could catch him, the earth-monster-thing scooped Dane onto its back and bounded back up the incline, the ground shuddering with its footfalls. Making a fisted gesture at the passing coal cars, guttural speech tumbled out of its mouth. It resonated like an internal landslide in Poppy's chest cavity. Her knees buckled against the pavement as she fought to stay conscious.

The creature limped up the hill, Dane clinging to its shoulders. On its heels, Thom slashed at its ankles. It backhanded him, sending his weapon flying – almost smashing Thom against a pillar. A blow from Ayden's weapon made it totter, but it caught itself with a fist, the impact shaking the ground. Recovering, it disappeared into the darkness at the top of the hill, its massive footsteps fading.

The pain inside of her diminished and Poppy staggered to her feet, gaping. *What was that?* The staff-weapon returned to Thom's fist – now the length of her arm. In pursuit, Thom mounted the stairs.

"Thom! Wait!" Ayden shouted, motioning to the train.

Thom halted. A crackling hiss began in Poppy's consciousness – it spread in her chest, burning like stomach acid. Both Ayden and Thom fisted their weapons, locked onto a twisting, smoky cloud billowing above the speeding coal cars. Poppy stared. *It's feeding. On the coal.*

The hiss within the darkness amplified, until it felt like an internal cat scratch. Hands over her ears, Poppy shook her head, trying to dispel the sensation.

The hiss transmuted into tinny voices, ragged and unintelligible. The dark cloud, now as big as a semi, arose and expanded above the train, popping and sparking like black powder.

Ayden made a face. "Crims."

Thom nudged Poppy's arm. "Tie your jacket around your nose and mouth. Stay with Ayden." He side-stepped, narrowing his eyes.

She didn't need to be told twice. *But what about you?*

Slithering on the air, the dark cloud divided, surrounding them like a murmuration, devouring the coal as the train raced underneath. The air crackled and spat and the landing lights diminished to sickly brown spots. Her eyes burned and watered. Beyond the landing, the streetlights flickered and dimmed.

A blast of heat shook the trees. Obscure forms appeared amidst the cloud, advancing, then drawing back, leaping around with strategic feints. Fire sparked in their slanting, long eyes, but the smog masked their other features.

Her lungs tightened like they were being wrung dry, and she wheezed. Grim with concentration, Thom stood his ground before her, while Ayden covered her back, his fists tight around the staff-weapon – which spread barrier-like between them.

With wiry appendages, the creatures sprang, their attacks swift like frog tongues. Darting around, Thom hacked and struck with the staff-weapon, breaking their limbs. Raspy cries echoed and darted around them.

Ayden herded Poppy away from the frontal attack. The darkness circled Thom. She choked on her scream as the cloud enveloped him.

The darkness ripped and popped, pricking with golden light. Two of the creatures dissolved into plumes of smoke and dust. His outline almost glowing, Thom appeared again, dashing a creature against the ground and pummeling its face. Rasping clicks and hisses intensified in the smoky darkness.

A shadow lunged for Poppy. Covering her head, she ducked. Ayden intercepted it with a deft swing.

"They're morphing!" Ayden yelled.

Under the blows the creature shuddered but continued advancing. Growling, he stabbed its eyes and impaled it through the throat. Spinning, he broke the legs of another. The dying creatures twitched and crumpled like tinfoil in acid.

The assault wavered, then surged again. Poppy fought to stay conscious, to breathe in the dirty air. Sweat beaded on her forehead. Stumbling against a bench, she clutched the edge. *Weapon. Look for a weapon.*

Weaving through the smog, Thom struck a section of the iron railing with his staff. The resulting clang was so piercing, she bit back a cry of pain. But instead of fading, the ringing amplified. The creatures hesitated, reoriented themselves, and continued attacking with erratic, handicapped stabs.

"Thom!" Ayden pummeled a convulsing creature. "Hurry!"

As the horrible resonance intensified, the cement around the posts cracked. Fissures raced across the street. The pavement buckled under her feet and she stumbled to her knees. The whole world trembled with the ringing timbre. Ayden crouched over her as she covered her ears, writhing. Black spots crowded her vision as her consciousness began to fade.

Again, Thom struck the iron. The vibration ceased and the railing near the street clattered to the pavement. Picking up a loose baluster, he threw it. The black swarm stuck to it like magnets, wrenched away into the night. Splashes came from the direction of the river. He launched another. As it spun away, the smog cleared and the air lightened.

Recovering, Poppy curled her hand around a piece of the scattered railing and staggered to her feet. Out of a shadow, a stray creature tackled Ayden. Wrestling, they hit the pavement. Wiry limbs oozed like diaphanous, black tentacles, assaulting his eyes, nose, and mouth.

No. You. Don't.

Swinging the baluster like a baseball bat, she struck. The creature flinched, dropping Ayden. With a noise like creaking metal, it lurched for her, slanted eyes stretching and merging, as if to suck her in like a fiery fissure. Heat prickled up her arms and a grating shriek made her cry out. She dropped the iron and landed hard on her rear, scrambling backward.

Thom's staff caught it under the chin. Its countenance shriveled and the remains of the creature twitched and sparked in the air. Blackened, twisted bones clattered to the pavement and dissolved, leaving ashes on her boot.

His chest heaving, Thom whirled, scanning the landing. Coughing up filth, Ayden climbed to his feet. Shaking, she got to her hands and knees. The baluster she'd used a moment ago rolled into the ashes, scattering around her.

The creatures were gone. The train had disappeared down the tracks. But instead of silence, the river roared eerily – as loud as pounding surf, as loud as the train had been. A whine began in the back of her mind, like an internal mosquito. On her heels, she grimaced, trying to clear her head.

"No!" Thom bellowed. Behind her, footsteps splashed. She spun. Just as Thom leapt for her, a cold grip bit into her calves, wrenching her away from him and across the landing.

"Poppy!" Ayden shouted, his voice ragged.

Scrabbling, she caught the leg of a bench. The watery hold tightened at her ankles, frigid and cruel. Her purchase slipped. Pulled in a tight fist of water, she flew over the track side railing, headed for the river.

A sudden grip at her arm halted her momentum. Gasping, she found herself suspended in a tentacle of water, Ayden's fingers tight around her wrist bone. With his other hand, he clutched the railing, keeping them from being pulled into the river. The water's hold was tight, like an anaconda squeezing and fighting for its prey, bruising her hips and thighs. The tug of war intensified, and her feet went numb.

The whispers became water-screams, transmuting into words. *Mine! Let go! NO! No! NO!* The water crept and slithered around Ayden, tendrils slapping at his flesh, creeping toward his neck.

Dragging her free arm out of the current, she clawed for the railing. He grimaced with the effort of holding her. Ayden's grip on her wrist started to slip. He shouted.

Thom clasped Poppy's outstretched arm. With a yell, he heaved her out of the water and onto the landing. Immediately, he grabbed Ayden's trembling wrist.

"Take her! Go!" Ayden shouted, just before the water crept over his face.

Poppy scrambled up to help, but a different wave rushed them, pounding the landing, trying to reclaim her, the force of the current lifting her body. Fighting to keep hold of Ayden, Thom wedged her tight against the railing with his hip. The thick iron began to tremble at its fastenings.

Just when she thought it would give way, the attacking wave retreated. Within the arm of water surrounding Ayden, Poppy glimpsed a flash, and then a silvery visage just behind him. Blinking water out of her eyes, she groped for Ayden's arm, meeting his gray eyes through the curtain of river water.

Don't lose him. Don't let go. Her hands clutched at his skin. *Ayden. Ayden Paquin.*

Thom still clutched Ayden's wrist, fighting to keep himself from being pulled into the current. The water began to creep and paw at him. Bracing herself against the railing, she pulled with every ounce of strength she could muster, her body straining alongside Thom's.

The landing trembled. A wave the size of a bus walloped them, knocking them backward. She tumbled over the concrete, covering her head. Nearby, Thom yelled, a sputtering curse. They collided with a car twenty feet away. Thom leapt up and splashed toward the railing, the staff-weapon again in his fist. Light trailed off of him like drops of rain.

"Ayden!" He halted, searching.

Dizzy, she stumbled after him.

"Poppy!" he shouted. "Stay back!"

Her heart hammering, she halted. The water on the landing slid together in pools and the whispers began again. Through the darkness, a glittering mass of water arose out of the Twin, like a river serpent. It slid up the banks and leapt the tracks, gathering strength as it slithered. Terrified, she froze.

Spinning, Thom maneuvered her up the stairs on the west of the landing, crouching behind a drenched bough. The serpent-wave searched, splashing at the threshold. He crouched between her and the water, the staff ready in his fist.

"Ayden!" His voice echoed.

No answer.

The searching arm of water darted for him. He struck it. On its surface, light exploded into platinum tendrils and withered, retreating. The water-whispers spat like an angry serpent.

"Ayden!" His voice held a dreadful edge.

Silence. Poppy's insides turned icy and sick. She wanted to cry out, to scream his name, but her throat constricted.

Thom struck the arm of water again, causing it to flinch and collapse. "Djöfullis andskoti!" His voice cracked with rage.

Sluggishly, as if it had expended all its energy, the water withdrew from the landing. The sinister voices faded into silence.

There was no sign of Ayden. *Ayden Paquin.*

From somewhere up the street, a dog bayed mournfully, the wail echoing off the waters of the Twin. Poppy slumped to her knees.

Chapter Ten

Hollow pain thrummed in Thom's chest. *Ayden.* His *Offysfyn*-brother and friend. *Poppy's brother!*

He clenched his jaw. *He's been through worse. And Mads was fighting in the water alongside him. Mads will get him to safety. If he's not too outnumbered.*

Next to him, Poppy's teeth chattered, and water dripped off her, pooling all over the stairs. Beneath his grip on her shoulder, she trembled.

Nothing you can do about it now. The pain gave way to anger, clouding his vision. *Dane! Fokking fifl!*

"What was—?" Poppy's voice shook. "Who…? I don't…!"

"Poppy." He tightened his grip, resisting the urge to shake her. "I need you to come with me. Now."

Her eyes widened as she stood. "What about Ayden?"

"Don't worry about him. He's been through worse."

"But, my mom! I can't. I need to find her!"

"The best thing you can do to help Ayden and Deidre is to come with me."

"How do you know?"

"Later."

Her brow furrowed, scanning him warily.

"It's your choice," he said, hoping he wouldn't regret the words.

"What…were?" Her shoulder tensed up. "All those…creatures?"

"Save it," he said. "We've got to move."

"Move? Where?"

"I can't explain right now. But I will later, if you come with me."

Her brow lowered, like she was about to argue. "Everything? Promise?"

Deliberately, he met her eyes. "Yes, Poppy. I promise."

She dipped her chin. Gripping her hand, Thom pulled her up behind him, scanning the stairs. Near the top, a jagged footprint dented the hillside. Anger blinded him again. *Morgedd. Dane. You jacked with the wrong guy.*

Her chest heaving, she squeezed his arm. "But the thing… the big thing! With Dane!"

No Ulli scent. "It's gone."

"How do you know?"

"Shhh. I need to think."

She tried to pull her hand free, but he pressed her into a crouch behind a boxwood hedge, scanning the yard of the

Victorian above the landing. Its bulk loomed dark against the overcast sky. The shadowy gardens surrounding it reminded him of a gothic horror novel – unkempt boxwood parterres, worn concrete statues, and overgrown roses.

Bass thumped inside the structure, rattling the dark windows. *Of course, Dane would try to handicap an attack with that racket.* He smirked. *It's not going to work.*

"What are we doing here?" Dappled light from a streetlamp wavered over her face.

He motioned to the house. "I have to go inside."

"Inside? Why?"

"Dane's in there."

Eyes wide, she swallowed. "I'm not staying out here."

"No, you're not." Scowling, he shoved his dripping hair out of his eyes. "You will stay with me. Right behind me. Unless I tell you otherwise." He gripped her shoulder for emphasis. "Okay? Poppy?"

Her expression galvanized. "Yeah, okay."

Motioning for her to follow, he crept along a curving brick path, gritting his teeth as the wind gusted through his wet clothes. To his ears, the chatter of her teeth sounded loud enough to give them away.

The path led to the eastern side of the mansion and then to a descending stairwell with a door at the bottom, steeped in darkness. Leaves scuttled in the corners, in time with the bass inside the house.

Prying the *cydern* off his wrist, he held it up, using it – in staff form – to illuminate the alcove. Spying the lock, he held it against the knob and after a moment, the door clicked and opened soundlessly, the metal responding to the persuasion of the elemental bone.

Inside, the darkness reverberated with pounding, black metal music. Moving slowly, he let his eyes adjust, gripping her hand to keep her close behind him. Rows of cabinets lined the walls of the room. A small table with few chairs huddled in the shadows. The air had a cave-like chill.

Beside him, Poppy's knees shook with each step. For a moment, his heart went out to her, and he thought to take her out of that place, to stow her somewhere safe. But no place *Erai*-side was safe anymore, not with the Grens after her, with Dane helping them.

Still, did his pursuit of Dane put her in too much danger? Maybe, but he had to discover if their escape had been compromised, who Dane was working with, and where they'd taken Deidre. He might not get another chance to score intel like this.

A short flight of stairs led up to another door. Faint yellow light shone at the bottom. He cracked the door, surveying the room beyond. The volume of the music washed over them, so loud he felt off balance.

They crept out and into a vestibule. Before them yawned a wide hallway with a faded runner and peeling foulard wallpaper. Skirting walnut paneled doors, backs against the wall, they inched down the hallway, their wet clothes leaving a dripping trail. The passage adjoined a high-ceiled great room lit by an iron chandelier. The music growled and screamed, so overpowering Thom had to fight to concentrate.

A sharp odor – rat piss and corpse flower – fi lled his nostrils, and Poppy covered her mouth and nose, her eyes widening with fear. *Ettars? In Uther-Erai?* Th om scowled. *What has he done?*

Motioning for Poppy to halt, he glanced up and down the halls and into the shadows. Seeing no immediate threat, he mouthed 'stay here', and peeked into the large room at the end of the hall. Just beyond a sofa, Dane crouched, tying a bandage over his forearm. Hurrying, he examined the contents of a red backpack and zipped it.

Using all of his weight, Th om sprung, launching himself over the sofa – tackling Dane, scattering bandages, cash, and food supplies across the Persian rug beneath them. Baring his teeth in a crazed grin, Dane struck his ribs and skull with both his fist and *cydern*. Thom wrenched the *cydern* from his grasp, and threw it, but with the effort, sacrificed his leverage. Dane rolled him to his back, but Thom blocked the restraint hold at his chest and unseated him with his hips, slamming him against the sofa. Wriggling, Dane worked an arm around his neck. Before he could get his legs around his body, Thom caught hold of his wrist, broke the attempted choke, thrusting his shoulder to the side, he spun out of the hold.

Chest heaving, Dane scrambled up and away, bouncing between his feet, circling behind the sofa. Thom crouched, his back leg planted, body angled in a ready position. The music growled and screamed. With a bloody grin, Dane turned up the volume – so loud Thom had to strain to keep from grimacing. *This has gone on long enough.*

As Dane lunged, Thom dodged, struck him across the jaw, the cheek, and under the chin, unbalancing him, finishing him with a palm at the base of the nose. Howling with pain, Dane crashed into the docking station. The music hissed then stopped. Grappling the wall, Dane caught hold of a glass shelf and launched it. Thom ducked. It shattered against the opposite wall. Glittering shards spun across the wood.

Their breathing ragged and loud, they circled each other. Dane's gaze swept the room, his grin bloody. "Where's Ayden?"

Keeping his face expressionless, Thom side-stepped. "Is money that important to you? That you'd betray everyone?"

"Why do you think?"

"How would I know?" Thom asked. "Explain. Or I'll quit being nice."

Dane shrugged. "Maybe I was bored. Maybe I wanted to see what the other side had to offer. Maybe I'd had it with shoveling Paquin shit. Maybe I want a taste of the good life for once." He spat blood. "If you had half my wits, you wouldn't have to ask."

He hurled a glass lamp. Thom dodged. It shattered against the wall nearest Poppy. Shrinking back around the corner, she drew her limbs close to her body.

Damn it! She was supposed to stay put! Thom forced his face to stay blank. *Get the information, Magnusson. Make him sing.*

Trying to lead Dane away from Poppy, Thom drifted further into the room. "Turn yourself in. Now. If you talk, he'll deal. I'll make sure of it."

Slowly, Poppy peeked around the corner.

Dane clicked his tongue. "You underestimate me." From behind a sofa cushion, Dane produced a black handgun. Grinning, he aimed it at Poppy. Her breath caught and her face went as gray as her hair. Thom felt his composure beginning to fray.

A mean grin crinkled Dane's face as his eyes flickered back to Thom. "This is the part where I take what I want and leave you feeling stupid or dead."

Rounding the sofa, he trained the gun at Thom and snatched up the red backpack, clutching it protectively.

*The moment he moves that gun…the moment he thinks he's won…*Thom shifted his weight to his back leg, ready to spring. "I gave you a chance."

Dane chuckled with derision. "Okay, beefcake, let me spell it out for you, even though you're too dense to get it." He gestured with the handgun. "This is a Glock 17. Not one of those useless twigs you're carrying. I got one as soon as Ayden told me you'd be stationed here. That was his first mistake. I knew something big was happening, if you were involved, gimp or not. And now," his grin widened, "who's won the prize?" Triumphant, he grinned at Poppy's pale face.

"She's not going anywhere with you."

"I don't think you're in a position to decide that." Dane scowled and spat blood again, massaging a swelling on his cheek. "I think you broke my jaw. Son of a—"

Springing, Thom slammed into him. Covering her head, Poppy dropped to her knees. The gun discharged. A window shattered. His ears rang and the acrid smell of powder bit the inside of his nose.

Banging the gun out of Dane's grip, Thom crushed his right hand. Dane howled. Thom kneed him in the chest and whacked his throat. The force of the blows creaked the floor. Writhing, Dane clutched his neck with his uninjured hand, struggling to breathe.

Removing the mag from the gun, Thom slid them to her, one by one. "Hold onto those."

Snatching up a shard of glass, Dane slashed at him. Taking up his *cydern* from his wrist, Thom sent it flying. He thwacked Dane across the jaw. Teeth flew across the floor. Planting a knee in the man's groin, Thom ground the staff-weapon at Dane's throat. "Time to sing, prize-winner."

Panting and thrashing, Dane's face purpled.

"The backpack." Glancing at Poppy, Thom nodded toward it. "Bring it here."

Trembling, she set the gun and mag on the rug and dragged the pack closer to him, away from Dane's pawing fingers. It appeared heavy, like it was full of water.

Gurgling, Dane coughed up blood.

Thom scowled at him. "I told you I'd quit being nice. It'll get worse if you don't start talking."

"Thom?" Poppy's voice, small and afraid.

She can wait.

"Who are you working with?" Thom let up the pressure of his staff, giving Dane a chance to answer.

The man only smirked. The backpack still next to her, Poppy scrabbled at his arm. "Thom!"

I'm not losing anyone else to these bastards.

Blood spluttered from Dane's lips as Thom slammed his head against the floor. "WHO?"

"THOM!"

A gray spider the size of a cat erupted out of the backpack, its pinchers poised to strike Poppy's face. It had white legs prickly with black hair, and bulbous eyes the color of blood. Choking on her scream, she threw her arms up.

Before he could react, the spider bit through her jacket. The flesh of her forearm ripped and long silver legs wrapped around her, claws raking. Releasing Dane, Thom struck the spider. It barked and scuttled away, up the wall, preparing to spray its toxic paralytic.

Grabbing the gun, Thom thrust the mag back in and sighted the ettar, just as little puffs rolled from its poison glands. *Not enough to paralyze.*

Dane leapt off the floor and ran, screaming. "Lilith! Come!"

Propelling itself off the wall, the spider sprang toward Dane.

Deciding between Dane and the ettar, Thom squeezed the trigger, grimacing at the report. Trembling on the floor, blood running through her fingers, Poppy moaned.

The floor shook with the weight of the spider. Limbs flailing, Lilith clicked and writhed. Dane shrieked, taking cover in the next room as Thom fired at him, missing. Leaping up, he crept toward Dane's hiding place, gun trained as he nudged at the ettar, checking it was dead.

The ettar shuddered and went still, its legs shriveling. Black blood drenched the rug. An unpleasant tang crowded the air, and his balanced pitched. *Hold your breath. Neutralize the threat.*

Dane glanced around the corner, but quickly took cover again. "NO!" His voice cracked with emotion.

Thom crept toward him. "Stop. Or I will shoot, and it will hurt in the worst way possible, but not kill you."

"Die, you murdering fuck!" Dane's voice went high and maniacal. "Tool! Priest! Come! KILL!"

Fleeing, Dane toppled the cabinet behind him, shattering the glass front, blocking Thom's path. Aiming at the running target he braced for another shot, but missed. The pounding of Dane's footsteps faded, and a door squeaked and banged.

Thom whirled around, crouching next to Poppy. She'd crumpled against the sofa, her bloody arm cradled in her lap. *Djöfulsins andskotans!*

Down the hallway, the shadows rustled with sudden movement, and spindly, clawed legs scraped on wood.

Chapter Eleven

Poppy's blood was warm on her palms. Her heart thundered with the aftershocks of fear as gunshots rang painfully in her ears. *Not good.* Trembling, she collapsed against the sofa, panting with the pain. The spider lay dead and twisted on the floor in front of her.

Was that thing poisonous?

She tried to get to her feet, but her body only flopped, like her limbs were asleep. A sudden surge of rotten-flesh odor coated her mouth and the room pitched. *No. Not more of them!* Her heartbeat spiked, frantic, as her eyes rolled, searching.

Kneeling, Thom appeared in front of her, examining her arm and wrapping it quickly with a cloth, before tying his jacket over his mouth and nose. She blinked up at him as he did the same for her with a blanket. *Am I going to die?*

More pain drilled up her arm. She choked back a sob. *More? Are there more of them?*

"Stay still and quiet, Poppy." He cupped her cheek. "It's going to be okay."

She blinked in response. Ripping the cushions off the couch, he stuck them around her, concealing her. Nearby, he crouched, as still as a waiting hunter.

Silence. Then scratching and clicks.

The gun discharged, jolting her. More pain. To keep from whimpering, she held her breath.

A loud thump shook the floor. Claws fumbled for traction on wood planks. Thom leapt up.

Warmth trickled into her lap. The smell of blood hit the back of her throat. Unable to control her body, she slid to the floor under the cushions, until her cheek found the rug. The pile was dusty and red—so red it hurt. *Is this what dying feels like? I don't want to go like this.*

A shadow flew through the air, screeching and grating. The couch trembled with an impact. She squeezed her eyes shut. Powerful blows, landing with bone-crunching force, competed with furious clicking.

Another gunshot. The floor vibrated with stomping. The pillows disappeared and hands gripped her shoulders.

"It's okay, Poppy." Thom's hazel eyes appeared inches from hers. "They're dead. You're going to be okay."

Shifting her upright, he worked his hands underneath her, cradling her wounded arm in her lap. She tried to help, but her limbs wouldn't work. Chilly night air wrapped around them and raindrops peppered her face. The jolt of steps caused her head to bounce against his shoulder and she bit her lip, tasting blood. Keys jingled and warmth surrounded them as he set her down on a cushiony surface.

"We're safe now," he said. "You're going to be okay."

Something heavy thumped on the floor and a key rattled in a lock. A fresh burst of agony flooded her veins, sending her vision into blurry spirals before it crystallized again, allowing her to see the room.

A lamp glowed on a side table, the base a carved owl. Nearby, a trunk revealed an orderly stash of clothes, papers, camping supplies, and stacks of cash. Thom rifled through contents of a medical kit thrown open in front of him. A smudge of red crossed one cheekbone, disappearing into his beard.

Blurriness again. Shivering. "Am–I–I–going–to–to–die?" she asked, her teeth chattering.

Thrusting a blanket under her calves, he shook a blue vial. "No."

He cut the sleeve of her jacket and shirt, revealing jagged gashes crisscrossing the flesh of her arm, oozing with blood. The room pitched like she was on a bad amusement park ride.

"I'm sorry, Poppy." He soaked a cloth with some liquid from a green glass bottle. "I shouldn't have asked you to get the backpack. I shouldn't have put you in danger like that."

His voice sounded far away. She opened her mouth to respond, but couldn't produce the words. He pressed the cloth on the rips in her forearm, and pain hammered up her arm. She moaned.

The syringe appeared, closer. Bursts of heat flooded her head and her stomach roiled. Stars clouded her vision before yielding to quiet darkness.

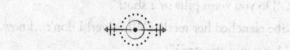

Poppy awoke to the rumble of thunder and the murmur of rain. As she moved, throbbing pain exploded in her right arm and her breath came in a whimper. Memories rushed into her, as raw and scary as the condition of her body; a gigantic spider munching on her arm, gunshots, teeth bouncing on a wooden floor, blood and pain. And Thom Magnusson – her coworker. Except, he wasn't.

This can't be happening. Tears slid out of her eyes, pooling in her ears.

The quiet rustle of movement neared the sofa. Under the duvet, she froze, terrified that a spider the size of a Labrador had saved her for breakfast. Thom knelt next to the couch, a deep v-wrinkle between his eyebrows.

A dappled bruise the size of an apple spread at his temple. On his neck, a butterfly bandage held together a laceration. He looked like a prizefighter, not a manager at Target. She shrunk away from him, not getting far.

"It's okay, Poppy." His voice was measured, careful. "You're safe."

Her large muscle groups went rigid with cramps, taking her breath away. Through the agony, she realized she was only wearing undergarments. Somehow, mortification joined her pain.

"You need something for the pain." He opened the medical kit. "Do you want pills or a shot?"

She clenched her teeth. "Whatever! I don't...know."

"Are you nauseated?"

"Muscles. Cramping. It...*hurts*."

Bottles chinked. The blood rushed and pounded in her head. Between the cramps, her arm throbbed like it was going to fall off.

Warmth surrounded her other arm. "You'll feel a stick."

Shutting her eyes, she held her breath.

"Don't hold your breath," he said. "Breathe through it. It'll help."

Keeping her eyes closed, she forced a breath in, a breath out, again and again – until other thoughts eclipsed the pain, questions crowing for attention. *Where are my clothes? What happened last night? Who's Thom Magnusson? Does anything in the near vicinity want to kill or eat us? Where am I? Just what the hell is going on?*

A vague memory of Ayden swam around the edges of her mind followed by a prick of regret. Was this somehow all her fault?

The thought took her breath away again. *Later, Poppy.* Now, she couldn't deal...She covered her face and breathed slowly until the hurt retreated into the medicine-fog clogging her brain cells.

Through rolls of thunder, rain drummed on the roof, trickling down the tall, narrow windows lining the living room. The muted light made her eyes heavy. Dishes chinked from somewhere and the smell of coffee wafted into her nose. Thom appeared again, with a glass of water and a bundle under his arm.

His expression brightened. "You look better."

"I'd be better if I was wearing clothes." Clutching the duvet to her neck, she sat up, hoping he didn't notice the color in her cheeks. "What did you give me anyway? I should've woken up last night. With the pain."

Handing her the water, he tossed a pair of jeans, a blue thermal, and some gray socks on the duvet. "Pain meds with a sedative. Drink…slowly. We can talk after you get dressed."

He disappeared around the corner. The sound of pouring liquid drifted from what she thought must be the kitchen.

"There's a bathroom down the hall," he called.

Grasping the clothes, she stumbled down the passage, her shoulder against the wall.

On her way back from the bathroom, fully clothed, she looked around. Birch floors creaked under her feet, bordered by thick ornate molding with layers of milky paint. A dusty chandelier hung from the ceiling, a Spanish style similar to the one last night – she shuddered, stiff-arming the memory.

A round window revealed a chilly view of her neighborhood, the angles of the houses softened by a thin mist. Squinting, she searched for her house in the gloom.

Mom!

She stumbled toward the smell of the coffee and burst into the kitchen, where he glanced up, his eyebrows lifting. "My mom! They took her! We need to call the police! There was a guy, a neighbor, dead. In our house."

Her vision crackled into white haze and she slumped against the counter. Hooking her uninjured arm, Thom guided her to a chair. A mug of coffee appeared in front of her, the steam caressing her nose.

Thom refilled his mug. "His name was Alan. Cerse saw to him, early this morning. Took him home."

"Cerse?"

"One of our cohort."

Sitting down in the chair across from her, he trained his eyes on the birdfeeder outside. A chickadee balanced on the edge, drilling at a seed, its black head bobbing. "The police can't be involved in this. They won't be any help." Leaning forward, he interlaced his fingers, his eyes catching hers. "We'll get her back, Poppy. And Ayden too."

Took him home. Cerse. Police can't be involved. Ayden. We'll get her back. She cleared her throat. "Explain. Please. I don't understand any of this."

"Drink your coffee. Let me collect my thoughts." He folded his arms and focused on the bird feeder. Fussing, the chickadee flitted away, and the coffee maker gurgled, loud in the silence.

Beneath the table, Poppy clenched her fists. *I don't want to drink coffee. I want answers.*

Glancing at her, his face smoothed into the cryptic, dispassionate expression she remembered from work – the same look he used on troublesome customers. He arose and returned, setting a jug of goat's milk and a bowl filled with golden raw sugar in front of her.

She couldn't move, she wouldn't move, until she had answers, no matter how damned intimidating he looked.

"You'll feel better if you eat. There's toast and cereal," he offered, leaning forward. "Or oatmeal."

Her stomach churned, ambivalent.

"I'm not explaining until you start to eat." He arose and opened a cabinet. "It'll help. Especially with the medication side effects. You'll think clearer."

White cabinets climbed up the walls of the kitchen. The speckled countertops were bare except for a toaster and the coffee maker. Against her will, she wondered what kind of cereal a guy like Thom ate, half-hoping it was multi-colored and had marshmallows. But no, a box of some health-food bran cereal appeared on the table in front of her, along with a spoon and a white bowl.

A knot of hunger twisted in her stomach, protesting the delay. Reluctantly, she downed the cereal and drank the coffee, watching the rain trickle down the pane in silver rivulets. Far below the house, the river traveled eastward, a ribbon of ominous purple-gray. Scanning the grounds, she realized they were on the top floor of the rickety Victorian above the landing.

Gulping the lukewarm coffee in the bottom of her mug, she refilled it. "It's time for you to start talking." Her thoughts stumbled on too many questions. "Why are we here, exactly?"

His eyes were greener than she remembered, the hue of a scotch pine in winter. "This is my apartment."

Drumming her fingers on the table, she waited.

Brushing aside the sugar on the table, he sighed, as if he knew his answer wouldn't be sufficient. "Dane lived in the apartment below – where we found him last night. We worked together, until recently. These quarters were provided as part of our employment."

"Okay," she said, after a minute. "Continue."

"I don't know where to start." He made a face, like someone who's just discovered a flat tire. "I wasn't supposed to be the one to explain this." He folded his arms. "And we don't have much time. Not enough time to do this right."

"What do you mean, not enough time?" she asked.

"We can't stay here. Dane will return. Soon." He glanced at his watch. "And he'll bring friends."

The questions tumbled out of her mouth. "Who is Dane? And who are you? Is this...because of my dad? Where's my mom? Who's Ayden?" Her voice rose. "I don't understand!"

He grimaced. "Slow down, Poppy."

She slammed her cup down, sloshing coffee on the table. "Slow down? Like hell! After this!" She held up her arm. "I want answers! All those, monster-things. And what happened to Ayden." Her voice broke. Lightheaded, she gripped the table, shutting her eyes. "Oh."

"Yeah. This needs to be slow. That bite could've killed you."

"I've never seen a spider that big." The bandages peeked out from underneath her shirt sleeve. "You didn't take me to a hospital." She didn't mean it to sound accusatory, but it did.

"If I had, you would've died."

"How'd you know what to do?"

The divots under his eyes were shadowy, the same color as the river. "Those spiders were ettars. A species native to," he made another face, "to where I live. I've been trained to treat attack wounds. And I've been bitten myself, though not as bad as you were. I had antivenom in my medical kit. It's standard issue."

"Where are you talking about?"

"The same place your parents are from. The same place you were born."

Her heartbeat kicked up. "I have a feeling you're not going to say Missouri. Or Ohio. Or somewhere normal."

Lines deepening on his forehead, he rubbed his chin.

"So? Out with it!" Her voice cracked. "I can take it."

"I don't think you'll believe me."

"I've actually been waiting for an explanation of a lot of really crazy shit for a long time now. So knock yourself out."

He rubbed the divot between his eyebrows. "The place is called Caelith. It's a realm weaved," he interlocked his fingers, "from the substance, the matter of this world. Connected by origin, but only just. The homeland of elemental beings." He paused, gauging her reaction. "It's difficult to explain."

She stared. "Try harder."

He leaned forward. "The creatures we encountered last night are elementals, beings originating out of the five elements. Caelith is their havenland, a place formed centuries ago after the original earth became uninhabitable for them.

The elementals from last night came here through a well, a passage where matter bends and stretches, because of unusual forces present in the earth. Here, it has something to do with this river." He glanced at the Twin. "If that makes sense."

NO. It doesn't make sense. Poppy's response shriveled in her throat, but her mouth stayed open.

The v-shaped wrinkle appeared between his eyebrows. "This is really difficult to explain. And I don't have time to do it right."

"What, like – a parallel universe?" She clenched and unclenched her fists.

"More like hidden spaces." The wrinkle between his eyebrows shifted, replaced by lines of concentration across his forehead. "Centuries ago, in specific areas, the earth...how to say it," he tugged the curls at the back of his neck, "stretched, shifted, expanded, becoming the lands of Caelith, eventually five regions, accessible throughout this world, but hidden. Some are similar to the earth landscapes they're located around, but some are different."

She snapped her jaw shut. "This isn't possible."

Scanning the view from the window, he stood. "Do you remember that big, smelly creature? That rescued Dane last night? That was real. Where do you think it came from?"

"Are you even from Iceland? Is your name actually Thom? Have you been shitting me this whole time?" She stood. "What am I doing here? I need to get home."

Like she was a spooked cat who might bolt, he rotated slowly. "Yes, Poppy. My name really is Thom. Thom Magnusson. I was born in Iceland and lived there until I was fourteen. Everything I'd told you is true. It just wasn't everything."

To her horror, tears burned behind her eyes. "But, my mom." Swallowing hard, she looked, away, setting her jaw. *Elementals? Caelith? How can this be real?*

"They took your mother to Caelith. And that's where we have to go. To get her back."

Shaking her head, she sunk back down.

"We'll find her, Poppy."

The conviction in his voice stirred longing, for reassurance, for hope of an ending that wasn't tragically dark, pregnant with inevitable loss and mental illness, outcomes she'd feared for so long. But, trusting him – it was too risky.

He glanced at his watch and his expression sobered. "We don't have much time." He motioned to the bandage around her forearm. "I need to look at your arm."

"Is that where my Dad's been all this time? This Caelith place?"

His eyebrows dipped, but he nodded.

Her head felt like it might float away from her body – grasping for something, anything to help her survive this. Was this revelation the answer to her Dad's mysterious absences? Maybe, just maybe, the reason behind them was actually good – noble. "Is he an elemental?"

Reaching for her arm, he shook his head.

Deflated by his answer, she dodged him. "Then why the hell is he there?"

"That'll take time to explain. I'll tell you more later." He managed to shift her arm away from her body. "Right now, I need to look at your arm, and we need to get moving."

She tried to protest, but he was unraveling the wrapping, and the sight startled her. The skin around the wounds had turned a violent red-purple. The jagged rips were closed with neat lines of black stitching, perhaps dozens, cinching the gashes. It was swollen, but nothing like the mess she'd seen last night.

Satisfied, he re-bandaged it with the skill of someone who'd had practice, producing supplies out of a canvas backpack the size of a small planet.

"Do you have pain anywhere else?" he asked, feeling her neck under her jaw. "Under your neck or arms?"

She shook her head. To see his eyes, to read his expression, she had to tilt her chin up. Abruptly, she remembered Dane's grip on her wrist, her bicep, his leering face. She shrunk away from him. Thom studied her for a moment, but turned away like nothing had happened.

"It's healing well. You'll be fine." He retrieved some bottled water out of the refrigerator. "Tell me when the pain gets bad. Sooner rather than later."

You don't even know him. Not really. What are you doing, Poppy? Fear coiled tight in her stomach. "Why should I go with you? I–I–don't even know you."

As the words hung between them, she remembered Thom dragging her out of the horrible arm of water, struggling to save Ayden, wrapping her bleeding arm in a shirt, reassuring her. Overnight, he'd become way more than a coworker. Conflicted, she sunk back onto the chair. *Besides, what other options do you have?*

His eyes below hers, he crouched next to the table. "Poppy, I know this is a shock."

That's putting it mildly, she thought. *All this time. They never said a word.*

He almost touched her shoulder, but instead curled his hand on his knee. "And this is the worst way to learn about this. But, will you trust me? For now?"

Why? Why would they hide so much from me? How does he know so much? Things that I should know? Anger and panic wrestled for control inside of her. *No. It's too much of a risk. Too much. I can't...*

Seeing the struggle play out across her face, Thom's expression softened, transparent. His face, that look – again, she experienced the powerful sense of familiarity. She knew him, more than she realized.

Something like a living dream hijacked her brain, dropping her in the middle of a meadow, at midday, surrounded by sunlight, waist high grass and wildflowers. A brilliant blue sky bowed above, dappled with sprawling white clouds, some glistening with rainbow colors. Sprigs of tiny yellow flowers tickled the skin of her arms. In a gentle breeze, purple plumes the size of fox tails swayed, and the scent of earthy heat and sweet, new green flirted with her senses.

The impression pierced something buried in Poppy. It exploded, an egg full of memories hatching.

She remembered a tree with craggy limbs, so tall it nudged the clouds. Sunlight fluttered on the leaves. The bark was gray and tidy, like leopard spots. Thom and Ayden perched high in its twisted boughs, beckoning her to follow them, to climb. A ladybug crawled on the trunk, at her eye level, its shell purple with amber dots. The intensity of the scene made her breath catch.

The vivid pictures faded, revealing Thom still crouched in front of her, his expression concerned. More visions elbowed their way into her mind, similar to when she'd driven him home, except now she knew what they were. *Memories.*

"I remember you!" she breathed. "We played in the Meadows together. And swam at the lake. You and Ayden. You had a pair of boots that I loved."

A corner of his mouth twitched.

"You let me flop around in them one day," she continued. "All afternoon, even though they swallowed my feet." She grabbed his arm. "You were so good with the horses. And you caught these gigantic red fish with purple spots. And we cooked them outside after dark. Under all the stars. There were so many..." Her voice faded to a whisper. "Please tell me this isn't all just..." She couldn't say it.

"You're remembering, Poppy." He took her hand and folded it gently between his. "We knew each other. In Cael-ith-Caldys. Years ago. I have the same memories."

"And Ayden was—" Her voice broke.

"Is." His expression galvanized. "He *is* your brother."

"But why did I not remember? Why did I not know you? Or him?"

"I'll explain when we're in a safer place. I promise."

Memories. It felt like she'd discovered a long-lost book which held the answers to her most important questions, but only had a moment to glance through it. She yearned to open it again, to immerse herself within it, to remember everything she'd forgotten.

If going with Thom meant more such glimpses – meant answers – she would follow him anywhere, regardless of the danger.

Chapter Twelve

Thom shrugged into his backpack and, peering through the leaded window in the front door, scanned the front yard and street. *We need to move,* the practical side of him insisted. He glanced back at Poppy. *But, look at her! She's been through hell.*

On the sofa, Poppy tugged on her boots, grimacing at the damp leather. Her face was a shade lighter than the gray upholstery and faint purple bruises rimmed her eyes – the effect of ettar poison. It reminded him of a Halloween costume. Standard care for similar bite wounds would normally be a week in hospital – impossible in their predicament. *If we don't move, they'll catch her, and her hell will get a lot worse.*

"We'll take it easy, okay? Tell me if you feel sick." He dug in the pocket of his jacket, his hand closing around the smooth surface of the blue, Caelithian stone he'd discovered, stowed in transparent silks beneath Dane's ettar, Lilith.

"Okay." When she didn't look up from her boots, he nudged her and held out the stone. Its weird static charge skittered over the silky surface into his palm. Did it contain elemental energy, and if so, how had it preserved it *Erai*-side?

Seeing the stone, her expression brightened and she closed her fingers around it, as if she was eager to hold it. "I thought I'd...How..." she cleared her throat, "did you end up with this?"

"The ettar had it. Wrapped up in silks beneath her."

"Dane's spider-thing?"

He nodded.

She pocketed it. "How did you know it was mine?"

Zipping up his jacket, he considered the question. "Deidre mentioned something about a Caelithian stone she'd given you, matching that description. It seemed important to her."

And if Dane considered it important enough to steal...what does that mean? He rubbed the frown crease between his eyebrows. *Save that riddle for later. We need to move.*

"Oh." She wobbled to her feet.

Watching her for pain, he handed her a backpack. Caelithian made, it was large and utilitarian, made of sturdy waxed canvas. Struggling with it like it was part of a costume, she slid the straps over her shoulders.

"We'll risk a stop at your house," he said. "You need clothes and shoes, and other things I don't have. Enough for a couple weeks. Do you have spare car keys?"

She nodded, her eyes skipping around, resting anywhere but on him. *Her world is in cataclysmic upheaval. Give her space, Magnusson.*

Outside, steep rickety stairs descended from the apartment. The wind was brisk, tossing Poppy's hair in cold, spitting blasts; the loose silver strands brushed his shoulder until she secured them under her collar. The sweet gum tree in the front yard blazed magenta and amber, striking against the gray, somber light.

On edge, Thom scanned the neighborhood. Cutting through a yard opposite the mansion, he jumped a chain-link fence, pivoted, and helped her clamber down from the frigid, wet metal. Soon they reached the opposite side of Weller St., just catty-corner from her house, in between an empty gingerbread rental and a neighboring bungalow.

The Paquin's car sat in front of her house, undisturbed. The porch light glowed next to the front window, the white curtains still drawn.

It's too quiet. He glanced up and down the street. "Anything about the house look unusual?"

"No. But nothing about this is normal, so I might be missing something."

"Fair enough," he said.

The spare house key waited beneath the garden gnome. As she unlocked the door, he scanned the street and then poked his head inside and listened. Closing the door behind them, he indicated to the foyer. "Wait here."

He swept through all the rooms on the first floor before pounding up the stairs, his footsteps creaking across the pine floors, checking in closets and behind beds. Behind a false panel in Deidre's room he retrieved a thick envelope of cash, a folder of documents, and stowed them in his backpack.

Returning downstairs, he found Poppy motionless at the entrance to the kitchen, staring at the dried blood staining the threshold to the laundry room, her face as colorless as the white walls. In her palm she clutched the blue stone, turning it over and over again.

A sharp pang threaded his ribcage. *We need to hurry.*

"The house is safe. Pack what you need. Layer as much as you can, so you don't have to carry everything."

Sniffing, she dug through a drawer and stowed the spare car keys in her backpack. While she trudged upstairs, he raided the closets, snagging a few heavy blankets. The stairs creaked and she appeared again, clad in black jeans and a thick gray sweater, lugging a full pack.

He eyed her converse. "How far can you walk in those?"

"Far enough."

"How's your arm?"

"Okay." Her eyes darted to the painting above the fireplace; the textured crimson of her hair shone in the dim light, like embers in a fireplace.

"There's one like it," he said, pausing in front of it. "In his quarters at base."

Clasping her arms across her chest, she angled her body away from him.

Say something, Magnusson. Something helpful. Something kind. He glanced toward the front door, rubbing his neck. *Nothing I can say about Felix Paquin will help, nothing that's true anyway. She should find out for herself.*

"The compass star." She pointed. "On his jacket. The same symbol is tattooed on your arm." Her voice cracked.

"It's a symbol of the *Offysfyn*. The coalition of elementals and humans that protect and guard Caelith." He pivoted for the door.

"Does everyone who serves have to be tattooed?"

"No." *Just the conscripts,* he thought, biting his tongue.

Outside, the overcast sky reflected silver off the puddles in the gravel driveway. Scanning the car's dashboard, he tossed the blankets and their packs in the back seat. *Andskotans helvítis.* It didn't look anything like the panel of Alan's motorcycle. Or the truck he'd driven in Snæfellsness. Could he operate this thing without killing them?

The keys jingled as Poppy fidgeted with them. "So, the last time I drove, things kinda went sideways."

Too risky. Not meeting her eyes, he straightened up. "I need you to drive."

"What? Why?" Her hand tensed around the keys.

"It'll be safer if you do." He ruffled the hair on the back of his head, sheepish as heat spread across his face. "I haven't driven a car since I was fourteen, in Iceland. And that was on rural backroads."

Her mouth twitched. "Wait, you can go all Jason Bourne, but you can't drive?"

A smile – no, a smirk – snuck onto her face and, for a heart-beat, he saw the Poppy he'd known long ago; the spirited, care-free kid – as alive as the Meadows of Clanglyn in Spring. If his embarrassment kept her smiling, keep her distracted, it was worth it. Realizing he was staring, he scanned the yard, the trees, the street.

Gooseflesh flooded his back and he stiffened, gripping the cuff at his wrist. A figure in a dark hooded sweater emerged from behind a hedge and halted at the edge of the driveway, clothed in the garb of a Gren mercenary – thick laced boots keyed with copper talismans, probably matching the leather armor hidden underneath the sweater. The man's shoulders bulged with the kind of heft that comes from habitually lifting heavy objects, or more likely, elemental *xust* or *dew* – illegal serums cooked to enhance non-hybrid humans.

Stiffening, Thom side-stepped in front of Poppy, murmuring. "Behind the car. Quickly."

The man pushed his hood back, revealing a bearded face with a sharp grin. His fair hair was trimmed close to his head and rows of small silver hoops glinted in his ears. The eye-lashes that rimmed his eyes were almost white. His eyes roved Poppy before snapping back to Thom.

Mack Morrison. Gemmed out to the Grens. Thom sighed.

Poppy moved with jerky steps, her eyes fixed on Morrison like he was a rabid grizzly.

"Thom Magnusson!" The grin revealed lots of teeth, but managed to not look happy. "I wasn't sure I'd ever see you again. Heard they messed you up pretty good. How big is your scar, then?" His voice rolled with a thick Scots burr.

"Morrison." Thom jerked his chin in a terse gesture, refusing to be distracted. "You're stupider than I thought, if you're working with Dane now. He'll screw you over in the end."

Shrugging, Morrison's eyes flickered to Poppy. "What makes you think I'm not playing him? I've found the two of you, and not a hair of him in sight. Cheers to me, I say."

A door banged across the street. A white-haired woman appeared on the front porch, bent over a walker.

Another complication. Calculating, Thom scoured their surroundings, his fingers surrounding his *cydern*, his quadriceps tense, ready to spring. He let a humorless smile crack his face. "So, I was right about stupider, then."

Across the street, the elderly woman tottered down the ramp to her driveway. Busy wiping at the rivulets of sweat crawling down his forehead, Morrison didn't notice her. "You know, Dane woulda cut you in, but you're too fucking honorable. And now he's pissed about Lilith." His grin faded as though he was too strained to hold it. "Wait till you see who is with him. You're going to wish you'd died last year."

He's bluffing, Thom thought, eyes darting from Poppy, to Morrison, to the white-haired figure tottering down the driveway. *No! He's stalling!*

"You'll be dead sooner if you keep dosing to sprint wells. You look like shit." Thom edged toward the vehicle, lowering his voice. "Get in the car, Poppy. Quickly."

"Stay where you are, sweetheart." A crooked black staff appeared in Morrison's hand. His gaze returned to Thom and he shrugged. "The risk is paying off so far."

Thom stiffened. *A Grimsvoht cydern.* Even from twenty paces, the thing vibrated with wicked power. The bones of *Grimsvoht* elementals made notoriously unpredictable weapons.

The elderly lady reached the end of the driveway, her walker scraping the concrete. Frowning, she squinted at the two men and produced a cellphone from the droopy pocket of her sweater. Behind the car, Poppy squeaked, shaking her head.

Morrison's smile disappeared; he still hadn't noticed the woman. "Do you really want to be on Paquin's side, Magnusson? They're losing ground every day." He took a measured step. "Sava would give a lot to have you with us. And Dane has to kiss his ass. All you need to do is hand her over. With the relic, of course." A line of sweat rolled down his neck. "Think about it."

Relic? Thom's expression sharpened. "Farðu til fjandans, helvítis mongólítinn þinn."

Morrison's eyebrows lifted. "Is that a no?"

"Definitely." Thom's fingers tightened around his *cydern.*

Squinting at her phone, the elderly woman fumbled with her glasses.

"Mrs. Tinsley!" Poppy waved from behind the car.

Her head wobbled around.

"Undercover cop!" Poppy gestured to him. "Busting a meth-head!" She pointed at Morrison. "Go back in the house! Please!"

Noticing Mrs. Tinsley, Morrison did a double-take. Scowling, she chucked her newspaper at him. "Get out of my neighborhood, ass-wipe!"

Seizing the distraction, Thom launched his *cydern*, muttering an elemental curse for extra punch. The weapon clocked Morrison's face, knocking him flat to the gravel at the edge of the street. Recovering, it made a spinning arc and returned to Thom's palm as he sprang for the car. Poppy was still crouched outside. "Get in, Poppy!"

Seeing Mrs. Tinsley turn her walker around, Poppy leapt into the driver's seat, gripping the keys, her face bone white.

Scowling, Morrison scrambled up, his expression livid under the blood streaming from his nose.

Before Thom reached the passenger side, the ominous whine of Morrison's *cydern* approached. Lunging, Thom deflected it. At the collision of the weapons, light flashed, accompanied by a gunshot-like bang. The car jolted and the windows on one side cracked. Poppy yelped in surprise. A painful charge shot up his arm, and his bicep muscles cramped.

The weapon rebounded to Morrison. His fists twisting it, he muttered – the rasp of elemental speech.

"Don't do it!" Thom yelled. *Not here! It's too risky!*

The ground trembled as Morrison charged them, his steps dragging.

Stupid fokker! Thom shook his muscles loose, fisting his staff. It was bad enough he had to fight a dosed-up idiot, now his elemental counterpart was about to show itself earth-side, with zero cover.

As the ground vibrated and rippled, a curtain of leaves burst up from the yard, toppling the garden gnome. The maple next to the driveway bucked wildly and the front yard collapsed and gave way. Teeth bared, Morrison charged him.

Their weapons collided, flashing like welding sparks, the impact louder than gunfire, but Thom was prepared for the impact. Recoiling, he wacked Morrison under the chin, sending a spray of sweat and blood through the air. Rolling, Morrison launched his staff, but it went awry, not meeting its mark.

With a dull tearing, the turf of the front yard folded up from the loam. The roots of the maple squirmed, shrinking from a widening fissure in the yard.

Thom sprinted for the car, but the ground yawned further, cracking the pavement, causing him to stumble. Leaping, Morrison tackled him, smashing his face into the gravel, trying to pin him down. Wrenching an arm loose, Thom elbowed Morrison in the eye. Grunting, his head flew back with the impact.

The earth inside the fissure arose like a geyser, shuddering. Dark soil rolled off it, revealing a lean figure with smooth, sandy skin. It had no eyes, mouth or nose, just subtle hints of features. *A kesili earthkind*. Intelligently, the *kesili* regarded them, stretching up to a height that competed with the dogwood tree across the street, debating if he wanted to suffocate him quickly or toy with him first.

Backing up, Thom's arm tightened under Morrison's chin, hoping to deter the elemental. But the man gurgled, spitting out an earthkind invocation. Releasing Morrison, Thom backed into a defensive stance, his *cydern* glimmering amber, becoming as long as a javelin. The elemental hesitated. Recovering, a mean grin stretched across Morrison's face and he repeated the words, getting to his feet.

The *kesili* advanced, the clinging mud melting away, quickening its movements. It ripped a thick branch off the cowering maple and flung it. Dodging, Thom rolled and jumped up. Swinging his *Grimsvoht*, Morrison joined in, doubling the attack. A searing blow tore through Thom's arm, ripping his shirt sleeve, just missing an artery. Evading attacks on both fronts, Thom whirled and dove.

"Thom!" Poppy shouted. "Move!"

Spying her behind the wheel of the car, he sprang out of the vehicle's path. The engine roared as she accelerated toward Morrison, ramming him. His body spun to the side and the car shuddered with the impact. Cranking the wheel, she plowed into the elemental. It collapsed, dissolving onto the hood. With a metallic screech, the paint ripped up and sand blasted the windshield. The *kesili* formed itself again and hit the windshield with a fist, cracking the glass. Yelping, she turned on the wipers, put the car in reverse, and zoomed backward, bumping over the curb and into the opposite side yard. The elemental tumbled off with a thud that shook the ground, sand flying everywhere.

Thom leapt inside. "Go!"

She plowed the car through a hedge and over the curb. The tires hit the road and she punched the accelerator, speeding to the corner of Weller and screeching around the turn.

Thom's chest heaved. At the end of the Meadows she jammed the brakes, scanning the road. A dark ripple of water gathered in the road at the bottom of the hill, too much to be rainwater.

"The storm must have flooded the creek," she said, breathless.

Frowning, he shook his head. "It floods at Sonnet. Not there."

With the power of a storm surge, it grew as they watched.

"No. No. No!" It came out under his breath.

Her eyes widened. "Thom? What is it?"

"Go right!" His voice echoed in the car. "Take the bridge!"

"The bridge?"

"Gun it, Poppy!"

Her knuckles white on the steering wheel, Poppy headed for the on-ramp that led the massive steel bridge spanning the Twin.

He glanced behind them, scanning for pursuing elementals. "Hurry! He meant to stall us! We've got to get out of Riverston. Quick!"

Chapter Thirteen

Poppy's arm throbbed in competition with her head. Gritting her teeth, she pushed the accelerator. Ahead, the stoplight glowed crimson and she slowed, scanning the intersection.

"Go, Poppy! Go!" Thom's voice hurt her ears.

She ploughed through the red light and took the on-ramp. The car reluctantly merged with lines of traffic headed for the bridge. By the time they reached the threshold, she'd pushed it to sixty.

Seeing the view from the bridge, she gasped in disbelief. The river was spreading in vast silver pools all over the flatlands of north Riverston, flooding the tiny municipal airport. The soccer fields were next. Occupants gaping and pointing, the cars cramming the highway slowed down.

"What the?" She stuttered. "How is this possible?"

"Faster!" He pounded the dashboard. "They mean to trap us!"

"I'm trying! It's a Taurus!"

A gawking car swerved in their lane. She leaned on the horn and the car veered away. As the lane emptied in front of them, she forced the gas pedal to the floor.

He glanced behind. "Faster!"

The needle edged one hundred. "You know this is a felony, right?" Her voice shook.

They left the bridge behind. Ahead, on both sides of the highway, the water surged at a low spot, crowding the shoulder, covering the southbound lanes.

Her knuckles whitened on the steering wheel. "There's water."

"We'll make it," he said, an edge in his voice.

Just as the right lane began to fill, the Taurus zoomed past. She blinked at the road ahead, gasping with the gallop of her heart. She'd never driven so fast, which was terrifying in itself, but considering what she'd just witnessed, she didn't feel safe enough to slow down. *Keep it together. Just drive.*

The road climbed as they headed north, speeding past tree-capped, rocky insides of the hills the highway cut through. Gradually, her heartbeat slowed, her wounded arm throbbed. The skin underneath the bandages felt hot and swimming. Was it bleeding? Or was her freaked-out brain on sensory overload?

Scanning the road behind them, Thom crouched down in the passenger seat. A gash on his arm dripped blood onto the console between them, but he didn't seem to notice.

What does he see? Not wanting to take a curve too fast, she let up on the gas pedal. The diffused brightness of the overcast sky made her squint, causing her head to ache like she'd been punched. After a few miles nausea joined the pain.

Frowning, Thom thumped down in his seat. Retrieving his pack, he wiped up the blood on the console, buckled his seat belt, and examined his arm before digging a first aid kit out of the pack.

"Are you okay?" he asked, making swift work of the laceration.

Afraid to loosen her grip on the steering wheel, she nodded stiffly.

He tied off the bandage. "Pull over."

Is it safe? The words stuck on her tongue.

"Right here." He motioned to the shoulder.

Signaling, she came to a stop, the world swimming around her. Dimly, she became aware of Thom at the driver's side, opening the door.

His arm slid behind her back. "Come on. Out you go."

Her feet barely touched the ground as they rounded the car. Sitting down in the passenger seat sent a jolt of pain through her arm. Sweat beaded on her temples and her muscles twitched and began to cramp. *Not this again!*

Thom appeared in the driver's seat.

"I thought you didn't know how to drive." Panic made the world spin faster.

Before she could grab the keys, his hand covered the ignition. "I think I can manage. It doesn't seem much different from Alan's motorcycle."

Stomach churning, she glanced between him and the cars zooming by. *Suddenly he knows how to drive?*

"This car is probably easier," he added, in a tone that failed to reassure her. "No gears."

Sinking back into the seat, she shut her eyes. *This can't be happening.*

From inside his pack, he produced a blue glass bottle with a handwritten label. A couple of pills appeared in her palm. They were gray and speckled, like a bird's egg, but only about the size of peas. He offered her water and an energy bar. She stared at them like she didn't know what to do. Moving – no, thinking – hurt.

"The longer you wait, the worse it's going to get," he said. "Take them. You'll be glad you did."

She turned away. "I'm afraid I'm going to puke."

He shrugged. "If you do, we'll just deal with it."

Before she could talk herself out of it, she swallowed the pills, gulped the water, and nibbled the food. *Any moment now*, she thought, *let it kick in. Let this horrible throbbing sick go away.*

He adjusted the heat, warming the interior. As her pain and nausea dulled, her shivering abated, and a calm seeped into her body. Out the passenger side window, a tree shone with amber leaves, fluttering in a crowd of army-green cedars. Poppy wondered what kind of tree it was; the bright yellow reminded her of sunbeams. Glancing around, she discovered him looking at her, his expression unreadable. Heat crept into her cheeks.

"Better now?" he asked.

"Better. Yes." Her voice croaked. "What are those pills anyway?"

A frown wrinkling his forehead, Thom examined the dashboard. "A multi-symptom painkiller and anti-nausea med. Caelithian made."

"They're safe?"

He nodded. "Yeah. I was on them for months."

She squeaked with horrified surprise. "Months! I'm going to feel like this for months?"

"No-no. Maybe a week or two."

Morrison's words surfaced in Poppy's memory, *How big is your scar then?*

"Why did you—" she began.

"You'll be completely recovered in three weeks." He signaled and looked over his shoulder, hand on the gear shift.

"Are you sure you know what you're doing?" She gripped the car door.

"Uh-huh." He surveyed the road. "The brake is on the right. No. The left." He tapped one experimentally. The engine vroomed. "I got this." He glanced down. "Which one is it again?"

Horrified, she stared at him.

The skin around his eyes wrinkled with a grin.

She grimaced. "Son of a bitch."

His grin didn't fade as he put the car in gear and pulled out onto the highway.

"Help me keep an eye out," he said. "For anything strange. Okay?"

Anything strange. She clenched her teeth. *Fantastic. Like multi-eyed monsters that appear out of the ground? Or golem-creatures made of sand? Or better yet, rivers that flood cities on purpose?*

"What was that back there? How does a river flood that fast?" She shook her head.

"That was the work of a waterkind called a *michawe*, an elemental of rivers. Several of them."

"How do you know," her voice shook, "that we're not going to be attacked by some monster at any moment?"

"Not a monster. An elemental."

She scowled. "What if an *elemental* decides to break the highway in two in front of us?"

His smile had faded, leaving a v-shaped wrinkle between his eyebrows. "I guess it probably wasn't the best moment to joke around. I just didn't want this to be so, heavy. Maybe it's too late for that."

"It's not too late to explain. Some of this. Any of this."

He twisted the cap off his water container and drank. His knuckles were red and scratched.

"So, what if?" Her voice went ragged. "After what I've just seen in the past twenty-four hours, how do you know that's not going to happen, sending us to our deaths in a flying heap of metal?"

"I don't, but it's unlikely." He put his elbow on the car door and tugged his hair. "Most elementals – not all, but most – can't stray too far from a well. Or they risk draining their life force. The amount of energy it would take to attack that way." He shook his head. "Dane will need different elementals to pursue us, if he tries. Not the kind born of earth or water. That big creature that carried him off last night, remember? It was an earthkind *ulli*, kin to basalt." Lost in his explanation, he frowned, concentrating. "Elementals' life and energy are tied to the Caelithian havenlands. They can't exist outside them, at least not indefinitely. This place kills them slowly. That gives us an advantage."

She grimaced. "Elementals? I need a study guide, or a cheat sheet or something."

Nodding, he adjusted the rear-view mirror. "Elementals – ancient beings that evolved out of the basic elements. Earth, air, water, fire, aether."

"Aether?"

"Spirit-matter, or dark matter. The least understood of the elements. Because it's so abstract."

She stared at him. His forehead wreathed in lines, he returned the look. When she didn't speak, he continued.

"Elementals are from an older time, before humans dominated the earth. They can appear as a humanoid – sort of like a human-friendly interface – or as a manifestation of their element. Or a mash-up of the two. The *michawe* – the river elemental in the Twin – attacked us in water form, last night.

It didn't waste its energy trying to manifest in a way we could interact with it. Because it just wanted to capture you."

"Friendly?"

"A form that makes interaction possible. Not necessarily...friendly."

"You make it sound...so normal."

"I've lived in Caelith-Caldys since I was fourteen. For me, they are normal." He glanced at her. "You spent your childhood around them too, in the same region. You just don't remember."

Poppy swallowed hard. "Caelith-Caldys?"

"One of the havenland regions. It's the closest, from here. There are five. Caldys, Enkka, Greya, Huldra, and Symsara."

"And humans live there?"

He nodded. "We're immigrants. Some accidental, some have more complicated stories. Most elementals pay us little mind. Some even like us, as long as we respect the havenlands. Many, but not all. It helps that humans in Caelith are outnumbered by elemental kind. We're not a threat. At least not yet. Things have changed in the last decade."

"What about my family?"

His fingers tightened on the steering wheel. "Your family, on both sides, has been in Caelith for generations. I'm not sure how they came to be there. There was a tapestry of record in your front hall, but I was rarely inside the house, so I can't tell you much about it."

Drab cedars and rocky hillsides flew by, but her thoughts kept her from seeing them. Part of her felt dissociated from his explanation, like she was only reading a fantasy book or watching a movie. But then she remembered – the creature in the river with lidless white eyes and a wrinkled hole of a mouth. "Is there a white elemental?" She blurted. "That would've been in the river? Different than the *michawe*?"

He frowned; the expression gave her a little shiver. "A *muiras*. An elemental of mists. They manifest properties of both air and water. That one was bated by Dane. He lured it to capture you."

Astounded, she faced him. "What? You knew? Was that you? Who pulled me out?"

He made a face and half-shrugged, which she took as assent.

"And you never explained? I thought I was crazy!"

Anger began to swim with the discoveries inside of her, like a crocodile waiting for the right moment to strike. Its hungry intensity, trembling in her fingers, scared her.

His hands tightened on the steering wheel. "I wanted to explain, but couldn't. That was Ayden's decision. He's been in charge of the operations protecting you and your mother. Alan, Neil, even Dane, were part of that outfit, long before I was." The v-wrinkle appeared between his brows. "There are complications. Caelith-side."

"Complications?"

"A while ago, Ayden became concerned for your safety, suspicious of some involved in the operation. He wasn't sure who he could trust here anymore, so he asked me to investigate. To advise on a way to extract you and Deidre, when necessary."

Her knuckles whitened on the door handle. "So, you've been babysitting me? All this time? This was just procedure?"

He sighed. "That's not how I meant it to sound."

Thom was some sort of glorified bodyguard. Not even a friend, and certainly not anything more. Heat prickled her cheeks. *It doesn't matter. Find Mom. Find Ayden. Get answers. Remember what you've forgotten. That's what matters.*

"Give yourself time, Poppy. This is a lot to take in." A curse vibrated in his throat. "This wasn't supposed to happen this way."

"How exactly was it supposed to happen?" she snapped.

"With your family in a safe place. Uncomplicated. Slow. As it is, I can't imagine how unsettling this is."

He sighed – a weary sound – and she felt a twinge of guilt. It wasn't his fault her family had hid so much from her. And he'd risked his life for her, which should've earned him a low level of trust. She hadn't asked for any of this, and he hadn't either. Thom was just doing his job.

"I'm sorry." She forced a deep breath, resetting herself. "This has been a lot to process."

"No apology necessary, Poppy. Just hang in there."

"Doing my best."

The adorable grin she'd become used to seeing at Target spread across his face. Quickly, she looked away. *Just a bodyguard.*

"Nice job back there," he said.

"What?"

He tapped the steering wheel. "Using the car to get us out of there. I was about to get my ass handed to me by that *kesili*."

Horror crept over her. "I – rammed him. That man."

"If you wouldn't of, there's a good chance he would've killed me and abducted you." His expression softened. "Don't lose sleep over it. He'll probably come to, and walk away from it."

Morrison's body flying through the air replayed in her memory. *How could anyone walk away from that?* Her stomach sickened. *Don't think about it.*

"Seriously." Thom nudged her, "He was dosing with elemental drugs that would've made his muscles like steel. He'll be fine."

She cleared her throat. "So, where are we going?"

He rubbed his neck and sighed. "The well in the Twin was our way into Caelith. With Dane and his lackeys using it, it's not an option anymore. So, we have to improvise. I retrieved some papers and cash from your house, part of a contingency plan, with the locations of other wells and borderlands. I'll have a better idea when I can look at those."

"Borderlands?"

"Openings into Caelith, sometimes miles wide. They're usually in remote locations. Difficult for humans to access." He glanced at her. "But they're easier to pass through than wells."

"Why?"

"I'm not sure, probably has to do with size and power of the energy fields involved. Wells take longer, sometimes hours, and are exhausting. Some require elemental assistance to pass through."

A sign flashed by: Centerville, 17 miles.

He continued, "We'll stop close to the interstate. Look at the papers. Get food and fuel up the car."

We're going into Caelith? Her heart kicked up, part excitement, part nerves. *How much danger lies between here and there, between the answers I need? And what other crazy things will I have to do to get there?*

She sat up straight. *I'll do whatever I have to do. For Ayden. For mom. To finally discover who I am.*

Chapter Fourteen

By the time Poppy spied the lights of Centerville winking brightly from both sides of the road, night had fallen. A gaudy display of truck stops, fast food joints, and stores with names like 'The Lion's Lair' made up the cluttered, interstate town. Thom exited and drove so slowly that a guy driving a gigantic truck laid on the horn, vroomed by, and flipped him off.

After another near collision with an impatient driver, Poppy grabbed the wheel and barked instructions. They made it to a Subway and parked. Fidgeting with the keys, he observed their surroundings. "Is this okay?" he asked, indicating the restaurant.

Returning the blue stone to her pocket, Poppy nodded, unsettled by how often she was discovering it in her palm.

They ate in a silence interrupted by the sporadic buzz of the ice machine. While she labored over a six-inch sub, he efficiently packed away a twelve inch. After the food hit her stomach, any hunger she'd had gave way to a sharp queasiness. Shoving her potato chips his way, she wrapped up the remainder of her turkey and cheddar and stowed it in her backpack.

Finishing his food, he scanned the papers he'd told her about in the car. His brow wrinkling with concentration, he shifted through blue social security cards, passports, maps with red circles, stacks and stacks of handwritten papers, and official documents with raised seals. Fidgeting with the zipper on her anorak, she watched, her tongue-tying over a hundred different questions, each more maddening than the last. Finally, she settled on one that had been nagging her like a rock in her shoe.

"Thom?"

His eyes flickered to hers. "Hmm?"

"Why were we – my mom and me – moved here in the first place?"

Letting the papers fall, he chewed his lip, his brow shadowing his eyes. As he considered his answer, the minute hand on the clock behind him circled once. "Your father, he jointly commands the *Offysfyn* – do you remember me explaining what that is?"

"Maybe." *No.* She palmed her face. "Explain again."

Glancing around, he lowered his voice. "The *Offysfyn* is a human and elemental alliance, operating under Caelith's elemental ruling council. It was formed because of problems with an extreme elemental sect called the Grens. Your father's role put you and your mother in danger. He thought moving you here would protect you."

"Why me and mom, and not Ayden?"

"Ayden had already enlisted in the *Offysfyn*."

Her eyes combed the papers he was hunched over, spread in ordered piles on the table. *But why conceal so much? Why keep my brother's existence from me?* She frowned. *Something isn't making sense.*

Under the table she passed the blue stone between her hands. "Why don't I remember anything? Why don't I remember Ayden? Or you? When I saw him – I thought he looked familiar, but not like family-familiar, more like a stranger you've seen once or twice. And you..." she shook her head, "sometimes I thought I recognized you. How could that all just disappear?" Anger spiked her emotions. "They said I was sick. Was that a lie?"

The deep v-wrinkle appeared between his eyebrows. "After passing through the Twin well, both you and Deidre became so ill, you almost died. So, no. It wasn't." He broke off, chewing his lip, focusing on a detailed map of Colorado.

You're not stopping there! Rankled, she almost snapped her fingers to regain his attention. "Why? Why would we get so sick? Was it a virus from here or something?"

Not meeting her eyes, he shook his head. "You were both vaccinated. Exhaustively. With vaccinations that aren't even available here."

"So why?" Her voice rose enough that several people in the restaurant glanced at them.

"I'm not sure." Thom returned the papers to his backpack, a frown wrinkling his forehead.

"No." She almost laughed. "That's not enough of an explanation."

Meeting her gaze, he murmured. "Not here."

Her eyes flashed. "I've waited long enough. So, yes here."

Backpack over his shoulder, he stood. "We can talk in the car."

Scowling, she followed him out. "*I'm* driving."

"Okay," he said. "We need fuel."

The nearest station was just yards across the parking lot, but still far enough for her to grow angrier about his reticence. A gigantic sign with red letters – Big Johnny's Truck Stop – glowed in the night sky, so enormous that it reminded her of a hideous hot air balloon. Rows and rows of Semi trucks idled in long angled parking slots, engines humming. A steady trickle of patrons rotated through the glass doors at the front.

Exiting the car, she wrinkled her nose at the oily smell around the pumps. Diligently, Thom scanned the place, further irritating her. Over the intercom, an attendant squawked something about pre-paying. As she rounded the car, he intercepted her, scrutinizing her hair with an odd expression. She patted it, heat flooding her face. After her last twenty-four hours, it was probably as tidy as a snowstorm. *Damn it.*

"Your jacket doesn't have a hood?" he asked.

"No." She had unzipped it somewhere and lost it.

"Do you have a hat?"

"They look weird on me." She pushed past him.

He fell into step beside her. "Get one. Or a hoodie. Get both."

She glowered. *He spoke in commands. Why did he always speak in commands?*

He opened one of the glass doors and stepped back. "Your hair is too noticeable, too easy to track. And we can't dye it. We've lost enough time as it is."

She produced a scathing look. "Come on. I've always wanted to go goth. I'm sure they have industrial strength dye in here somewhere. It might even last twenty-four hours." Grimacing, she tugged on a rippling strand – under the fluorescents it glowed like an elderly firefly.

"We don't have time for that. Get a hat. Get a hoodie." Putting some cash in her hand, he faced the counter, grabbed a pre-paid phone, and slid a wad of bills toward the attendant, folding the rest in his pocket.

Watching him exit, irritation spiked in her chest. Tempted, she wandered around the convenience store. What would Thom do if she came out of the restroom with black hair?

Feeling the cash in her pocket, she paused in front of a hat display. Most of the hats had sports logos – she hated those. There were piles of adjustable mesh ones with route 66 patches – not much better. Beside those hung some hunting camos with wide brims and chin straps. *Yuck.*

In the adjoining diner a motley collection of guys lounged around a table. They had the look of truckers taking the required rest time before their next shift. The remains of burgers and fries, beer bottles, cash, and a poker game littered the grubby tabletop. One of them, a guy with a long brown beard, looked her up and down with a hungry expression. Her shoulders tensed.

"That piece of ass would make my night." he said.

"Maybe she's for hire." Replied another, staring.

The hoodies were near their table. Deliberating her next move, she pretended to be interested in the sunglasses display.

Another sneered. "I'm more interested in her boyfriend's cash."

Several of the men sat up straighter. "I'm listening," one muttered, the toothpick in his mouth bobbing. As they put their heads together, the jingle of a nearby lotto machine hid their conversation.

Her knees wobbly with anxiety, she headed for the door. Thom entered and halted, scanning her. A frown appeared between his eyebrows; it wasn't a small one.

"Okay," he said. "If you're not going to get them, I will."

He grabbed the first cap he saw and made a beeline for the hoodies.

"Thom listen—"

"Poppy. This is serious."

"Okay. Yeah, I get it." She lowered her voice, putting a hand on his arm. "But listen. I heard…"

Still gathered around the table, the guys were all watching them now.

She whispered, "let's buy them somewhere else."

The frown remained heavy on Thom's brow. "No."

One of the men, a guy in a camo hunting jacket, stood up. "Why don't you come over here sweetheart? We'll treat you better than that guy."

They laughed. The toothpick juddered some more.

A guy wearing a faded Tool t-shirt cracked his knuckles. "I bet this tough guy won't be so tough without you to pick on."

The other occupants of the diner went eerily still. A histrionic laugh bubbled inside of her – the situation was unbelievably ridiculous. How had she gotten them in trouble this fast, even without dangerous elementals?

"Let's go." Thom clamped a hand on her shoulder and turned her toward the exit.

One of the men sauntered between them and the door, the bulge of his hairy belly showing under his t-shirt. Thom stiffened, his hand falling away from her shoulder.

The biggest man of the group, a guy with spiky blond hair, drifted toward them, his freckled face smug. "See, we's got a theory. You got all this cash you don't know what to do with. And you need some help." His grin revealed a chipped front tooth. "We've decided to be generous and help you out. Or you can let us spend some time with your girlfriend here." He winked at her as roars of agreement came from the table. "You pick. Or we will."

Poppy swallowed. Her head felt like it was floating away from her body.

Folding his arms, Thom cocked his head, like he was regarding an insect. "No. Let's not."

"What did you say?" His grin stretched wider.

"No. Let's. Not." Thom repeated slowly, his tone mocking.

He glanced at his buddies, his grin incredulous. "Is this guy for real?" He faced Thom. "Can you count?"

"Really," Poppy stammered, "we don't want any trouble."

"Go to the car." Thom didn't look away from the men.

Thom's plaid sleeves were rolled up, his tattoos standing out like an invitation for a fight. The fluorescent lighting made the dark circles under his eyes pronounced and deep, his bruises motley. More than any of the truckers, he looked like he'd just driven a twelve-hour shift.

She'd been too busy being angry to notice how tired he was. *If only I'd just bought a hat*, she thought. Now, Big Johnny's was about to play host to Centerville fight-night – the seven against one bracket.

As she shifted toward the door, a hot voice spoke at her ear, rank with the odor of cigarettes. "Hey now, don't you go yet." A hand pawed at her ass.

Ready to strike, she whirled around. But the guy didn't have a chance to smirk; his nose kissed the floor faster than she could blink. She didn't even see how Thom did it.

His expression menacing, Thom faced the others. "Anyone else?"

For a stunned moment, they stared at him. A second later, spewing obscenities, the blond man charged. Using his momentum, Thom propelled him onto the table, catching Tool-guy in the process. The table folded under their weight. Plates shattered and flatware slid across the floor. Spit flying, the bearded guy rushed him. Dodging, Thom grabbed his arm, flung him around, and smashed him into a lotto machine.

Stumbling back, Poppy saw toothpick-man reaching for the gun at his waistband. Grabbing a plate, she brought it down on the top of his head – the force of the impact stung her hands. He dropped like a bowling pin, his gun clattering to the floor. Hands shaking, she scooped up the weapon and dumped it in the trash bin by the door.

Camo-jacket guy threw a slow punch. Deftly, Thom caught his fist and twisted his arm. There was a nauseating crack, followed by a shriek as the man clutched his forearm. Tool-guy ended up on top of him, flipped off Thom's back. The prostrate men rolled into the path of the hairy-belly-guy who tried to swerve, but Thom swept his feet and broke his nose with a knee, adding to the pile.

The attendant screamed into the phone. The onlookers from the corner bar halted. Gaping, Poppy stumbled backward toward the exit. *Thom was cleaning the floor with these guys… one man against seven.* Looking back up, her breath caught in her throat.

A man with a tattooed fist circled Thom, a gun trained at his head. "Cash," he growled. "Now."

In a millisecond, Thom disarmed him, slammed him into the hat display, flipped him, and thrust his forehead against the wall. The man slumped, unconscious, hats scattered all around him.

The bearded guy scrambled up. "You, nasty piece a—"

Dodging his right hook, Thom pummeled him in the gut. The guy folded. Thom laid him out flat with an elbow in the kidney and a kick across the jaw.

Back on his feet, the blonde rushed Thom with a broken beer bottle. Blocking it with a chair, he sent it smashing into a window. Flinging the chair around, Thom struck the man's chin, and he spun, face-planting on another table.

One of the men struggled to get back up.

"Don't get up!" yelled a guy from the bar.

Stunned, Poppy wheezed. Glimpsing the scowl that had settled into the lines of Thom's face, her legs went watery.

His chest heaving, Thom marched away from the pile of men. As he neared, the attendant made a face like she was sucking in her cheeks.

"For the damage." He put a stack of cash on the counter.

The phone slid out of her grasp and clattered to the floor.

Stone-faced, he held the door open for Poppy. She shuffled out, holding her breath. Before she could get in the driver's seat, he claimed it. In the confines of the car, his anger simmered, quiet but intense, like heat off concrete in July.

Thom exited the service station, driving cautiously until he found the on-ramp to the interstate. Once they merged onto interstate seventy, he floored it, heading west.

Poppy gripped the handle of the car door, afraid to look at him. *What had she gotten herself into?*

Chapter Fifteen

In the driver's seat, Thom breathed deliberately – a short inhale through his nose, a slow release through his mouth – concentrating on the headlights illuminating the highway.

Vacate the scene. He coached himself. *Then get off the interstate. Get small.*

Recalling his training, he resisted his body's exaggerated adrenaline response – the panic ramming through his veins. *The fight's over,* he told himself. *Calm down. Focus. Review strategy.*

Despite his efforts, sweat dampened his temples, and his vision pitched. On the highway, the headlights shone in tunnels, like he was trapped. Danger felt a hairsbreadth away, poised to skewer him to the ground. *And Poppy…the Grens would take her and only Cael-Astrett knew what would happen to her…how they would use her…*

He wiped the sweat out of his eyes and fought to ground himself. *I'm in a car, in Uther-Erai. It's the month of October. It is night. Poppy is with me. Safe. She's safe. I'm safe.*

Muffled and distant, Poppy's voice broke his concentration. "Thom? Are you okay?"

Not taking his eyes from the road, he spoke between his teeth. "Give me a moment."

He repeated the grounding cues until his heartbeat slowed. *Car, steering wheel, road, headlights, October, Poppy, safe.* Beginning with his jaw, he unclenched his muscles one by one.

When his muscles no longer felt like they were going to crack open, he opened a bottle of water and chugged it. *Car, steering wheel, road, headlights, October, Poppy, safe.* He finally caught up with his own breathing. *Come on, Magnusson. Get your shit together. Reassess.*

"Thom?" Poppy's voice wobbled, like a sapling caught in a gale. Simultaneously, he experienced a spark of irritation and a surge of compassion, cage-fighting each other, muddling his brain. His back muscles tensed up again, and pain spiraled through his left side. *Come on! Not the pain! Not now!*

Through the needles in his side, he forced out a response. "Look for an exit. We need to get off the interstate. Every highway patrol from here to Nevada's going to be on the lookout for a green Taurus, a girl with silver hair, and a tattooed guy who messed-up six truckers. After a report like that, they don't tend to give you the benefit of the doubt."

"It was seven truckers, actually." Her voice died off in a whisper.

Helvítis! He didn't mean to glare at her, but he did. Poppy's face turned as ashen as her hair; her naked fear jolted him. He focused on the road. *Nice job. Terrifying the very person you're supposed to protect.*

"I–I'm sorry," she whispered.

The pain in his side lessened. "Poppy, what happened wasn't your fault. My anger doesn't have anything to do with you. Okay?"

"Yeah, okay." She stared out at the night-shrouded landscape, twisting her hands in her lap.

Andskotans, he thought. *All of this, so sudden. So foreign.* He was used to this life. She wasn't. And for a novice, she'd really held it together.

"I'm serious, Poppy. None of this is your fault. You're doing better than a lot of people would in your situation."

She blinked.

"Your quick thinking with the gun…" His shoulders tensed again. "But, please don't do anything like that again. You're in enough danger as it is. Especially with me being stupid about the cash. That didn't help us."

An exit sign flew by in the headlights. When the off-ramp appeared, he took it, screeching around the turn and onto a dark, narrow road.

"You can't take corners that fast!" She pumped an imaginary brake pedal. "Brake around turns! Brake!"

Helvítis. The sooner I stop driving the better. He took his foot off the accelerator.

"Where are we going?" she asked.

"I need to pull over, to think. We should stay off the main roads for a while. Some sleep might help too." Scanning the darkened roadside, he shrugged. "I'll know when I see it."

The narrow, bumpy road ambled through acres of farmland peppered with cattle. Thom caught himself longing to explore the countryside – it had been so long since he'd been free of the stink and noise of the city. Now that his body had mostly healed, he itched to move, to immerse himself in the wilderness again.

Her voice interrupted his thoughts. "How did you learn to fight like that?"

The bluish light from the dashboard illuminated the freckled skin across her nose and cheeks; he couldn't decide whether he saw fear or curiosity in her face. *What do I say to that? Does she think I'm a monster?*

"Everyone who serves in the *Offysfyn* is trained." Internally, he cringed at the half-truth.

"Trained to fight seven guys at once?"

"They were drunk."

Her forehead wrinkled in a vexed expression, but relaxed when she glimpsed the grin twitching at his mouth. "Oh yeah, that makes a big difference." She shook her head. "Guns! They had guns! And they wanted to use them!"

He shrugged. "Guns make people overconfident. More likely to make mistakes."

"Yeah, like shooting someone!" She gestured. Her posture shrunk and she hissed, a noise of pain.

"How's your pain?" he asked, studying her.

"It's okay."

She needs to rest. Frowning, he glanced at his watch.

A road sign labeled CC leapt into the headlights. Soon after, the road came to a T and they took a right. At a crawl, they passed a cluster of silos, a convenience store, a bowling alley, and a Dairy Queen. They needed a place to hide – a place no one would think twice about a stopped car. Near the road, a row of darkened cars appeared beside a hand-painted billboard: First-Rate Robert's Used Cars. *That'll do,* he thought. Pulling into the lot, he parked the car on the end of the row.

Rummaging in his pack, he found the flashlight. Cringing, she shielded her face against the sudden brightness. The pill bottle clattered as he tipped it, and finding some water, he nudged her. Wordlessly, she gulped down the medication.

A thin film of sweat shone on her temples and her eyes seemed colorless in the light, like she was more ghost than human. Deflated, she settled back into the seat, staring into the night. *I need to look at that wound.* He thought. *But she's exhausted. Let sleep do its healing.*

A cut prickled on his jawline. Examining it in the visor mirror, he cleaned the blood off his neck and closed the cut with surgical tape. Shutting the mirror, he tossed his pack onto the back seat, grabbed the blankets, and unfolded them, his movement shaking the car.

"We need to sleep," he said, spreading the thick blue blanket over her. "No one will find us here." He clicked off the flashlight and darkness invaded the car.

"Thom?" She whispered, her voice as fragile as a moth's wing.

He shifted, trying to see her in the dark.

"I'm sorry I...that things got so...complicated."

"It wasn't your fault, Poppy. I'm sorry I got so angry. I don't like bullies." The car tremored as he shifted. "We'll be okay. We'll figure it out."

Leaning the seat back, he pulled the blanket up to his chin and tried to get comfortable. Stars dotted the sky, shining between intermittent clouds, bathing the car lot in faint silver light. Crickets sung in weak bursts and a Texaco sign across the street squeaked in the wind.

He didn't think he was ever going to sleep – he probably shouldn't. *No one will find us here.* Just a guess. A calculated one, but still, there was always a risk. Dane was cunning. And Thom wagered he wasn't about to let them get away.

But the blood in his veins felt leaden, weighing on his eyelids. The night before, he'd kept watch – monitoring Poppy's condition after the ettar attack – concerned about what was happening Caelith-side, about Deidre, Ayden, the Twin well, how long they had before Dane returned, and how he was going to explain everything to Poppy. To make matters worse, he was still recovering from his swift vault through the well to warn Ayden. Even with aching knuckles and a throbbing bruise across his bicep, a deep sleep overtook him.

Sometime in the early hours of the morning, Thom awoke, his heart thundering in his ears, pulsing in his chest cavity. The dream was fading fast, but he could still see the hand of liquid red ember stretching toward him, touching his forehead, brushing his hair away. He still felt himself cringing away from it, even as he panted from the remembered pain of his wounds, the frigidness of the ground beneath him.

His muscles clenched in wild spasms. Breathing instinctively, he sat up, clutching where the scar forked across his side, forcing himself to think, to rationalize. *No different than usual, Magnusson. Push through it.*

He breathed. *Car, steering wheel, dashboard, stars, Poppy, safe.*

Magnetically, his gaze snapped to Poppy. Inches from his arm, she lay curled on her side, huddled under the shadow of the blanket, her breathing slow and quiet, like the sough of night wind.

Cora Blackhorse – the surgeon who'd become his friend during his convalescence – said he would get over the trauma eventually. And it had lessened, especially after he'd been stationed in Riverston. Watching over the Paquins – Ayden entrusting his family to him – had consumed his thoughts, providing a focused, outward purpose; a powerful method of rehabilitation.

The faint light just illuminated the curve of Poppy's bottom lip. In unguarded moments, he still expected to see the Poppy he knew when she was just barely twelve – an awkward and long-legged kid, crimson hair braided carelessly down her back, spoiling for adventure. Then she had been a sister to him, almost as much as she was to Ayden.

But now everything was different; the first time he'd seen Poppy in Riverston, that ambushed him like a sucker-punch. The bleached colorlessness of her hair didn't take him off guard nearly as much as her shape – all hips and waist and breasts. Poppy had a bewitching sort of beauty, rendered more potent by her choices; her patient kindness with Deidre, her curiosity, her passion for geology. And she had a beguiling wry streak. Knowing her as an eighteen-year-old was both wonderful and unnerving.

Eighteen. Clenching his jaw, Thom turned away, squirming in the cramped space of the driver's side seat. Allowing himself to think about Poppy was misguided. Unwise. *Remain detached.* He told himself, for the hundredth time. *Suppress any attraction like her life depends on it, because it just might.*

Besides, she probably thinks you're too old. And there were other reasons, beginning and ending with Felix Paquin. *Why torment yourself?*

Settling the blanket around him, he gazed at the glittering night sky, breathing until his pain faded to a dull prodding, waiting for the gray of dawn.

Chapter Sixteen

Agony and cold forced Poppy awake. Pain cramped her body, radiating in waves through her arm and up into her temples, as if her blood was laced with it. She squeezed her eyes shut, the memory of a spider munching on her arm returning in an awful rush. Flashbacks accompanied the pain: Alan's bashed-in bloody head, her mom's strangled cry, Ayden's fingers slipping on her wrist.

Keys jingled and the car roared to life. She clenched her teeth and curled into a ball. The cold, impervious to her coat and blanket, seemed to magnify the pain, biting her in cruel jaws. A pill bottle clattered.

"Poppy." Thom's voice rumbled, barely a whisper.

The predawn light shadowed his face, hiding his expression. Wrapping her fingers around the pills, he held out the water container. Sitting up, she gulped the medicine and shut her eyes, waiting for the pain to subside. Her teeth chattered as the icy liquid hit her stomach. Another blanket settled on top of her, although she barely registered its weight.

"Breathe," he said. "Try not to be tense. It makes it worse."

In ragged gasps, she forced her lungs to work, feeling the heat slowly infiltrate the cold. She longed to wrap it all over her body like hot towels, or drink it like chamomile tea with honey – to feel it warm her from the inside out. For it to make everything better, to rescue everyone she loved, or at least reassure her that they would be okay.

Thom rummaged in the back seat, remained still for a while, then opened the glove box and shuffled through some papers.

As the warmth usurped the cold, her pain relented, leaving her muscles feeling as though they floated inside her body. Taking her arm, Thom unwrapped the bandages, removing the packing covering her wound, inspecting it with the flashlight. It stung a little, but the look of relief crossing his face when he saw it was enough to make her forget the soreness.

"It's healing well." He met her eyes. "Does it feel hot to you?"

Shaking her head, she watched him rebandage the wound, covering the gnarly line of Frankenstein stitches marring her forearm. *I'll have a scar the size of Texas.* A disappointed pang accompanied the thought.

A hint of weak, lemony sunlight peaked over the trees behind the car lot, gilding Thom's hair as he packed up the medical kit and hunched over the map he had bought the night before. His dark brown locks curled in unruly waves around his ears, the color of wheat where the sun touched it. Stifling a yawn, he held a pen over a notebook resting on the middle console. Dark circles still camped out under his eyes, and she wondered if he'd slept at all. In a smitten fog, Poppy gazed at him.

"I'm going to see if Robert's posted his hours." Thom eyed the shack behind the cars. "Hopefully he doesn't come in early."

The car door opened and shut in a swirl of frosty air. She watched his tall form through the fogging windows, stiff-arming her questions about what lay ahead of them – about Ayden, about her mom – content to rest while she had the chance.

When he returned, he held the license plates from the Taurus and some paperwork. "Ready to go? We're switching cars."

Sitting up, she gaped at him, choking on her question. *Another felony?*

He made a face, crinkling the bridge of his nose. "I hate doing this, but I don't see any other option. We need to get moving."

Gathering her things, she staggered out of the car, her boots crunching in frosty grass. Keys jingling, he unlocked a Lumina with chipped white paint and a bumper sticker that read 'Sasquatch doesn't believe in you either.' Temp tags fluttered on the back. Inside, the seats were covered in fuzzy gray upholstery and smelled like dust and pine air freshener.

The key turned in the ignition and it shuddered to life. He adjusted the heat, steered through the bumpy car lot, and rolled onto the road. Huddled in the passenger seat, she put her elbow on the door and palmed her face. *I'm an accomplice to car theft. That has to be a felony. I need coffee.*

Near the interstate, he turned into a bustling Kum and Go and parked at the pumps, awry enough that Poppy wished she hadn't taken the pain medication, so she could take over the driving. Furtively, he dumped the plates from the Taurus in a trash receptacle. While the fuel was pumping, he unzipped his backpack and threw her a black hooded jacket.

"I should've given you that last night," he said, apologetically.

She shrugged. "You were tired. We both were."

A corner of his mouth went up and their eyes merged. Just as she was going to offer to fetch breakfast, the dispenser clicked and he turned back to the pumps.

Remembering the night before, she watched the roll of his broad shoulders underneath his canvas jacket. Despite the fact he was probably the most dangerous person she knew, he was still the same Thom she'd worked with – the guy who cared about their elderly coworker Rose, and Cheri's kids' welfare. Somehow, the realization made their situation less daunting than it seemed last night.

She slid into his jacket and layered her anorak over it. The jacket swallowed her, like wearing a blanket. The sun streamed in through the windows and flooded her with warmth. Still, her limbs felt sluggish and leaden, as though she could sleep for days and still be tired.

After disappearing into the convenience store, he returned with coffee, steaming in the cool morning. Grinning, she thanked him. It tasted like coffee-flavored dirt, but he'd put cream and sugar in it, just how she liked it. A bag dangled from his arm, containing peanut butter, wheat bread, apples and bananas, string cheese, and Greek yogurt. After she selected a banana and a yogurt, he methodically inhaled a dizzying portion of the food. Stowing the remainder in the back, they set out on the interstate, the road growling and bumpy beneath the tires.

Rubbing his eyes, he dropped his empty coffee cup in the middle console. A red-purple splotch crossed his cheek and trailed into his bearded jawline. White bandages peeked out from a rip in his plaid shirt. Over veined wrists as thick as tree branches, he still wore the unusual cuff bracelet she'd noticed during work at Target.

He's as handsome as the sky is blue, she thought. She focused on the view outside. The sun glided fields, sleepy with mist, dotted with hay bales, and brown and white cows. *He's just a bodyguard, remember?*

"What did you find out from those papers last night?" she asked.

He glanced at her. "There's a borderland in Colorado, near the national park in the Rockies. It's the closest one from here. That's where we're headed. Look through the papers if you want."

Her forehead wrinkling, she emptied the folder and shuffled through the papers. "Borderland? Explain that again."

"The intersection of here – *Uther-Erai* – and Caelith is like a rabbit warren. A labyrinth of large and small passages connecting the worlds. Some are so wide the spaces shift and blur, these are borderlands. They're easily passable, relatively at least, as opposed to a well. Wells are narrow and twisty, hard to access. Dangerous. You have to know where they are, and how to navigate them. They're difficult to pass through, for humans. Sometimes they require elemental assistance." Checking for comprehension, he glanced at her. "Compared to borderlands, wells are numerous. Borderlands are rare." Pausing, he worried his lip. "I'm hoping that a borderland will be easier on you."

Could I lose my memory again? The thought unsettled her breakfast.

She faced him. "Could the Twin well have caused my illness?"

"It's a good guess, although what happened to you and Deidre hasn't happened to others, that I know of. Ayden was determined to figure out what exactly caused it, but…" He grimaced, "other things got in the way." An expression she didn't recognize crossed his face. "You might be onto something."

"Other things?"

"The conflict with the Grens. The threat they posed to peace in Caelith."

"Conflict? Like, a war?"

"Not war, at least, not as you know it here. Not yet." He kept his eyes on the road. "More," he frowned, "like skirmishes. Disappearances. And in some places, genocide."

"That big Scots guy said something about Paquin losing ground? About wanting you on their side, handing me over?"

"He was trying to mess with me." Propping an elbow on the car door, he rubbed his temple. "But, it's somewhat true. About two years ago, tensions escalated in Caelith, putting a strain on the *Offysfyn*. Ayden took over Riverston operations then. Your father had too much to manage as it was. We're keeping our heads above water, but only just."

Heat spread in her chest. *So, Dad had a good reason for leaving us. For missing so much.* But still, it didn't explain everything. Poppy found the blue stone and palmed it, rubbing it with her thumb as though it might absorb her anxiety. "Why didn't they tell me? About Ayden? About Caelith?"

His chest rose and fell. "I can speculate, but really you should ask them."

He's right. Don't put him in this position.

"Will I forget everything again? Passing through the borderlands?" *I don't want to forget again. To be lost in my own skin.*

"You're older now. It could've been the strain on your body, as a child. Or it could've been that particular well. And the circumstances weren't the best," The shadows under his eyes seem to deepen, casting the hazel into a gray-brown. "I'm not going to lie to you, Poppy. I don't know what to expect, when we pass through. But we don't have a lot of good options. Dane will regroup and pursue us, if he hasn't already. I'd like to do this differently, but…" He broke off, shaking his head.

"It's worth the risk," she said, setting her chin. "I want to find my mom. Ayden. I want answers, to see Caelith." *Home.* She thought the word, but couldn't bring herself to say it aloud. "But, I don't want to end up – lost. Again. There's still so much I have to remember, that I want to remember."

"I want you to remember too." He glanced at her, the green in his eyes taking on a summer hue. "And I'll do everything I can to help you. Whether here or there, I promise."

"Thank you, Thom."

He might be only a bodyguard, but he's a damn good one.

A horn blast from a semi-truck snapped Thom's attention back to the road, and he straightened the car between the highway stripes.

Although his driving skills could use some work.

She turned the blue stone in her fingers. "So, what happened? If we were supposed to be safe in Riverston, what changed?"

"The well in the Twin was a protected secret." His fingers tightened around the steering wheel. "Someone leaked its location – probably Dane. I'd been trying to prove he was compromised for a while, even before the *muiras* attacked you. But his plans were too far along. That's why Ayden was here. He was going to assist with moving you and Deidre. To help her explain."

She gritted her teeth, thinking of Dane's unctuous expression, his sickening, oil-colored eyes. *Bastard.*

"Why was Dane there at all?" Shuddering, she remembered the buried alive feeling she'd had around him. "He was…awful. I felt…" She swallowed the words, not wanting to remember.

A growl vibrated in his throat. "Dane was useful for people without social security numbers. Clever at fraud. I don't think Ayden was right to trust him as much as he did, but when he enlisted him, Dane was on another path."

"There was something weird about him. He…" She shook her head. "I don't know."

"Dane's *unnusti*. An offspring of a human and an elemental. He has an *ulli* father."

She almost dropped the stone. "That happens? How?"

"How?" His expression grew both strained and amused.

"I know *how*, but how can *that* happen?"

"Elementals, especially the higher forms, can manifest in an interface that allows all kinds of interaction. Some can even pass as human. That's how." His mouth twitched. "Does that explain it, or should I go into more detail?"

Subject change! Poppy fanned herself with the papers. "No. I'm good." She gestured with the stone. "So, what is this? I mean, it's got to be from Caelith. It actually helped me fight Dane off."

"Fight him off?" The tendons in his wrists went rigid. "Is that how you got all those bruises?"

Her face burning, she faced the window.

"What happened, Poppy?"

I don't want to talk about it. I don't want to remember. She gestured with the blue stone. "I asked about this first."

The sun glinted across a speckled blue whorl on the stone, sending speckles of blue light across the ceiling of the car. It resembled a nebula or the night sky unpolluted by artificial light, pocked by sparks. A cloud dimmed the sun and it became a nondescript blue stone again. Poppy hid it in the shadows. She couldn't say why, but it felt a little like holding a grenade.

Under his breath, he muttered something that sounded Icelandic. "I'm not sure what that is. Ayden didn't mention it. And Deidre wasn't big on specifics. Sometimes we had to decipher if she was having a bad day, or actually remembering something important from Caelith."

Frowning, she faced him. "It's just a rock then?"

He shook his head. "If I had to guess, I'd say it's some kind of relic or elemental token of favor. It's definitely storing Caelithian energy. Objects like that are uncommon." Shadows collected under his eyes. "How did the stone help you?" His voice softened, careful and low. "It might help us understand what it is. It might be important."

She wished his argument wasn't so compelling. Her voice halting, she recounted that morning at Target, intending to brush over most of the incident, to focus on the stone, but ended up spilling details before she could stop herself. The buried-alive feeling when Dane had grabbed her, the strength in her limbs when she'd dropped the rock, the multi-colored flames at her fingertips and around the stone itself. How she'd been able to throw Dane against the wall, so hard it cracked, and the tremor that had raced through the ground, and the resulting flames – attacking him, fighting him off.

Thom listened without interrupting. By the time she'd finished, his expression darkened further, so much the shadows inside the car seemed to deepen. Other than thanking her when she'd finished, he remained silent, his forehead crisscrossed with deep lines, the tendons cording the back of his hands rigid. Their speed fluctuated from the minimum of fifty mph to hover around sixty.

Anxiously, she turned the stone over and over, gliding it through her fingers, wondering if reliving such an awful moment had helped clarify anything.

Chapter Seventeen

As Thom drove, the brilliant blue of the stone Poppy cradled seemed to flicker in the corner of his eye, as if it was a captured flame instead of the colorful Caldysian bedrock he'd believed it was. *Helvítis andskotans!* As if he didn't already have enough trouble on his hands without an obscure elemental relic showing up in *Uther-Erai*, in human hands, vulnerable to Gren capture.

The multi-colored flames Poppy had described didn't resemble any elemental he knew of, but the Paquins were an old *utherling* family. Who knew what their vaults contained? The power it displayed was extraordinary, especially for a non-*cydern* object. No wonder Dane wanted it. What if it represented some sort of alliance or elemental connection the Grens had yet to make?

The thought almost made Thom tack the gas pedal to the floor. If there was any chance of claiming such a relic for the Grens Dane would be inexorable in his pursuit of them – thirsty for the considerable payout from its procurement, regardless of its elemental origin.

An exit sign dotted with restaurant icons appeared as a highway town emerged on both sides of the road. As if on cue, Poppy's stomach growled.

"Panera!" She indicated the sign. "They have decent coffee. And I doubt truckers eat there. Not six or seven at a time, anyway."

Despite his apprehension, his mouth twitched with a grin.

"And you should let me drive," she added. "If I don't, we'll never get to Colorado."

He gave in to the smile. "No pulling punches, then?"

Her grin reached her eyes. "Just keeping it real."

Might not be a bad idea to let her drive. His smile faded. "Am I really doing that bad?"

She shrugged. "I don't know, you're better than my mom, that's for sure. I'm not sure how she survived before I got my license."

He grimaced. "Oh, thanks. Ouch!"

"Come on, Thom. You can't be good at everything. That's just unfair."

A laugh burst out of his chest. Her cheeks flushed, cradling a charming, wide grin. The rosy color spreading over her cheeks matched her lips. *Focus, Magnusson.* He forced his eyes back to the road. *Keep your mind on the mission.*

Should they take the time to stop? So far, there weren't any indications they were being followed. They would benefit from a good meal and the break might give him some time to deliberate. Decided, he exited.

In the parking lot of the restaurant, sunlight highlighted the red-purple of the Maple trees loitering around the Panera, the colors setting off the bluebird hue of the afternoon sky. Thom stretched and yawned, happy to relinquish the wheel. Fighting with the gusty winds, Poppy concealed the bright silver of her hair with the hood of his jacket, tucking away the errant wavy locks, free of braids for once – and really quite lovely. *Stop it*, his thoughts berated.

After they ordered their food, they settled at corner table with a wide vantage. Sitting with his back to the wall, he cased the restaurant. Poppy sat next to him in a ribbon of sun, slipping her coat off. Her knee almost grazed his and, on pretense of retying his boot, he scooted over enough so they wouldn't touch.

Shedding his canvas jacket, he rolled up the sleeves of his plaid shirt. On his forearm, the crisp black lines and the amber, russet, and navy hues of a sun tattoo peaked out from underneath his sleeve. He hated that one because of what it represented. It felt good not to worry about it being visible. Here, the symbol meant nothing.

As if his notice of the tattoo had been a sign, the room pitched and the sounds of the restaurant slowed to a crawl in his ears. Under the table, he clenched his fists. *No! Not here! Not now!*

The atmosphere in the restaurant fractured subtly, as the presence he sensed approached, Etin. Catching sight of her, he cursed under his breath. The *cym* elemental had manifested as a woman so striking she could have landed a walk-on role in a major film, even disguised in a drab Panera visor and apron, though not too different from how she appeared in Caelith. Her blond hair rippled, mermaid-like, matching her skin; both were flawless. Even her eyes were gold, as if her chromosomes had been engineered with precision. She was too flawless, preternaturally flawless, like she had real-time photo-shop. While that might not have been obvious to the multitudes of ogling eyes, it was to Thom – he knew this particular *cym* and her disguises all too well.

But why is she here, of all places? Playing games instead of just being direct? He scowled. *This is Etin, remember? A tiger can't change her stripes.*

As Poppy's salad and squash soup sloshed to a stop in front of her, she blinked up at Etin, and her expression went rigid, like she'd just been waited on by a zombie instead of a human. The moment stretched like taffy, and the sounds of the restaurant echoed around them.

Keeping his expression as frosty as a glacier, Thom met Etin's golden eyes. *Give me my damn sandwich. And let me eat in peace.*

Cocking her head, she dropped his sandwich and glided away with locomotion so effortless it shouldn't have been possible for anyone, except maybe a Russian ballet dancer. As she disappeared, the room settled into normalcy again, like a spell had been lifted. Focusing on her soup, Poppy picked up her spoon, worried little lines settling between her eyebrows.

She knows, he thought. *Clever girl. But how much, if anything, does she remember? Living Cael-Astrett, nothing at all, I hope.*

Wordlessly, Thom consumed his turkey and bacon sandwich, telling himself he'd think clearer without hunger gnawing at his gut. Afterwards he'd deal with Etin, see whatever scheme she was peddling to worm her way into the oxygen around him. Then he'd explain to Poppy – possibly. Or maybe Etin would just leave them alone. He scowled. *We've a better chance of finding an instant well to Caelith in the parking lot.*

Forcing down tiny mouthfuls, Poppy fidgeted with her spoon, and squeezed her eyes shut, like she was praying she wouldn't upchuck all over the table. When she opened them, she noticed him looking at her and her eyes darted to her salad.

"It's the ettar poison," he said. "It can mess with your appetite, make you nauseated."

She swallowed hard. "That explains a lot."

Rubbing his shoulder, he scanned the restaurant again, wincing at the soreness. He'd finished his sandwich, but the last thing he wanted to do was confront Etin.

"Tell me more about Caelith." Stalling, she stirred her soup. "What sort of jobs do hey have there? What types of industries?"

"Which question do you want me to answer first?"

"I don't care."

He frowned at how little she'd eaten. "You need to eat."

Suppressing a shudder, she took a bite. "Your turn."

Sighing, he leaned back. They shouldn't delay. They needed to move. And he needed to squelch whatever scheme Etin had brewing before it metastasized and screwed them all. But the curious spark in Poppy's eyes was beguiling.

Leaning forward, he lowered his voice. "Caelith's biggest industry is research and geological engineering. Using elemental resources and byproducts for energy, in ways that don't affect the ecosystem." Hoping to not see Etin, he scanned the restaurant again. "We have medical and pharmaceutical co-ops, but it's different than here, both in scale and ideology. Agriculture and hunting are important. And construction, especially in the last decade. But Caelithian methods aren't like here. They're regulated by the elemental council. Much smaller in scale and environmental footprint. Our trade and supply chains are community based. Before the conflict, most humans lived off the land, growing their own food, making their own medicines, crafting what they needed if they could. Or trading with neighbors."

Her lips parted, the curiosity in her expression morphing into shock or fascination – which, he couldn't decipher. Frowning, he clenched his jaw. *I sound like I'm teaching a class.*

"So, it's different," he continued, searching for humanity to add to his description. "But the people are the same. They work, create, form communities, disagree, compromise, fall in love, and have families. We just don't have all the stuff and scale of waste that's here. We have markets, but nothing like Target. It's a lot simpler." His eyebrows contracted. "The conflict has been really hard on people."

Fidgeting with his napkin, he fell silent.

"What did you do there?" Eyes wide, she chewed a mouthful of salad.

This could get tricky. He folded his arms, considering his words. "I was—," he couldn't stop the scowl from settling into the lines of his face, "forced into the conflict, when the serious problems were just beginning."

She dropped her spoon. "As a soldier?"

He nodded.

"And you're still in the *Offysfyn*?" she asked.

"I'm covert liaison now."

"Like a spy?"

He shook his head. "More like an intelligence gatherer, contact seeker, protector, negotiator. When I'm not *Uther-Erai* side."

She stared. "What did you do before then?"

"What I had to. Mostly farm labor."

Tension flooded his muscles. He hadn't realized how much he didn't want to talk about that time in his life – to keep his past to himself. The whole truth of the circumstances would hurt her, and that was the last thing she needed right now. They needed to stay focused.

She waited a moment, her forehead wrinkling. "How did we know each other? In Caelith?"

"I lived close." He glanced at her untouched food. "Eat. We need to get moving."

She chewed a forkful of salad. "How do humans end up there?"

Nervously, he bounced his heel on the grimy tile beneath the table. *Cael-Astrett*, she asked good questions, but he still had Etin to deal with.

But his desire to talk *with* Poppy triumphed. "It varies. There are a few places in the world – like in Iceland – with borderlands that are easy to pass through. People can wander in and not even know they're there. Sometimes they can't find their way out." He rubbed his neck. "Sometimes it's because of elemental intervention. Some groups of people were rescued by elementals from an existence that became impossible here, because of imperialism, or wars, or natural disasters. There're a lot of different stories. Some people – a vetted few –even straddle both worlds. Like many of our researchers. But they're trained."

"Do people speak English in Caelith?"

He nodded. "It's a common tongue. There are also Welsh and Gaelic communities, and a lot of Native American, African tribal, aboriginal dialects. Some have worked hard to preserve their heritage. Some cultures have evolved, along with the languages. But elementals understand most tongues."

In his line of sight, Etin appeared, pretending – badly – to bus a nearby table. His temples began to throb. *Best lance this boil before it gets worse.*

"How did you?" Poppy began.

But Etin swept up to the table, so close he felt the warmth off her skin. "May I take your plate, darlin'?"

Thom almost smirked. Etin's inflection sounded lifeless and wrong, like a robot unsuccessfully copying a cultural expression. Still, her voice echoed with power, like the room's acoustics were askew. Poppy's hand tightened around her fork.

Keeping his expression stony, he jerked his head toward his plate, and then to the hall beyond the foyer. Etin scooped it up and retreated, unceremoniously dumping the whole lot in a trash can before disappearing into the back.

Bemused, Poppy gaped in the direction of the dumped plates, dropping the fork.

"I'll be right back." Not waiting for Poppy's response, he marched off. Grounding himself with each step, he rounded the corner near the bathrooms and leaned against the yellow wallpaper to wait.

The first time Thom saw Etin he thought her a hallucination, a prelude to death throes.

Lost in the wintery wilds of Snæfellsness, it had been a week since he'd eaten anything other than moss, and drank anything other than melted snow. A day had passed since he'd had feeling in his fingers and toes, and he'd been wondering if it would be better to give up the ghost than to live maimed. Warming frostbitten extremities was excruciating and, with each passing hour, fading into the numb cold of Iceland forever became a better option.

After all, he'd found the remains of Sylvie's tent, but failed to find her, and not bringing his sister back wasn't an option. With his failure to find her, his future hopes unraveled and frayed like old rope. If he could still bring her back, alive and safe, it would make losing a few fingers worth it. Maybe he should just keep moving...try and get warm. Eventually he would find a familiar landmark. Or her frozen body. That would make his dilemma an easy one.

But he couldn't continue walking, because a Goddess of a woman blocked his path, clothed in a weird, gold body-suit, resembling sunbeams. To bypass her, required clambering over moss-covered mounds of lava rock, sharp enough to shred leather. Stopping, he'd rubbed his eyes, wondering if he was already dead.

Stiff-arming the distant memory, Thom shook his head, trying to refocus on the present. Through a swinging door to his right, clatter from the steamy kitchens filled the dimly lit hallway.

Etin appeared beside him, a coy expression hovering on her brow, much like that day. Now, nine years later, he knew she wasn't a hallucination, or a huldufolk as his Amma would've believed. No, she was a *cym*, a rare lightkind elemental, kin to air and aether. And a devious trickster who could give the most malignant of narcissists an inferiority complex. At present, more than anything, he wanted rid of her.

I'll play, he thought. *See what she wants. Let her think she's in control.* Concentrating, he allowed a practiced calm to master his demeanor.

"Hello, Thom," she said. The visor and apron had been replaced by sand-colored fatigues.

Thom kept his expression stony. "What do you want?"

Exhaling, she tilted her head. "Why so unfriendly? I thought you were above holding grudges."

"I did too, until the Maris plateau. Remember that?"

"They knew what they signed up for. Even if I'd been there—"

"Stop. Just stop. What do you want?"

Gesturing in Poppy's direction, she leaned her shoulder against the wall. "What are you doing?"

Exasperated, he half-spun. "I can't believe you would ask me that."

"You keep killing yourself for them, when they couldn't care less. When they don't deserve it. You've given enough—"

"You're wasting my time." He took a step away, but she restrained him with her palm.

"Don't. Touch. Me." He said it through his teeth. *This was a bad idea.*

Her eyebrows lifted, but her hand fell away. "I'm trying to help you."

"Well help, then. Or leave me alone."

With an almost uncertain look, Etin bit her lip, and her eyes darted to the right, concentrating.

She's trying to manipulate me. I'm out of here.

Before he could walk off, her expression melted into urgency. "I have vital intel for you, but it'll have to wait. You're being tracked by a sortie of *orysi*, the best and most powerful of the Grens. Dane has spared no expense in calling in favors. In fact, they're gathering right outside. You are, what is the expression? Fucked, I think?"

Too much of a coincidence to be a lie. He slid on his backpack and fisted his *cydern*. Her fingers slid around his forearm, where the tattooed sun marred his skin. He shuddered and pulled away.

"I can help you, Thom!" Her expression twitched, almost pleading. It wasn't a look he'd seen before.

"I think we both know how that works out. I'll take my chances."

Her face fell. "Thom…I—"

"Thom!" Poppy's shout echoed down the hallway, ragged with fear.

Cydern in his fist, Thom sprung away from Etin toward Poppy's voice.

Chapter Eighteen

Drumming the balls of her feet on the floor, Poppy turned her coffee cup round and round between her fingers, waiting for Thom. A gust of wind rattled the windows of the restaurant. Shivering, she shrugged back into her anorak.

In her pocket, the blue stone twitched. Involuntarily, she cupped it in her palm. Feather-soft, static electricity tickled her skin, like the drag of invisible spider-webs.

A voice leapt inside her chest, *Move, Poppy, move!*

She startled. *What?* Dread shivered down her neck and she felt her eyes drawn out the window.

Through a jagged rent in the southeast sky, low, ominous clouds dove toward the restaurant, churning like they were being mixed by gigantic hand blenders. Shreds of angry purple and gray sky dipped lower and lower, obscuring the view of the highway, approaching with the speed of a bullet train. As she watched, they broke apart, transmuting into multiple tornado-like entities. A tinny howling started in an indistinct corner of her chest. Her legs shaking, she stood, stumbling past tables, afraid to look away.

Two-hundred yards distant, one of the tornado-things engulfed a tree. The leaves swirled into the churning stack of clouds, coloring it in streaks of crimson. The tree shuddered as the cloud ripped it out of the ground and, with a resonating crack, snapped it in two. It seemed to happen in seconds – enough time to inhale and exhale.

The building shuddered and creaked in the wind gusts. A woman let out a strangled scream and a man shouted to get away from the windows.

"Thom!" She lunged out of the seating area. "We have a problem! Thom! Where are you?"

As she reached the lobby, Thom burst out of the hall and propelled her into the breezeway, his hand tight on her shoulder. "We're leaving."

She squeaked. "Leaving? Have you looked outside?"

His expression didn't change, and she wondered if he was ever surprised about anything. Shoving the car keys into her palm, he spun her, hoisted her pack onto her shoulders, tied the straps around her waist, whirled her around, and positioned her in front of the door.

Heat pulsed in her jeans pocket. Her hand went to it. *The stone.*

The staff-weapon from the landing gleamed in his hand. "Whatever happens, keep running. Focus on the car. I'll be right next to you."

A gale exploded into the breezeway, so strong it knocked her back into his chest. He'd already started forward, compelling her out of the doorway like a racehorse. The glass door shattered behind them. Yelping, she covered her face.

A voice rumbled in her chest, licking her insides like gentle lightning, *Be brave, Poppy. Be brave!*

More heat radiated from the stone in her pocket, simmering in her limbs, melding into the outlandish strength, almost glimmering across her skin. Gulping air, she pinpointed the car. The keys felt sharp in her hand, and she gripped them harder, stumbling over the foreignness invading her body.

The din of the storm pounded heavy and deafening in her chest, vibrating like a kick drum. A murmuration of red leaves flew by in front of her, followed by a tree, ripped out of the ground. It flipped, bounced, and tumbled into a line of vehicles in the next parking lot, shattering the windows. Dirt pelted her, stinging her skin. The wail of a car alarm echoed in and out of the roaring wind.

She stumbled, almost landing on her knees. Hooking her arm, Thom kept her on her feet, propelling her onward. His weapon glowing, he held it before them like a shield, and debris bounced away without hitting them, allowing them to fight through to the car.

They were within ten paces of the vehicle when the air surrounding them collapsed, sucked away by a potent force. Pain spread in her chest and her legs crumpled. The violence of the storm went eerily quiet. The ground shuddered with the impact of the atmospheric change and the air boiled with heat.

Thom slammed into her, his arms surrounding her, shielding her with his chest, his palm covering her eyes. Light rolled over them, as bright as if she'd face-planted onto mega-watt stadium lights. The flash faded and sounds crashed into her ears; a deafening mob of alien voices, vibrations, screams, and roars. Yanking her to her feet, they were at the car, fumbling at the doors and leaping inside. Her hands were slick with sweat as he wrenched her backpack off.

"Get on the highway! Westbound!" He sounded far away. "Hurry!"

The warmth from the stone pumped alive and vibrant in her cells, like when Dane had attacked her, but stronger. A louder, wildfire voice, *Be brave, Poppy.*

The warmth spread up the back of her neck and into her head, clearing the light imprint from her retinas. With an agility foreign to her, she maneuvered the car out of the parking lot, dodging tree limbs, scanning the road, calculating the fastest path to escape.

The tires screeched, weaving between stopped vehicles. Gunning the Lumina down the left turn lane, she threaded an opening, avoided an intersection by speeding through a corner gas station, careened across a grass embankment, and zoomed onto the highway. The intensity of her focus blocked her from seeing anything other than the way out.

Thom crouched in the passenger seat, the staff-weapon tight in his hand, absorbed with the scene behind them. Punching the accelerator to the floor, she scanned the rear-view mirror. Low black clouds hovered and swirled around the restaurant, lit up with sulfurous lightning, lightning without rain or thunder. With fear, or something worse, the length of her spine shivered, her forehead damp with cooling sweat.

Her heart pulsed in her fingertips, and the aching in her wounded arm returned. The pressure and the flash replayed in her brain, followed by the angry roar of the tornado-like clouds. She clutched the steering wheel, her hands going numb.

"Are you okay?" Thom's voice rumbled, the same maddening, calm tone as in the restaurant.

Trying to answer, she swallowed hard. Her hand started to smart where the keys had dug into the middle of her palm.

"What happened back there?" She strained to keep her voice steady. "What was that?"

"Elementals. Tracking us. Trying to capture you." He put his elbow up on the door, clenching and unclenching his fist.

"Elementals are tornados?" She spat the words, incredulous. "This is unreal." *But you saw them, with your own eyes, Poppy. People in the restaurant saw them*. Frantically, she scanned the rear-view mirror. "Did we get away? What about the people in the restaurant? Will they be okay?"

He nodded. "Yes. And yes. Just barely. They were *orysi*. Elementals that harness the wind and sometimes the weather, if there are enough of them. They only mimic tornados."

Yeah, that makes perfect sense. She bit back the words. "And the light explosion?"

"That was a *cym*. A lightkind elemental. That was how we escaped."

"How we escaped?"

Again, a terse dip of his chin, as if he didn't want to acknowledge it himself.

A memory detonated in Poppy's head, the malicious golden visage, an awful welling of fear in her belly. The inhuman woman in Panera. *I knew it!* "The blonde server. *She* was the *cym*."

His expression turned stony. "Yes."

Poppy didn't lower her voice. "But she helped us escape? What am I missing here? And why didn't you say something?"

Clutching at his seatbelt, he scanned behind them again, his expression distant, as if he hadn't heard her. Just when she was about to explode, he pointed at a semi-truck ahead. "Pull in behind this truck and stay there. The draft and the fumes might hide us if we're being pursued." Out the windshield, he squinted at the graying sky. "Night will help too."

She followed his directions, her anger cooling, leaving her shaky and worn. Just when she'd given up hope of a response, he began to speak, his voice subdued.

"Her name is Etin." Over the rumble of the car, Poppy strained to hear him. "She was my elemental counterpart in the *Offysfyn*. This *cydern*," he placed the staff-weapon back onto his wrist where it became the leather cuff, "came from her."

She gaped at the cuff, finally connecting the dots – the polymorphic weapon he'd been using. *"Cydern?"*

"An elemental bone. It can take many forms. It's our only protection from elemental attacks."

His voice rumbled flat, with a melancholy edge. Poppy's chest buzzed with a strong emotion she couldn't place, or didn't want to acknowledge. The *cydern*, his super-important weapon, came from a gorgeous elemental – his *Offysfyn* counterpart? That sounded – intimate. Her stomach turned over. *He's just a bodyguard, remember?*

"How?"

"Higher forms of elementals can regenerate, so it wasn't a loss." Thom bit off the words like they tasted sour.

"What's her problem? With me?" She glanced at him. "It seemed like she had a problem with me."

Eyes shut, he rubbed the bridge of his nose. "To some elementals humans seem more of a liability than they're worth."

Wow. I don't know how to respond to that. Confused warmth flooded her cheeks – she didn't know if she was hurt or angry or just plain terrified. "She wants you to ditch me?"

His expression cloaked his thoughts. "If I'm around she'll behave. She has reasons for being loyal to me. You don't need to worry about her."

Nope. Angry – I'm definitely angry. "Well, that's cryptic." Poppy snapped. "Are you saying we're going to encounter her again?"

A muscle in his jaw jumped. "We have bigger problems at present. She's not one of them."

"You didn't answer."

"I don't know."

"But—"

"Enough!" His voice echoed in the car, making her jump. Stung, she clamped her mouth shut.

Unfolding the map, he scanned it in the light from the window, his brow furrowed. In his fingers, the pen dented the paper as he glanced between the map and the notebook, his fist tight. Her heart throbbed in her chest, she glared at the back of the semi, her fingers tight around the steering wheel. For several miles, the only sound was the rumble of the road beneath the tires.

When he nudged her, she forced her wide-eyed startle into a glare.

Undeterred, he met her eyes. "I'm sorry, Poppy. I shouldn't have been so harsh."

Catching the weariness in his expression, she remembered the shitstorm he'd been thrown into, one he'd tried to prevent. *Cut him some slack. It wasn't like you didn't lose your temper either.*

"I'm sorry too." She whispered. "It is true. This would be a lot easier not having to drag me along."

His hand curled into a fist. "You're *not* a liability."

"But, it—"

"No! That perspective is not right. My job is to walk alongside you, and take the hits if I need to. I'm honored to do that. That's the truth. Etin and I see our worlds very differently."

The rigidness inside her ribcage dissolved, leaving a cloud-soft warmth spreading through her veins. "I don't want you to take the hits, Thom."

A subdued grin replaced his scowl. "If we're lucky enough, I won't have to. But that doesn't mean I won't."

"And it doesn't mean I can't. Surely there's something I can do other than just…" She broke off, shaking her head.

"Driving fast? Taking guns from truck drivers?" He shook his head. "I have a feeling you're just getting started."

A smile tugged at her mouth. "Glad we've come to an understanding then."

"Let's not get carried away."

"No take-backs."

"Fokking fokk." He muttered it under his breath.

She laughed. "Curse all you want, if it helps you accept the inevitable."

"It does." His mock scowl gave way to his adorable, crooked grin.

Poppy returned the smile, feeling more like herself than since she'd been swept into their outlandish adventure.

Chapter Nineteen

A lovely, mauve dusk gave way to full night. Poppy focused on driving, while Thom scoured the map and noted exit signs. Soon he directed her to take an exit that read: Nebraska 87, where they stopped at a rest station for fuel. When she returned to the car, he'd commandeered the driver's seat. Instead of returning to the interstate, he took the outer road, squinting at road signs.

His demeanor had returned to its bag-of-rocks opacity; she didn't have to strain her intuition to know he was troubled. Quickly noting the map again, he turned down a narrow two-lane road. It felt like driving into a dark tunnel.

"Where're we going?" she asked.

He handed her the map. "We're headed west through Nebraska, up into northwest Wyoming. You should sleep. I'll drive for as long as I can. Try and get us there by morning."

"Wyoming? Not Colorado?"

"Change of plans. Because of the *orysi*." He rolled a shoulder. "There's a little known, minor borderland in the Tetons. They won't expect us to go that way. It will be a harder road. Not ideal." He glanced at her. "Rest while you can. We'll have to do a lot of walking later."

"These *orys* things are really serious, aren't they?" she asked, already feeling the answer in the pit of her stomach.

The corners of his mouth lifted, but the smile didn't touch his eyes. "Don't worry. I'm just being cautious."

She leaned the seat back, trying to find a comfortable position to rest her arm, which throbbed with every jolt and bump of the road. The passing landscape glowed in the spray of the headlights and thin ribbons of gray rippled in the northern sky, reminding her of the bizarre lightning outside of Panera, of the way she'd been able to drive them to safety with the skill of a stunt-driver.

Coalescing with her increasing feelings for Thom – her *just a bodyguard* mantra became less effective every time he smiled at her – Poppy felt as though a vast realm of nerve-endings had been awakened, like she'd grown an extra limb and didn't know how to use it. Were these senses, along with the voice she kept hearing, connected with the blue stone? or was it some other Caelithian power from her past she didn't remember? The recollection of the static electricity crawling over her skin and invading her cells, rattled her, making it difficult to take Thom's advice and rest while she could.

Inches away, his restless energy thickened in the cramped space of the car, as if he fought with inner adversaries, or was having intense conversations with himself. The sense bled into her mind, mingling with her disquiet, making sleep elusive. As the road dove deeper into the night, she kept her questions to herself, watching clouds from the south overtake the stars.

When sleep overtook Poppy, she dreamt.

In the dream, a floor of pine planks stretched beneath her toes, rippling with orange light and purple shadow. She peeked through the slit of a cracked door, an unseen observer. Inside, her mother sobbed into her hands, her hair spilling over her fingers in shiny waves, reflecting the strange, lavender light of a nearby lantern.

Over the sobs, her father's voice rose, gruff and impatient. "Don't you understand, Deidre?" He paced, grinding his fist in his palm. "This is the only way to keep her safe. It's the only way!"

Deidre shook her head, dragging the back of her hands over her eyes.

"God knows how long those fire bastards have been after her!" Felix pivoted, the lines on his face harsh in the lantern light. "Do you know how lucky we are they haven't already taken her?"

"There has to be another way. There has to...I can't..." The agony of Deidre's voice made Poppy's stomach curdle.

With a frustrated growl, Felix grabbed Deidre's wrists and yanked them away from her face, revealing her mother's reddened eyes, trails of mucous oozing from her nose. "Are you listening to me?"

Startled at her father's shout, Poppy darted away from the door, flattening herself against the wall.

His voice hurting her ears, he continued. "It's getting too dangerous to travel. This is the best place I've found! They'll never find her there. We *are* doing this. There's no other way!"

Covering her ears, Poppy peeked through the crack of the door again.

"But, our home. We can't take her from here." Deidre choked. "We'll be all alone. In the *Uther*."

"Do you want to keep her safe?" Felix's hand tightened on her shoulder.

Deidre didn't respond, her body swaying as he shook her. "They'll drag her away. They'll do worse to her than the Grens will, for certain."

Removing her hands, Poppy held her breath. *What?*

Nodding, Deidre's face crumpled.

"It has to be done." He let go of her shoulder and she pitched forward, almost falling.

"You'll go through the well within a fortnight. You and Poppy. Ayden will stay with me."

No. They can't mean it. Poppy's heart skipped and writhed.

"Find a way to cope." Her father walked back to his desk in front of the window, shuffling through the maps cluttering the surface.

Her mother had gone very still, staring at her hands, folded in her lap. They reminded Poppy of the limp wings of the dead sparrow she'd seen lying outside the sitting room window.

Warmth nudged Poppy's shoulder, and she gasped, throwing up her hands as if she'd been caught. Intent on listening, she'd forgotten Addis – her *rif* friend – who'd brought her to overhear the conversation. His orange and purple flames reflected off the polished wood floor, warming her bare feet, her shoulder. Level to her chin, his cat-like black eyes blinked, for he was no bigger than a child. No bigger than she was.

'You needed to hear, Poppy,' he said. *'To know your danger. Felix will take you to Uther-Erai. Dangerous for you. For your mother.'*

She trembled, biting her lip. *No. They wouldn't.*

The elemental stroked her arm, consoling, beckoning. *'Will Poppy come now? With Addis? My master will protect you. If you come. We will keep you safe. You won't have to leave Caelith. We will take care of you. Always.'*

Fire bastards. That's what her Dad had said. Poppy blinked at Addis's flaming form, realization souring in her stomach.

Felix had insisted she stay away from the Firekind, making her recite the warning rhyme until she hated every syllable. He'd told her they meant no good. But they'd been so friendly, so harmless – her only friends, besides her brother and Thom. And she was so lonely. She hadn't listened, hadn't believed him, carefully hiding her escapades with her *rif* friends.

This was all her fault.

Tears choked her. Spinning, she fled down the hall, her feet slapping the stone floor of the kitchen. As she flung it open, the back door creaked and banged against the stone of the house.

Crisp night air shook loose her scarlet braid as she ran, the grass shocking her bare feet. The sky had surrendered to navy twilight; with cold brilliance, the stars winked across the darkness.

The hated rhyme whispered inside of her – the rhyme meant to warn Caelith's children, especially ones like her.

> *Crimson hair*
> *Beware! Beware!*
> *He rises out of firelight*
> *All around burn at the sight*
> *Of violet coal and scarlet fright*
> *His groaning roars, his flames alight*
> *Crimson hair*
> *Beware! Beware!*

Poppy ran faster, breath harsh in her lungs. Following her effortlessly, Addis bounced from tree to rock to bush, suppressing the glow of his flames. Sprinting, she concentrated on each step, wanting to outrun him, to be alone.

By the gate, the *fyn* inside the lantern called her name, but she ignored it. They'd betrayed her – she didn't want to understand, to hear them anymore, no matter how special it made her feel.

> *Burning for the crimson one*
> *Who fled from him undone undone*
> *For whom his grief*
> *Will always run*

Now she would be punished. Her mother along with her. And Ayden…tears choked her again.

Her feet carried her through the kitchen gardens, past the slumbering beehives, across the sheep pasture. Desperate hope nudged her. *I'll be safe with Thom.* she thought. *He'll know what to do. He'll make it better. He always does.*

As she turned toward the barn, the rhyme continued, raking across her thoughts like splintered wood.

> *Crimson hair*
> *Beware! Beware!*
> *He ascends in red moonlight*
> *Enchanting, slaying by his might*
> *Steals her to his home of fire*
> *Chains her to his flame desire*

Her father's anger, his desperation, gave the words new meaning – like a long dead thing flopping around. Glimpsing Addis's flames behind her, she sprinted blindly, fear watery in her gut.

The dark shapes of the horses loomed in the meadow. She hopped the fence and skirted them. The peak of the barn appeared ahead, black against the purple night, the windows glowing. Bursting through the wooden doors, she tackled Thom in a fierce hug.

Dropping the bucket he was holding, he returned the embrace, and the rhyme's chant died away like a snuffed candle. Chest heaving with sobs, she burrowed into his arms, until she could feel Addis spying on her from somewhere unseen.

Pulling back, she blinked up at Thom's bemused face. "They want to take me away!"

Her tears blotched the front of his wool sweater. Embarrassment crept hot up her neck, but before it took hold, another wave of fear suppressed it.

Guiding her to a stool, he slid a tin cup of water into her hand. Straw prickled and stuck to her muddy feet.

Across from her, he sunk down on a hay bale. Stubble darkened his jaw line – in the shadowy light, he looked almost grown up, like Ayden. Ashamed, she squirmed, suddenly not wanting to meet his eyes. The dusty, animal-pungent air made her sneeze.

"What happened, Poppy?" he said.

Her breath rattled in her chest, but she began, haltingly. "Tonight. Da said – it was dangerous for me." She squeezed her eyes shut. "He wants to take me away! Me and mam. To the *Erai*. Away from Ayden. Away from here."

I can't tell him. I can't tell him what I've really done.

Thom's eyes darkened with thought. "Maybe you misunderstood. Maybe—"

"I didn't! I know what I heard!" Her voice echoed harsh in the barn.

'Does he hurt you, Poppy?' Addis's voice came from the flame of a hanging lantern, taking on an orange and purple cast.

"No!" Rising to her feet, she shook a fist at it. "Leave me alone!"

Thom glanced between her and the lantern, a frown gathering on his forehead. "You overheard them?"

Sinking back down, she bit her lip, trying to keep it from quivering.

He learned forward. "Poppy, you can trust your parents. I think they might be upset if they knew you were here, talking to me, instead of them."

She blinked hard. He wasn't going to understand. Trying not to blubber, she held her breath, sitting up straight, trying to be brave, to be grown up, like him.

Thom's weight sunk onto the hay bale next to her. "Let's go back. Before they get worried. We can ask them, together. What do you think?"

He doesn't know what I've really done. Maybe I deserve this. To be sent away.

The fire inside of her extinguished, she acquiesced, blinking back tears. Saddling a horse, he boosted her into the worn leather seat, and mounted behind. Again, the chanting began inside of her, like the throb of a headache. Smashing her hands over her ears, she doubled up, cringing. What was worse? losing her home? or the betrayal of elementals she'd believed were her friends? *You were warned. It's your fault.*

"It's okay," his voice murmured. "You're going to be okay, Poppy."

Snapping the reigns, Thom clicked his tongue, and the horse struck out in the night, its hooves thudding in the grass, keeping time with the rasp of the night insects.

On the path before them, Felix and Ayden appeared, their faces white and strained in the lantern light, their chests heaving with running. Seeing her, relief passed over Ayden's face, but her father's jaw clenched, the red flush across his cheeks visible, even in the half-light.

Thom slid off the horse. "I was bringing Poppy—"

"DON'T you come near my daughter AGAIN!"

"Da!" Ayden and Poppy protested simultaneously.

Angry tears sprung to her eyes. *Why would he talk to Thom that way?*

Felix shoved Thom and dragged her off of the horse, yanking her behind him, his fingers pinching her bicep.

"No! Da!" She choked on the words. "It's my doing! This is—"

Without pausing, he thrust her toward Ayden and lunged at Thom, halting inches from his face. Thom didn't flinch, but his eyebrows lifted for a hair of a second.

Not sparing her a glance, Felix boomed at Ayden. "Take your sister back to the house!"

Mouth ajar, Ayden looked between them, as if he couldn't believe what he was seeing. The horse pawed the ground. Thom planted his feet, loosely holding the reins, his expression even. Poppy struggled, trying to go back to Thom, to defend him.

His face twisting with anger, Felix blocked her way. "Ayden! NOW!"

"But—" Ayden's temper ignited.

"NOW!" Felix shoved her back toward Ayden, causing her to teeter.

Before her knees hit the ground, her brother caught her. Scowling at Felix's back, Ayden hustled her away as shouts echoed in the night, her father's words indiscernible with rage. The rhyme became a crescendo in her head, to the cue of his shouting.

Crimson hair
Beware! Beware!

Chapter Twenty

Poppy awoke with a gasp, gripping the dashboard, the door handle, the seat, reeling with the fading dream. The scent of the hay, the lantern light, the ringing of her father's shouts, the worn leather under her fingertips – it was as if a three-dimensional movie had been uploaded to her brain as she slept. How could something so real have been a dream? Even now, the flame-lit landscape of the dream obscured her vision. Rubbing her eyes, she blinked in the dark. In her pocket, the blue stone tremored with heat, glowing through the fabric.

Weird. Removing it, she squinted at the brilliant orange of captured flames, roaring at its edges, glowing with blue speckles in the center. They shriveled, leaving her in darkness. Trembling, she thrust it on the dashboard, abruptly loathing the way it felt against her skin – remembering the rhyme, her father's warning, the fear in his eyes.

The wind w*Uthe*red and shook the motionless car. Curtains of rain drummed across the windshield and gusts ripped at the trees outside, dappling the windows with sodden leaves. The atmosphere hummed, pressurized with the storm. A damp chill had settled like invisible fog in the interior of the vehicle.

In a flash of lightning, she glimpsed Thom's silhouette, crammed in the driver's seat. The plaid blanket from her house covered him; his arm was thrown over his forehead in sleep. Letting the stiff remnants of fear dissolve in her body, she sunk back into her seat, the vivid pictures still whirling behind her eyes. She snatched at them, wanting to gather them up and save them, like the blown pages of a term paper. Could it be she was remembering her life in Caelith? The thought stabbed her. Maybe she didn't want to remember...

The car shook as Thom twitched in his sleep, mumbling in Icelandic. Watching him, she smiled. She should look away, give him privacy. But she kept looking, both enchanted and guilty at the moment of stolen intimacy. Thunder bounced around the night-shrouded world, chasing flashes of lightning.

As sudden as the thunder, a noise of agonized fury burst from his throat.

The car shuddered as his head bumped the ceiling. His knees hit the steering wheel, and there was a muffed smack as his elbow collided with the window. Unable to catch his breath, he gasped, the ragged sound echoing in the interior over the rain. His forehead came to rest on the top of the steering wheel, his shoulders rising and falling.

For a moment, she stared, breathless. "Thom?" Hand shaking, she touched his shoulder.

He restrained her arm, his grip crushing. Pain flooded her wrist and she yelped. Startled, he released her. Wrist throbbing, she shrank back against the door.

Thom seemed to come to, as if he'd surfaced from deep water. "Poppy – I'm sorry." His chest heaved in between the words.

"Are we in danger?" she blurted. "Did the *orysi* find us?" Squinting in the lightning flashes, she rotated.

"No." Still, his chest heaved, like he'd just sprinted a half-mile.

"What's wrong? Thom?"

Shivering, he shook his head. Starting the car, she turned the heat up. The light from the dashboard illuminated him; his left arm was clamped tight around his middle. "Are you okay? Are you hurt?"

"It's nothing."

"I'm serious, Thom. You don't seem okay."

"I'm okay." Doubling up again, he clenched his teeth. "Just need. Some time."

"What can I do?"

"It's just," his chest heaved, "an old injury."

Poppy remembered what the Scots guy had said back in Riverston; *How big's your scar, then?*

"Do you need meds?" She reached for his backpack.

"Won't help. With this." His voice went hoarse. "It'll pass."

She touched his shoulder – it was all she could think of to do. When he didn't flinch, she found his hand and gripped it. The car shuddered with a gust of wind. His breath caught and his hand went rigid.

"If you're tense it'll be worse," she whispered. "I remember you telling me that. Try and breathe through it."

Little by little, his tension dissolved. He attempted to breathe, his inhale and exhale ragged and forced, like the effort pained him. *What hell has he been through?* And then close on the heels of that thought, *What's really going on in Caelith?*

As his breathing slowed, she coaxed him back into his seat. Grimacing, he dragged his other hand over his face. "I'm sorry," He made a frustrated noise in his throat. "This isn't… I'm supposed to be taking care of you."

She gave a little snort. "At the moment I'm doing pretty well taking care of myself. Let me enjoy it while I can."

He almost chuckled, but a grunt of pain stunted it. She retrieved his blanket off the floor, and he tensed up again, as if her sudden movement had startled him.

"It's cold." She tucked the blanket over him. "This'll help."

His hand wrapped around hers with a grip bordering uncomfortable, as though he might squeeze comfort from her proximity. *I must be doing something right*, she thought.

The storm moved on, and his breathing grew steady and deep, the tension in his arm and shoulder melting. Heat radiated off his body. Feeling the cadence of his breathing slow, she relaxed. *He's going to be okay. We're going to be okay.*

The warmth and the darkness, and perhaps the intimacy of the moment, calmed her more than she had been in two days, coaxing her eyes shut. With the rise and fall of his chest, her head slumped onto his shoulder. He shifted so that she settled more against him, his beard resting on her forehead, soft and prickly.

All those weeks at Target, she'd never been, or expected to be, this close to Thom Magnusson – close enough to feel the warmth of his breath, the sharpness of his jawline, the heaviness of his palm draped over the back of her hand.

The proximity was becoming headier by the minute; the bulk of his arm and shoulder next to hers, the pulsing heat of his hand, the rise and fall of his chest, and his smell; wood smoke, sage, and salt. It might as well have been a love potion concocted for her. More awake with each moment, her stomach tightened and persuasive, liquid arousal trickled into her veins, feeding an ache in her belly that was becoming difficult to ignore.

Her breath caught and his hand tightened around hers, her nerves crackling with a delicious electricity. The ache became an insistent throbbing. Was this feeling just her? Hardly daring to breathe, she lifted her chin, searching for an answer in his eyes.

Somehow, their lips met, slowly, then deliberately. His hand slid along her cheek, cradling the back of her neck, the touch gentle, but also taut. The kiss deepened, wet and soft. Not the fumbling desperation of inexperience, but restrained, waiting, held in check by her surprised intake of breath. An involuntary moan in her throat, she melted into him. He melted into her, both his arms surrounding her waist beneath her anorak, erasing the distance between them.

Outstripping restraint, the kiss intensified, the play of his lips decisive and adept, her tongue responding against his. She stroked the bones of his collarbone, his shoulders, felt his biceps contracting. Responding to her touch, his arms tightened, and he drew her against his chest, crashing together like they were tides pulled by the moon. The center console dug into her thigh, but she barely noticed.

His hands were hot on the skin of her waist, her back, and fireworks of pleasure crackled along her skin. Her heart galloping, she forced his coat off his shoulders and tossed it aside, tugging at his collar. The momentum was coaxing her into his lap. Despite a quiver of nervousness, of inexperience, she had no objection to going there.

As she nestled into his lap, his shoulder blade dug into her forearm and she yelped and shrank away, hitting the steering wheel. As if coming out of a dream, he stiffened. "What am I? *Helvítis*. I'm sorry. Poppy. I–I–wasn't thinking." Like he couldn't retreat fast enough, he extracted his arms from around her waist.

"It's nothing. Just my arm." Her lips grazed his again, but he turned away, clenching his jaw.

"Poppy. We can't. This can't happen."

Intoxicated with the hot roar in her veins, she didn't comprehend his words. "What?" Pressing her lips along his jawline, she stroked the hair at the base of his neck.

"*No.* Not like this. I can't." His shoulders tensed, just short of pushing her away.

A sick, hollow feeling invaded her chest and she shrank back into her seat, her pulse hammering in her ears, her fingertips, her belly. *What have I done?*

"Look, if things hadn't changed, if we were still working at Target," he drew in a harsh breath, "we wouldn't be in this situation. You've had a lot thrown at you. Don't rush into something that—"

"Rush? Thom! I've liked you for…that's not for you to decide!" She was going to say liked him for months, but that wasn't possible, even if her feelings belied the facts. "Are you saying you don't like me *that* way?"

He rubbed the dent between his eyebrows. "I'm saying this situation isn't fair to you. You've had too much thrown at you the past three days to even think about…for me to consider this okay."

Her breath came in an exasperated huff. "Maybe I don't care!"

"I promised to protect you!" His voice rose. "And getting off like this isn't keeping that promise. Not to me. Not like this."

The wind howled. The sick feeling spread through her insides. The ache still crowed uncomfortably between her legs, a humiliating reminder of how much she'd let her inhibitions down.

"We're in too much danger, here." He murmured, so softly she almost couldn't hear him. "This isn't about what I want. If it was about what I wanted." He shook his head.

"You wouldn't be here," she finished, bitterly.

"That's not what I was going to say!" Anger flared around him, so sudden her breath caught.

Pushing her hair out of her face, she crossed her arms. Her lips felt raw and tingly. In less than five minutes her Thom-specific defenses had been irreparably damaged. Embarrassment and shame lashed at her thoughts. *Was she behaving like a petulant child who didn't get her way? Is that how he saw her?*

"Am I too young?" she asked. "Is that it?"

He laughed, a mirthless bark. "Poppy." He shook his head. "No." His voice cracked. "That's not. It's…there're a lot of reasons, but that isn't one of them."

Mortified heat spread in her face. "A lot of reasons?"

A frustrated noise vibrated in his throat. "Nothing that I wouldn't ignore in a heartbeat if I could. Please don't push me on this. I'm just trying to do the right thing."

Twisting, he rummaged in his pack and the beam of a flashlight interrupted the darkness. She threw up a hand to block the light.

"Sorry," he said.

What now? The leg she'd folded up beneath her tingled with pins and needles, and she settled back down in the seat. She could still feel his hands on her skin. *How do I even talk to him now?*

Struggling, he held the flashlight between his teeth, illuminating the map, scanning for the route he'd marked…doing a bad job of it. She took it and held it for him. His eyes flickered to hers. "Thanks."

His finger traced highway eighty-seven, up into Wyoming, stopping in the middle, his brow furrowing. "I think we're somewhere around here." He said, almost to himself, before meeting her eyes again. Her face growing hot, she glanced away.

"I'm sorry, Poppy." His voice cracked again.

She shook her head. "Well, I'm not. Not really. Not if I'm honest."

"You misunderstand me then."

Bemused, she glanced at him. but he was folding up the map, his fingers trembling. In an awful rush, Poppy remembered his pain, how it all started.

"What happened?" she asked. "To you?"

Facing the dashboard, he scanned the night. "The rain was so heavy I couldn't see to drive. Had to stop."

"No. You were in a lot of pain. I was really worried."

His face furrowed, as if the memory hurt him. Putting the car into drive, he glanced toward the road. "I don't feel like talking about it right now. We need to make up for lost time."

She arched an eyebrow. "Well then, let *me* drive, silly."

They traded places, and as she settled into the driver's seat, she felt the weight of his gaze. *What is it now?* She thrust her hair behind her ear and looked at him. Thom gazed at her like there was no sight in the worlds that gave him more pleasure. Heat flooded her face, her hands, her ribcage.

He swallowed. "Thank you, Poppy. For helping me. Tonight. It was nice to not go through that alone, for once."

Could he hear her heart racing? She started the car. "Anytime." If she wasn't belted in the car she might float away. Maybe Thom Magnusson's stony and disciplined heart might be more malleable than he let on.

Chapter Twenty-One

Thom was grateful and more than impressed; with Poppy at the wheel, they traveled much faster than he'd could've ever managed. They might outmaneuver the *orysi* after all.

Despite what had happened between them – *don't think about it, Magnusson, for the love of Cael, don't think about it* – the early morning silence between them felt comfortable, as natural as when they used to fish together in the shallows at Dream Lake. He hadn't meant to nod off, but on the heels of the night before he was knackered.

But now, in the afternoon light, her face was as gray as her hair, and the purple circles around her eyes had deepened. He shouldn't have slept. He should've switched with her earlier. The thoughts dug a guilty, anxious hole in his chest.

Squinting in the amber sunlight, he glanced around. "Where are we?"

"A Conoco." Her mouth twitched.

Rubbing his eyes, he grinned. "Okay, smart ass. Where are we in Wyoming?"

"Somewhere in the middle." She pointed. "I think those are the mountains."

The surrounding town huddled under a stunning backdrop of snowy peaks towering into silver blue sky – bearing the distinctive shape of Grand Tetons. He grinned at her. "Yes, those are the mountains. You got us here fast."

She smirked – a satisfied smile, but it quickly morphed into a yawn. "Yeah. The drive was pretty uneventful." Adjusting her arm, she grimaced. "Kinda nice for a change."

How much did her arm hurt? Ettar bites were as excruciating to the nervous system as jellyfish stings – he knew from experience. But, when he'd been bitten, he'd had time to rest and recover. Poppy hadn't had that advantage, and had pushed herself. How would the borderlands affect her? Should they change course, go slower? But the *orysi*. *Too much of a risk.* This task felt like walking an invisible tightrope.

"Where to next?" She turned the blue stone over in her fingers.

Twisting, he surveyed the adjacent streets. Across from the gas station, billboards advertised tours, camping supplies, ski and cabin rentals, kayak and rafting trips, and little motel haunts. The local signs all had some sort of rustic depiction of wildlife; moose silhouettes, wolves, or carved wooden bears.

When she cracked the window, the wind snapped in and flooded his arms with goosebumps. Except for the stink of exhaust fumes, it reminded him of home – of Caldys.

"We need to buy gear for the hike. Coats, boots." He unfolded the road map. "I need a detailed map of the mountains."

Grabbing their packs, they set out toward the row of stores across the street, Poppy clutching her jacket at the neck, shivering. Beyond the town's edge, foothills like thick emerald blankets covered the knees of the mountains. The immense scale of the land made it difficult to estimate the distance, but they were still miles from their destination – an obscure canyon in the heart of the Tetons, the hiding location the borderland, if his memory served him well.

At the camping store, they selected down-filled parkas with hoods, waterproof trousers and gloves, and fur-lined hiking boots to replace Poppy's converse. While she tried everything for size, he chatted with the owner about conditions in the mountains.

Indicating the flat-screen mounted on a nearby wall, the woman shrugged. "First snowfall's gonna dump a lot. Probably not a blizzard though, so that's good. Especially for skiing." She eyed their supplies. "Probably not the best time to hike, unless you're experienced. The park trails are closed."

He shrugged into the parka. "Great, thanks."

Poppy caught sight of the snowfall projections displayed on the TV in waves of red, pink, gray, and white. Her eyes widened. Wearing most of their gear, they exited the store, Poppy glancing back at the continuing weather report.

"Did you see that – about the snow?" she asked.

Nodding, he patted his backpack. "I bought thermals."

"You're not worried?" she asked.

"Not about that."

"It's not an elemental? A snow one? Trying to catch us?"

"A *nors*." He shook his head. "The Grens don't have enough *norsi* allies to produce a storm like that. And *norsi* wouldn't cross the borderlands, not for Dane." He shaded his eyes against the sun. "I'm more worried about the *orysi* finding us again. And the hike." He studied her face. *And you.*

It was too late to hike to the borderland, and she needed to rest. They needed to find somewhere to hole up for a while, get a good night's sleep. Colorful flyers littered the window of the camping store, and he paused, scanning the pictures of wildlife and rafting tours, mountaineering guides. The wind tugged at his hair, and he shoved it up under his cap, spying a picture of a cabin; *Grand Grizzly Lodges*. He squinted at the little map printed at the bottom, a red star marking the location, at the base of the Cathedral Group.

One moment Poppy hovered at his elbow, fidgeting with the zippers on her new coat, then wandered to the corner to gaze at the mountains. When he looked up again, she'd vanished. Heart in his throat, he pivoted, searching, tension flooding his muscles. "Poppy?" He jogged to the corner. Except for the view of the Tetons and the brisk whine of the wind, the alley was empty.

His pulse pounded in his throat. He spun. *How could I have lost her?* The sharp rushing of the wind, the rattle of the metal sign of the repair shop next door, the car engines accelerating down the adjoining street – the noise made it impossible to hear beyond. The repair shop blocked his view of the sky. He sprinted down the alley and around another building until the view opened up.

There! A disturbance in the air, like a mirage, a blot of silver moving with the wind. An *orys* scout! How could he have let it grab her right under his nose? He clenched his fists, a hurricane of rage heating his blood.

The sharp ping of a wrench came from the repair shop, then the sudden roar of a motorcycle. Thom sprinted toward the sound. A man in a gray jumpsuit adjusted the kickstand and faced his toolchest. Before the man turned around, Thom leapt on the motorcycle and zoomed out of the bay, dodging the cars clogging the road until only open road and the mountains lay in front of him.

The *orys* had gained so much distance that the ripple of its diaphanous body was difficult to make out. It had climbed in altitude – higher than the trees. Thom gritted his teeth and pushed the bike to its limits, his vision collapsing to a tunnel. He'd never be able to catch them!

The blurry slash of silver made a sudden dive, and blue sparks trailed behind it, like the tail of a comet. It dipped and wobbled behind a grove of trees, and zoomed back up to twice as high, as wild in flight as a balloon releasing air. Barely breathing, Thom turned the motorcycle off road, following them through sagebrush, bumping over the rough terrain. *Cael please. Don't let her fall!*

The bike jostled, rattling Thom's teeth, obscuring his vision, but he didn't let up. An explosion of pale blue fire skimmed the ground and zoomed back up into the air, nearing enough that he could see the *orys's* long limbs and fingers surrounding Poppy's back, clutching under her backside as she bucked and struggled. Another burst of sparks, and the *orys* let out a wail, audible even over the roar of the motorcycle. Blue sparks? The stone, had helped Poppy fight off Dane. Could it be helping her now?

The *orys's* bones blackened within its diaphanous form, as thought it was charring from the inside. The blue light intensified, spiked with orange, tinging Poppy's hair multi-colored, like she was a punk wasp with fiery wings instead of a human.

Baffled amazement flooded Thom's body, and goosebumps prickled up his arms. The bike roared as he accelerated again. A divot in the field of sage brush neared – the Snake River, cutting through the landscape in a wide arc.

Trapped within the spidery arms of the elemental, Poppy squirmed. The blue light burned around her with a white-hot center, as brilliant as platinum. The wind carried a scream, and the light careened down into the riverbed, out of sight. The brilliance left an imprint on his eyes, and he couldn't tell if it was afterburn, or pieces of the *orys*, or human, floating down through the air. *Poppy!* Fear pummeled him harder than any fist.

He brought the motorcycle to a skidding stop at the edge of the riverbed and scrambled down the rocky incline. Sprinting along the edge, he searched the deep blue rapids of the Snake River. Glimpsing a bobbing pale form, he shed his pack and coat, dove into the current, and punched his strength into each stroke, gaining on the current. A sunset flash reflected over the water, clasped in a struggling hand. Poppy splashed and rotated, unable to reach the bank; the current kept spinning her back into the middle of the river, and her head dipped beneath the water, as though she'd used all her strength up in the fight.

"Poppy!" He shouted, and her head whipped to face him, her eyes wide. Her arms flailed.

And then he reached her, and never had he been so relieved to feel the grip of her hand, the pointed end of her elbow colliding with his shoulder. He thrust his arm behind her back, and she slumped against him, spitting water. The feeling that the worlds' precipitous wobble had tipped back into balance melted over him. *I've got you, Poppy. I've got you.* And he realized he was saying it aloud, and she was clinging to him, gasping, her eyes red.

Around them, the waters of the Snake River were frigid, soaking her down coat until it felt as heavy as sandbags. But Thom barely felt the effort of ferrying her to the shore. *She's okay. Poppy's back in my arms.*

He'd been such a fool. To think he could suppress his feelings for her. To think he could protect her. But he was the best chance she had, and better he die trying than allow something to happen to her.

Sprawled in the muddy gravel of the riverbed, Poppy gripped a handful of his shirt, and wouldn't let go. Her other hand held the stone to her shuddering chest. One by one, he loosened each of her fingers, and brought her hand to his lips and kissed it.

"Oh, Thom." Her teeth chattered. "You came."

The words landed like a left hook. As if there was ever any hesitation in his mind. "Of course I came. I will always come, Poppy."

The hand holding the still-gleaming stone fell to the gravel. "What just happened? What is this thing?"

His lips parted, but he couldn't produce an answer.

He would be even more foolish if he still believed she was only an *Uther*, just the daughter of Felix Paquin, the *Uther-ling*-Steward. The serendipitous owner of a powerful elemental relic. To have even half a chance of keeping her safe, he had to answer that question, to decipher this precious mystery that was Poppy Paquin.

Chapter Twenty-Two

By the time Thom hauled her to the bike, Poppy could barely walk for trembling, shock, and exhaustion. It felt as if the battle had stolen her red blood cells, the marrow in her bones, the fight in her muscles. Even worse, she feared at any moment she might be snatched into the sky. With every blink, every step, she feared the ground might suddenly be a hundred feet below her, and she would fall like a stone, her bones shattering like pottery.

Thom shed her sodden coat, and wrapped her in his dry one, but on the motorcycle, *where had he found a motorcycle?* she wondered. The wind cut like knives. Maybe it was wishful thinking, but the set of his back, the turn of his chin, seemed to have purpose, as though he had a plan, or knew where he was going. *This is Thom, of course he has a plan.*

Water dripped off his curls, and his shoulders tremored, tensed up, then shook again. She tightened her arms around his waist as though she could keep him warm. They passed a sign that read: *Grand Grizzly Lodges*, and his shoulders rose and fell and slumped as he shifted the gears and turned the bike.

The 'lovebirds' cabin nestled in the shadow of the magnificent Cathedral Group, the snowcaps gleaming in the growing dark. If Poppy hadn't been so cold, she'd have wanted to linger outside, watching the approach of night over the Tetons, in the bright twinkle of the stars above.

Without a word, Thom shunted her in the bathroom, immediately cranking the shower on. In the mirror her lips were blue, her face was as white as fresh paper, and she couldn't stop shivering. She blinked. *Oh shit. Not good.*

With both of them in the bathroom, she could barely move. The ends of Thom's hair had dried in the wind, and the curls skimmed his hazel eyes; they were narrow with concern as he tested the temperature of the water.

Poppy almost laughed. Of course, the moment she might actually succeed at seducing him, she had hypothermia. Pressed awkwardly against the towel bar, she struggled with the button on her jeans, but her fingers were too numb to undo it.

He ripped off her sweater and, not bothering with the rest of her clothes, maneuvered her under the warm water. Slumping against the shower stall, she groaned as a burning tingle spread through her hands and toes, heating the blood in her veins.

Before she could stutter something clever or suggestive, he shut the door behind him. She steadied herself against the tub walls. He wouldn't have fit anyway.

The door opened again. Thom's voice, "Here, some dry clothes."

"Thom?" She cleared her throat. "Are you okay?"

"I cranked the heat out here. I'll be okay." His silhouette hesitated at the door. "Are you still shivering?"

"Sort of. I'm better. I'm warming up."

"Don't get out until you feel warm again."

"But what about you?"

The door clicked shut. Poppy made a face. Thom was probably blaming himself, suffering needlessly. They both just needed a good night's sleep in an actual bed. No elementals or creeps or baddies chasing them. She didn't want to use all the hot water, so she peeled out of her clothes, let her skin warm a bit longer, and cut the flow. The stitches that crisscrossed her forearm stood out as she peeled off the wet bandages. The wound was still tender, but the pain didn't make her nauseated and dizzy anymore. *Curious.*

On the edge of the sink, Thom had left a pair of his jeans and a plaid shirt. She'd dropped her pack somewhere between the camping store and the river. Carrying her sodden clothes, she exited, squirming at how the waistband of his jeans hugged the soft flesh of her hips.

Clothed in black jersey pants, Thom stood in front of the washer and dryer, rubbing his hair with the towel. Draping the towel over his bare shoulder, he shoved her parka into the dryer and started it. Dropping her clothes, Poppy stopped, half-grinning, half-gawking at witnessing a Thom being all domestic. She looked closer and had more reason to gawk. *Thom Magnusson. Without a shirt.*

The light cast the muscles of his arms and back beautifully. Shadow hid most of his chest, but then he twisted, and the light illuminated a red scar across his left side, the length of her forearm. It puckered his skin as it snaked around his waist, ending at his hipbone.

That explains a lot. She must have made a little noise in her throat, because he glanced up, his expression jolting like he'd been startled out of his thoughts. The v-shaped frown appeared between his eyebrows and he stopped in front of her, resting the back of his hand against her cheek, her forehead. Goosebumps flooded his arms. "Thom, you need to warm up." She snapped her gaze away from the scar. The frown still held fast to his lips, but it was heavy with something else; pain, guilt, shame.

"I'm so sorry, Poppy." She barely heard him over the roar of the heater.

She touched his arm. "Absolutely not. You're not wasting another minute apologizing for a situation you have no control over."

Grief shuddered in his expression, and his eyes darted to the window, his mouth twisting, his I'm-about-to-argue face.

She shook her head. "No, sir. Don't fight me on this."

He licked his lips, and a shiver went through him. Pivoting she snatched the coverlet off the bed and threw it around his shoulders. "Why is it so hard for you to take care of yourself? Hmm?"

The day's events, paired with her exhaustion, stripped away any fear or reserve she felt standing before him, leaving her as candid as if she'd downed a few shots of vodka. She let her hand trail down his chest to the scar. "I hate that you've given so much. And you're still here. Putting yourself in danger for me. Even when I don't really understand what you've been through. How could I?"

"I almost lost you." He flinched, and his jaw worked, as though the old wound still hurt him. Maybe it did. "I never should've let that happen." Poppy stopped his mouth with her finger. She would've kissed him, but what he'd said the night before held her back. And with his back so straight she couldn't reach his mouth with hers.

Lines tightened around his forehead, and the green of his irises shone emerald next to the reddened whites of his eyes; the copper fleck in his right eye reminded her of colorful artic mosses. His jaw worked; he held back tears, and she hated that he took so much upon himself. How could she help him see? "Oh Thom." It came out a sigh. "It's not all up to you. We're in this together."

He bent, brushing his lips over hers, as though he meant to give her one careful kiss. But feeling the heat of his bare chest so close, a little groan escaped her throat. A shock went through him and his arms slid around her, pulling her against him. Her fingers swept over the hard line of his jaw, the soft prickle of his beard, the curls at the nape of his neck, the broad slope of his shoulders, capturing his lips with open-mouthed enthusiasm. His hand tightened on her hip, his arm surrounding her waist, pressing her body against his as if he couldn't get close enough, short-circuiting her brain, plunging her into a honeyed monsoon of desire. The blanket puddled at their feet.

Just as he began to pull away, she wrapped her arms tighter around his neck, on her tiptoes. The kiss became fierce, a breathless tangle of lips, teeth, tongue. The blood sprinted through her fingers, her belly, her thighs, firing with a thirsty kind of pleasure. His lips trailed down her neck to her collarbone, and the too-big plaid shirt gaped, revealing her bare shoulder. She threw her weight against him, pushing him down on the bed. Effortlessly, he cradled her in his lap, chests pressed together, lips meeting again and again, their desire spreading a wildfire kind of heat around them.

Maybe he's changed his mind. Maybe he feels right about… me. About this. After all, making love should be a good way to get warm.

Her brain clouded over with his salty scent, the warmth and movement of their bodies, the tingle of her lips, the groan in his throat, coalescing into a sacred connecting of souls. She found the scar curving around his side and caressed it deliberately. He stiffened, and his jawline went sharp, but she kissed him, and wriggled her body, compelling him down on the bed, fumbling at the buttons of the shirt he'd let her borrow. There was no one else she would rather be with, for her first time. Thom Magnusson was as good a man as they came, a better man than any she'd ever *known*. Maybe it was the spaces in her memory; but he was already there, a protector, a friend, a constant.

But a jarring rumble approached, like the roar of an oversized diesel engine, stinging her chest cavity. He startled, and all the breath rushed out of his chest. Suddenly being next to him felt like trying to cuddle a brick wall.

Not meeting her eyes, he slid her off his lap onto the bed and thrust on his coat.

Her legs wobbly with fading euphoria, she stood. "Thom? What is it?"

Focused on tying his boots, he only shook his head. The vibration leveled off, but hovered around the cabin, its energy familiar. A glimmering flash peaked through the curtains.

Etin. "Thom? What are you doing?"

He looked like he'd seen a ghost, so haggard it stunned her. "I won't be long." He forced the words out through clenched teeth.

"Don't do this to me, Thom." She felt pathetic, saying it, but she couldn't take the words back.

He sighed and faced her. "I will explain everything. I promise. Do you trust me?"

The lines of his face held years of pain, but his eyes were still the brilliant, captivating shade of green. A gut-level response, she nodded. Pressing his lips to hers, he whispered, "Stay inside and keep warm? Okay?"

He shrugged into his coat and a pair of wool socks. Frigid air rushed into the cabin as he flung open the door. He pulled it shut with a force that rattled the lamp near the bed.

Tucking the blanket around her shoulders, she slid into the chair by the window, watching him as he sunk down onto the stairs outside in front of Etin's glowing figure. The blue stone lay on the coffee table in front of her, and Poppy palmed it. What would Etin do, face to face with this? Interrupt her and Thom again, and she just might find out.

Chapter Twenty-Three

Thom found his gloves and wrenched them on. Slowing his breathing, he surveyed the dark, gusty landscape. In between fast-moving clouds, the faint light of the stars glowed on the mountains like cobwebs of silver. The sagebrush around the cabin rasped in the wind and the gusts chilled his nose.

Sinking down on the steps, he rubbed his hand over his swollen knuckles, his breath fogging. *Andskotans!* At least there was no sign of imminent attack from the *orysi*.

Sensing her watching him, he scowled into the darkness. "What do you want, Etin? Make it quick."

In front of him, her golden luminescence gradually appeared. Etin's presence and warmth spread around him, the abrupt change in the molecules aching in his bruised arm and shoulder.

"Oh, Thom." She sighed, and tapped her foot. "I thought you knew better."

Stretching his back, he grimaced. "I didn't come out here for conversation."

"You've figured out what she is right?"

Memories of the *orys's* bones charring scrolled through his mind, followed by the flickering radiance of the stone, the subtle glimmer off her skin. "She's *unnusti*." *So what?*

Etin's countenance darkened. "Yes, but what kind?"

"Does it matter? That's *never* mattered to me."

Etin gritted her teeth. "Hear me out. The traits Poppy displays are unusual, Firekind, but not. Probably of high value to the right bidder." Her eyebrows lowered into a scowl. "I don't know *what* she is, and that makes her dangerous, especially the closer you get to Caelith. So you're going to abandon this foolish mission right now."

Thom considered. That would explain why Poppy got so sick when she was moved to *Uther-Erai*. Going back into Caelith might shock her system, but it might be way less dangerous than he feared. He let a wry smile cross his face. "I don't know why that would change anything. She sounds like my type."

Etin's voice, raw with emotion. "She's a *red-hair*, *and* an *unnusti*! Have you been *Erai*-side so long you've forgotten? Before her father sent her away, Firekind were crawling around their estate! *He* was terrified – Felix Paquin! The *Utherling*-Steward! The same man who's charmed the whole elemental council! After losing her all those years ago, what do you think the Firekind will do to *you* if you set foot back in Caelith with her in tow? Have you thought about that?"

"What happens to me isn't your concern."

Etin continued like she hadn't heard him. "They'll steamroll you, Thom. Into an ashy corpse. Just like they would've steamrolled Felix, little Ayden, and sixteen-year-old you, if she hadn't been hidden here." She arched an eyebrow. "Elemental kind that powerful always get what they want."

He rubbed his eyes. *This is going nowhere. I've already made my choice. I made it a long time ago.* "Didn't you say you had information for me? Back at the restaurant?"

Her lips puckered. "I don't want you dead, Thom. Not then. Not now. Someone has to look out for you."

That's it. Anger snapped inside him. "I'm going to ignore the cruel irony of that statement." He stood. "It's simple. Information. Now. Or are you going to dangle it until I grovel? Try to weasel me into another *slagere?* That's what you really want isn't it?" From the look on her face he could tell he'd nailed it.

"This is about protecting you from yourself." Etin's eyes darted around, widening with each word. "You think you can help her, help Ayden, but you can't. The Firekind are too powerful. And I'm not going to let you—"

"That's not your choice."

"You were safer with me!"

"That's debatable. No, I was miserable for sure."

She poked his chest. "Do you think when she realizes who she is, who *you* are, that she won't regret tying herself to you?" Her voice grew low and silky. "Firekind notwithstanding, you're deceiving yourself if you think this'll play out any other way. It'll never take, you and her. You weren't happy with me, you won't be happy with an *unnusti*, especially one with a father like Felix Paquin."

Helvítis djöfulsins andskotans. That was low. Thom folded his arms. He wouldn't let it show how much that stung. *Stay focused.* "Does this mean you're not sharing the intel?"

Scowling, she sunk onto the step, picking dry strands of grass and shredding them.

"Because if not, I'm going back inside, and continuing right where Poppy and I left off."

A gleam of light resembling hackles flickered across her shoulders.

"Fine. Don't say I didn't warn you." Her expression galvanized, as if she was about to throw a gut punch. "The night you almost caught Dane in Riverston, he fled to Caldys. He reported to Felix Paquin that you and Ayden conspired together against the *Offysfyn*. For leverage, you abducted Deidre and Poppy Paquin, and are now hiding them until Ayden directs you otherwise."

Thom stared.

Her tone biting, Etin continued. "Dane has convinced the *Offysfyn* that Ayden is demanding Felix's resignation because he wants the stewardship for himself. If Felix doesn't acquiesce, Ayden will go to the Grens and share valuable intelligence, and Felix will never see his wife and daughter again." Etin's lips curled with a sneer. "Felix believed him. And why should he not? Father and son have always been so cozy. And you already know what he believes about you and his little Poppy. Sometimes you *utherlings* really are despicable." She cursed under her breath. "Ayden is supposedly camped at Awys beach in Caelith-Greya, awaiting your father's decision. You're supposedly taking Deidre and Poppy into one of the havens and hiding them. And the whole *Offysfyn* thinks the two of you are traitors now, so there's that."

Thom sunk back down on the stairs, running his hands through his hair. *Fokking fokk.*

"And the best part, Felix has set out to Greya with half of Caldys's forces in tow, to reason with Ayden, I suppose. He rewarded Dane's service with joint authority at Caldys in his absence."

The blood in Thom's veins went leaden. *Worse. So much worse...* He didn't notice that Etin had stopped relishing her punches.

"Dane is now using his newly obtained resources to capture you. They're probably searching for you, even as we speak." Her eyes stopped on the mountains.

Without seeing them, he stared at the peaks, storing away the information, cross-checking it with his plans. He stood, pacing, strategizing. *I can fix this. I'll find a way.*

"Thom?"

Rubbing his chin distractedly, he faced her.

"Are you going to abandon this foolishness now?" Etin crossed her legs, trying to squelch the pleased expression on her face. She actually thought she had him.

"Of course not." He reached for the door. "I've got to plan."

Clutching his coat sleeve, Etin's eyes widened with something like fear, an expression he'd never seen on her face before. "Please don't."

Your turn to be the ruthless player, Magnusson.

The power dynamic between them had shifted, and Thom was going to use every ounce of newfound leverage he had. "I needed that information hours ago. Now, agree to help us, or I never want to see you again."

Chapter Twenty-Four

Poppy stepped back as the door opened in a rush of gelid mountain air. Beyond Thom's shoulder, the gold of Etin's luminescence faded into the night. He closed the door with a soft click and faced her, his expression stoic, but astute.

The scotch-pine green of his eyes had been replaced by a weary charcoal hue. Fear chilled the heat rising in her face. What now? Her heart jangled and raced, so much so that she felt dizzy. *You've figured out what she is, right?* That was bad enough, but the words she'd overheard continued. *I don't know what she is and that makes her dangerous.* Even worse, *Felix Paquin, her father, was terrified!* Then the awful, nebulous words, *Steamroll Thom into an ashy corpse. Firekind, Firekind, Firekind.*

Poppy was dangerous, that much was clear. Every moment Thom stayed with her, she put him in danger. So what kind of *unnusti* monster was she?

Questions darted around in her head like swallows, she stuttered like a frightened idiot in front of the man she'd fallen hard for, the man she feared for.

He studied her face. "You heard most of that?"

She nodded.

Thom's hand covered her shoulder, his touch feather-light. "We'll figure this out, Poppy. It'll be okay."

"What am I, Thom?" She didn't know how she choked out the question, but it resounded like a gong between them.

He gazed at her a moment, and then drew her into his chest, his arms surrounding her. But she pushed away. "No! Every second I'm with you I put you in danger. I won't do that to you."

Poppy didn't want to believe that her and Thom were doomed before they'd even started, but the revelations had star-crossed tragedy written all over them.

Thom's throat bobbed with a swallow. "Poppy, you don't know Etin. She twists information so it fits her ends. You're going to have to trust me."

"Are you saying I don't put you in danger?" *What was a slagere anyway?* Her heart twisted. *Who was Etin to him, really?*

"I'm saying it's no different than what I signed up for. I'd already guessed at a lot of what you heard. And it doesn't change anything. Not for me."

Poppy turned away, biting the inside of her cheek against the prickle behind her eyes. "When were you going to tell me, Thom?"

"I'd only just put it together." His voice rumbled, but it was quiet, subdued, as if he was breaking bad news. "After what you did to that *orys*. It's the only explanation for the way the stone responds to you. Why you became so sick here. You and your mother. The adjustment to *Uther-Erai* – to this world – would've been difficult for an *unnusti*." His voice cracked. "You're lucky you lived."

"Does that mean Felix Paquin isn't my father?" Poppy braced herself against the counter, as if the floor might vanish beneath her feet.

He shook his head. "It just means you have elemental blood in your line. I'd guess it's on your mother's side. Hereditary surprises aren't unusual in Caelith."

A memory detonated in her brain. "In the car last night, I had this dream…it felt. Real." She shook her head. "I wondered… Oh, I don't know…"

He steered her to the little sofa in the front room. "Tell me."

Haltingly, she recounted the dream, the *rif*, overhearing her parents, finding Thom in the barn, the rhyme, and her father's anger when he found her with him. His brow low in concentration, he listened, worrying his lip. By the time she came to the end of the dream, a frown shadowed his expression. His arm snaked around her shoulder and she slumped into his embrace.

"I have the same memory of that night." His cheekbones turned scarlet. "At least the part in the barn, and afterwards."

It was real. I'm remembering! Understanding quickly evaporated her elation. "I got you in trouble, didn't I?"

His face remained impassive, thinking. "I didn't know about the *rif* though. It makes more sense now, knowing that."

She swallowed hard. "I made things a lot worse for you, didn't I?" *I disobeyed my father about the rifs. I got Thom in trouble. What didn't I screw up?*

His chest rose and fell. "Not really. My circumstances were already difficult. I was grateful for you and Ayden. Your friendship."

"But—"

"Poppy, I wouldn't have done anything differently." He steered her chin so they were face to face. A little shiver went through her, remembering what his lips had felt like on hers. *Focus Poppy.* "Maybe some other decisions, but nothing with you or Ayden or that night."

"But what does it mean? The *rif* – the elemental from my dream – is Firekind?" she asked.

He nodded. "If a flame manifested in such a form, it wouldn't be any other elementalkind." His expression went stony-serious. "You have to understand, Poppy. *Rifs* are rare elementals. Most Caelithians have never seen Firekind, except for *fyns* – a lower order of elemental that resemble fireflies. But *rifs*." He shook his head.

She pressed on before she lost her other questions. "Etin said that Firekind were crawling around our estate? That my father was terrified of them?"

"He would've been concerned about *feys* – Firekind warriors. They are larger and clever than *rifs*." A muscle in his jaw twitched. "Firekind are no friend to humans. Caelithian folklore is steeped in their brutality and wildness. They're so primitive they don't even associate with other elementalkinds. In some regions, it's said they abduct red-haired children at certain moon cycles. Use them as *slagerei*, death-bound slaves." His eyes darted to her. "If I had to guess, the *rif* might have been trying to lure you away, make you an easier target, probably for a *fey*. Your father probably thought that too. So, yeah, he would've been terrified."

Her shoulders tensed, remembering her illicit forest escapades with the *rifs*. *Why didn't they take me then?*

In her pocket, she felt the smooth surface of the blue stone, and produced it. It shone in the weak glow of the overhead light, a weight between them. "What about this? It made Dane's clothes catch fire. And it burned that *orys* to ash. Could it be a Firekind thing?"

The v-wrinkle appeared between his eyebrows. "Deidre wouldn't have given you a dangerous elementalkind relic."

"Unless she didn't know what it was."

"True. But that doesn't explain how she obtained such a relic." Deep lines crossed his forehead. "Best guess, it could be an aether relic, that's definitely the kind of thing Felix Paquin has access to. I wish I knew, but I don't think it matters right now. We just need to keep it out of Gren hands. Once we enter Caelith, we'll ask my elemental contacts."

His jaw was sharp against her forehead, his sage-salt scent surrounded her, comforting. Squeezing her eyes shut, she wished they could linger at the 'lovebirds lodge' and forget everything. *This feels impossible.*

"We'll get through this, okay?" He squeezed her shoulders.

But Ayden. Mom. Dad! I can't give up!

"So, what about the intel Etin brought? What's the plan?"

Thom leaned forward, rubbing his temples, as though he shouldered a heavy weight. "When we get into Caelith, we'll go after your father. Hopefully he'll listen to us. Realize Dane has deceived the *Offysfyn*. Before something really catastrophic happens." He stalked to the kitchen, filled a glass of water, and drank. "These circumstances are bad for the entire *Offysfyn*, for all of Caelith. It could escalate the conflict." He filled a glass for her, his expression grim.

What if we're captured? She wouldn't voice her fear, but tense lines sprung up around his mouth, as though he'd guessed what she was thinking.

He rubbed the bridge of his nose. "Etin said she'll help us."

She almost choked. "Is that supposed to make me feel better?"

He grimaced. "We're in a tight spot. It's better than nothing."

"What about you?" The water went cold in her stomach. "There has to be some other way to do this! You've already risked too much for me!" She sprung up and started pacing, biting her thumbnail.

He shrugged. "I've been in worse situations. We're far from being beaten, Poppy. Things are just complicated."

She didn't want to voice the question, but it snuck out. "Does this mean Ayden is...is dead? If he's not there to contradict?"

"The *micahawes* probably captured him, like they captured Deidre. Took him to a Gren encampment." Seeing her concern, he added, "He's valuable. And he's tough. As soon as we wade through the shitstorm we've been handed, I'll find him, I promise you."

She crossed her arms. "*We'll* find him."

His lips twitched. "You'll have to debate me on that."

"Count on it."

There was still the mystery of him and Etin. *Do I even want to know?* Goosebumps flooded her legs as she remembered Thom's lips against hers, his crooked smile. *Yes, I do.* "What's with you and Etin?"

Leaning back, he looked at the ceiling, his expression pained. "You want to talk about that now?"

"Why not?"

He flicked aside the curtain at the sink, and glanced at his watch. "Because we should rest. Tomorrow will be a hard day."

"You've delayed. And changed the subject. And deflected. And—"

"I'm ashamed, Poppy." His voice was low and quiet, the wrinkles around his eyes deepening. "I don't want you to know this part. To know me, as I was then."

A vulnerable kind of pain had seeped into his expression. Poppy wished he trusted her more. So much had happened between them, it seemed like she'd earned it. "I've seen enough of you to know who you really are, no matter what I discover. But I want to understand."

He leaned back against the cabinets, his knuckles white around the edges, one knee bent. His throat bobbed with a swallow. "When I was thirteen, my sister Katla disappeared near our home in Snæfellsness. After the searches for her had been called off, I continued looking for her, for months, even into the winter. On a hunch, I waited until the aurora was similar to the night she'd disappeared, and set out, my route plotted. The map should've kept me from getting lost. But like Katla, I stumbled through the borderlands into Cael-ith-Caldys. The opening had expanded with the aurora."

Frown lines deepened on his forehead. "I was lost for days. Ran out of food. By the time Etin happened upon me, I was almost dead from exposure. She offered food and shelter *if* I made a bargain with her."

Poppy's stomach soured and she held her breath.

"I agreed, only to find out the bargain was a *slagere*. There was much more to it than she'd disclosed." Not meeting her eyes, he shoved up his sleeve, exposing the star-sun tattoo.

Her fists clenched, nails digging into her palms.

He continued, impassively, like he was reading a textbook. "A *slagere* is a term of service to an elemental, like an indentured servant. It's illegal, but it used to be common practice among elementals in Caelith's early days. In some places, there's little effort to crack down on it, especially if you don't have a tribe or family protecting you." He cleared his throat. "So, I ended up belonging to Etin."

"That's. Not. Right." Poppy's shoulders tensed with anger. *That horrible woman-thing.*

"*Cyms* have a very different system of morality, if you can call it that."

"Did you try to?" She bit her lip. Of course, he'd tried to escape.

He nodded, following her thinking.

"How did you get out?" *Panic.* "*Did* you get out?"

He nodded. "I did." Calculating, he squinted outside again. "But that part will have to wait. I need to prepare, review our route. And we need to sleep."

"What about your sister?"

A cryptic expression crossed his face. "She was much luckier in her elemental friends than I."

"She lived?"

Thom nodded, his expression as closed as a midnight storefront. Fetching the map, he spread it over the table and hunched over it, not meeting her eyes. "I'll sleep on the couch."

Slumber didn't come easy for Poppy that night. The dryer rattled and hummed, drying their soaked clothes. Her heart raced, imagining how Thom had lived all those years in *slagere*, and her brain insisted on devising clever ways to introduce Etin's face to a baseball bat. When the gentle nudge at her shoulder woke her, she felt like she hadn't really rested.

"It's about five-thirty," Thom's voice, a soft murmur. "It's snowing. We need to get moving."

In an up-too-early fog, she stumbled to the bathroom. Bundled in winter gear, Poppy stared at her reflection. *What awaited them in the snowy wilderness? The borderlands…passing through…what's going to happen to us? How will it affect me? Will we escape capture?*

She blinked at her ghostly gray eyes, memory walloping her like a sneaky left hook. *I'm unnusti. A hybrid. Dangerous.* What does that even mean? Maybe it was something like the crescendo of anger she felt when the *orys* scout had snatched her. Trapped in its clutches, she realized Thom would be frantic, would blame himself, and determination burned like a hot coal in her ribcage. When her hand closed around the stone, it was primed, one with her desire. Something like spontaneous combustion surged through it, through her, until the *orys's* grip dissolved, and her body plummeted toward the water.

Her breath caught, as frozen as if she were on stage enduring a jeering crowd, hearing Etin's horrible words, *"I don't know what she is, and that makes her dangerous — especially the closer you get to Caelith. So you're going to abandon this foolish mission right now"*

What kind of *thing* was she? Would she ever find out? Again, did she put him in danger, just standing next to him? But what would she do without him? How would she ever make it? She wouldn't.

In the sitting room, Thom waited on the couch, his expression far away. Seeing her, he stood and adjusted his green knitted cap over his ears. Glancing at her attire, his chin dipped in a curt nod. The muffled silence of the snow seemed to have crept into the interior of the cabin. It clogged the acute flash-flood of her psyche.

Maybe it's better not to know. Maybe that's why my parents never told me. Pulling on her gloves she blinked out at the misty landscape, now gray with dawn, avoiding his eyes. She didn't want him to see she was terrified.

"I don't want to put you in danger, Thom. If there's another way, I want to take it, now. I want you to be safe."

Thom held the door for her, his expression softening into grin lines. "I wouldn't miss this for the world. And danger seems to find me anyway. Ready for a hike?"

His familiar, crooked grin melted her fear. If he could smile at a moment like this, so could she, no matter what lay ahead. Taking his offered hand, she produced a wobbly grin. "With you? Of course."

Chapter Twenty-Five

The snow-covered roads made the motorcycle ride perilous. Poppy held her breath for much of the journey up into the foothills. Somehow, Thom managed to coax the motorcycle up the service road which bordered the canyon he'd shown her on the map. Creeping along, they followed the patched blacktop until it deteriorated into a deep-rutted mess of puddles, snow, and gravel, forcing them to ditch the bike. Together, they paused at the mouth of the canyon, the mountains surrounding them like horned monsters hiding in the snowy air.

Scanning the vast forested canyon before them, Poppy's eyes widened, entranced and intimidated at the gorgeous wildness of the Tetons – a geology-lover's paradise. She wished she could see the marbled gneiss rock that made up much of the peaks, but the snowfall obscured it.

"We're headed northwest, to a glacial lake with a waterfall." Thom indicated the magnificent view. "It's at the end of this canyon." He shook the snow off his cap. "The water makes it risky in the winter, but it might give us a tactical advantage. We'll have to be stealthy." The lines on his forehead disappeared under the knitted green wool.

"Falls?" Thinking of gigantic icicles, her heart deflated. "The borderland is a waterfall?"

"Not the falls. It stretches across the lake and up the side of the canyon. Hopefully the sorties will be busy with easier borderlands."

"Yeah, hopefully." Fear dropped like a stone in her gut. She followed him as he set out down the snowy slope.

Chunky boulders the size of cars punctured the hill, along with overgrown grasses, bent over with snow.

As if he knew she needed a distraction, he continued. "This region has an unusual concentration of borderlands – maybe a dozen of them, counting the ones in Yellowstone. And some wells that are too dangerous for humans." He squinted around at high walls of the cirque. "Tell me if you sense anything. You might notice an elemental presence before I do." He squeezed her hand.

Because I'm unnusti. She felt colder than the snow-lashed wind. Again, their conversation from the night before tumbled into her head.

Wordlessly, he headed for a spruce copse, gathered at the bottom of the glaciated valley. Above them the rocky snow-brushed peaks towered in the misty air, half-concealed by thick silver clouds, their presence palpable and vigilant.

She cleared her throat, half-dreading asking the question, but she had to know. "Last night, you said you got out, from the *slagere*?"

His lips made a thin line.

"Is that why you were in our barn? Were you working for my father?"

His throat bobbed with a swallow. "Etin lent me to your father. In exchange for keeping quiet about the *slagere*, she gave him favors. Favor with her kin, and my labor." Setting out again, he half-shrugged. "It happens more than it should."

All this time, sorrow and shame tightened her throat, *I thought my father was one of the good guys.*

Thom continued, "After that night – the night you dreamed about – he conscripted me into the *Offysfyn* for five years, dissolving the *slagere*. He wanted me gone, away from Ayden. Away from you."

Poppy felt like another hole had been knocked into her heart. "Thom, I'm so sorry." Her voice shook.

"They were your father's actions, Poppy. Not yours."

She blinked, not seeing the mountains anymore. *How could he?*

They came to an incline, their way cutting up through snow-covered vegetation, mounds of boulders, and tree roots, the way was taxing. She was glad because it gave her a moment to regain her composure.

"You and Ayden were good friends," Thom continued, helping her on ice-coated rocks. "I'll always be grateful for that." He studied her. "That's what I think of when I look at you. Not Felix Paquin."

Her shame lessened, leaving a hollow pain in its wake.

"When Ayden discovered what Felix had done, he enlisted in the *Offysfyn*. Used his influence to advocate for me." He squinted at the sky. "What happened to me, it sounds trite, but I'm better because of it. Wiser. And I'm lucky, to have the friends I do. The experiences I've learned from."

His words were comforting, as pleasant as the sight of the snowflakes on his eyelashes. Emotion crystallized in her soul. Her silly Thom-crush wasn't silly. Or a crush. It was something pure and enduring. Real. Scary serious. Maybe even serendipitous for an eighteen-year-old, even an old soul like hers, to stumble into *loving* such a genuine good man. Because that's what this was: *love*.

Even if he did come ragged around the edges, ill-used, honor-bound, and with some dangerous elemental baggage, her heart had been pricked by his needle and thread. The unexpected discovery stole her breath, more than the climb. *But does he feel the same?*

Her courage wilted under the intensity of her unanswered questions, her doubts, their circumstances. *Too soon. Too many other problems to think about that.*

Deliberately not looking at him, she surveyed the wild terrain, misty with snowfall. "If you were freed from the *slagere*, why is Etin still hounding you?"

He made a face. "Etin didn't want to give me up. She resented Felix for meddling. So, she followed me into the *Offysfyn*, charming her way into my units, making trouble where she could. My cohort could've been saved, if she'd done her job. We were ambushed on the Maris plateau." He made a stiff gesture to the scar on his left side. "She agreed to scout that day and did not, unaware of how much her actions would cost the *Offysfyn*. Would cost me. Her pestering now is an attempt to make amends, I assume." His eyebrows lowered. "There's a collection order for her bones. But, the *Offysfyn* has been too taxed to catch her."

Poppy tucked away that nugget of information into her revenge file. Now, she had even more reason to dislike the *cym*.

A copse of spruce closed around them, swishing and creaking in the wind, shedding snow in white cascades. Within the trees, they discovered another incline barring their path. Her shoulders drooped.

Spying a crevice between snow-blanketed rocks, he helped Poppy ascend the slope, the set of his shoulders relaxed as though scaling snowy mountains was routine. As she struggled for footing, he always seemed to find purchase with an uncanny acuity. She couldn't help feeling grateful, a little impressed, and rueful the hike wasn't just for fun.

They crested the incline, threaded a cluster of young aspens, headed down for a time, and then plunged into another regiment of evergreens. Cascades of granite boulders and ancient trunks of fallen trees – weatherworn like old bones – led down to a lower track of rocky ground. As they trekked deeper into the wild, the light shifted, taking on a subtle gray cast.

"Everything's so quiet." Her voice felt tiny in the landscape.

"Part of it's the falls." He paused. "Listen."

Cocking her head, she stopped, the warmth of their breath clouding the chilly air around them. Beneath the fallen snow, the ground felt animated, containing a roar of power, just detectable beyond the tiny thump of snowflakes.

"That's good," he said. "I was afraid it might be frozen already. The more active the falls, the better. The energy makes the passage wider, easier to find the borderland."

Goosebumps, that had nothing to do with the cold, spread up her arms. Were elementals and *Offysfyn* soldiers around the next boulder? Waiting to ambush them? Would she sense them? How would she know if she did? Maybe she was just nervous about the borderland, about everything.

He whirled around, his body tensing.

"What is it?" She whispered, ducking into the trees.

Crouching next to her, he scrutinized the snowy landscape, his eyebrows drawn tight.

A tense minute of observation passed. All she discerned was her own heartbeat, racing itself.

"Probably nothing," he murmured, finally. "Let's move."

Thom abandoned his measured pace, and soon her breath came in gasps. The falling snow obscured the terrain ahead of them and her boots began to sink into the white mounds instead of crushing them. The murmur of the falls played gently around the canyon. How much longer until they came into view?

After another strenuous hour they halted, again scouring the landscape. The rumble of the falls and the heaviness of the snow suppressed other sounds. The slopes of the mountains crowded closer, populated by indifferent snow-covered evergreens.

As far as she could tell, they were alone in a vast wilderness. They could've been in Caelith for all she knew; the thought made it difficult to regain her breath. A week ago, she'd been ringing up Halloween candy at Target.

Out of the snow loomed a forested incline, steeper than the last. Their way scaled yet another mountain slope. *I'll die walking before I let Thom down,* she thought. Steeling herself, she gulped the air and leaned into the incline, following his zigzagging path. The pearly sky took on a depressing cast. How long before dark? The snowy expanse seemed bent on hiding that important scrap of information, at least from her.

Just when she thought she couldn't endure another ascent they came to a level swath of ground, carpeted with snow to her calves. The echo of the falls had changed; the rumble drifted up from below.

They paused for a rest, Thom somber and watchful. Clearing the snow on a fallen tree, she sunk onto it, studying him while she caught her breath. He sat next to her, his elbows on his knees. Between them, they finished a bottle of water and downed a couple of protein bars.

"We've met up with a backpacking trail." Murmuring in her ear, he motioned to the snow-covered track alongside their resting place. "There's a steep drop-off at the right."

Pressing on, the track led them through a forest of aspen and spruce clinging to the edge of the canyon; the spiky heads of their cousins tumbled down the slopes beneath them, proud to be thriving in such a precarious home. Soon the trees thinned, and the snow tapered off, revealing a spectacular view of the mountains.

The trail veered sharply to the left, leading over a tumble of boulders, clustered at the edge of a precipice, clogged with snow. The height made her head spin. Helping her scale the rocks, he gripped her arm so tightly it throbbed when he released it. Her legs trembled as she caught her breath, dusting snow off her coat and gloves.

An opening in the trees revealed the view below. Across a slim valley, a ribbon of water snaked down the mountain, leaping off a sheer face into a churning pool, hundreds of feet below. A modest roaring frolicked around the walls of the canyon. If there was a way to get to the water's edge, she couldn't see it.

She gaped. "How?"

He drew her next to him and pointed, speaking in her ear. "The path goes down the edge. Gradually. Can you see it?"

Finally, she did – a winding snowy trail, bordered by tall evergreens and mountain fir, interrupted by boulders, following the slope of the canyon wall to a flat expanse of snow-covered ground below. The terrain at the bottom was isolated from any other path, cut off by the canyon walls and the rippling waters of the lake.

"Is the border invisible?" she asked.

He nodded.

"How do people not wander in accidentally, like you did?" she whispered.

He shrugged. "It's possible." He pointed to the sheer face opposite. "But most of it's inaccessible to humans, unless you can free climb, or know what you're looking for in the lake."

They continued, wading through the heavy, wet snow. The path trickled down a gently sloping part of the canyon. They were high and far enough away that the freezing mist of the falls didn't reach them. But the cold invaded her lungs with each breath and her feet grew numb.

Hinting at evening, the sky grayed further, and the descent became arduous and slippery. After an icy spot landed her on her backside, he slowed their pace, shielding her from steep drop-offs, eventually hauling her along like another backpack, his arm about her waist.

The light was dismal with twilight when they came to the level ground she'd seen at the top; a table of rock so wide it felt strangely spacious. The falls were more than three hundred feet away; the icy shore of the lake lay forty paces away, at the edge of a sloping snow-covered bank. Naked aspens, alder, and fuzzy spruce rose to meet the walls of the canyon all around them, in places grazing the lake, in others hanging – poised as if they were about to fall and then decided to grow again. Overhead, the mountains towered. A fresh burst of snow swirled on the wind; the rushing through the trees sounded like a thousand whispers. The air grew luminous and silvery.

Her legs begged to sit down, somewhere, anywhere. *This is it. The borderlands.* Blinking at the rippling water beyond the ice rim at the edge, her body felt like it could float away.

Thom looked away from the shadowy woodland and met her eyes for the space of three heartbeats, taking her hands in his. "It's going to be okay, Poppy." His gloved hand lingered at her cheek, tucking a stray lock behind her ear. "Don't give up, promise?"

The question confused her. But before she could ask, a sharp voice rang out.

"Thomas Magnusson! Step away from the woman and lift your hands! By order of the *Utherling*-Steward, submit to capture!"

Chapter Twenty-Six

Like shapes out of a fog, a dozen figures clothed in mottled gray appeared out of the snowy woodland. Thom didn't look at them – he kept his eyes on Poppy's wide gray ones. The flash of fear across her face almost undid his composure.

"It's okay, Poppy." He whispered. "We'll get through this. Trust me."

Her eyes narrowed as the *Offysfyn* sortie approached, her face graying with shock. But then, she glanced at him and her chin dipped with a quick nod. Relief settled and refocused him. *Now Etin better do her fokking job!*

Thom knew the *orys* scout he'd detected earlier would alert the sortie searching the Caldys borderland. Their capture had always been a strong possibility; he'd planned for it. Even more than he disliked relying on Etin, he disliked concealing his plans from Poppy. He hoped the less she knew, the less burden she carried – the safer she'd be if she encountered Dane again. Glancing between the sortie and his face, she gripped his hands.

He kept his voice calm and quiet. "It'll be okay, Poppy."

"Don't speak!" The woman's voice battered his ears. "Back away from her, NOW!"

The voice came from a russet-skinned woman, her face etched with a frown as rigid as the rock face above, her cheekbones sharp beneath her dark skin. *Rasha of the Red Rocks Clan. Could've been worse,* he thought. *We can work with this.*

Tension hummed on the air. Lifting his hands, Thom shifted away from Poppy, keeping his eyes locked with hers. *You've got this,* he tried to say with his expression. A deep wrinkle appeared between her eyes and her chest heaved, like the air was too thick to breathe.

Rasha nodded to the lithe *kesili* elemental next to her, barely visible in the half-light. "Confiscate his *cydern*."

Thom stiffened, loathe to let it close to him, to lose his weapon.

The elemental's limbs stretched and flexed sinuously, its half-manifested features mysterious and shrouded, but no less lethal – a *kesili* could suffocate an *utherling* without a *cydern* in less than a minute. With its locomotion, the ground vibrated on a different key than the falls, as if it called to the silica embedded in the granite beneath them.

Poppy hissed between her teeth, and her fingers curled into tight fists. A glimmer of light sprouted from her coat pocket, visible even through the thick fabric. *The relic! This should be interesting.*

Barely more than a form of iridescent girt, the *kesili* seized his *cydern* from his wrist and rearranged itself beside Rasha, a translucent henchman.

"Where's Etin?" Rasha's voice rattled off the canyon walls.

Thom shrugged. One of the soldiers startled at the movement and a collective twitch of fear rippled through the group.

Twenty-five Offysfyn. For me and Poppy. Thom frowned. *What atrocities did Dane spin about me to get them so wound up?*

Thom let his hands drift to his sides. "How should I know? After Maris, we parted ways."

"Lace your hands behind your head, Magnusson!" She growled. "Turn around and walk backward, nice and slow."

"No!" Poppy stumbled forward. "NO! You're making a *mistake!*"

Hands still laced on his head, he shook his head. *It's okay. Stay calm. Stay safe.*

A group of men surged forward, grabbing him so violently he staggered. The burliest man of the group seized his wrists, knotting the chord so tightly his fingers began to numb. One of them pressed a *cydern* against his chest. It was pointed at one end, like a skewer. In their mottled gray gear, they were indistinguishable, and kept stealing nervous glances around the canyon, as if expecting sniper-fire.

Poppy's breath came in gasps. Thom craned his neck. "Poppy, it'll be okay."

"Quiet!" The burly man jabbed him in the kidneys.

Cringing at the blow, Poppy shouted. "If you're following Dane's orders! If you believe anything he says, you're making a mistake! He's working with the Grens! He's betrayed you! He's betrayed the *Offysfyn*!"

A man fisting a restraint headed for Poppy. Halting, Thom dug his heels in. "Hey! No restraints for her! Passing through the border will be dangerous enough!" He scowled at Rasha, wrestling his captors. "Rasha! Stop this!"

Consulting with another *soldati*, she ignored him.

Backing away, Poppy shouted, "Thom Magnusson is no traitor! I would be dead if it weren't for him! This is wrong!"

Her voice echoed off the water, crackling, raising goose-bumps on his arms, laced with an outlandish sort of power. Straining, Thom pivoted, it wasn't difficult as the men restraining him had slackened their grip, studying Poppy with naked curiosity.

Fisting the restraint, the *soldati* approached her, his expression conflicted.

Evading him, Poppy continued, shouting. "Dane is the traitor! And I have proof!"

Flinging off her coat, she let it fall in the snow, causing several of the *Offysfyn* to start forward. Poppy hauled up her shirt sleeves, ripped off the bandages, and exposed the bruised lines of stitching. Snowflakes melted on her flesh.

"*Dane* tried to abduct me, using an *ettar*! Thom killed it before it could finish the job. *He's* been protecting me. *He's* the only reason I'm still alive!"

The *Offysfyn* sortie stared. No one had expected this. Thom's heart went cold, fear prodding him. More than anything, he wanted Poppy safe, camouflaged instead of revealing how much she knew. If she compromised Dane's plans, he wouldn't hesitate to remove her from the equation. "Poppy!" Shaking his head, he tried to catch her attention.

But Poppy's voice echoed, louder. "Dane revealed the location of the Riverston gate to the Grens! If it weren't for Thom, I would've been captured days ago!" Poppy's voice went hoarse, and a low rumble went through the ground at her feet. As though seized by an invisible grip, her body jolted, but clutching the stone, she managed to stay upright.

Several of the *Offysfyn soldati* shifted nervously.

Approaching Poppy, Rasha shoved aside the man with the restraints. "*Ettars*? In the *Uther-Erai*?" She laughed, but the sound wasn't humorous. "They wouldn't survive the border."

Poppy's fists curled. "Are you saying I'm lying?" Another earthquake-like rumble went through the ground, strong enough that Thom had to plant his feet to keep his balance. Eyes narrowing, he scanned the snow-covered mountains surrounding them, dim in the fading light.

"No. You're confused." Rasha's nose stopped inches from Poppy's forehead.

Poppy had to look up to meet her eyes. "I. Am. NOT. Confused." Another rumble, this time shaking the rock beneath them.

Rasha's hand shot out to the *soldati*. "Restraints. Now."

The man hesitated. "She's the Steward's daughter. Not a prisoner. We should let her talk. The information could be relevant."

"He speaks wisdom," Thom said, his voice carrying. "I wonder what the Steward will do when he hears his daughter was bound like a prisoner."

Teeth barred, Rasha whirled on him. "Shut him up."

One of his captors struck his left side. Pain spiraled through the scar tissue there, vacating his brain of all thought except agony. He sunk to his knees, gasping for breath. Poppy's cry transmuted into a growl of rage, and the sortie gasped and drew back, as if she'd struck at them like a cobra.

Gritting his teeth, he blinked through the pain haze. Multi-colored flame rippled like water from Poppy's fist, closed tight around a jewel-like ray of light, vivid in the snowy dusk. Another tremor went through the ground, so deep it felt like it nudged the mountains.

No! Too dangerous! He scanned the mountains again. *Etin! Where are you?* The earth groaned and a web of cracks spread in the snow covering the table of rock beneath them.

"Let him go, or I swear bad shit is going to happen." Poppy's face held an internal storm, and her eyes shone like the reflection of cat's eyes. Spidery veins of copper lightning leapt up and down her frame, in tandem with the flames, overshadowing her humanness.

Andskotans. His mouth fell open, mirroring the company around him.

The wind and snow changed directions. On the surrounding slopes, the spruce trees shook, shedding their coats of snow.

In the blue stone's light, Rasha's eyes glinted hard. "She has the relic!" Her voice echoed, and the angles of her face became more pronounced. "Seize it!" Her hand an outstretched claw, she lunged, as the sortie's elementals charged Poppy.

"Poppy!" Thom bellowed. "Throw it!"

Pivoting, Poppy launched the flaming blue stone toward the falls, her throw at least one-hundred feet, eliciting a gasp from the man next to him.

The elementals changed direction, sweeping after its fiery path, reflecting across the water.

"Etin!" Thom shouted.

A single powerful current swept over the lake, leaving whitecaps in its wake. The falling snow surged, turning against the direction of the wind. Before the stone touched the water, a burst of rainbow luminosity swallowed it, the hot draft making the *soldati* totter as Etin swept past and disappeared. Thom's shoulders sunk with relief.

But high on the western slope above the canyon, an innocent puff of snowy air arose. The earth tremored and cascades of snow began to race down the incline like white waterfalls. The slope-bound cloud burgeoned, and a distant roar shook the earth, so powerful it tremored beneath his ribs, magnifying with each passing second. Rasha's eyes widened, comprehension flooding her face, and she pivoted, shouting.

Off-balancing his captors, Thom lunged against his bonds. *Poppy! Must get to Poppy!*

The rumbling intensified. A white fog the size of a storm cloud obscured the western slopes, the avalanche approaching with a roar as dreadful as a thousand death knells, consuming the forested slopes above them. If they didn't run for the borderland now, they'd be buried.

Thom struck with his heel and one of his captors toppled over, clutching his thigh. Thom felled another with a bone-jarring head-butt, landing on the *cydern* as it fell from his hands, using it to free his bonds.

Order dissolved as the *soldati* scrambled for the water, Rasha shouting somewhere in the lead. The *kesili* had already disappeared beneath the surface, leaving the slower *utherlings* behind.

"Make for the border!" Thom shouted to the remaining company, sprinting toward Poppy; her form glimmered like a sunset in the dim light.

Poppy's body was angled quizzically toward the avalanche, as if the snowy world had suddenly become abstract, and she didn't comprehend the meaning of the white mass speeding toward them. Abruptly, her body seized, and the light surrounding her went from ochre to red-purple and then nothing. Falling to her knees, she crumpled over sideways in the snow.

The *Offysfyn* sortie were all in the lake now, disappearing as they entered the currents of the borderland. The rumble of the approaching avalanche dominated Thom's senses. Sliding in the snow, he scooped Poppy over his shoulder and sprinted to the bank, hoping the trees at the edge would slow the brunt of the impact if they didn't reach the water in time.

Ripping off his cap, he pressed it over Poppy's mouth and nose, propelling them off the icy edge, leaping as close to the location of the border as he could get. As they hit the frigid water, the ground quaked with the impact of snow and ice. The water surged around them, going black as the avalanche consumed the light of dusk. Underwater, he struggled to swim and hold onto her, fighting the shock of the cold. Snow poured into the lake, the momentum driving them deep into the icy waters. The current tried to rip her away, but he clutched her body to his, sacrificing his hold on the cap.

Kicking hard, he swam, his vision a field of black, feeling for the border's current, hoping against hope to see the light-glimmer surrounding it, kinetic like the aurora borealis. His lungs burned, and he felt himself fading, losing strength.

All at once, it broke upon him, a flash of light slamming into the cells of his body.

Waves of undulating color cascaded into his vision, and he crushed her to his chest as a dizzying speed hooked them. Just as the pressure felt like it would break his ribs, it shifted and lessened. Blinking, he found himself prostrate upon mossy ground, Poppy still clasped in his arms, her soaked hair snow-white against chartreuse vegetation, her countenance gray.

Check respiration. Chest heaving, he knelt, turning her. *Cael, please! Let her be okay.* But someone grabbed his biceps and dragged him away from Poppy's motionless body. Growling, he fought, spinning out of the hold, flinging a man to the ground and throwing punches at others. Dimly, he heard shouts, and then a loud *thwack* on the back of his head sent him face-first to the spongy moss. His vision faded to black.

Chapter Twenty-Seven

Soaring like a sparrow in a vast, dark sky, waves of crimson and purple cascaded in Poppy's vision, undulating like the northern lights. Far below, ghostly mountains sped by – their forms shattered and angular like panes of stained glass. An aurora of colorful flame burst around her, throwing shadows on the alien landscape, interrupting her flight.

'Poppy!'

The voice resounded like the shockwave of an explosion, filling the vast world below, cramming the air around her – a voice she'd heard before. The crimson faded from her vision, and the ground sped up toward her like a military jet. Terror seized her limbs.

With a gasp, she opened her eyes, expecting pain. Instead she felt the softness of blankets, tucked tight around her. A heavy down-stuffed quilt lay over her chest and legs, vivid with cobalt waves, orange flames, and faceted shapes of violet and red. She inhaled deeply; the breath tingled in her toes, but her heart raced with fear and confusion, memory just out of reach.

Where am I?

A hearth glowing with embers cast dim light into the room. The plaster above the mantle was molded in an elaborate compass star, the lines crisp and vivid in the faint illumination. She'd seen that symbol before. *What is this place?*

Longing for a familiar smoothness, her fingers closed – searching – but her palm was empty. *What am I missing?* Within her skull, her brain seemed to shudder, take a deep breath, and resettle, as if the different regions had traded places and were now traumatized. Resisting tears, she blinked, wrestling the aftershocks of terror and loss.

What happened? Come on! Remember!

As though scrambling up a cliffside, she fought with her consciousness, hanging on with raw fingers, fighting for the memories. Her temples began to pound, the pain arcing behind her eyes. She emptied her mind and retreated, resting up for another try.

The pain faded and she opened her eyes. A sunken window punctuated the wall to her right, its panes dark with night. The plank floor was strewn with rag rugs sewn into puzzle-like shapes. Pushing herself onto her elbows, she sat up, studying the room for clues.

Caged iron sconces hung on each side of the wrought iron bed; one was dark, the other glowing. An orb of light shone in a tall glass cloche on a square wooden table, next to a mirror and a washbasin. The quality of the light was strange; not yellowish incandescent, or the unnatural gray of LEDs, or even similar to firelight. It glowed and shifted with diverse pure hues, too rapid to pinpoint, and vibrant – almost as if she was seeing color for the first time.

At her movement, the room stirred as though surprised. Whispered voices came from all directions, pinging off a deep place inside of her before quieting. They resonated in her chest cavity more than she wanted to. A light orb the size of a baseball floated by in front of her, bouncing on the opposite wall before passing her again, rotating and spinning in midair.

She gripped the covers. *What the hell is that?* A clank startled her and she threw back the quilt. A metal shackle surrounded her wrist, connected to a chain fastened to the bed frame. Her heart began to pound, and sweat beaded on her temples. Marks on her arm caught her eye.

Her shirt sleeve, an unfamiliar white knit, was scrunched up to her elbow, revealing her forearm – splotched and crossed with jagged healing wounds that looked like they'd been stitched up. The stitches were gone. As if from a great distance, her brain recalled something about the wounds.

Memories exploded in her head; the legs of the gigantic spider wrapping around her, gunshots, the owl lamp. Thom appearing next to her, hazel eyes soft, his expression concerned. *Thom!*

Covering her face, she lay back, weaving her fingers in her hair. Tears ran down her chin and dripped onto the quilt. Memories battered her; the Tetons, the discovery of her father's cruelty, their capture at the falls, her body – electric with a power she couldn't control, overwhelming her, a destructive, consuming power. The avalanche. The nauseating feeling she'd made a big mistake as the life drained out of her.

There were holes in the fabric of her recollections, but remembering something was better than nothing.

'Poppy.'

The quiet whisper morphed into ordered sounds inside of her, somewhere between her heart and brain. The quality of the sound resonated vibrantly, as if she experienced hearing in a new way. Gulping down her tears, she glanced around.

'Poppy. Why do you weep?'

A reticulating flame, about the size of a child, materialized at the foot of the bed as another, nearly identical, approached from the side. Startled, she clutched the blanket to her chin. The fiery bodies drifted, as if they walked on air. As she studied them their features became clearer and more humanlike, the flames calmer, almost as if they were accommodating her intuitively.

'Do you hurt?' They watched her, waiting.

As if from a great distance, she remembered; Thom had called these elementals *rifs*. Yes, *rifs* – the name settled naturally inside of her. *Firekind*.

"Not my body. My heart, hurts." It felt like someone had pumped her soul full of buckshot.

'Does medicine help that?' Their voices murmured in wispy crackles. It was difficult to discern which of them spoke, or if they spoke in unison.

She shook her head. "No. It doesn't." *Where is Thom? Where am I? What am I going to do?*

The *rifs* crowded up against the bed. *'What will help?'*

"Knowing that Thom is okay."

She didn't expect them to understand that. Laying back, she stared at the thick wooden beams across the ceiling. For a time, the *rifs* crackled with subdued staccato noises.

'Thomas Magnusson?'

Blinking, their violet eyes gleamed next to the bed, shifting with tiny thermals, as bright and alert as puppies.

"Yes. Thom Magnusson."

They looked at each other. *'The* cym *will know.'* The *rifs* focused on Poppy. *'Should we fetch her?'*

Etin? Desperate for information, she nodded.

One of the *rifs* trickled under the thick wooden door to her left, its red-orange light fading until the crack underneath darkened again.

The other *rif* remained, watching her silently. Its energy dove into a place near her heart; familiar, but also disquieting. *Caelith*, she grounded herself. *I'm in Caelith.*

The *rif's* eyes stayed trained on her face.

"Why are you staring at me?" she asked.

The purple eyes widened. *'Poppy was lost. She is found again. Addis is moved. It is...'* His clear visage wavered, *'difficult to express.'*

She sat up. The shackle around her wrist clanked. "Addis? Is that your name?"

The flames inclined in a motion that resembled a bow.

"And the other?"

'Jinsen. My sister. Addis and Jinsen watched over Poppy many turns. Until Poppy was lost. She will not be lost again.'

Snatches of distant memory nudged her, just out of reach, a fuzzy sense of warning. Shutting her eyes, she rested for a moment, thinking. *I need a plan. To figure out what I have to work with.*

The heat of the *rif's* flames neared and she withdrew involuntarily, clanking the chain attached to the shackle. "Can you do anything about this?" She shook it, scowling.

Addis slumped. *'Too strong. The* cym *will have to break the* kysim.*'*

Addis's flames billowed. The iron around her wrist tingled. His flames dimmed. *'I tell it to let go. It doesn't. I would hurt you if I tried harder. So I will persuade the* cym *to break it.'* He shuddered. *'She has been very cross.'*

Poppy gave up abusing the shackle. "Isn't that a state of being for her?"

Little bubbles fizzed on the air – laughter. Addis cracked a smile.

"How long have I been here?"

'One turn of moons. One of sun. The moons begin again.'

Thankfully those dots weren't difficult to connect.

"Who shackled me?"

Addis folded his arms with disdain. *'We don't concern ourselves with the others, unless they threaten. He says to watch over Poppy, and Poppy we watch over.'*

"He?" Her heart squirmed. "Whom do you mean?"

His demeanor spiked, like a cat arching its back and puffing up its fur. *'Etin comes.'*

An aggravated vibration shivered the air, rattling the table next to the bed. A trickle of orange and yellow light bloomed in the middle of the room – bright cracks spreading in midair. The other *rif* appeared and hovered by the hearth, ragged and puffed. A tremor jarred the room and Etin appeared, her arms crossed. Steeling herself, Poppy sat up as straight and tall as she could with the shackle.

Etin appeared substantial, as she had in the restaurant, but her skin was textured, as though dusted with powdered diamonds. A conspiracy theorist would've taken her for an angel or alien, because of her luminosity. But her aura was anything but angelic.

Her golden locks were pulled back in a complicated series of knots, her eyes angled in a scowl, unnaturally wide. A tailored seamless garment of a color resembling sunbeams, clung to her cat-like frame. Poppy was again struck by her beauty; her tongue in knots.

Appearing unimpressed, Jinsen motioned to the shackle. *'The* kysim *won't yield to us. Remove it. Without damaging Poppy.'*

In a fluid movement too quick to follow, Etin struck it, and the shackle groaned, fell off Poppy's wrist, and clattered to the floor, crawling under the bed, trembling. Poppy's arm throbbed with a fading charge.

Etin's scowl deepened. "The fireball said you wanted to talk to me. I'm in the middle of something much more important, so I give you three breaths to speak."

"I–I–just woke up. And I don't know what's going on, or where Thom is."

"And you want to know?"

"Of course."

"You really want to know?" Turning heel, she began to pace. "What if I told you Dane was letting an *ettar* rip into him? Would you still want to know?"

Poppy's breath came in a horrified wheeze.

Etin glared. "Not going to answer then?"

"That would—" Poppy choked, "will kill him." Thrusting the covers aside, she wobbled to her feet. "We've got to do something!"

"We? You'll just slow me down."

"Why haven't you done anything then?" Poppy struggled to find equilibrium – her balance felt like it had been knocked around.

Etin continued pacing. "It's complicated."

Steadying herself, Poppy gripped the iron bed. "Can you get me out?" She wobbled over to the window. The view revealed snow-covered evergreens, shrouded in darkness, three stories up.

"You'll just slow us down. You should let him go."

Silently, the *rifs* looked back and forth between them, their expressions alert.

Poppy straightened, ready to fight. "He won't leave without me and you know it."

Etin turned her back, light prickling and sparking off her skin.

"Come on! You either care about him, or you don't." Gripping the doorknob, she rattled it. *Locked.* "We have to do something! Get me out of here!" Her hand closed again, frantically searching for something, and she remembered – she no longer had the blue stone. Poppy couldn't remember what had happened to it – the effort to recall curdled her brain.

But she remembered something else. She whirled on Etin. "You're afraid of getting caught! By the *Offysfyn!*"

Eyes flashing, Etin turned on her. "You don't know anything, *utherling.* You're useless."

Poppy cringed. The flames of the *rifs* spiked, and the air in the room tensed with an imbalanced charge.

"We're wasting time!" Poppy gritted her teeth. "Take me to him or I'll find out a way to go myself!"

The *rifs* crowded around her, currents of warm air tugging at her nightgown. *'Poppy goes with us.'*

"I'm not going anywhere with anyone without Thom!" Her voice rose, ragged in her throat.

A key rattled in the lock of the door.

Etin vanished and the *rifs* merged with the embers in the hearth. Scrambling back into the bed, Poppy hid her bare wrist in the folds of the quilt.

Chapter Twenty-Eight

A woman in a gray jumpsuit with a green scarf tied over her hair entered, pushing a wooden cart, followed by a man in a white coat. Ominously, the door clicked shut.

"Poppy," The man's lips stretched in a placid smile. "I see you're awake."

A chair scraped and the man sat, crossing his legs, keen eyes studying her. His trimmed gray hair traveled down his face into an even neater beard, accented with horned spectacles perched on his nose. Beneath his white lab coat, he wore a tweed jacket, an intricately knotted necktie, and pressed gray pants. As the woman handed him a clipboard, he licked an index finger and flipped through the papers.

Poppy burrowed deeper in the quilt. "Who are you?" Her voice was hoarse after screaming.

He leaned forward, extending a hand she did not take. "I'm Lars Youngblood." He smiled, a maddeningly calm expression, withdrawing his hand after a moment. "You would refer to me as a psychiatrist. In your familiar environment."

Familiar environment? I don't have time for this shit.

"You must be wondering where you are." His eyes combed the papers before him.

"I'm in Caelith. One of the havenlands. Caldys, I think." Despite the cold fear slithering down her back, Poppy didn't suppress the venom in her tone. "I remember everything. So, spare me the psychoanalysis."

His eyes flitted up from the clipboard, his mouth again forming the placid smile. Letting the papers fall, he took off his glasses, tucking them into his front jacket pocket. "I'm glad you feel you're doing so well, Poppy. Would you like to talk about why you were so upset before I entered the room?"

"That's none of your business."

Lars turned to the woman. "Prepare a partial of the amsen. And then thirty of the bloc."

Nodding, she shook a glass vial, keeping her eyes on her preparations. The fumes from the liquid in the vials made Poppy's head spin.

Lars put a hand on her arm. She recoiled. Nothing about this man said trust-me-with-your-secrets. If anything, she wanted to run, or offer him to Etin as a toy.

"Passing through the borderlands can be traumatic," he said. "Especially for someone who has experienced trauma as you have. You're in a delicate phase of your recovery, Poppy.

It could be easy for you to think you know what really happened, when your brain is just accepting what you were made to believe."

Poppy kept her forearms under the quilt. There was no way she wanted him knowing the shackle was gone. "That's the prettiest load of bullshit I've ever heard, *Doctor.* Sounds exactly like what you're trying to do to me."

Out of the corner of her eye, the assistant held up a metal and glass syringe, the size of a tapered candle.

Poppy tensed. "No."

"I know it's hard to accept this." Dr. Youngblood smiled again. "But you'll come to realize we're doing the right thing for you, by letting you rest. By allowing your brain to suspend thought." Delicately, he took the syringe and flicked it, nodded, and laid it on a white cloth on the cart. "There's a term for what we're trying to help you recover from, from the world you've been living in. Stockholm Syndrome. Maybe you've heard of it?"

"That's not right." Poppy shook her head. "That's not what happened."

The embers in the hearth muttered and spat, crimson flames leaping up among the ashes, but Lars and the assistant didn't notice.

"Stop. This. Now." Poppy snarled the words. "Or you'll have Felix Paquin to answer to."

Examining another vial, Lars didn't respond. Her expression blank, the assistant rounded the bed, clutching the huge syringe.

"Don't!" Poppy shrank away. "I don't want that!" She flailed around so the assistant couldn't get a hold of her. A grim, angry look tightened at the woman's lips. Flinging back the covers, Poppy kicked her in the stomach. The syringe clattered to the floor, cracking, releasing an eye-watering odor.

Clutching her stomach, the assistant staggered for the door. "We need another restraint."

"No! No! No!" Poppy jumped up and ran to the window, searching for an escape.

The energy of the room quivered with anger, merging and simmering in Poppy's veins, fuzzing her vision.

His placid expression gone, Lars tossed the clipboard on the bed, and approached her, smashing his tongue between his lips. The assistant slipped past him, rushing into the hall.

"Poppy." He attempted a placating tone. "You're making this harder on yourself. This medicine is an important part of your recovery."

"NO! NO!" She dodged him, surprised at her agility.

Does he hurt you, Poppy? The *rifs'* voices crackled livid, somewhere in her consciousness.

Backed into a corner, she slipped on one of the rugs, and his crushing grip wrapped around her bicep, pulling her off balance, throwing her to the floor. Lars's weight pressed against her, forcing the breath out of her chest in an *oof.* Unable to speak, her shoulder smarting from the impact, she struggled to gasp, to answer the *rifs.* Her eyes rolled in horror as his legs snaked around hers, his pelvis tight against her crotch, exposed by the short nightshirt.

An angry groan in her throat, she called to the fire in the grate, spitting in a language that smarted on her tongue. Straining away from his awful red face, she imagined she could feel the stone, still clutched in her palm. The *rifs'* eyes appeared within the embers, scowling like jack-o-lanterns.

Fire snaked out of the grate and grabbed Dr. Youngblood's shoulder. Feeling the heat, he spluttered, scrambling back on his hands and feet, diving into a rug to snuff the flames out. An oily, burnt smell filled the room as he dropped the rug, exposing the angry red flesh on his shoulder beneath a burnt hole in his jacket. Poppy skittered into a corner, scooping up the broken syringe and launching it at him with a feral snarl.

Dodging the projectile, he retreated, slamming the door behind him. The key clicked in the lock followed by the sound of muffled curses fading down the passage.

Chapter Twenty-Nine

Damn. *Damn. Damn.* Poppy's breath came ragged. Before she could even stand, Addis and Jinsen exploded into view, buzzing and sparking with anxiety.

'Poppy. We must go. We must go now.'

Rattled by the assault, her head spun. "Go? Where? No—"

'We need to keep you safe. If something happens to you, he'll be angry.'

A different vein of anxiety shifted inside of her. "Who are you talking about?"

Their flames pawed at her, their warmth soothing and gentle. *'Come with us. You must come. We will keep you safe.'*

Buried memories surfaced and Poppy's brain made a shaky connection, the *rifs* had an agenda of their own, one she didn't understand, yet. But they wanted to keep her safe. Maybe she could use that for her own ends.

She stood. "Who? Tell me!"

'No time. Explain later. Must go now.'

"I'm not going anywhere without Thom!"

'No. Poppy. Come with us now!' They sputtered in desperation. *'You must!'*

"It's out of the question, *unless* you help me save him first."

The *rifs* muttered to each other like they had a problem they couldn't solve.

Looking for clothes, Poppy pillaged the room, dumping the contents of a chest of drawers, shivering. The chest held linens and more gowns like the one she wore. No coat, clothes, or boots. The gown billowed around her bare legs, as substantial as a jellyfish.

Staccato noises emanated from the *rifs* as they murmured to each other, hindering the translation to conceal their discussion.

Rubbing the goosebumps on her legs, she shivered. The gown barely came to her knees and took flight at the smallest puff of air. It wouldn't do, but it was all she had. Pulling another one out of the dresser, she tied the arms around her hips to hold it down, rehearsing her impromptu scheme of how she was going to get Thom and her out of here, wherever here was, and how she was going to press Addis and Jinsen to go along with it.

There wasn't much to rehearse. *I'm in trouble.*

Like it had been seized by an earthquake, the room vibrated and Etin appeared in a nebula of light.

"They've left Thom!" Her eyes were wide, the golden irises almost fearful. "We've got to move! NOW!"

Blinking through the imprints on her retinas, Poppy staggered.

The *rifs* buzzed, agitated. *'Poppy comes with us!'*

"She comes with me," Etin scowled. "Because Thom won't leave without her. Tag along if you like."

The flames crackled. *'We have Adym close. We'll call Adym.'*

"Fine. More to help then." She whirled on Poppy. "Are you coming or not?"

Adym? Poppy straightened. "Of course, I'm coming. Let's go."

Etin marched to the window. It came open at a tap of her finger and a gust of frosty wind swept into the room. Twisting and shrinking in on themselves, the *rifs* compacted their blazes, their expressions vexed.

"Come on." Without a backward glance, Etin sprung out the window.

Poppy rushed to the opening. The room was situated about three stories up, in a vast stone structure, surrounded by a forest of spruce towering about twenty feet out from the window, dark against the snow on the ground. In front of her, Etin appeared, alight with distain.

Surveying the drop, Poppy glared. "What do you expect me to do? Exactly?"

Expelling a frustrated puff of air, Etin grabbed her arm, her touch tingling like a science experiment gone wrong. Before she could protest, Etin launched her out of the window. Her strangled scream was loud in her ears, but it didn't echo in the frosty night.

Poppy expected to smash into the ground with a crunching of bone, but she landed as if she'd only jumped a fence – rattled but unhurt. Etin tore off with the speed of an Olympic sprinter. Scrambling to her feet, Poppy followed, the chill shocking her bare skin. At her side, the glow of the *rifs* reflected on dry leaves, scattered and frosty on the snow.

"Hurry!" Etin hissed at Addis and Jinsen. "Hide yourselves."

"What should I do?" Poppy asked.

"I'll hide you. Now run!"

Like a ghost, Etin glowed in the night-shrouded forest, her energy pulling on Poppy. Bewildered at the strength flooding her muscles, Poppy kept pace, through a forest of conifers and giant oak trees, her feet navigating snowy ground littered with pinecones, branches, and tangled underbrush. More than once, the presence of something more alive than just a plant or a breeze filtered around them. At these moments, Etin enveloped Poppy, shunting her at a dizzying speed.

Random lights twinkled among the trees, some viridian green, others ghostly blue. Vivid pinging and rumbling quivered in Poppy's chest cavity – eerie elemental sounds. The elemental part of her was expanding; becoming sharper. Wary like cats on the hunt, Addis and Jinsen crowded her heels, easily keeping pace.

The opening of a cave appeared in a swell of deciduous forest, wavering with lavender light. A slender track weaved in and out of the trees, leading to the opening. Halting, Etin studied the entrance for a time, before enveloping Poppy, and diving into the opening with the speed of a falcon, crashing through a locked gate.

For a cave, the interior was well lit and dry. After a short passageway it opened up into a large cavern crammed with hundreds of wooden barrels, stacked crates, and worn leather tackle and gear. Caged lights hung from the ceiling, glowing with a strange luminosity, similar to the room she'd just vacated. Before Poppy could look any closer, Etin nabbed her and shot above the supplies at lightning speed, dodging the lights, heading for an iron-reinforced plank door at the back of the chamber.

Before they reached it, the door flew open with a violent crack, splintering. Following a passage that forked to the left, Etin rounded a corner and thrust Poppy headfirst into an alcove with a wood floor. Splinters dug into her shins.

A man shouted and there was a hot, brilliant flash. Beneath her knees, the floor shook and creaked. The light and heat dissipated quickly. Sweat beading on her forehead, Poppy spun around. They had come to a large stone guardroom, with adjoining cells at the left. A passage to the right led to a tall arched doorway.

Etin loomed above two guards rolling on the floor, clutching their faces. Poppy thought she recognized one from the canyon; his eyes blinked rapidly, weeping and red as though they'd been burnt.

The other squinted. "I—I—can't see." He whimpered, pawing around for a lever mounted on the wall.

"Quiet." Etin whispered, menacing. "Unless you wish for permanent blindness."

They froze. One in each hand, she shoved them against the wall, her gleaming countenance inches from their noses. Cowering, they squeezed their eyes shut, their bodies stiff with fear.

"Please don't." One choked out. "We'll do whatever you want."

"Get the keys." Glancing at Poppy, Etin motioned to the ring on the other's belt.

Poppy lunged and snatched them, wondering why Etin couldn't just pop open the cell with her superpowers. At her heels, the *rifs* clung to her like mini tailgating vehicles.

"Now restraints," Etin pointed. "In there."

Poppy fished the corded ties out of a drawer at the guard's station.

The other man struggled, his eyes wide and panicked, reflecting the *rifs's* flames.

"Remember what I said?" Etin prodded him and he stilled. Flipping the men simultaneously, she shoved their chests against the wall, smashing their faces against the stone.

Leaping forward, Poppy tightened the cords around their wrists.

"Quiet now, boys." Etin flung them in a chamber off the guard station and shut the door.

Without glancing at Poppy, she charged down the cell-block passage. Breathless, Poppy sprinted after her, past clean, empty cells, her bare feet slipping on the flagstones, the sweat growing cold on her back. Etin paused at a cell at the end of the passage, one that twisted back into a corner with blackened stone walls. The bars across the front were as thick as her wrists, buzzing and vibrating with power. Keys clanked and iron rattled as Etin forced the door open.

Curled up near the back wall, Thom lay with his hands bound behind his back, his clothing in shreds, his body a mess of bloody lacerations and scarlet bruises. The smell of damp filth and blood filled her nostrils, earthy and sickening. Sinking to her knees beside him, the floor dampened her gown, even as warmth of the *rifs* touched her heels.

As Etin nudged him, his eyes opened a little. "I'm not leaving without—" His expression jolted. "Poppy, are you... okay?"

"We're getting you out of here." Etin snapped the cord around his wrists.

Speechless, Poppy shook her head, cupping his face and kissing his forehead. His hand found one of hers and the strength of his grip surprised her.

"It's not as bad," he winced, "as it looks."

"This absurd little reunion will have to wait." Etin glanced down the cell block, her body glowing with hackles of light. "We must hurry. They'll return soon."

"I'm not going to be able to hurry." Rolling onto his back, Thom hissed through his teeth.

Working her hands under his arms, Poppy hauled him upright, grunting with the effort. Clenching his swollen jaw, he squeezed his eyes and leaned back against the wall, blood trickling down his chest from a deep gash near his clavicle, revealing bone. The sight made her want to hurt somebody.

"I can't carry both of you." Etin's voice was icy as the snowy ground.

"Take him. Leave me." Poppy glanced at the *rifs*. "They'll get me out."

"Certainly." Etin's countenance lightened.

His eyes widening, Thom gaped at Addis and Jinsen. "NO!" His voice strengthened and, staggering, he pushed himself up the wall to his feet. More blood oozed from the deepest wound, trickling down his chest through hair, green filth, and lacerations.

Etin tossed her the keys. "Find him some clothes. Hurry."

Poppy sprinted back to the guard's station, the *rifs* shadowing her as she rummaged through the wooden cabinets lining the walls, nabbing a roll of bandages, some boots, socks.

A vibration in the air. The *rifs* sizzled. '*Down, Poppy! Hide!*'

The floor shook with approaching footsteps. Diving under the guard's counter, she held her breath as a flinty, pungent smell filled the room, followed by a throaty breathing. A rotting stench made her gag. The suck and plop of sloshing faded down the hall. Their light muted, the *rifs* crouched protectively next to her.

The elementals turned down the cell block, one a massive sable form, rippling with spikes and muscles, dotted with white eyes – the *ulli*, the same elemental that had erupted out of the ground by the landing. As it ducked under the ceiling rafters, each step made her teeth rattle.

The other resembled a rolling mass of swampy filth – like an organic droid. Malicious anticipation and a thirst for violence accompanied them.

"Thom," she whispered, her fists clenching.

The *rifs* stroked her with warm currents. *'Etin will protect him.'*

A clatter echoed down the cell block, followed by a roar and a burst of light. Gritting her teeth, Poppy leapt out from under the counter and continued searching the cabinets, this time for a weapon, although she wasn't sure what she could do against a creature like the *ulli*. The floor trembled, light flashed, and Etin wailed a metallic battle cry. A deafening shatter and a watery explosion hurt her ears. Warm currents of air gusted through the cell block like angry winds.

Poppy almost ripped a cabinet door off its hinges. Still no weapons. But, a familiar coat fell out – Thom's! Snatching it up, she gathered the clothes stowed around it.

The *rifs* hissed. Poppy froze.

Dane loomed in the doorway to the guard's station, an *ettar* halting next to him, its pinchers rasping together. Dropping the clothes, Poppy backed against the cabinets.

"Oh!" Dane's mouth stretched into a grin. "What do we have here?"

A silver eye tooth gleamed under his lips. She gulped and straightened, trying to think of something frightening to say. On either side of her, Addis and Jinsen quivered. Dane's eyes flitted over them with a surprised, hungry light before returning to her. He stopped so close the stubble of his jaw scraped against her cheek, murmuring in her ear. "I was going to visit you in your room tonight, but now's just fine. Thom can wait."

"Sick bastard." Her voice trembled.

"Sick bastard." His eyebrow twitched. "I like it when you talk to me that way."

The *ettar* clicked, its desire to rip into her intense. Her knees wobbled, and she clawed the edge of the cabinets behind her. *Weapon. I need a weapon.*

Dane's irises were suffocating and as black as oil, lingering on her body as he gestured to the ettar. "What do you think, Ozzie? Is the rest of her as fiery as her mouth?"

Ozzie rubbed his pinchers and clicked again. Grazing her hip, Dane lifted the gown, enough to discover her lack of underwear. Resisting the numb panic metastasizing in her limbs, she recoiled, her face reddening with anger.

He grinned. "Come now, sweets. Don't judge me for going after what I desire. It's what everyone really wants to do, if they're honest. Most just don't have the stones to go for it." His eyes moved up and down her, as though deciding where to start. "Can't say it hasn't worked out for me."

Eyes darting between him and the *ettar*, she inched away.

"That's why Thom will always end up losing. His principles castrate him." His hands rough, he forced her chin toward him. "Lucky for you, I'm willing to overlook your resistance to my charms." His fingers surrounded her bicep.

She clobbered him across the jaw, stinging the bones of her hand and wrist. In response, he only blinked.

"We could do a lot for each other." He eyed the *rifs*. "Especially with your little friends here. Think about it."

Snarls and crashes resonated in the cellblock, rattling the bars of the cells. Poppy wanted a chair to smash over his head. A knee in the groin would have to do.

Sidestepping her attack, he backhanded her across the face. The force of the blow knocked her against the cabinets, and she crumpled to the floor, pain crawling through her head. The *rifs* raged and buzzed, their words muddling in her consciousness.

"Oh my. So rude." Dane's words distorted, like a radio transmission breaking up and clearing. "You've been taking lessons from that hero has-been in there." Yanking her upright, his lips brushed her ear. "Oz is going for his man-junk next. For Lilith." He shoved her down the hall. "You want to watch?"

She fell against the stone, skinning her knees raw. "No!"

Hot at her elbow, the *rifs* boiled and sputtered, their smoke stinging her eyes. *DOES HE HURT YOU, POPPY?*

She drew a gasping breath. "Yes!"

A blistering, explosive rush of heat filled the guardroom as Addis and Jinsen's flames combined, erupting around Dane, his eyes widening as the storm of fire enveloped him. The *ettar* screeched and lunged for her, its claws scraping the flesh of her shoulder, but the *rifs'* flames snatched it, dragging it into the fury, where it shuddered, its legs popping and shriveling.

Choking on the smoke and oily fumes, she scrambled away, cringing as a tinny scream mingled with the suck and rip of the flames. Writhing, Dane's blackened body staggered, collapsing on the floor. Eyes stinging, she scooted back and hit the wall, her breath ragged.

Dane's charred body stilled as the *ettar* shuddered and crumpled, half its body turning to ash. Releasing them, Addis and Jinsen returned to their serene *rif* forms. It had gone so quiet in the cell block she could hear the pop and snap of roasting bones.

Snatching up the clothes, Poppy stumbled down the cell-block, her heart pumping with fear.

The *ulli* was crumpled against the wall across from the cell, motionless. Green and sulfur slime splattered the walls along-side jagged cracks and crumbling dents. Orange barnacle-like bones littered the floor and a restless hum vibrated on the air.

His back striped with gaping bloody rents, Thom knelt over Etin, cradling her head. The elemental's hair trailed onto the stone floor, lank and loose, her luminescence wavering like a guttering candle.

"Don't." His voice caught with emotion.

Her hands like claws, Etin gripped his arms. The air around them shimmered and her light diminished. Grunting, Thom doubled over as some of the wounds on his back closed up, the skin knitting itself, the marks fading to silver lines.

"Stop arguing." Etin's voice, breathy and faint. "Let me do what I can."

He shook his head.

Feeling sick, Poppy braced herself against the wall.

"I know you think I don't love you," Etin's slender fingers gripped his shoulders. "Let me prove that I do. In my own way, at least."

His shoulders trembling, Thom embraced her and her light merged with his body, healing the remaining gashes, knitting his broken ribs in powerful ripples. Etin's form grayed as she placed his hand around her right wrist. "Take it." Her voice was so faint it sounded like distant wind over prairie. "A *cydern*…given in passing. Most…powerful."

In dusty ripples of luminescence, Etin faded away, until Thom held only a ridged bone the color of gold leaf. The stone lay next to him on the floor, a dull glow of blue and orange in glittering dust. Wiping his face on his arm, he picked it up, and stood like one unsure of the stability of his legs.

Dumbstruck, Poppy stumbled toward him. Tensing, he spun around. Seeing her, his shoulders relaxed, he took the clothes she offered in a white-knuckled grip.

"Thanks." he said, as if nothing had happened.

Dried blood crusted his chest, but his serious wounds had been healed – though his face was drawn, as if pain still rankled him. He dropped his tattered garments to the floor and Poppy stared at the flagstones, her cheeks reddening.

"Are you okay?" His voice muffled as he tugged a sweater on.

She swallowed. "Thom, I'm so sorry."

Regarding Addis and Jinsen, his brow wrinkled with a mixture of disbelief and bemusement. "Is she okay?" His accent sounded clipped and odd, as if Caelith gave him leave to speak naturally.

Startling, the *rifs* peered up at Thom, their expressions puzzled. 'Yes. *We keep her safe and warm. But—*'

"Good." Thrusting on his coat, he rolled his shoulders with a grimace, stowing the stone in his pocket.

In an errant breeze, Poppy's nightgown billowed, showing a good twelve inches of her thighs. Forcing it down, she grimaced.

His frown deepened. "We need to find you some clothes."

"Wait," she said. "You can understand…Firekind? You said that wasn't—"

"Later, Poppy." He funneled her toward the opening. "Clothes."

The bars rattled as the *ulli* sprung into the cell, blocking the way, fingers grappling for Poppy's throat. The *rifs* snarled, but Thom leapt between them, blocking the reaching arm and striking the creature between the eyes. Slipping on a slimy spot, she fell, almost cracking her head. Billowing with multi-colored flames, the *rifs* dove between her and the fight.

The creature recovered, launching itself off the bars, denting them. The power of Thom's *cydern* raised the hair on her arms. As it connected with the creature's bicep, it exploded in a burst of rock, clattering in pieces all over the cell. Her ears rang and she threw her arms over her face. The floor vibrated as Thom struck the *ulli* repeatedly, unbalancing the elemental, so it flailed and grunted, tottering on its feet.

With a hoarse yell, Thom drove the weapon into its chest. The *ulli* uttered a sickening, guttural noise. Withdrawing the weapon, Thom spun it, impaling it in the throat. The elemental crumpled and rock and bones shattered on the floor in dull, brown splinters.

With a heave, Thom hoisted her up and over the fragments. The *rifs* following, they rushed down the cellblock. Dane's charred remains lay in their path, stiff on the blackened flagstones. Thom's jaw dropped.

Her stomach went queasy. "Dane got on the wrong side of Addis and Jinsen." She eyed the *rifs*. "Ozzie did too."

"Ozzie?"

"The *ettar*."

Thom's expression stiffened and she had the impression that he was more acquainted with Ozzie than he cared to be. Skirting the ashes, they opened cabinets, raking the contents onto the floor until she found a suitable pair of pants, undergarments, a thick wool sweater, boots, and a coat trimmed with fur.

"Hurry." Thom jogged to the entrance of the guard room, and peered around the door frame, head cocked, listening.

Poppy scooped up the clothes and ducked into an empty cell to change. Sparking, Addis and Jinsen trailed after her, their flames spiky with ire.

"What's going on with you guys?" Glad to be rid of the nightgown, she slithered into the stiff, warm garments.

Addis made a face like a child pouting. '*Thom shouldn't understand us.*'

Jinsen flared. *'We don't know why Thom hears us. He didn't before. He shouldn't now.'*

Wishing she understood more, she shrugged into the sweater, suddenly nervous about the *rifs'* intentions. "Well, it'll make communicating less complicated, won't it?"

Little sparks exploded off them, bouncing across the floor.

"Careful guys!" *What was their end game here?*

They quieted. Tying her boots, she crouched in front of them, thinking fast. "If something happens to Thom, I'll die. You know that right?"

Not exactly true, but after what she saw them do to Dane, she wasn't taking any chances.

Aloof, they acted like they didn't hear her, although she got the sense they did. *'We will ask Adym why. Adym will know.'*

"Who's Adym?"

"Poppy." Thom appeared around the corner. "Are you ready? We've got to go."

Shrugging into the coat, she jogged after him, the *rifs* at her heels. They would tell her later. She would make sure of it.

Chapter Thirty

Poppy studied Thom's gait as he led them into the store-room. *He's favoring his left side. Better watch him closely.* If she'd learnt one thing, it was that Thom would push himself too far, give too much. "Are you okay?"

"I will be." Scanning the barrels and crates, he spun. "We need supplies."

In minutes, they'd filled canteens at the water pump, and crammed foodstuffs and gear into packs, and fled the cave for the cover of the woodland. Hemming them in, the forest thickened over the snow-covered track, luminous in the snow, but also dark with wind-tumbled shadows, broken by the flickering of the *rifs*.

Even with the darkness, Thom set a brisk pace. Poppy surprised herself by keeping stride with his long legs. The *rifs* glimmered, one in front of them, one behind – lithe orange

streaks in the night, lighting the rutted trail. Thom kept stealing glances at them, clenching his jaw like he was chewing on
a problem he couldn't solve. She couldn't help but remember
his face when he'd seen them with her; he'd been shocked,
troubled. Why?

Because the *rifs* had helped them escape. The questions
would keep for when they'd escaped, at least somewhere safe,
preferably out of earshot of her new friends.

Thom deviated from the track, and the rough terrain of
mountainous forest swallowed them. Lingering behind, Addis
manipulated their tracks to hide their trail.

The woodland reminded Poppy of the forest around the
lake in the Tetons. Evergreens shielded them from powerful
snowy gusts. Tall ghostly trunks of a tree she didn't recognize
rose into the canopy with massive hollies and gnarled twists of
woody vines. Mist and snow blotted out the night sky, obscuring the treetops, but she got the sense the trees towered high
above them, like skyscrapers. The *rifs'* flames reflected off of
the snow, painting the shadows blue and purple; without the
elementals' light, they wouldn't have been able to see.

The farther they went, the darker and more immense the
woodland became, with inclines as brutal as their recent hike.
Even with the obstacles they pressed on at a pace that, after
an hour, burned her lungs and knifed her side. The downward
slopes provided a little reprieve when the grade was mild. Still,
she was amazed she was able to keep up. Was it adrenaline
fueling her strength? or something else?

The forest followed their progress, its energy peculiar and observant. The whisper of the falling snow coalesced with the murmur of the wind and the creak of the branches, peaceable, but alive. Goosebumps spread up her back. *Did the forest allow them to pass unmolested because of the rifs?* Questions troubled her, but putting distance between them and the base was imperative. That simple fact explained Thom's brutal pace. The farther they plunged into the wilderness, the less she sensed the buzzing presence of elementals, and she hoped that was a good sign.

Much later, the night sky still misty with snowfall, Thom halted in a small clearing, turning in place, squinting at a compass. Gulping air, she crawled onto a snow-covered log, slumping onto her knees. Eying Thom, Addis and Jinsen huddled next to her, muttering in hushed tones.

Standing still, he remained quiet, head cocking in all directions, listening for long enough that her heartbeat slowed. Then, with a stunted sigh, he sunk down next to her, taking the canteen she offered.

"Are you okay?" he asked, between gulps. "This pace is rough."

She grunted. "I'm not the one who was tortured."

Half-shrugging, he made a face. "I don't want to get captured again."

His eyes were shadowed in the light from the *rifs'* flames, but she could still see him frowning at the Firekind like they were a life-or-death riddle he couldn't solve, his jaw clenched between drinks of water.

Poppy faced them. "Addis, Jinsen, will you go back and scan the path behind us, see if we're being followed?"

'Yes, Poppy.' Their fiery forms drifted away, leaving them in frigid darkness.

As soon as they were out of earshot, Thom gripped her arm, his whisper low and urgent. "Where did they come from?"

"They were in the room with me, when I woke up. They helped me, and Etin." She frowned, thinking. "They wanted me to come with them." His grip tightened and her heart kicked up again. "Are they?" Her breath stopped. She was going to say dangerous, but the memory of Dane's blackened body answered her question, followed by snatches of what Thom had told her about the Firekind, back in the Tetons. She shut her eyes. No wonder Thom was so worried. *Out of one net, only to be tangled in another.* "What are we going to do?"

Thom's arm slid around her shoulders, drawing her close so he could speak in her ear. "I'd like to ditch them, but we won't be able to see without them, and we'd probably freeze. Our only option is to keep going, and hope they don't make any trouble."

Glimmers of flame appeared in the trees, growing closer.

His voice became the smallest of whispers. "We'll look for a chance to escape, when we can."

"And then where will we go?"

"We'll try and intercept your father. Warn him of Dane, and the Caldera's vulnerability."

Floating nonchalantly over the snowy ground Addis approached, his bright eyes blinking.

Shivering, she rubbed her palms on her thighs. "How much farther?"

"We should cut northeast soon," Thom spoke normally. "Depending on conditions, and how long we stop to rest, we could reach the *Kairyn* outpost by noon."

She pressed her shoulder against his. The lines around his mouth cut harsher than normal. "And you? Are you really okay?"

"Don't worry about me. Etin patched me up pretty well, considering."

He's not telling me everything. Through his shoulder against hers, pain leaked from his body, trickling into some new awareness in her cells. Thom would martyr himself before he showed weakness. *Watch him.* She told herself. *Don't let his trauma or his overdeveloped sense of duty call the shots.*

Addis huddled by her, his heat pouring around them in comforting waves. Glancing around, Poppy stood, swiveling. "Addis, where's Jinsen?"

Eyes averted, he shrugged and drew a fiery limb across the snow.

"Fokking fáviti!" Thom flew to his feet, looking up.

Two-hundred feet above them, Jinsen flared at the crown of a spruce tree; a pulsing, fiery signal in the night, the light diffused by the mist.

"Jinsen!" Poppy called. "Come down! Now!"

'Poppy doesn't tell us what to do.' Addis muttered.

Thom loomed over Addis, menacing. "There might be search parties from Caldys by now. You could be leading them right to her."

Addis avoided his eyes. *'We need Adym. We call Adym. He comes. Poppy wouldn't be in danger if she just came with us.'*

"Who's Adym?" Thom's eyes hardened.

Nose in the air, Addis turned his back. Thom pelted him with an armload of snow.

Sparking, the *rif* spluttered, shook the watery mess off, and charged Thom. With a cry, Poppy threw herself between them, remembering Dane's fiery fate. She wouldn't let that happen to Thom, no matter what.

Addis halted. *'Not fair, Poppy! Thomas Magnusson plays mean!'*

Still wary, she kept herself between them. "Answer his question."

Wrinkling his nose, Addis glared sidelong at Thom. *'Adym is our fey-master.'*

"*Fey*-master?" Poppy repeated, dim memory crawling up her spine.

Thom pivoted, rubbing his neck.

She loomed over Addis. "What's a *fey*-master?"

Innocently, the *rif* blinked up at her. *'Poppy doesn't know? How could you not know?'*

Thom growl-sighed in his throat. "We'll find out soon enough."

Warm gusts surrounded them, crackling the air like hot water over ice.

Her expression smug, Jinsen hopped down next to Addis. *'Adym comes.'*

Why did I trust them? Her neck prickled with embarrassed rage. "You promised me you would explain! So, what's going on? Who's this 'he' you keep mentioning?"

Addis and Jinsen glanced at one another.

"Who are you working for? This Adym? Your *fey*-master?"

Jinsen shuddered like a bird puffing its feathers. *'We serve Adym. Adym serves the ith-astrett, Ryn of Maris, father of the Firekind, lord of liquid earth-fire, watcher of the borderlands, lostaja of all elemental kin.'*

Ryn. The name pricked her memory, injecting her with dread. A tense silence crowded the dark clearing, as though the forest had quieted at the sound of the name.

A muscle twitched in Thom's bearded jaw. *"Ryn?"*

The *rifs* nodded, their expressions reverent with an awe that, under other circumstances, might've been comical.

"How does he know she's here?" Snow-pale skin replaced the angry flush on Thom's face.

'Ryn has searched for Poppy many, many years. Only days ago, her talisman passed the gates.'

Poppy gulped, grasping for Thom's hand.

"A *Mesian*?" Thom asked, like the question tasted awful in his mouth. "The *Ryn* of legend?"

The *rifs* nodded. "Yes. *Lostaja.* That one."

Thom's skin surrendered the last of its color.

A warm gust shook the trees. More snow fell. Anticipating the *fey's* arrival, the *rifs* quivered.

I don't understand. Fear trickled into Poppy's stomach. "What does any of this have to do with me?"

The stone. A Poppy-specific talisman. She felt in her pocket for it. Reading her thoughts, Thom extracted it from his coat and handed it to her.

Poppy whirled on the *rifs.* "Is this the talisman?" The stone blazed, the light tremulous with the shaking of her hand, magnified by the snow. "If it's yours, or any of the Firekinds', just take it! I don't want it! I never wanted it!"

The *rifs* didn't move. *'The talisman isn't ours to take. It was bestowed as a warding to the daughters of Crymson.'*

Against her palm, Thom's hand went rigid and he shut his eyes – an expression as unsettling as the *rifs'* revelations.

Crimson? Like my middle name? "I still don't understand," she said. "What does this have to do with me?"

'We don't question Adym. We do as we are bidden. And what we are bidden, we do.'

"So you're just sycophants? I thought you were…" She was going to say *my friends*, but that sounded silly and naïve.

Memory bobbed to the surface of her consciousness. The rhyme from her dream – her father's warning about the Firekind.

> *Crimson hair*
> *Beware! Beware!*
> *He rises out of firelight*
> *And all around burn at the sight*
> *Of violet coal and scarlet fright*
> *His mourning roars, his flames alight*
> *Burning for the crimson one*

Who fled from him undone undone
For whom his grief
Will always run

More memories came with it; crouched on the hard chair in the kitchen, she'd had to write out the rhyme over and over again, until her fingers were black with ink, gazing longingly at the sunlit outdoors. Resenting her father for making her do it.

Crimson hair
Beware! Beware!
He ascends in red moonlight
Enchanting, slaying by his might
Steals her to his home of fire
Chains her to his flame desire

Addis and Jinsen's blank, mild visages, gazed at her, as unfeeling as soldiers. She'd been a fool to think they'd wanted to help her, to let herself be lulled into trusting them.

Orange light filtered across the sky from the north.

Wide-eyed, she looked at Thom. *I'm sorry. This is all my fault.* The words choked her.

Dark circles rimmed his eyes. The pressure of his fingers gentle, his hand slid into hers. "It'll be okay, Poppy. We'll think of something."

Scorching anger filled her chest. This couldn't be her fate, to be a trophy of some elemental psychopath! Thom wouldn't be swept up in her shitstorm. She wouldn't allow it. But what could she do?

The air grew warmer, the light intense and rosy. A nearby pine jolted under the weight of a brilliant crimson flame, sending clumps of snow to the ground with soft thuds. The flame leapt down the tree and approached without pause, sparks following like a cape, the air around him rippling with thermals.

Thom's arm tightened around her and she leaned into him, her knees watery, even as she felt the surge of power from the *cydern*, clutched in his other hand, tremor through his body.

The approaching *fey* stood as tall as a lamppost, his physique more exact than the *rifs*, as if his flames were contained by invisible skin. Tendrils of fire raced over his muscles, so they continually shifted in color and size. Adym was the most magnificent elemental she'd seen thus far. Not necessarily pleasant, but certainly a stand-out.

His appearance lost none of its majesty as he approached, though he seemed to shrink, his flames diminishing as his flesh took on the appearance of bronze skin, hinting at fiery insides. Blackened markings, like geometric tattoos, ringed his wrists and biceps and patterned his chest. A long mohawk of mahogany hair rippled in the wind, crowning a strong forehead. Unlike the *rifs*, his cloak of humanness made him terrifying.

Their flames spiking, Addis and Jinsen bounced around him like puppies, rippling the kilt-like garment around the *fey's* hips.

'Adym! Adym! We have Poppy. Look! Poppy!'

"Be still." Adym's voice crackled and sucked at the air.

The *fey* spun in a liquid movement, facing her, his eyes like sable jewels, backlit by fire. His eyebrows arched, painting his appearance almost sultan-like, except the mohawk. If she hadn't been so frightened, she would've thought him gorgeous in a jaw-dropping, terrifying, sort-of way.

A sense of wonder swam around him, mingled with consternation. And there was something else, but it was too muted for her to get a fix on.

His gaze shifted to Thom and Thom's brows dipped in a scowl. A cryptic exchange occurred between them. Poppy didn't know how she knew this, but it made her stomach drop. A sly grin crossed Adym's face, and Thom dropped his gaze, sweat beading on his temples. Self-satisfied, the elemental turned away. *What was that?*

Addis and Jinsen had contained themselves, as much as *rif*-puppies could. Like they waited for a treat, they bobbed and scurried around Adym, tracking his every move.

Adym's voice echoed among the evergreens. "Jinsen, Addis, calm yourselves."

Addis tugged on a corner of the *fey's* garment. *'The man, Thomas Magnusson, understands us, speaks our tongue, even cloaked. We don't know why.'*

His chest rumbled with a noise that might have been a laugh. He motioned to Thom and Poppy. "They are tied, these two. That is one reason. We will not discuss the other here."

A bizarre combination of sparks and snorts emanated from the *rifs*, like they were giggling.

Digging her heels in the snow, she glanced at Thom. *What did they mean, tied?* The expression in his eyes made her heart leap. Maybe she already knew.

Thom's expression melded into indifference. "Well, as interesting as this has been, now that you lot have found each other, Poppy and I will be moving on." He steered her away.

"What is your business in the Caldera wilds?" Adym cast his coal-bright eyes between them, lingering on her. "This weather is dangerous. Your reason must be important."

Thom cocked an eyebrow, half-grinning. "Why should I trust you with our business?"

"Fair enough." Adym clasped his powerful hands behind his back. "Nevertheless, I would be apprised of your direction. At the least."

'They go to the Kairyn passage. They hope to find the Uterling-Steward, Felix Paquin.'

Bastards. She scowled at Addis and Jinsen.

"I see." Adym grinned like a fox with a full belly. "As we happen to be traveling in the same direction, we wish to accompany you, offering warm assistance. *Kairyn's* weather is perilous just now."

"We don't need your help." Thom's body tensed, but his expression remained unconcerned.

Adym's eyes flickered to hers. "I'd like to make sure Poppy's safe."

Poppy's heart sickened. The *fey* sought *her*. They were in danger because of *her*. She had to do something.

She squared her shoulders. "I don't believe you. What do you really want?" She produced the stone, bright with jeweled flames, its colors painting her skin, the snow. "Is it this?" She chucked it at his feet. "Take it to your boss, and let us go. We have enough trouble as it is."

Adym's eyes widened with consternation, flickering between her face and the stone. He took a step back. "I will not touch it. It isn't mine to take."

His trepidation gave her a scintilla of hope she had more power in the situation than she'd realized. Perhaps she could figure out a way out of this mess, or least procure safety for Thom. *He's given enough as it is.*

"Well, what then?" Her eyes not leaving the *fey*, she scooped up the stone, returning it to her pocket. "What do you want?"

Adym's expression neutralized, as calculated as a spy's. "It's as I have said. I'm interested in your safety."

"Right." *Slagerei need to be healthy so they last longer.* She crossed her arms, not even close to mollified. The *fey's* lack of transparency was, at best disconcerting, at worst ominous. But she had a plan, if a rudimentary one. The Firekind desired her safety, at all costs. That was her leverage, and she would wait for the right moment to use it.

"Come," Adym said, civilly extending his arm. "I have slowed you enough."

A questioning eyebrow raised, she glanced at Thom. His eyes glittered with anger, but lips pressed into a grim line, and his shoulder rose in a weary shrug. Onward they went.

Chapter Thirty-One

T hom was itching to bring the full weight of his wrath down upon the head of the smug *fey*. But the vague feeling that somehow he'd oiled the machine of their wicked plans addled him, as agonizing as the pain throbbing in his collarbone.

At least they didn't try to take my cydern. His fist curled around the weapon. *I might be smaller than Adym, but a bee sting can still kill, and I'll make sure that self-assured asshat will regret fokking around with me and mine, the first chance I get.*

In prickly silence, the company set out through the woodland, Adym at the rear. The *rifs* dimmed, so much so that they threw only the faintest of shadows. The darkness concealed much of the surrounding terrain, but the way was choked, as if the vines, boulders, and dense thickets hindered them intentionally. Wind ripped through the treetops, shaking the spruces and dumping snow from the underbrush down their necks and into their sleeves. It didn't trouble Adym, but the *rifs* cowered beneath him in heavy banks of the stuff.

More than once, Adym halted, warning of elemental scouts. At these times, the Firekind vanished while he and Poppy darted under the cover of the nearest thicket and waited, shivering. When danger passed, the Firekind reappeared – dim blooms of warmth, like breezes from the south, and they continued toward the *Kairyn* outpost.

Sometime during the trek, the snowfall diminished, and a faint roar, different than the wind, mingled with the chinking tree branches and their muffled footfalls.

Leaning against Thom, she whispered. "What's that sound?"

"Probably the Tors," he replied, his lips brushing her ear. "It's rapids at this point. Eventually we'll have to cross it."

Her eyes widened. Pivoting, he addressed Adym. "Crossing the Tors at night will be our death. We'll find a place to rest until dawn."

Unconcerned, Adym's chin dipped in acknowledgment.

After culling a level area of the mountainous forest, they found meager shelter in a gathering of evergreens, with branches that dipped low to the ground. The *rifs* simmered together like a gigantic campfire, creating a muted warmth – enough to keep them from freezing, but not enough to make a watery mess. Thom cut evergreen branches and spread them beneath a colossal alpine spruce, where the snow wasn't as abundant.

They ate the supplies they'd gathered from the storeroom; chewy flatbread, dried gamey meat, apples, and Caldysian nuts and seeds. Her jaw working at the meat, Poppy eyed the elementals, her gaze darting away when Adym's coal-bright eyes found hers.

She choked down food until Thom told her to take it easy or she'd be sick. Her hunger was a good sign that she'd detoxed from the ettar venom. His stomach seemed to resent what he was able to swallow. Compartmentalizing his concern, he ignored the queasiness, instead reviewing his knowledge of the terrain ahead, thinking of places they might be able to slip away unnoticed.

Drops of moisture slid off the trees, plopping into the snow. Distant howls and yips echoed over the landscape, the sounds bouncing, coming from all directions. The Firekind crackled, whispering covertly among themselves, low enough that Thom couldn't discern if they purposely hindered the translation.

Curling up on her side, her knees to her chest, Poppy turned away from the Firekind, the branches creaking with her weight. The fragrance of evergreen tickled his nose.

Settling next to her, he whispered. "Poppy?"

"Hmm?" The glow of the Firekind cast an ochre light across her face.

"Did they vaccinate you? At Caldys?"

The question had been nagging at him, since he'd seen her in the med-ward gown. How many people had been around her, breathing on her, potentially exposing her to a myriad of foreign viruses her body had no immunity to? *Surely, they thought of that? Surely, they took precautions?*

She rubbed her eyes. "I don't know. I only woke up today, so I don't remember much. I think they were sedating me."

"*Djöfullinn,*" he muttered under his breath. Favoring his collarbone, he arranged the backpack as pillow for them, unfolding a wool blanket and tossing it over her with a heavy thump.

"Unfasten your coat. It'll be warmer."

Her gloved fingers fumbled at her coat buttons. As he tucked her head under his chin, warmth burgeoned between them, smelling of dried blood and the tang of evergreen. Not exactly what he'd had in mind when he'd dreamed about sharing her bed.

"Are you okay?" he asked, keeping his voice a whisper.

"I'm okay. I'm more worried about you. After...what they did to you. And what happened with Etin."

His breath hitched at the pain stabbing his clavicle. "Don't worry about me."

Before he realized it, his eyes drifted shut.

"Thom?"

"Hmm?" Inches from his, her eyes shone with a ghostly beauty.

"What did the *rifs* mean, about Crimson and her daughters? It meant something. To you."

So that wasn't pain haze. He sighed again, gathering the story to him like pieces of broken glass. He didn't want this part to be real, but it had become unavoidable. "I probably should've told you sooner. But I wanted to be certain. More than certain."

"Told me what?"

His throat bobbed with a swallow, the words like cotton in his mouth. "I didn't think it was possible that you could have a connection to the Firekind, even as an *unnusti*. I ignored the clues." Pain slid in waves between his temples. "I shouldn't have brought you here."

"This was my choice, Thom. Even if it didn't happen how we intended it to, none of this is your doing."

"No, I should've figured it out sooner. The connection. Between you and them."

"I don't understand."

Searching for a less painful position, he slid his arm under his head. The branches creaked. "There is a legend, part of Caelithian folklore."

Her expression galvanized. "Tell me."

Brushing her hair out of her eyes, he tucked a stray tendril behind her ear. At her temple, the roots were darkening. Thom wouldn't let himself think about what that might mean, about her slipping from his grasp forever. His failure to protect her, to protect everyone he ever loved. "When humans first found their way into Caelith, a small settlement flourished in the shadow of the Wysterwilds, in Caelith-Huldra."

She tilted her ear toward his mouth, her brow wrinkling in concentration.

"Among them lived a woman named Crymson, spelled with a Y. In ancient elemental tongue this translates as *she-flame*. She was named this because her red hair resembled flames."

Her lips parted. "That's my middle name."

Thoughts darted across her face, almost vivid enough to read.

He continued. "One day, Crymson and her siblings set out to explore the wilder places of the Wysterwilds. Drawn to the color of her hair, a shadow-beast captured her. *Ryn*, a *Mesian* gatekeeper of Caelith, had been tracking the shadow, driving it from the Caldera region of Caelith-Caldys. Seeing it had taken a human, he confronted it. After several days of battle with the creature, *Ryn* prevailed, freeing Crymson. He fed the beast to the Maris volcano."

"A shadow-beast?"

He nodded. "A *nephyl*. They're rare. In older times, the *Mesian* – the *lostaja* – protected Caelithians from them."

"*Mesian*?"

"A *lostaja* is the elder of each elementalkind. Keepers of the gates. Guardians of their kind. The *Mesian* is the Firekind *lostaja*." Concentrating through a burst of pain, Thom shut his eyes. "Evading *Ryn*, the shadow-beast had taken Crymson far away – traveling between havens. Weary, disorientated, and wounded from her ordeal, she didn't know the way back to her settlement. *Ryn* and the Firekind took care of her, providing her with a refuge among them, as they searched for her homeland. Despite missing her kin, she enjoyed seeing new lands and *Ryn*'s companionship. As time passed, their hearts knitted together, tied with a love-bond. The search for her kin continued, but Crymson found contentment with *Ryn* and with the Firekind."

Momentarily, the pain in his shoulder took his breath away. Shutting his eyes, he tried to find his place in the story, to conceal his discomfort. *Don't let her see. She has enough to deal with.*

Thom found his way back, continuing the story. "*Ryn* and Crymson had a daughter, an *unnusti* resembling her. It seemed nothing could steal their joy. But then, pursuing another shadow-beast, *Ryn* discovered Crymson's lost kin, beyond the Wyster in Huldra. His fear of losing her and his daughter to them became so great, he concealed this."

Poppy's eyes narrowed.

"Somehow, Crymson learned of *Ryn*'s secret. Angered with his betrayal, she fled, taking their child, and returned to the family of her birth, spurning *Ryn* and his kind. Consumed with anguish, *Ryn* pursued them, causing fire and ash to erupt from the land for many days, darkening the sky. The ground shuddered and cracked open from Caldys to Huldra – even spilling across the borders into the *Uther-Erai*. Crymson's kin and the whole of their village were terrified and fled, seeking protection with another *lostaja*, who gave Crymson's family aid, hiding them from *Ryn* and his Firekind kin."

"Nursing a powerful grudge, *Ryn* and the Firekind spurned all others, growing wild and savage. But *Ryn* never gave up trying to reclaim his lost family. To this day, he searches for his offspring, the line of Crymson's flame-haired daughters. In retribution, any *red-hair* is ripe for the taking." His voice fell to a murmur. "It is said that *Ryn* made a vow that if he could not have his daughter, he would have her daughters and her daughters after that, haunting her line forever. All Firekind pledged devotion to him and this purpose."

Her eyes widened, as though she'd finally glimpsed what stalked them, and she recognized it.

"That is the legend, as I learned it." Grimacing, he adjusted his shoulder.

She swallowed thickly. "And you–you–think, I'm one of Crymson's daughters?"

"I'm not sure." The pain spiraled from his shoulder to clench the left side of his chest. "But I don't think it's my opinion that matters."

"But my hair's gray. Wouldn't—" she cringed, as though she already knew the answer, "that put them off?"

Gently, he brushed her hair away from her temples. "Poppy, the roots of your hair are coming in, as red as a sunset."

Her eyes round, Poppy sat up. "What?" She pawed at her hair, pulling at it as though she might stretch it enough to see.

Under her weight, the branches splayed, poking his shoulder. Seeing his grimace, she sunk back down next to him. He cast a wary eye past her shoulder at the Firekind. Unblinking, Adym returned his glare, his expression penetrating, self-assured. The *rifs* glowed like embers in a campfire, slumbering.

"What does that mean? My hair?" She whispered.

He forced himself to grin. "That you're as lovely as ever, no matter what color your hair is."

"You know what I mean, Thom."

"Maybe your body knows you're home." He let his smile fade. "I don't know. And I don't care. I just want to get away from our elemental hitchhikers." Thom's eyes shut of their own accord. "We should rest."

Chapter Thirty-Two

I t took some scooting and shifting, Thom grimaced as each movement yanked at his collarbone, but eventually Poppy succumbed to exhausted slumber, the sunset glow of the Firekind painting the hair at her temples in like hues. Thom had intended to stay awake, to watch over her as she slept, but sleep crept up on him despite his pain.

Fatigue should've brought a dreamless sleep, but Adym had troubled him beyond the obvious, and past trauma hemorrhaged once again into his mind, the reoccurring nightmare he had never been able to leave behind.

In the dream, he lay on the Maris battlefield, death heavy all around him; an open-air sarcophagus. He wanted to move, but his limbs were unresponsive, as if they no longer obeyed his spinal cord. Each heartbeat pumped his blood onto the ground around him in a thick, coppery puddle. Evading death grew more improbable with each second.

His mouth was gritty with the sand that blew across the frigid, rocky ground. Even clothed in winter gear, frostbite had him in its gullet, swallowing him whole. The heat of life had been siphoned out of his fingers, his biceps, his thighs, his chest. His vision sifted to a monochrome, mottled gray. In his left side, dull pain quivered like it was the only part of him alive.

As his sight went dark, a stab of bright, potent heat swiped at his face. He didn't want it, to feel, to see the brightness. But the heat grabbed his jaw, ripped off his wool hood, and struck him; a dull, painless *thunk* on his cheek.

Pictures bloomed in his head, swimming in translucent, glided waves; his mother making a pie; her forearms white with flour, dusting his nose, laughing as he sneezed. His father blowing on a mug of coffee, smiling through the steam, poking at the embers of the fire. The ripples of the Emerald Lake, cold on his ankles, jumping with speckled trout. A ginger cat weaving around his ankles in the barn. The jolt of the mare's hindquarters, her hooves thudding in the meadow, the bracing wind in his ears.

Tears wet his face. Pain in his side twitched and reared, and he groaned, clenching his teeth. Another blow. The air buzzed and crackled, stretching, morphing into words buzzing around him.

"Master. Leave him. If you remove the shard, he'll bleed out in one breath, as dead as the rest of them. You'll learn nothing."

Blinking, Thom glimpsed the glassy piece of obsidian rock embedded in his left abdomen and hip, pinning him to the ground – as fatal a wound as he'd ever seen. He wasn't walking away this time. *Fokking orysi. And Etin…how could she?*

Warmth covered his forehead. The golden pictures spun wildly, pouring out of him with his blood, separating, materializing in the darkness above him like animated constellations; his memories, the sum of his life playing out before him.

The warm, caramel flank of a draft horse. His mother clutching a suitcase, her face streaming with tears. Hay dust in a fall afternoon. The rings in Katla's nose and at her eyebrows, glinting over a wry smile as she packed her camping gear. Around a bonfire, the twang of a harp joining the heartbeat of a handheld drum. A rosy moon in the night sky. Ayden pointing, as the opal crescent gave way to red shadow. Poppy, half-asleep, leaning against Ayden, clutching the wooden horse he'd carved for her, her hair gleaming like fire in the twilight.

And then Ayden again, his shoulders hunched, muttering in miserable tones, "Poppy has been taken to the *Uther-Erai*. A well in *Symsara*. No one can know."

"There!" Another voice; this one made the earth tremble, reaching hot fingers into his veins. "He knows where they've taken her!"

The golden memory-pictures broke before an apocalyptic pain in his side. Fire all around him, fire inside of him, invading through the wound in his side. He could endure, as long as death came on wings. But this death delayed, searing with the pain of hundred lives that wouldn't stop living.

"Master! *Utherlings* cannot endure suffering as this. Let him pass!"

"NO! He must live!"

A noble, terrifying visage filled his pain-hazed vision; eyes like amber coals, sable hair aflame, but not burning. Firekind.

He held Thom's face so he couldn't turn away. Thom's gray vision exploded into the kinetic color of life. Sweat beaded on his temples, and a thunderous rushing and crackling filled his ears. The pain swelled, seizing his body in a tug of war. The elemental spoke and the ground trembled beneath him.

"Find her! Swear it upon the blood I stem. The flesh I burn. The life I recapture."

"Find—" Thom's voice creaked liked he'd forgotten how to use it, "who?"

"Find her! Thomas Magnusson! Swear it!"

The voice, the fire, filled his consciousness, like venom inside of him, enough to end a thousand lives. A yell exploded from his throat.

Thom awoke, his chest heaving, pain turning in his chest and shoulder like a screw, his forehead damp with sweat. Between the towering spruce trees, the sky hinted at dawn. Closer, the light was tinged with a subtle flickering. He grimaced. *Cael-cursed Firekind.*

Poppy lay against him, her eyelashes motionless on her cheeks, her lips parted, no longer the child he'd seen in the golden, living constellations of his dream. The offspring the *Mesian* sought with inexorable passion – an *unnusti*, a daughter of Crymson. *What have I enabled? All this time – working to save her, to bring her home – have my actions been her doom?*

Hundreds of times, he'd strained to recall the events after the fatal ambush on the Maris plateau. The field medic – and his friend – Russ Blackhorse, had taken one look at his wounds and asked, "How the ruddy blazes did you walk out of that, Magnusson? Cauterized wounds yourself? You're either the luckiest bastard alive, or your mother was an aether."

Russ had hit the nail on the proverbial head. Being impaled with a shard of obsidian the size of an oar should've shattered his pelvis. So how had he, and he alone, ended up unconscious, at the threshold of the *Offysfyn* medical tent, a half-hour's walk from the field of battle? Especially when he remembered other details without difficulty; the awful *thunk* of Jacques's head falling in the dust, the shouts of *regroup* as knives of rock shredded the mossy turf, efficiently impaling Shi-Shi through the eye, and severing Kwame's leg at the thigh. The unbearable pressure throwing him to the ground, pinning him tight, stealing the breath from his chest. After that, the details had always failed him, except for scant, fiery recollections – the sense of being burnt alive.

After a debriefing at the Caldys med-ward, Ayden had decided dumping him half-alive at the outskirts of the camp had been the Grens' attempt to send a message. As a result of the blood loss Thom had endured, Cora – his surgeon – explained that his recollection of the incident would either never return, or if it did, it wouldn't be accurate.

So, Thom ignored the dreams, spurned the flames – breathing through them, just as he breathed through the pain of the first steps he took, and the increasingly longer walks through the med-ward grounds. All the while, he shunned the impression that something observed his recovery with interest.

He couldn't shake it, the feeling that he needed to heal fast. There was something he was meant to do. An important task, a vital mission; he'd been saved for a reason.

So, when Ayden approached him with discharge papers, every cell in Thom's body protested. It didn't make sense; he'd always wanted to go his own way, to find Katla again, to escape his conscription into the *Offysfyn*.

Ayden burned the discharge papers in the hearth. Over pints, Thom had asked Ayden about Poppy, giving voice to an unshakable, vague concern for her. Ayden's face had lit up and he slammed his fist on the table. *Of course!* he'd said. *I need someone there with your skills. This couldn't be more perfect if I'd planned it!*

And, just like that, Thom had been reassigned to *Uther-Erai*, Riverston, protection detail for Poppy and Deidre Paquin. Serendipity. At least that's what he'd thought at the time. Now he wondered if there hadn't been a more sinister design behind the circumstances, a crafty elemental trap he should've discerned.

Lingering from his dream, memory of the fiery visage burned brightly in his conscience, along with the booming voice, imploring him to find her. To find Poppy.

What had he done? And was it too late to set it right?

Chapter Thirty-Three

Poppy groaned at the soreness in her muscles. Overnight, her bones had frozen with the cold, brittle like
they might break if she moved too quickly. The scent
of evergreen pinched her nose and her throat felt like she'd
swallowed some of the needles during the night. Pearly light
illuminated the snowy, dim forest, looming around them like
creatures in a haunted house.

Inches from hers, Thom's eyes were open, the v-shaped
wrinkle creasing the skin between his eyebrows. In the light,
his eyes looked gray-green, like moss in a boreal forest. The
lines around his mouth and eyes gave him a sorrowful, strained
look. But then a corner of his mouth lifted in a smile, lighting his face like sunshine on snow.

When she'd first seen him at Target, she'd thought him
handsome. But now every detail of his appearance crystal-

lized; the angles of his face, the rumpled hair under his cap, his scruffy beard, the lines framing his eyes. Handsome wilted in comparison. He was breathtaking now that she knew him – really knew him.

The reason they were sleeping in the wilderness interrupted the moment. His sadness, the burden, she hadn't imagined it. Burying her forehead into his sweater, his arms tightened around her waist, drawing her so close she felt the ridges of his chest muscles. As morning approached, the light shifted faintly above the treetops.

"Thom?" she whispered.

He stroked her hair. "Hmm?"

"What did Adym mean about us being tied?"

A corner of his mouth twitched. "You can't guess?"

"I don't want to guess."

His eyes brightened, the hue of summer grass. "I love you." His voice rumbled, so she felt it in his chest. "I think I always have in some way, but, knowing you now, it changed into something more – amorous. Love, a wholesome sort of love, when shared, creates an involuntary bond between souls, a tie that elementals can see."

Her heart leapt. "I never told you."

He kissed the top of her head. "You didn't have to."

"But still," she pulled away, looking between his eyes. "I do." Heat spread in her ribcage. "Love. You."

A grin tugged at his lips. "Demonstrations are good too."

She pressed her lips to his until she thought her heart might burst – like they were back in Riverston at the landing, or on the red bench in front of Target. Or in the barn she'd remembered in Caelith. All the time they never had to be together. Letting her lips tell him what she couldn't form into words, reveling in his response.

His beard scratched pleasantly against her cheeks, contrasting with the softness of his tongue. A tingling started in her lips, coursing through her body to her feet, winding tighter and tighter. His coat scraped on the branches as she tried to get closer to him, and the blanket tangled in the undergrowth.

But another energy pricked the moment, tinging their intimacy. Tears came to her eyes, mingling with their lips, and she tasted salt. What was to become of them? Would they ever really get to be together? A blast of heat poked at them, stirring her hair, rippling the blanket. Reluctantly, she pulled away, resenting the Firekind to the marrow of her bones.

The *rifs* muttered and heat licked her back, as hot as sunlight. The hazel of his eyes clouding, Thom scowled over her shoulder. Clutching the front of his sweater, she buried her face in his chest.

Twigs snapped and the clearing began to stir with Firekind movement. Untangling himself, Thom withdrew, rolling his shoulder with a sharp grimace. Cold rushed between them and their moment vanished as quickly as it had begun.

Bleary-eyed and hunched beneath the blanket, she sat up. Adym's gaze found her immediately, hints of his intent hiding themselves before she could read them. Nothing had changed; the *fey* had more in mind than helping them remain unfrozen, especially if she was who they thought she was.

"The searchers from Caldys were looking." His expression smug, Adym rose to his full height, his tattoos smoky against his skin. "But they had to yield. They didn't have a *fey* to assist them."

The *rifs* gazed up at him and purred.

Busy digging through the pack, Thom cursed under his breath. Water and some food appeared, they shared a portion before they vacated the shelter. With each step, Poppy winced; every muscle in her body had rebelled during the night.

Soon, she forgot her sore muscles. Weak sun wavered through thin clouds, illuminating a vast mountain forest, glittering in the snow. From their vantage point, the north and west were choked with majestic rocky peaks; mountains that resembled the Tetons, though almost – backward. She gaped. "Is that…what I think it is?"

Thom nodded. "Don't ask me to explain." His mouth twitched. "Not today."

To the east, the land dropped into a wide valley, rimmed by the distant blue of more mountains. Tree-covered slopes spread outwards in silvery undulations. The view of the south was blocked by the towering spruce trees they'd sheltered under.

The acuity of her vision amazed her. Icicles sparkled one-hundred paces away, tiny drops winking on the tips. An eagle wheeled a thousand feet above, its amber eye fixed on them. Two-hundred yards away, a magnificent beast of an elk paused on a crest, his tiered antlers soft and velvety.

The journey had landed them in a nature documentary, a rare a privilege to see such beauty, undisturbed. Poppy felt as though a lost soul-cog had been oiled, set into its proper place inside of her, and was now joyfully spinning. But she also felt intimidated. The outdoorsy backpacking thing had never been her. And Caelith probably didn't have ski lodges. Or hospitals in the middle of nowhere.

She nudged Thom. "Where are we?"

"Caelith." His mouth twitched.

She thumped him on the arm. "*Where* in Caelith, smart ass?"

He grinned. "We're in the center of the Caldera region… the oldest of the havens. West Caldys – where we began – is southeast of here." He pointed. "We're in the middle of the Eirian Range, which runs north, northwest. Northwest is the wildest part of the Caldera, the location of the Maris volcano and the border of the Wyster, where Caldys meets the Huldra havenlands. Beyond the Asys…" he turned her east-northeast, pointing to the distant mountains, "is Greya."

Shielding her eyes, she concentrated on his description, wishing for a glimpse of the map inside his head, a glimpse of the Maris volcano. *A volcano!*

"Your father took a direct route from Caldys to Greya, the usual way. We would've been caught if we went in that direction. So, we go to the Norsen, which is north, northeast of here, making up time on the river. The *Kairyn* passage cuts through the Eirians to the flatlands before the Asys. There's an outpost there." Thom eyed the *fey.* "That's our destination. At least for today."

Adym waxed self-assured. Unease prodded Poppy again.

They headed north. Ahead, just visible through the woodland, a gorge bisected their path. Misty trees perched on the opposite edge and the sound of rapids echoed around the forest, making their location difficult to pinpoint, but she guessed the watercourse lay at the bottom.

They weaved through the woodland, passing towers of granite erupting out of the forest floor and knots of boulders and fallen evergreens, thick with snow. After a breathless incline, the ground leveled, and they came to the drop-off. As she had anticipated, it was a gorge with a wide bottom, bisected by a massive, frothy watercourse, two-hundred feet below.

The edge dipped into a slender track crawling down the walls of the gorge, at times no more than a series of tree roots to scramble over. Gripping the rock face, she found her footing behind Thom, every step of the descent was painstaking.

With something resembling disinterest, the Firekind watched them. When she and Thom were a quarter of the way down, the elementals leapt off the edge, sailing on powerful thermals created by the warmth of their flames, Adym using translucent fire-wings the size of bed sheets. The downward progression of their colorful forms was dizzying. Strangely appealing.

Feeling traitorous, Poppy clutched the granite at her cheek, focusing on Thom. His pallor reminded her of the snow crowding the riverbed below. Worry crowded out her reluctant fascination with the Firekind.

As Adym's feet touched the bottom of the gorge, his flames disappeared. The *rifs* flared, shuddered, and turned lazily to see if they'd been watched. They tracked her progress like a bobcat stalking a fat squirrel in a tree.

The tepid sun had almost reached the peak of the sky when their feet touched the snow-covered debris crowding the banks of the rapids. The icy waterway flowed fast and turbulent; so potent, in seconds it could've swept them downstream to where rocks punctuated the waterway, if the ice chunks didn't shred them first. It stretched so wide she doubted she could throw a rock across.

Adym's fists closed around a barren pine tree at the edge of the water; it must've been four stories tall. With a spray of frozen dirt and a cracking that echoed up and down the gorge, he ripped the tree out of the ground and let it crash down over a cluttered part of the rapids. On the opposite bank, it bounced on a heap of driftwood. Snow tumbled into the water and melted as it sluiced downstream. The Firekind rushed across, their footfalls barely touching the spiked trunk. As they reached the opposite bank the *rifs'* forms shrunk into dull resting states, conserving energy.

Frowning, Thom nudged it with his boot, studying the river and the opposite bank. He made a noise in his throat. "I'm not using this." He scanned the gorge, looking for another way across.

Tentatively, she touched one of the splintered roots. *He's right. It's not going to hold.*

Just as the thought solidified inside of her, the tree shuddered and creaked and the rapids curled over it, inhaling it like an appetizer. The trunk split, the pieces spun around, and were dragged down river like the struggling limbs of a drowning person.

The blood drained from her face. She faced Thom, murmuring, "Is this our chance to run for it? To escape *them*?"

A muscle in his jaw twitched. "Fording the river at this point is the only way to get to the *Kairyn* passage. They know we don't have another option, except to go back and be captured."

"What do they expect us to do then?" Poppy threw Adym a withering look. His poker-face would've rivaled Thom's if it hadn't been so unctuous. The *rifs* appeared to be playing a game with a pile of pebbles, taking no notice of events in front of them.

Thom crossed his arms. "I'm sure he has something in mind."

Adym dipped his foot into the waters, concentrating on the frothy mass. A tremor began in an indistinct place inside her chest, an internal sifting, as her awareness of different elemental energies separated, focused, and crystalized.

In response to Adym, another invisible elemental power strengthened around them, taking on a distinct, but terrible familiarity in her awareness. Poppy gripped Thom's arm. "What's happening? What is that?"

"He's challenging the river's *losta*."

The rapids grew ambivalent and testy. The tremor became a roaring that popped her ears, teeming with whispering-death voices, longing to flood the lungs in the vicinity. The night at the landing in Riverston came back to her with awful clarity; the watery arm dragging her into the river. Heart jackrabbiting, she shrank against him. "The voices. It's like at the Twin."

Thom's arm surrounded her. "It's just a solitary *michawe*. These are Roe's waters. She's probably insulted they crossed without her permission. Adym's negotiating." Thom's tone was reassuring, but the set of his back was as tense as if they were facing a firing squad.

With a shudder she felt in her bones, warmth surged through the gorge, like tempestuous spring breezes. On the opposite bank, the Firekind crowded at the edge of the rapids, their flames billowing like wildfire, reflecting across the water.

Wisps of steamy fog appeared, dappling the surface of the water. The rapids cowered, scurrying away from the flames, retreating to the walls of the gorge in places, leaving her and Thom standing before a small passage dividing the river and leading to the Firekind. The stone boiled in her pocket. Thom grabbed her hand, and propelled her into the pebbled riverbed, as fast as they could navigate the slick stones.

The *fey's* aura was so powerful it made her head spin. Using every ounce of his authority, he reined the waters, in tandem with the *rifs*. Their flames moved in a mesmerizing slow dance, quieting the voices in her chest, replacing them with a deep chant, almost hypnotic in quality.

At midpoint, a deep rumble began farther down the gorge and the water shuddered, as if it was about to invade the breach. Water began to trickle and rise amidst the stones, wetting their feet. Pulling her to him, Thom struck the water with his *cydern*, and an explosion of light consumed the world for a blinding moment, shrinking everything to the hot white center of the impact. As Poppy's eyes cleared, and the gorge reappeared around them, she saw currents of light skittering across the water and up the walls of the gorge.

Hissing, the waters recoiled further. Panting, they made it to the bank, Thom's face pale with exertion, his knuckles white around the weapon. The Firekind released their hold and, with a groan, the rapids crashed back into the riverbed, spluttering watery curses.

Thom snapped at Adym. "Nice job pissing off an ancient. Roe can flood this ravine quicker than we can climb out."

A disconcerting tremor went through the ground and the rapids churned and roared.

"Rest assured," Adym said. "Poppy will leave this gorge safely."

Poppy glared. "Not without Thom I won't."

A motley jumble of snow-covered branches, ice floes, driftwood, boulders tossed like playground balls, littered the riverbank – the remnants of Roe's tantrums. The obstacles required climbing, slowing their pace to a crawl. One eye on the frothing rapids, she shuddered at the memory of the waterway snapping the pine tree as if it had been no more than a pinky bone.

The rapids chased them for a time, splashing up against the sides of the gorge, so they had to hold on to roots not to be swept back into the sluice, soaking them through. More than once, Thom's arm around her waist, or his grip on her wrist, kept her from being pulled into the current, although she suspected, if she'd been in mortal danger, Adym would've dried up half the gorge. The water seemed reticent to approach the Firekind, who led them like they were prisoners of war.

After Roe desisted, they slowed to an energy-conserving pace, the Firekind almost jaded with the ease of the trek. They manipulated air currents in a way that gave them a frightening advantage, but their heat kept her and Thom from freezing, drying their garments. When one of them disappeared or moved away, the resulting chill made her teeth chatter. As angry as she was, she was grateful for the warmth, especially as Thom's color hadn't improved. He tried to hide the chatter of his teeth, and the worry for him began to dominate her thoughts.

By the time they left the gorge behind, the sun had angled across the sky. The gorge, the river crossing, and rough terrain had taken its toll, forcing them to rest and eat something, even though the Firekind protested the delay. Thom stomached only a scrap of bread, his face haggard and white at the edges, like internal pain gnawed at him. Poppy watched for an opportunity to speak with him privately, but none came.

Free of the gorge, they plunged into a thick, sloping mountain forest, the snow lessening as the elevation decreased. By late afternoon, the trees thinned and the way leveled out into a rocky mesa with a spectacular mountain view. They'd reached an overlook at the edge of the valley she'd seen from their camp that morning, a small distance considering their efforts.

The Asys loomed purple-blue in the distance, highlighted with snow. Closer, the valley dipped and curved in and around the foothills of the Eirians, giving way to moors of speckled gray-green, lacking the snow of the higher elevations. The terrain was untamed and severe, but also beautiful in a way that made her breath catch.

Stopping at the edge, Thom produced a small reticulating telescope from the pack. As he focused the instrument, Poppy saw the tendons in his wrist go rigid.

Squinting, she followed Thom's line of sight. A shadow spread in a northern curve of the terrain, a dark earth-bound cloud, roiling and creeping over the ground east of the moors, headed south. "What is that?"

Thom handed her the spyglass. "See for yourself."

Through the lens, the shadow became horrifyingly clearer – an unnatural, dark fog surrounding lines of marchers, though still too far to discern much detail. "What is that?"

"The Grens. Marching to attack Caldys. Making this a war." Gray with anger – or exhaustion – Thom mopped his forehead with his sleeve. "That was Dane's design, this whole time. Divert the Steward. Signal the Grens to attack." He rubbed the bridge of his nose and shut his eyes. "They'll have sacked the *Kairyn* outpost overnight and captured any out-riders. Caldys won't know they're coming."

Adym approached. "Why have we stopped?" Uninterested, he blinked at the valley, his eyes focusing as he spied the army. Oblivious, Addis and Jinsen chased each other around a boulder the size of a car.

Taking the telescope from her, Thom closed it with a snap. "The *Offysfyn* won't recover from an assault like this. And the civilians sheltering in Caldys – elderly, women, children – both elemental and *utherling* – thousands. The entire Caldera could fall." His expression galvanized. "We have to warn them." Thom picked up the pack. "We've no time to lose."

Adym crossed his arms. "I cannot allow that."

Ignoring him, Thom passed the *rifs*, traversing the slope that led into the valley.

Before Poppy could cry out in warning, the *rifs* growled and charged. At their heels, Adym leapt into the air and landed in front of Thom, blocking his path. *Cydern* fisted, Thom threw his arms up, flinching at the blast of heat. The *fey's* body shone with a colossal plume of orange and red flame, wreathing his form, the heat whooshing through the landscape like a shockwave. Stumbling from the hot current, Poppy almost lost her balance.

"Do as I say, or you'll die, Thomas Magnusson." Adym's voice ripped the air like wildfire thermals. "Though my master will not be pleased at your death."

Sweat burst on Thom's forehead. His face reddened and scrunched as his *cydern* expanded into a transparent shield-like barrier.

"No!" Poppy screamed, lunging for him.

"Stay away, Poppy!" Thom shouted above the roar.

"They won't hurt me!" She halted between them. The heat roared, withering the ends of her hair, stinging her exposed skin.

Eyes widening, Adym withdrew, his flames evaporating in an instant. The *rifs* mimicked him.

"Stop! Please!" Poppy swiveled, her eyes watering. "There has to be a solution that doesn't involve combustion!"

"You will come with us! Both of you!" Adym growled, his flames quivering.

"Yeah! You made that pretty clear!" Her chest heaved, part fear, part exertion. "But, look!" She gestured to the army. "Don't you care?"

Adym's eyes flickered to the shadow creeping over the moors. Displeased, Addis and Jinsen roiled and merged, their flames spiking like the fur of angry cats. Thom's expression had gone dispassionate, but the grip around his *cydern* was spring-loaded.

The *fey's* gaze returned to Poppy. "I must see to my mission. Others will see to theirs."

Cursing, Thom lunged at Adym. Poppy thrust herself between them.

Just short of knocking her down, Thom froze, his jaw clenched, his eyes flashing. "It's in your power to warn them? And you do nothing! Fokkaðu þér, andskotans fíflið þitt!"

Adym's expression soured into disgust. "You know nothing, *utherling cym-slag.*"

"At least warn them! At the very least, send one of your little fáviti," he gestured at the *rifs*. "for Cael's consecrated lands!"

The shadow of the army slithered behind them, an inexorable creep of death.

I can fix this. Poppy faced Adym. "Let Thom leave, to warn them. I'll go with you."

Thom whirled on her. "No. Absolutely not."

Adym's eyes flickered between them, and an edgy silence took over, punctuated by the rustle of the *rifs* and the crackling wafting from the hot rock beneath them.

In an almost surreal, sluggish motion, Thom's knees buckled and he collapsed on the rocky ground, unconscious. Stunned, she went to her knees, moving his head onto her lap, feeling the fever reddening his cheeks, the sweat darkening the hair at his temples. *I should've made him stop, rest...I should've tried to do something...anything.*

Even unconscious, his body trembled, and his knuckles whitened around the *cydern*, as if its power kept him alive.

Adym's chest rose and fell. "Even if I could allow that, Poppy, Thomas Magnusson wouldn't make it there alive."

Chapter Thirty-Four

Thom shuddered from the blow at his cheek as it knocked the other side of his face to the cold rock underneath him. His eyelids fluttered, and spark-like gold dust spread around him, disappearing as quickly as a thought, like his dreams of dying on the Maris plateau. A sickening dread, crept upon him with consciousness, mingling with his pain and fever. But the peril marching across the moors toward Caldys was so much worse than his pain.

The *Offysfyn*. His *soldati*, his friends. The refugees in Caldys. He'd glimpsed the peril approaching them. They would be slaughtered without warning. The Grens' had probably taken out the *soldati* at the *Kairyn* outpost, before they'd even spotted their forces. If any outriders escaped, they would've been mostly likely hunted down and killed. Caldys was blind. It would be a bloodbath. And it wouldn't stop there.

"Thom?" A gentle hand smoothed his rumpled hair away from his eyes. *Poppy*.

He pushed up to his elbow, biting his cheek against the pain spiraling in his collarbone. The awful *fey* loomed just behind her, again manifested as a Firekind-warrior, the flames that had threatened both of them extinguished. *Must protect Poppy*. It was all he could think, over and over again, against all hope.

Adym's tattoos seemed sharper, more ominous, as if they were a beware-of-elemental warning. "We've delayed too long." he said, frowning.

"Stay down, Thom," she coaxed him, her hands gentle.

Pushing her away, he crawled to his hands and knees, concentrating on every movement, assessing their situation, the danger the Firekind presented. Adym conferred with the *rifs* in secretive rumbles. As Thom staggered to his feet, Addis scaled a tree and launched himself into the sky, rising slowly as he warmed the air.

"Where's he going?" Poppy cried.

Adym watched as the *rif* harnessed an invisible current of wind, high above the tree tops. Soon his brilliant form disappeared, carried at a pace faster than a bird's wing.

"He has business to attend to." Without a glance at them, Adym set off again, this time in the lead.

I'm done with this bullshit. Clenching his jaw, Thom slid in front of the *fey*, halting nose to nose with him. "What's your real business with Poppy?"

Adym folded his arms, regarding him with mild amusement. "At the moment, none of yours. Conserve your strength instead of wasting your energy on things beyond you."

"Beyond me?" He tightened his fingers around his *cydern*. "I doubt that."

"You've accomplished your mission. Now it's time for others to do theirs."

Baffled, Thom's eyes flickered between Adym and Jinsen, as though they might explain. The *rif* only blinked at him, rotating to gaze after where Addis had disappeared.

Poppy edged her way between them, putting a hand on his chest; the touch sent a shiver of pain through him.

But he wasn't done yet. "Where are you taking us?" His voice rasped, gravelly. "And why?"

The *fey* arched an eyebrow. "You do not know?"

"No, I'm just asking for the fun of it, fáviti!" He clenched his jaw against another wave of blinding pain.

Jinsen billowed, causing a ricochet of sparks off the rocky ground.

"My master called you *eldfjall hrogn*, Thomas Magnusson," said Adym, his expression darkening. "And now I understand why. Your willfulness tries my patience."

"*Eldfjall hrogn*?" Poppy stuttered.

"Stubborn mountain." Adym's eyes didn't leave his face. "You mean to tell me you don't sense his desire humming around us? Stirring in the earth? For Crymson's lost daughters?"

Thom's stomach sickened. *Not this. Anything but this.*
Despite being chilled, heat spread at his cheekbones, somehow
making him feel sicker. "I know the story. Just as all Caelithians are taught."

"Yes, just as all Caelithians are taught. Whatever that's
worth." Adym's lips curled, mocking. "You already agreed to
help my master. Why do you slow us now? At your own peril?"

Thom's mind raced; his psyche felt unusually fragile, as
brittle as thinly blown glass. Looking between them, Poppy
held her breath, her eyes wide, as though waiting for a blow.

He forced himself to speak. "I agreed to nothing."

Adym stabbed a finger at Thom's chest. "You were snatched
from death. By my master. Your broken body restored. To
protect her in the *Uther-Erai* when we could not. To return
her to Caelith."

She flinched as Adym turned his eyes on her. "You were
lost, Poppy. We have labored to bring you home. And home
you will be."

Jumbled memories pounded his brain and the protest froze
on his lips. Any moment now, his heart would crumple...*I
could never remember. But that can't be what happened. I wouldn't
have bartered her freedom for my life. I would've died before that.*

He felt the heat in his cheeks cool, his body straining to
hold up his weight, to draw words from his soul. "Everything I've done was for Poppy," he bellowed, "her safety, her
freedom! Nothing was for you or your *fokking lostaja* master!"

Adym approached, his black eyes burning above his, his smoky scent clogging his nostrils. "You owe my master your life. And now you claim you acted out of your own power?"

"I owe him nothing! And yes! I did!"

Adym's eyebrows made an angry double arch. "I was there, Thomas Magnusson. I saw you dying. I saw the accord between you and my master materialize, in liquid gold. There were many witnesses."

"No!" Dragging his hands through his hair, Thom spun. "I was dying! I should've died! With everyone else. No—" Memories poured into his brain. *Am I being deceived somehow? Could I really have done as Adym claims?* His hand went to where the scar crossed his side. "I agreed to nothing." His shoulders slumped as he sensed Poppy's confusion.

A sly grin twitched at Adym's mouth. "He remembers. Finally."

'He remembers. He remembers his promise.' Jinsen chanted, sing-song.

At his shoulder, Poppy nudged him. "Thom?"

He fought to make sense, to explain. "I lost consciousness… and then…" Shaking his head, his chin dropped to his chest.

"This *utherling*, Thomas Magnusson," Adym fixed his dark eyes on Poppy. "has acted, on your behalf, as an agent of my master, *Ryn* of Maris. Unbeknownst to him, our scouts followed him for many years, until that day in the Maris vale, where his life blood spilled out of his side. As his soul departed, my master glimpsed knowledge of his lost daughter living in the memories within. His blood was returned to his body and bound there, and the accord made between them. To find you, protect you, and bring you into Caelith. To be delivered unto my master."

The blood rushed in his head. *All this time. How could I have put her in so much danger?*

"Thom?" Her voice trembled.

How could I have let her down so spectacularly? Her gray eyes were wide in her lovely, freckled face. "I didn't know, Poppy. I couldn't remember." *No excuses. Fight!* He whirled on Adym. "I did *not* agree to this. And I will fight it with what remains of my life."

"That you will have to take up with my master." Adym arched an eyebrow triumphantly, facing Poppy. "I suppose you're feeling betrayed now, but that will fade when you're home. Despite his service, Thomas Magnusson is a living example of the Firekind's dealings with *utherlings*. They're inconstant and deceptive creatures. Always falling short of honor. Bringers of sadness. Mates of death."

The words landed like sharp blows. *He's right. Your sacrifices will never mean anything. You might as well have given up the ghost out there on Maris…Poppy wouldn't be here now. She wouldn't be in danger.*

But she wasn't looking at Adym. "Thom."

Not meeting her eyes, he opened and closed his mouth, but he couldn't muster words; he had none. He felt as bare and defenseless as a newborn. *I can't. I can't look at her.*

Her palm came to rest on his cheek, nudging his chin up. Her face glowed with emotion, with memories – almost material, feeding on the tie between them. No scorn or disdain, or disappointment. Poppy saw him as he was, without turning away or spiting him, even in his mistakes. His heart pounded, daring to hope.

With tiger-like ferocity, she whirled on Adym. "Inconstant? Deceptive? You're calling *Thom* short of honor? If that's what you believe then you don't know him at all!" Advancing, she poked his chest for emphasis. "And coercing him into an agreement when he's mortally wounded? That's not exactly moral high ground, you," she struggled for an insult with some punch, "walking natural-disaster!"

Adym backed up, his eyebrows lifting, his eyes glinting with the reflection of multi-colored flames. All the breath whooshed from Thom's chest as she pivoted, seizing his hand. Prism-like flames shimmered over her skin, highlighting the crimson roots at her hair, the silver in her eyes – a striking elemental essence he'd never seen the like of before.

She faced him again. "I love you, Thom. And nothing I discover is going to change that."

Like a spring thaw, his soul softened, relaxing the muscles in his shoulders and neck, smoothing the wrinkles of his face. Even through his physical pain, a corner of his mouth twitched. Their understanding – the tie between them – was true.

Glimpsing the flames around her, Poppy's eyes widened, rotating her arms in disbelief as the luminescence faded. It reminded him of the glow he'd seen around his *cydern*, except it wasn't subtle or monochrome. Stunned, she brushed at it, flicking her fingers. Poppy was stunning, like no *unnusti* or elemental he'd ever known, but he would've loved her even if she were only an ordinary *Uther*.

Jinsen made awed noises. Adym's expression rearranged itself back into stolidness.

"Now that that's settled," Thom shot a triumphant side-eye at Adym, "tonight is going to be colder. We'll need shelter." He faced Adym, his expression hardening. "You should let us go."

Jinsen hissed.

Adym's expression darkened and a fiery glow hinted at the edges of his body. "I will never spite my master's wishes."

Thom grimaced. "Fine. Where must we go?"

The *fey* took his time answering. "We go to Lyls."

Jinsen quivered with alacrity, as though the journey couldn't begin fast enough.

"*Ryn* has private business with Poppy." Adym added. "He wishes to see you as well. But there will be trouble if you resist."

Fear flitted across Poppy's face, and Thom caught her hand with his.

Not waiting for a response, the *fey* set out, his bare feet impervious to the rocky ground. Gripping each other's hands, they followed, Thom's body slumping with the jarring pain of the first step, like some invisible support had been removed. Questioning, she raised an eyebrow.

"Lyls is a valley northwest of here," he murmured. "We'll be there by sundown."

"Are you going to be okay?" she whispered.

Thom mustered a curt nod, knowing it would fail to convince her.

Waiting, Adym loomed before them. "We race the sun. Let's move."

Jinsen had already disappeared into the woodland ahead. Letting them pass, the *fey* herded them onward, his pace nipping at their heels.

Chapter Thirty-Five

The plains where the Grens' army advanced faded from sight, disappearing behind a screen of evergreens, swaying in a stiff wind. The wind through the boughs followed them like haunts, chilling Poppy to the bone. Fallen trees cluttered the way and scree complicated their footing. Thom's countenance was set and determined, but it paled as they progressed. Every time she touched him, pain radiated through her like a slap to the face.

More than once they encountered Jinsen, waiting impatiently. Adym burned at her heels, but Poppy dragged her feet, slowing their pace, thinking of Thom. *If he couldn't go on, would the Firekind just leave him?* What might she do if it came to that? Wrap her arms around him and refuse to let go? She couldn't devise anything better.

They delved deeper into the wilds of the Caldera. The scree gave way to solid ground; often they hiked across tables of solid granite so large they dwarfed the Target parking lot. The mountains tipped the sun and cold air surrounded them, thickening with the fading light.

As he shuddered with fever-chills, Thom's steps began to drag. She took the backpack from him and settled it on her shoulders. *He's given so much for me. Now it's my turn.* Frowning, Adym glanced sidelong at him, as if he thought Thom should be put out of his misery.

Close to dusk, they paused for a drink, hanging back, out of earshot. Lines of pain deepened around Thom's mouth. Rivulets of sweat trickled through the dirt on his face.

"How much farther can you go?" she whispered.

He nodded to a shadowy forest stretching between the nearby mountains. "That's Lyls. We'll get to rest soon." She leaned in to hear him. "Don't worry about me."

Still, her chest ached, sick with anxiety, but she kept a brave face. *Just get to shelter. One step at a time.*

As they neared Lyls, the terrain slanted downward. The surrounding mountain slopes were forested, and steeper than any they'd encountered during their recent journeys. A stone's throw ahead, Jinsen entered a spectral forest, her flames glinting off twisty branches of gray trees. The canopy hung so thick Poppy wouldn't have been surprised if the sun never touched the floor.

The snow cover diminished, as much of it had caught on the branches, and soon a profusion of gray-green mosses dominated the ground, spreading over rock and trunk and musty undergrowth, much like the army she'd seen earlier in the valley, except this was more like an orgy of vegetation than something violent and unwanted. Tendrils of lime green moss hung like green ghosts from the trees. The place felt serene, but watchful. Ancient.

Where the roots of the mountains met, cold, dry air rolled down multiple slopes and mingled at the bottom in a frigid crowd. With the dying of the day, the temperature plummeted further. The chill was pervasive, even with Adym close. It felt like swimming through frozen air.

With every step, Thom trembled. She propped her arm around his back. He winced but let her support him, his weight almost knocking her over.

The forest loomed above them, the trees as tall as skyscrapers, their substance dampening the Firekind's radiance. The ground leveled out and a pool appeared ahead of them, the water rippling with furtive disturbances, almost hidden by a heavy cloud of warm steam.

A hot spring, she thought, amazed. Behind the pool, the ground rose again in chunks of rock, some the size of elephants. They had reached the toes of the mountains. Delicate water-whispers emanated from the pool, tickling her insides. If it weren't for Thom's sickness, the phenomena would've fascinated her.

Jinsen's flames illuminated the mossy, forested slopes, steep enough that one needed to climb to manage the incline. Farther up, patches of snow glistened silvery on the ground.

Adjacent to the pool, a dark blot punctuated the slope; the mouth of a cave, jagged with tree roots.

Buoyed by the possibility of sheltering Thom from the cold, she pointed. "Could we shelter there?"

Thom squinted at it and nodded.

"I'll check it out." Dropping the pack, she steadied Thom next to a tree.

He grunted in protest, restraining her. In the faint radiance of the flames, the shadows under his eyes were pronounced, his cheeks hollowed, as though death hounded him. It took her breath away.

"Jinsen will do it." Adym said.

Jinsen darted up to the opening, illuminating the mouth of the cave with orange light. Seconds later, she returned on a warm puff of air. *'Cave is dry. Safe for Poppy.'*

Not waiting for Adym's permission, Poppy hoisted the pack on her shoulders and tried to help Thom, but he shrugged her off, waiting until she reached the cave to follow.

The cavern was just big enough for two humans and a *rif*. Other than an abundance of tree roots, a gritty floor, and the faint odor of sulfur, it wasn't too shabby. Jinsen's warmth reflected off the walls, heating the space enough that Thom's teeth stopped chattering. And other than the *rif*, it felt private. Freedom from Adym's relentless scrutiny gave her some space to think, collect herself, and anticipate what might be next.

Thom leaned back against the wall of the cave, his long legs bent in front of him, eyes shut, jaw clenched. The tendons in the backs of his hands bulged as he tried not to shiver.

Jinsen settled at the mouth of the cave like a jailer. Outside the firelight darted about the forest like the gleam of light across water. Poppy rummaged in the pack, producing the canteen and a wrapped bundle of food. Gently, she spread the blanket over her and Thom.

"You should eat something," she said.

His Adam's apple bobbed. He tore off a piece of bread and chewed.

She murmured. "You asked about vaccinations. Are you sick?"

"No. This is from…earlier. Dane's handiwork."

The bread she'd swallowed lodged in her throat.

'Thom is ailing.' Jinsen stared at Thom, wide-eyed. *'Etin couldn't fix everything.'*

Poppy looked between them. "Thom? What is she saying?"

Thom regarded the bread in his hands as if it were a chunk of wood he had to eat. Deliberately, he deposited it on the food bundle and shoved it away. He shrugged out of his coat and fumbled with his sweater. "You'll have to look for me."

Gingerly, she helped him remove the garment. He began to unbutton his shirt, but she pushed his hands away and undid them herself. At his collarbone, the garment underneath was soaked with blood. A metallic smell filled the cave. *No.* She struggled to keep her face blank and unconcerned.

Grimacing, Thom wretched the bloody undershirt over his head, exposing the deep wound below his collarbone that Etin had healed. It had split open, festering with a silvery ooze, smelling similar to the odor cheap jewelry leaves on fingers.

Teeth chattering, he tried to look, but abandoned the effort, making a noise in his throat as he leaned back against the wall of the cave and squeezed his eyes shut.

Oh, God. No. Swallowing her tears, she beckoned to Jinsen. "Come closer. Warm him."

Jinsen's warmth crammed the cave.

Thom tried to look at the wound again. "I can't see it. Is it...bleeding?"

As his chest moved, a trickle of blood and fluid oozed out of the wound. Taking the shirt from him, she pressed it against the wound. *Stay calm, Poppy. You'll think of something.*

Willing her voice not to shake, she asked, "Is it infected?"

"Some venom must have gotten...in...during," he gritted his teeth, "that's why it didn't heal right...I...need...antivenom."

"Where can we get that?"

"Maybe...at the...outpost. But I don't know. It was...probably ransacked."

She faced Jinsen. "Can you do anything for him?"

Jinsen shook her head.

"What about Adym?"

'I will ask.' Jinsen faded, leaving them in darkness.

When she returned, her downcast face made Poppy grind her teeth in anger. *Of course, that retched fey won't help us! They'd already gotten what they wanted from him!*

She examined the wound. "Would it help to—to—clean it?"

"Wouldn't hurt." His mouth twitched.

"Cute, Thom. Really cute."

He smiled wryly. "The kit's in the pack."

By the time she'd cleaned the wound and fastened the scant amount of bandaging around his shoulder, her hands shook, betraying her composure. Using her scarf to mop up his chest, she helped him into his shirt, sweater, and coat, an awkward feat in the cramped cave. As slowly as an old man, he curled up on the floor of the cave and shut his eyes. She slid the pack under his head and covered him with the blanket.

When she was sure she could keep her voice steady she spoke. "Can you make it to the outpost?"

"I think we've got bigger concerns at the moment." He lifted the blanket and patted the ground next to him. She crumpled into him, rubbing at her eyes with the arm of her coat.

A chuckle started deep in his throat.

"What's so funny?" she asked.

"I was remembering. Today. How you told Adym off." He chuckled again. "What did you say? A walking natural-disaster?" A laugh rumbled in his throat.

She sniffed. "I guess you've rubbed off on me."

He made a skeptical noise in his throat. "I knew you as a child, remember? You were just as fiery then. When the moment called for it. And sometimes when it didn't." A grin infused his voice. "These Firekind, they don't realize what they've gotten themselves into, with you." His arm surrounded her waist and he snuggled her against his chest.

She tried to see herself from his perspective, as if she'd done something intentionally brave, as opposed to just reacting in the moment, but couldn't convince herself. "I don't know,

Thom." She put her forehead to his chest. The close heat of his fever was as warm as Jinsen. "I'm pretty scared."

"Nothing wrong with that."

"I wish I knew what to expect. What he wants."

Thom's chest moved and his breath caught, pain stiffening his body. She clenched her jaw. *He won't see me cry. Not now. Not like this.*

"Poppy, I'm so sorry. About all this."

"No, Thom—"

"I'm going to do whatever I can to make this right—"

"Thom, think—"

"You won't be forced into anything."

She rolled onto an elbow, frowning. "Listen!"

He blinked at her.

In earnest, she held his eyes. "This is not your fault. Understood?"

Exhausted lines creased his forehead.

She continued, her voice a whisper. "Maybe if I pretend to cooperate, they might heal you, like *Ryn* healed you before. And then you can go to Caldys and bring back help. My father could mediate. We've just got to think of a solution."

At her own words, she grimaced. *Your father won't help. He'll be too busy picking up the pieces after the Offysfyn is routed and scattered. If anyone is even left alive.*

Thom cleared his throat. "These Firekind, I find it hard to believe they just want to talk. Adym made it clear they don't trust *utherlings*, so they would be reluctant to mediate. And Caldys...I don't even know if," shaking his head, he broke off, "*Ryn*, if he takes you…" He swallowed hard and rubbed the bridge of his nose.

Remembering the rhyme, her stomach clenched with foreboding.

> *Steals her to his home of fire*
> *Chains her to his flame desire*

She clasped his hands. "But you did what *Ryn* asked. You returned me to Caelith. Maybe that will mean something to him. Maybe we can use that. Maybe I can persuade him."

"I'm not going to leave you. With them, alone." His voice fell to a whisper.

What if you don't have a choice? She let her head fall to the pack. His hair, darkened with sweat, tickled her cheek. Tears prickled behind her eyes. Warmth spread in her coat pocket at her thigh. Fishing around inside of it, she pulled out the stone.

It blazed like a multi-colored fragment of captured beauty, glowing on the walls of the cave like blurry rainbows. In the light Thom's eyes looked as green as summer leaves, even glazed over with pain. Resisting an angry urge to chuck it out of the cave opening, she stuffed it back into her pocket.

What had she done by choosing to go with Thom that rainy morning, days ago? Now she, and maybe Thom, were about to be imprisoned by an elemental of legendary power. And this, after they'd finally connected in a way she hadn't dreamt would ever happen. After she'd finally began to get answers about her family, her identity, her homeland. And if that wasn't enough, her homeland was about to be devastated by the Grens' savage army.

Kissing her forehead, Thom sighed and drew her close. Whatever the circumstances, she wouldn't have chosen differently. That would mean eschewing all she had learned and experienced, the beauty and the adventure, the choice to break out of the empty monotony of her life. No, she would never regret that, and Thom, him especially. Regardless of what the next day brought.

She'd decided. *I won't be cowed by this Ryn, no matter how scary that damned rhyme is.*

Chapter Thirty-Six

Pressure on Poppy's arm shook her half-awake.

Thom's voice. "Poppy. Wake up."

Exhaustion and pain wrinkled his countenance. Jinsen burned curiously in the cave opening. Next to her, Addis flickered, blinking his violet eyes.

Poppy wobbled up. Addis had returned. Nerves came to life in her stomach, wriggling like leeches. There must be news.

'Come Poppy. Master of masters awaits.' Eerily, they spoke in unison.

Master of masters? The warmth of the stone in her pocket prodded her fully awake. Her hair had stuck to her face while she slept, and she shoved it aside, ignoring the gritty, cave-like feel of her mouth.

'Come.' Still crooning in unison, the *rifs* beckoned, somber, but also quivering with anticipation.

Thom's face was pinched and colorless, as if sitting up had
taken all of his strength. Meeting her eyes evenly, he offered
her the canteen. Taking it, she squeezed his hand, finding
comfort in his palm's silent, gentle reply. Gulping water, she
slid across the cave floor to the opening. Following, Thom
braced himself next to a tree before beginning the descent.
With buoyant enthusiasm, Addis and Jinsen sped down the
incline, their glow merging with the otherworldly luminosity filling Lyls to the brim.

Gaping, Poppy halted. Scores of crimson and amber *rifs*
simmered around the clearing, tucked next to trees, resting
on boulders, hovering over moss, their colors conflating with
the violet and navy shadows cast by the trees. Dozens of *feys*,
similar to Adym, were gathered in a circle, entertaining themselves with a ring dance, the percussion seeming to come out
of nowhere. She had expected *Ryn*, and maybe a guard or
something. But hundreds of Firekind? Her stomach dropped
to her toes.

The varied hues of the Firekind reflected across the pool,
a rippling patchwork of light, tinting the steam pink. Their
energy and heat quivered upon the air and, upon seeing her
and Thom, the *feys* stopped and stared. Crackles stirred the
morning stillness, as if the Firekind began murmuring all at
once.

The tree branches stretching toward the dawn sky gleamed
with russet and orange highlights. The air held the scent of
heat turning with frost, devoid of burning, spiked with amber

and hickory – an otherworldly, delicious fragrance. Poppy drew in great, fortifying breaths of it.

Thom gave no indication of apprehension. Despite his pallor, he appeared ready, as if he had been born for moments such as these. Poppy wished she felt the same. Unsure of what to do, they paused next to the pool.

The *rifs* were the most numerous, identical to Addis and Jinsen, except some were tinged emerald green, others magenta, others amber. The *feys* were dimmer, with the same bronze skin as Adym, but more varied in overall appearance. Their hair was dark and shiny – some braided and spiked it elaborately, others left it loose and flowing. One fey caught her attention, her tanned face was elegant with feline angles, more stunning than Etin. And probably more dangerous.

Poppy gripped Thom's hand and his fingers tightened around hers, sweaty with fever, but retaining their strength. Studying them, the Firekind bristled with anticipation. She thought she saw gemstones changing hands. Addis had said master of masters. *Has Ryn come to Lyls? Are they going to drag me away? What about Thom?* Her legs went watery and she locked her knees. If there was ever a time to be brave, it was now.

Adym appeared; it took her a few heartbeats to recognize his sable eyes and mohawk in the brilliance of the surroundings. He gestured to a dell overhung by moss, where a cloth dyed the colors of the night sky had been spread. Wooden bowls of strange fruits, greens, flatbreads, and cheeses perched atop. A bottle of oil and containers of preserves and nuts waited next to wooden cups and plates.

"You will replenish yourself, with my master's compliments."

She gaped. *Is this some kind of joke? Or does Ryn like his prisoners fattened up?* With a snap, she clenched her jaw. *If they think I'm going to cooperate this easily, they've got another thing coming.*

Scowling, she made a chopping motion with the flat of her hand. "Not while Thom is sick. He needs antivenom. And if you refuse to help him, then I refuse to eat."

Thom made a noise in his throat that might have been a chuckle.

Adym blinked at her. "Antivenom? What is antivenom?"

Poppy tried to hide her disgust, but not too hard. "He has a wound from an ettar. He needs medicine, for the poison." Her heart dropped. Speaking it aloud gave a dreadful weight to the urgency of Thom's predicament.

Adym beckoned to a *fey* in the shadows, tall with skin the color of copper. Thin black braids weaved with blue beads fell to her hips, framing dark and intelligent eyes. She wore a tailored garment trimmed with tawny fur. Her elegant-boned feet were bare and twice the size of Poppy's.

She approached Thom with the air of a medical professional accustomed to performing painful procedures, assessing him with an up and down sweep. Thom faced her, looking up to meet her eyes. Opening his shirt, she wrinkled her nose and pressed her palm to his chest, her expression concerted.

Sweat broke out on Thom's forehead and he doubled over. Holding him upright, the *fey* grimaced and said something unintelligible, but curse-like. Adym's forehead creased with vexation.

Gossamer-thin crimson flames entwined with an amber-white glow, radiating like dust off of Thom's skin. The differing glows merged and entwined for a breathless moment, but then the light vanished and Thom's knees buckled as the *fey* let go of him abruptly. Poppy lunged, breaking his fall.

The Firekind started talking at once, like the chatter of insects in summer. Adym and another *fey* lifted Poppy like they were inspecting a treasured object for damage. Squirming away from them, she crouched protectively over Thom.

"What's happened?" she growled. "What did you do to him?"

Her expression as unyielding as granite, the healer-*fey* shrugged. "He is too much *cym* for my abilities. Maybe I help him some, but he will succumb to poison if he does not have medicine." She made a chopping gesture that Poppy didn't care for.

"Too much of *cym*?" she asked.

Thom's eyes opened, closed, and opened again. His face had a faraway look, as if he didn't know where he was. He saw Poppy and drew in a sudden breath, grimacing.

"He needs to rest," continued the healer-*fey*. "To be still. Slow his body."

Adym replied so quickly Poppy didn't catch his words. She disappeared into the shadows. The air slithered around

Poppy, toying with her sense of gravity, muddling her vision. *This. Cant. Be. Happening. After all we've been through. I won't let it happen.*

Rubbing his face, Thom sat up, draping his arms over his knees. "It means too many of my cells were regenerated by Etin, too recently." He met her eyes. "They can't help me."

Adym nudged her. "You must replenish yourself now."

She whirled on him. "Not until we have antivenom!" she spat. "And not with an audience gawking at us!"

Adym looked bemused, but held up a fist, a cryptic signal. In an instant, the forest bordering the pool grew shadowed and dim as Firekind vanished, leaving only Addis and Jinsen, Adym, and another *fey*. This *fey* stood shorter than Adym; his arms and chest corded with muscles and dappled with black tattoos that reminded her of cave drawings. His shiny black hair was gathered in three spiked crowns across the top of his head, fastened with blue beads, shaved at the sides and the back of his head.

Her heart hammering with fear and rage, she stood. "I don't want your food! We need antivenom! Addis and Jinsen can guide us to the outpost! I know they can! Let us go!"

The two *feys* stared, perplexed.

"If you let us go, if you let us get the antivenom," she went hoarse but railroaded on, "even though it is a monstrous injustice, I'll return and do as your master wishes. Although *I* will never call him master. Those are my terms." At least she could pretend she had bargaining power.

"Poppy. No." Shaking his head, Thom staggered to his feet.

She produced the stone. "And here is the wretched thing." She tossed it to the ground; concussions of brilliant flame burst around it. "I didn't want it to begin with!"

The ground trembled, shaking the mountains. Wide-eyed, the *feys* went deathly still. They bristled, flames appearing at the edges of their bodies. But their response wasn't about her. Like in the presence of a wild animal, they revolved toward the deepest, darkest area of the surrounding forest, just beyond the cave.

Within the trees, smoky darkness billowed, like storm clouds separating from the night sky. Branches creaking, the forest deferred to the smoke, which advanced with slow deliberation. The ground trembled again, a long low vibration, as if magma stirred within the earth.

Poppy clutched her sternum; the vibration was so powerful it felt like her heart shifted across her chest. Thom hunched over with pain, but still, his arm encircled her, his face regaining its defiant expression. The *feys* straightened and attended the coming plume, reverent.

The darkness transmuted, and then it was as if an image appeared on top of the smoke in liquid fire, or else the smoke was dissipating where the form moved, because suddenly he was there, weaving toward them with languid strides. Liquid fire seemed to drip, revealing the form as it walked, untroubled by the mountainous landscape, his bare-footed strides the embodiment of power and grace. *Is this bewitchment? A trick?*

He resembled the *fey*, but then he did not. This Firekind shone like liquid copper, like the light of the cosmos come to earth. The smoke hung about him like a cloak and the earth trembled with his footfalls. When each foot lifted, the ground was awed, but unmolested. *How did the earth not crack under such power?*

Her hair whipped across her face with warm gusts, reminiscent of a summer day. As the elemental neared, the space in her chest vibrated on key, harmonizing with her spirit. Awestruck. Undone.

And then the form of molten copper became like – and yet unlike – a man, with the same russet skin and shiny dark hair as the *feys*. The feeling of being undone spread to her toes. Introductions were superfluous.

Ryn's amber-brown eyes glinted roguishly. His black hair was sheared on the sides and tied back, framing a strong-boned, clean-shaven face. Black markings started at his neck and went all the way down his shoulders and arms, encircling them at the biceps and wrists, accented with blue diamond like shapes. Even though he wasn't much larger than the *fey*, they looked small next to him. He wore a fur vest and a black garment resembling a draped kilt, revealing plenty of muscular leg.

Regarding her dispassionately, *Ryn* halted in front of her. The longer she returned his gaze, her chin defiant, the less colossal he appeared. The resonance in her chest diminished and her mind cleared. This was his intent. A powerful sense of familiarity washed over her.

In an imperceptible, fluid movement the blue stone appeared on a black chord around his neck, in rank with a row of similar stones, veined with fiery light, joined by gossamer platinum strings like constellations.

"Welcome, Poppy." He dipped his chin to her and then Thom. "Thomas Magnusson."

His fingers brushed the stone. "I am pleased to have this again. Thank you for returning it."

His voice resonated in her chest, like fire's warmth on a winter's night. Not realizing she had been holding her breath, she let it out in a wheeze.

"Now," *Ryn*'s tone was light, as if he spoke of the weather. "I believe I need to clear up a misunderstanding, if I can."

The more she heard it, the more she knew that voice. Its baritone distilled within her a painful longing she didn't understand. A series of electric-like pops skipped through her head, followed by jumbled pictures so vivid they made her temples throb. *Memory.*

"I—I—" she stammered.

Ryn watched her intently, his expression growing somber.

And then she knew. His voice was the same voice she'd been hearing since she'd been given the stone. The voice exhorting her to be brave. And his face, she *knew* his face.

"I know you. *Ryness.*" The name was on her lips before her brain comprehended it.

The corners of his mouth turned up. "Yes, that is what you called me, as a child. And you may call me that still, if you wish."

In her memory, the elemental before her reclined by Emerald Lake. Splashed in the waters with her, while the *rifs* pouted onshore. Transformed into a magnificent, winged creature of flame. Laughed at her mirth and delight. She knew him like she knew Thom, but the essence of their connection was different. *Paternal.*

Her chest cavity pinged and twisted. "I don't understand."

Sadness crossed his face. "Much damage was done, when you were taken from this world, into the *Uther-Erai.* Your spirit is still darkened in places. Disjointed. I'm afraid you might be like a bone needing to be broken and reset."

Thom made a noise like a growl. "NO. She's been through enough. Stop speaking in riddles and state your intent, or let us go!"

Ryn arched an eyebrow. "Thomas Magnusson. I'm sorry to see you near death again. When it comes to you, *Cael-Astrett* doesn't swerve the storm."

"Helvítis fokking fokk! It's Thom! Just *Thom!*" His jaw clenched. "Cut this mystic, elemental shit and—"

Ryn's arm shot out lightning fast and gripped Thom's shoulder. His eyes rolled back in his head and he crumpled as if his bones had liquified.

A cry flew from her throat. "What did you do?" She fell to her knees, feeling for his pulse, fearing the worst. "Thom!" Why had she let her guard down?

But *Ryn* knelt with her next to Thom, his expression somber. "*Thom* needed to rest, and rest I gave him." He felt his forehead. "He'll have more time this way. We can talk without his life melting like sand before water."

"He needs antivenom." She blinked hard, her voice reedy.

*Ryn*ess studied her evenly, as if assessing her mettle. "Yes. He needs medicines we don't have. Without them, he'll die. But he'll not die without me helping him live. He's the first man I've thought to have faith in for years upon years. I've no wish for his death."

Unsure of how to respond, she stared. Nothing about this *Ryn*, this day, was turning out as she had anticipated. But did he speak the truth? Could he be trusted?

Ryn turned to the feys. "Adym, Nox. See to him. Have Umai use the *comfreyi*."

Reverently, Adym approached and placed a golden fur blanket on the ground. Nox moved Thom onto the blanket and covered him with another. They stood next to him like alien sentinels. Swallowing the knot in her throat, she tucked the blanket under his chin, unable to keep herself from feeling the faint pulse in his neck.

"Now, Poppy." *Ryn*ess stood. "May we talk?"

Chapter Thirty-Seven

Delicate breezes crept around Lyls, swaying the mosses like strange green curtains. *Ryn* offered his arm, a polite, urbane gesture that confused Poppy further. Where was the ravaging monster the rhyme taught her to beware of? Swallowing hard, she glanced down at Thom.

A noise rumbled in *Ryn*'s throat. "We'll see to him soon, I promise."

The electric pictures in her mind became clearer, but they were still jumbled, rapid, and interspaced with familiar faces; Thom, Ayden, her mother and father. It made them even more difficult to decipher, difficult to keep her wits.

His hand pleasantly warm, *Ryn*ess guided her to the food. The banquet was now enclosed in a tent, as if the smoke had materialized into fabric of grays, blues, and purples. Thick cushions of similar fabric, patterned with designs resembling

Firekind markings, littered the ground, piled thick with fur blankets and smaller cushions. Some were so large three of her could've fit on one. The gentle music of chimes sang on the breeze.

To her alarm, her eyes felt heavy. Was he bewitching her? She stood straighter, digging her fingernails in her palms. She glanced back at Thom, bundled in the furs, motionless like one ready for burial.

"You're worried." He settled on a cushion and gestured for her to do the same. Tears stiffening her throat, she hesitated.

"But see." He gestured. Adym and Nox bent over Thom's prostrate form, rubbing a copper substance into the wound at his collarbone. "The tonic will fight the poison in his blood. He still needs," his tongue paused on the word before enunciating, "*antivenom*, but this will stabilize him. For now."

Her legs watery, she sunk onto the nearest cushion, twisting her hands in her lap.

A thoughtful frown settled on his forehead. "The pain of loving is often overlooked. Sometimes there's as much suffering in love as there is joy. That's the way of it. Even in the havenlands."

His words were like an ocean; layers of currents, climates, shafts of light and patches of dark. One could dwell upon such words for ages and still not reach the bottom.

"Tell me more," she heard herself asking, "about that."

*Ryn*ess's chest rose and fell. Taking a wooden cup from the table, he poured a generous amount of purple-black liquid from a woven jug and offered it to her. The smell of autumn nights, thyme, cardamom, and clove made her mouth water. As she took it, he poured a portion for himself.

"In answer, I'll tell you a story. Perhaps it is one you've even heard. Perhaps not."

Watching him over her cup, she sipped the beverage. The flavor exploded in her mouth; blueberries, smoke, black-currant, fresh cut wood the color of honey. Involuntarily, she gasped, her tongue singing.

He grinned. "We make that ourselves."

The drink revealed itself in languid, delicious layers, dulling the edge of her shock. Her stomach gurgled, demanding sustenance beyond wine. Glancing at Thom, she nibbled at some bread, thinking she didn't really want to hear a story, but she wanted her questions answered. And if listening got her what she wanted...

Sipping his drink, *Ryn*ess continued. "This story is about your great-great-great-great grandmother, as you speak of in *utherling* terms."

Surprised, she choked. *Ryn* thumped her back, as though she were a baby that needed a good burping.

"Who are you?" She choked out, her eyes wide.

*Ryn*ess's expression took on a faraway cast. "Listen, if you will. And I will tell you. At *Uther-Erai's* fall, darkness and death threatened all elemental kind to near extinction. Seeing that the *Erai* was no longer suitable for elemental kind, *Cael-Astrett* stretched the foundation of that world, and thus the realm of Caelith was born. *Cael-Astrett* charged five elementals to watch over our kind during our passage from *Uther-*

Erai to our new home, naming them *lostaja* – ones who guide the lost. I am one of these five. And, for many years, we led and guarded all elemental kind as they passed into Caelith. But the darkness was cunning and secretly followed us in, in the form of many beasts. Our kind were beset by these beasts, and I and my kin pursued them, binding them and feeding them to the fire of the earth."

"One spring I chased one of the beasts, a *nephyl*, and found in its clutches an *utherling*." He rested his hand on his chest. "I knew the *astrettur* in my soul. The *good way*. I had to help her, elemental or *utherling*, whether she belonged here or not; the distinction wasn't important. So, I battled the *nephyl*, freed her, and fed the beast to the heart of Caelith."

"The *utherling's* name was Crymson. I don't know why the *nephyl* had taken her. He might have mistook her for one of our kind, she was so fire-like. Like no other, she moved me, but I concealed this, for she was weary and distressed, and longed for her *utherling* kin. I bound her wounds, fed and clothed her, surrounded her with peace. And I searched for them, her kin. Her longing was mine, as was her sorrow. Many months passed, and we visited wild and tame places of the havens, seeking them."

"With each conversation, each look that passed between us, the new paths we followed together, our souls knitted, and love grew along that tie like a garden. Despite my misgivings, I could ignore my heart no longer. To my joy, Crymson returned my love, and so we were bonded, and joy was ours."

The words of his story were like perfume. Yes, she'd heard Thom tell the same story just days ago, but these words came alive around her with whispers and glimmering dusty images, like sentient golden smoke.

Pausing, his gaze rested on the cup. "We soon had an *unnusti* – a beloved. When she came," a smile played upon his lips, "she was so like her mother. Crimson hair, eyes like the gray sea." His eyes traced her features. "So very like you, in fact, the first time I saw you I couldn't help but think of her. We named her Etayn. And as she grew, she exhibited extraordinary abilities, empathy and compassion for others, but also Firekind traits. Powers difficult to tame. Confusing for a child. Slowly, I began training her, instructing her in using these abilities. Ever surprised at what she could do."

His expression tightened with sadness.

"We continued searching for Crymson's family, so they could share in our *unnui*. But the Caelith havens are vast, ever-expanding beyond their original borders. Finding a small community of *utherlings*, especially with their subtle energies, is a difficult task, even for a *lostaja*. Etayn was eleven of years by the time I found them. Her family was overjoyed to see Crymson again, but they were frightened at the sight of a caravan of nomad Firekind appearing next to their village. They were unfamiliar with us, distrusting of our kind. But we were friendly, and didn't find offense, even where it was meant."

Ryn's face darkened. Capillaries of fire appeared in his hands, and veins glimmered at his temples. Poppy held her breath.

Some of the darkness left his face, snuffed out by grief. "Unbeknownst to us, Crymson's family, believing her bewitched by me, approached the elemental council of that region, asking for assistance in dissolving our bond. Of course, *astrettur-bonds* cannot be dissolved. Even death only alters them." He shook his head. "One of the council members was most disturbed by Etayn and her gifts, Sava - a *Gren*, kin to obsidian." *Ryn*'s lip curled with derision. "He devised a plan, with Crymson's kin, to take her and Etayn and hide them. To keep the elemental bloodlines pure, he secretly planned to kill Etayn, but the council discovered and prevented this."

Poppy closed her eyes. The pain behind his expression became a thunderous churning in her chest. She listened intently.

"So, Crymson's family held a feast celebrating her return with the entire village and our Firekind clan. In the clamor of the festivities they drugged Crymson and Etayn, and rendez-voused with the council. They hid her entire family far away, using an aetherkind, even before the wine had been finished. Because I had brought forth *unnusti* offspring, Sava used his influence to exile me from elementalkind. It wasn't as accepted then, as it is now." He frowned. "The Firekind followed me in my exile and assisted me in searching for my stolen family."

Her throat ached. How could she respond to such pain?

Ryn sighed, and the earth around them seemed to tremor. "Nine years passed before we found them. My Crymson had succumbed to an illness, and had passed into eternity." A pallid shadow crossed his face. "Etayn was grown and *uther-*

ling-bonded, with a child of her own. She fled from the *rifs* sent to greet her, barring her doors, afraid. She had been shamed and deceived, most viciously, about her origins. About the evils of the fireborn." He fell silent, his expression faraway. "Treated harshly enough she lacked the strength to wield her abilities."

"Still, I couldn't help but love her and her child. I vowed to watch over them, secretly, wherever they should be, however numerous they grew. And because I'm responsible for the dormant *unnusti* powers my offspring hold."

He leaned forward, his arms resting on his knees.

"They didn't grow numerous. Sons showed no Firekind traits. But as my *unnusti* daughters grew their Firekind heritage eventually showed itself. They were feared, mistreated, shunned, or used for ill purposes. We sheltered many over the years. Even so, some were too afraid to accept our help, because of the tales told of our kind."

"Because of these hardships, eventually, only one of my daughters remained outside our care; a kind and sensitive *unnusti*, trained by her father to hide, to suppress, her Firekind heritage. Because of her beauty, a very old and influential *utherling* family, with peculiar influence in elemental politics, took an interest in her, and she was joined to their eldest son, Felix."

Poppy's breath caught.

"They did not know of her heritage, and I'm not certain they would've allowed the match if they had." His expression darkened. "The Paquins have aether heritage, a trait which they've hidden well, and used to their advantage in *utherling* circles. They wouldn't have wanted the risk of aether and Firekind mingling, much less Firekind itself. Felix proved to be just as ambitious as his father. But ambition is often like grabbing a snake by the tail. One has a sense of mastery, but also the expectation that it is about to swivel and bite the hand. He was a natural leader, but an uncompassionate love-partner. A harsh parent." His eyes rested on her, softening. "As you matured your heritage became unmistakable to us, even capricious, at times."

"Perhaps we should've been more careful with our watchers, but I was concerned for you, lonely as you were, and didn't try to restrain Addis and Jinsen. Most of all, we were worried what Felix would do if he discovered your Firekind heritage, how he would want to use it. Because of myths of our kind, when Felix grew aware of us, he misread our intentions. We tried to warn him against hiding you in the *Uther-Erai*, knowing it would hurt you, because of your elemental blood. But he ignored and threatened my messengers. I only excuse his foolishness because it was out of desire to protect you."

*Ryn*ess filled his goblet and leaned back, closing his eyes and tasting it.

"I feared the worst when my watchers were evaded, and you and your mother disappeared. Still we searched for any trace of you. We couldn't come close to Felix and Ayden, for their mistrust of our kind was dogged, and they had alerted the council to our presence." His gaze found Thom. "So we observed Thom, for there was already a friendship-bond between you and him, and we hoped it would help us discover where Felix had hidden you."

"Years later, at the massacre in the Maris vale, I discovered Thom did have knowledge of your whereabouts. And now, here you are." His eyes merged with hers. "You, and your mother, are the last of Crymson's line, the last of my *unnusti* daughters. Long I've wished to sit before you and tell this story."

Poppy met his eyes for several breathless moments. The story was beautiful, illuminating, and heartbreaking. It felt at home in her, but it also felt as though it had rubbed her raw, or like she'd stepped into a costume of an understudy unprepared to fill her role. "I was told a similar story." She glanced at Thom. "Except it ended much differently."

He nodded. "Yes. Crymson's family spun another version, so often and so long the lie became accepted, significant in Caelithian folklore." He set his goblet on the ground. "But I concealed nothing from Crymson. I had no need to. There was no fear in our love." His brow furrowed. "Fear birthed the evil and darkness that corrupted *Uther-Erai*, making monsters of *utherlings* and elementals alike. The same fear allowed Crymson's kin to lie, and eventually believe those lies, enabling evils to take root in Caelith that would've withered otherwise."

Poppy's eyes went to the stone, gleaming at his chest. "Tell me about the stone."

Ryness touched it. "This is a *lostaja's* relic. A talisman of many properties and merits. Addis slipped it to Deidre, as a precaution, in case you were taken into the *Uther-Erai*. We hoped it would track and protect both of you, enable a distant connection between worlds. But it didn't work until the ele-mental part of you had been reawakened."

The discoveries steeped and settled into her consciousness. Poppy finally worked up the courage to ask. "Do you know where my mother is?"

His mouth twitched with a pleased grin. "Come, Deidre, my *innuia*. Comfort your daughter."

Chapter Thirty-Eight

A cry escaped Poppy's lips as Deidre approached, striding through the cushions toward her, arms outstretched beneath a garment of smoky sapphire. Her braided auburn hair shone with silver, and her cheeks had filled out. As her mother embraced her, Poppy wheezed, stunned. Deidre's arms were still bony, but warm and much stronger than the last time they'd held a wine glass in front of the television.

"Mom," she choked, tears wetting her eyes. "I was so worried. How?"

Deidre's eyes flickered from her hands, to her face, to the hair at her temples. "I always hoped your crimson hair would return."

Looking between her and *Ryn*ess, Poppy gripped Deidre's hand. "But, how?"

"The moment that *ulli* dragged me through the Twin well, he was doomed." She glanced at *Ryn*. "I don't know how long those *feys* had been waiting, but they were ready."

"So, you've been safe, with the Firekind, all this time?"

"Yes, safe. I'm home, more at home than I've ever been. And now you're here." Her expression melted into joy, before sobering. "I'm so sorry, Poppy. We should've told you long ago, about Caelith, about everything. Felix convinced me – I'd convinced myself – that we were just protecting you, making the loss easier. And I'd always hoped I didn't pass on those traits to you."

"It doesn't matter now." Poppy dragged her sleeve across her eyes. "So much has happened." With a jolt, she remembered Thom's peril, and wobbled to her feet. "Thom! We need to help him." She clutched Deidre's hand. "Without him, I would've been captured, maybe even died. He saved me, over and over again."

Abruptly, Poppy remembered the creeping darkness of the army, advancing on Caldys. "And the Grens are marching across the moors toward the city of Caldys, to attack! Thom said thousands of *utherlings* and elementals are at risk!"

Ryn's expression darkened. "Addis apprised me. But the Caldysian *Offysfyn* spurned our messengers."

Poppy's heart leapt. "You warned them?"

"I'm afraid the word of a Firekind is as trusted as one of Sava's *slagerei*."

"They didn't listen?" She sunk down, staring at Thom's still form lying cocooned in the furs. His countenance shone pale against the brown fur, as still as death. Watching the army from the overlook, he'd been so troubled by the fate bearing down upon his friends. What would he say if he woke up and discovered Caldys had fallen? That the *Offysfyn* had been crushed?

*Ryn*ess leaned forward, his hand wrapping around hers. "While the elemental council, the *Offysfyn*, and the *Utherling-Steward* have been busy with Sava and his Gren *slagerei*, they've missed the biggest threat to this realm – the *nephyl* and his minions. But the Firekind, and the other *lostaja*, haven't. The same evil that Sava has decided to serve – the same evil which robbed me of my family – springs from the shadow they cast. The havenlands are being corrupted exponentially."

Poppy concentrated; *Ryn*'s discourse was difficult to follow. He leapt ahead of her, while she limped, falling farther and farther behind. She glanced at Deidre – her mother's face had sobered.

*Ryn*ess continued, "For too long, we've allowed this evil sway. It's time for the *lostaja* to move against the *nephyl*. Your gifts would be invaluable in this fight. Firekind and aether traits haven't ever mingled in an *utherling* before. We don't know what marvelous things you're capable of. But I leave that decision up to you. We would welcome Thom's bravery and character. There are so few of us now." His dark eyes found Thom. "We'll find medicine to treat him. But we need to leave Lyls immediately."

Her heart leapt. Thom! Alive and recovered! The two of them, together, working with noble purpose! It had seemed impossible an hour ago. Why then, did a cryptic uneasiness keep pace with her happiness?

Is it my father? Ambivalent, Poppy frowned. *I should at least give him the chance to explain, to see things from his perspective. People make mistakes. Maybe he regrets his.*

"What about Dad?" Poppy asked, facing Deidre.

Unease flickered over her mother's face. "Poppy, I think it's best you avoid your father, until you know how to handle your abilities. In a way, he loves us, and always will, but he loves power too much. I don't trust him with you. Maybe when the darkness is gone." She shook her head. "I can always hope."

Poppy had expected it, but it still stung. Still, she decided to suspend judgment about Felix. She wanted to decide for herself. "And Ayden?"

"We have *fey*-trackers and *fyns* searching for him," *Ryn* said. "They'll send word when he's found."

A little of her angst lessened, but the prick at her conscience remained. The memory of the Grens marching toward Caldys loomed over her like a punch about to be thrown. *How can I ignore the danger to so many? Wouldn't it be right to intervene, regardless of the circumstances, regardless of the Offysfyn's, the council's mistakes?*

And wouldn't it prove a point? Cause other elementals to see the Firekind in a light other than the one spread by false folklore and ignorant prejudice? Wouldn't it highlight the bigger threat to Caelith — recruit others to fight the nephyl as well?

Her eyes flickered from Thom to *Ryn*ess. "Thom said the *Offysfyn* wouldn't recover from such an attack."

"They have chosen not to heed our warnings." Sadness passed over *Ryn*'s expression, the glow of his veins fading. "They have chosen their prejudice."

"What about the elementals, the *utherlings* sheltering there?" she pressed. "Isn't there anything you can do? It doesn't seem right to just–just leave. To bow out when you have the power to stop the Grens."

Pressing his fingers together, he leaned forward. "It would be a great risk for our kind. A risk perhaps better saved for battling the *nephyl*. And we would frighten them."

"Not if they saw you fighting the Grens, defending Caldys. This might be the Firekind's chance to prove you're not the monsters folklore says you are, to influence the *Offysfyn* to join in the real fight. As it is, it'll be a massacre at Caldys. Half of the *Offysfyn* are across the sea with my father. Even if they did heed the warning, they won't be able to reach them until it's over."

Ryn's gaze swept the forest. Thoughtfully, he rubbed his chin. The forest seemed deliberately quiet, listening to the conversation. An expression she couldn't pinpoint leapt into *Ryn*'s eyes. He stayed silent for heartbeats upon heartbeats.

Finally, he spoke. "Poppy, I can't save both Caldys and Thom. If the Firekind go to Caldys' aid, I must go with them. They can't be without my protection and authority, especially against Sava. And we must go this very moment, for the slaughter will have already begun. You'll be left with only Jinsen and Addis to help you. And no medicine as I promised. Those who don't fight will have to watch over our elders and young."

Her heart felt as though it had been dropped off a cliff, fallen into darkness. The feeling left her breathless and sick. Still, she knew what Thom would choose. She knew the *good way.* If she dwelt on the choice much longer, she wouldn't have the courage to make it.

Through a ragged breath, she whispered, "Go then. Save Caldys. But I'm going to try and help Thom. To get to the outpost, somehow."

Deidre covered her mouth with her hands, her eyes reddening with tears.

"It's what Thom would do. I can't let him down."

*Ryn*ess regarded her for a moment, his expression unreadable. "It's a very great risk. A void I can't see beyond."

Hurry up already! Pain seizing inside of her, she nodded.

Ryn signaled to Adym and Nox. A deep rumble began, shaking the curtains of moss and the pebbles at her feet. In curtains of sparks, Firekind appeared all around them. As *Ryn*ess stood, she and Deidre arose, hands clasped.

His expression softened. "I didn't expect..." His voice cracked, strangely incongruent with his majesty. Then his face galvanized, and he removed the blue stone from around his neck and slid it into her hands.

Turning away, his voice rose to a sonorous roar, apprising the Firekind of the danger Caldys faced. Her heart leapt into her throat. *They're going to Caldys!* The realization was both sweet and acrimonious.

When she returned with the pack, *Ryn*ess had Thom conscious and on his feet. Addis and Jinsen hovered next to them, their flames jagged, crackling with static electricity. Before she reached them, Deidre pulled her aside, embracing her. "Be careful, Treefrog." Glancing back as though she didn't want to leave her, Deidre stumbled away, gathering with a ragtag bunch of *rifs* and other Firekind.

The forest clearing glowed and flickered with amassing Firekind warriors. An eerie roar of power simmered on the air, just out of range of her hearing, resonating in the elemental space in her chest like a beating of raptor wings. *The Grens' were about to get their asses handed to them.* She wished she could be there to see it. But the sight of Thom made her insides feel hollow.

Thom hunched over, hands on his knees, observing the mustering of the Firekind with wide, confused eyes. The hair on his forehead was dark with sweat, his face stiff with pain. Seeing her, his expression smoothed and he straightened, weaving with the effort.

She sidled under one of Thom's arms, glancing up at *Ryn*ess. "Will you, will the Firekind, be okay?"

Thom grunted in surprise.

*Ryn*ess's expression grew intense, as though his soul roiled and fought with itself. He faced Addis and Jinsen. "Watch over Poppy and Thom. Do whatever is in your power to assist them."

The *rifs* nodded gravely.

Facing her again, he embraced her briskly, his aura sizzling with a heady charge of power. "As soon as the battle is over, I will return. And we will find medicine." Pulling back, he fixed her with a thoughtful gaze, his eyes flickering to the blue stone. "If you aren't here. I will find you. Remember, I don't even know what you're capable of. So, persist. Be brave."

Stepping back, the glow of the Firekind intensified, as though they coalesced their essences, pooling energy from the tiniest corner of their cells. She watched, fascinated, feeling the pull in the elemental place inside of her, an almost magnetic connection. The rock trembled in her hand, as though it longed to follow, to call to the micro elements of Caelith as the Firekind did now. Through the rings of firefly sparks lapping them, *Ryn* fixed Addis and Jinsen with a sort-of reminding look.

Just before they were swallowed up by the glimmering light, pride, adoration, and sorrow crossed *Ryness's* face, the last thing she glimpsed as the Firekind disappeared.

A dormant part of her soul stretched and pinged, as though asking why she didn't follow, and multi-colored glimmering wisps of flame appeared over her skin.

What if? Wondering, she shifted her concentration to the tiniest particles holding Caelith together, clasping the stone, thinking of the mitochondria, the DNA, the nucleus of the cells, and the surrounding particles, sensing their movement, their energies.

"Poppy? What's going on? I don't understand." The pain in Thom's voice almost jolted her out of the mysterious power building around her. She curled his fingers around his shoulder and squeezed. Now that she'd found herself, now that she knew who she was, she was turning a corner, tapping into a miraculous beckoning.

A hum joined her consciousness, an otherworldly melody, a familiar, and yet unfamiliar strain. She longed for it to be louder, to plug it into her ears and crank it, but it wasn't quite music either. A rushing tingle of icy-hot touched her other hand, the one holding the stone. Jinsen had grasped her fingers, surrounding them with gentle flickers. Addis's flaming limbs stretched to join Jinsen and Thom, creating a radiant oval. The ineffable sound grew louder, vibrating inside of her, resonating and growing as though her cells were magnifying it.

Closing her eyes, she thought about the particles making up antivenom, their unique bonds and elements. And she called to them, not really knowing what she was doing – stumbling through matter, acting out of the desperation thrumming in her soul, running toward the mystery at the heart of all living things.

Then, with a shudder, a million cells rushed at her, all at once, streaming through the elemental space in her chest. The hum and rhythm intensified – lovely, but wholly uncivilized. Concentrating, she balanced her awareness of the magnetic pull and movement of the atoms, and her grip on Thom's shoulder. The green world of Lyls went nebulous and dizzy in a whirl of sunset color.

Poppy felt a jolt, and the world around her rushed outward, righting itself into sparks and amber-violet flames, fading to reveal a landscape she'd never seen before. The hum had been replaced by the howl of wind, and she felt like weeping, as though she'd lost something precious. Feeling like her blood had stopped moving in her veins, her knees wobbled and collapsed, thudding into tough heather studded with tiny, white flowers shaped like stars.

Chapter Thirty-Nine

This must be delirium. Agony thrummed in Thom's body and the sparks danced in his vision. *But this pain. Cael-Astrett, it can't be just in my head.* He stared at the anomaly of light surrounding Poppy, surrounding them, glimpsing open sky through the rippling luminescence, his eyes widening. *Impossible.*

As amber-violet sparks shrank in around them, his pain surged like a current of electricity. Through the agony, he felt only a minuscule tug in different directions, a feather-light crackling sensation on his face, as though he'd been doused with fizzy water. As the light faded, the sensation disappeared, driven away by a gust of wind, strong enough to make him totter. The scent of rain entered his nostrils. Tottering in thick alpine heather, he planted his feet, grunting with pain.

Next to him, Poppy fell to her knees, slumping. He gripped her shoulders, studying her face, fearing the worst. But her countenance glowed with life, almost illuminated by the red glow of her crimson hair, crowding her temples. Her eyes widened with bemusement, scanning the terrain. Her fingers stroked the pentas flowers at her knees.

Meeting his eyes, she read his question. "It's okay, Thom. I hoped maybe…" She swiveled, scanning the terrain around them. "I don't know where I've brought us."

The sky boiled with black clouds, overshadowing scraggly gray-green turf. Directly to the west, a stone's throw away, the terrain leapt into rocky foothills and beyond, the forbidding snowy peaks of Maris. Far to the northeast, the Asys mountains loomed, cutting into the sky. Just before them, the sterling ribbon of the Norsen River curved through the landscape, disappearing between the Eirians. Realization jolting him, he dragged his gaze directly north. The *Kairyn* outpost. *Incredible.*

"The outpost." Thom pointed to a cliff just northwest, towering above the moors. He couldn't help but grin. "You've brought us to the outpost."

Spying the gray boxy shapes, incongruous with the forested cliff, climbing up the side of the incline, she smiled. The bulk of the outpost arose into off-set cylindrical stone towers, providing a spectacular view of the whole of the moors. If they kept to the edge of the foothills to the west, the distance probably wasn't more than a half a mile. He clenched his jaw. "Let's go."

Barren moors stretched between them and the outpost. Battling the wind, Addis and Jinsen shrank, huddling together. Thom eyed them. Were they still captives of the Firekind?

He staggered, and Poppy thrust her shoulder under his arm, her face stony. Stiff-arming pride, he let her take a little of his weight, even though as he did her eyes widened. *Just. Keep. Moving.*

The light huddled around them, sickly and gray. The wind hissed over the moors in adversarial gusts. Scanning the sky, the *rifs* shuddered.

'Must hurry.'

'This is dangerous country.'

'Must take care. Take care.'

Wary eyes on the storm clouds, Jinsen and Addis fled toward the outpost, speeding close to the ground like foxes. It wasn't long before he and Poppy lagged far behind. Bobbing anxiously, the *rifs* halted, urging them onward.

With his heartbeat, with each drag of his feet, pain lanced his body. A small walled courtyard and guard house became visible, enclosing the bulk of the outpost – obscured in the dim light, but still standing. He'd hoped for this much. Burning the outpost would've nullified the Gren's advantage of surprise, attracting the attention of the *Offysfyn* at Caldys. *But did they leave the medicines?*

Under his weight, Poppy's breath came in gasps. When he tried to pull away, she muttered. "No, Thom…don't…you… dare."

Knowing she wouldn't be able to break his fall if he lost his footing, he concentrated on placing each step in the tough heather before lifting his other boot. The stone turret of the watchtower came to loom against the sky above them, soaring over the moors. *Almost there.*

"Do you think it's safe?" Breathless, she scanned the structures.

"Difficult...to tell," he uttered between clenched teeth. "But we would've been hailed by now...if it wasn't."

A fork of blue lightning rent the clouds, casting ominous shadows inside the flexing purple mass. Thunder rumbled and shook the ground. Addis quivered and shot toward the outpost like a bird in flight. Jinsen scurried back to them, her countenance pinched with fear. *'We must reach shelter. Addis goes ahead, to see if the outpost is safe.'*

Poppy nodded, wiping sweat from her eyes. Jinsen shot away, following Addis.

Unsteady under his weight, her feet skidded and she almost fell. He grunted, managing to keep them upright. In their path, shiny blue bones littered the heather, mingled with a thick ashy dust. Paces away, stained patches marred the vegetation. A gust of wind brought an icky, pungent smell to his nose. Retching, he clamped an arm over his stomach.

The outpost and surrounding landscape had hosted a massacre a day or two before. The fortress was as good as a crypt, for both *utherlings* and elementals. "Poppy—"

"Save your breath, Thom."

"No! This," he indicated the outpost. "It's going...to be... gruesome."

Her face went white, but she didn't slow her pace, guiding them around the bones, avoiding the bloody ground. Thunder shook the moors like the inside of a kettle drum.

Sweat dripped off his jaw. "Almost there."

Thirty paces ahead, Addis wavered in the opening to the courtyard and stables, his light reflecting across an arched stone gate, vivid in the stormy light. The gates lay smashed on the ground, like they'd been made of cardboard. Her flames jagged with agitation, Jinsen urged them onward, cowering before a fast approaching wall of rain.

The outpost appeared deserted, its windows dark. Another scattering of elemental bones littered the nearby turf. A powerful gust brought a cold smattering of rain with it, nipping at their heels. Taking cover, the *rifs* disappeared into the guardhouse as the deluge overtook them.

The mossy wall rose before them, slick with rain. They crossed the threshold of the gate, Poppy recoiling at the odor of death pouring from the guardhouse. A bloody smear marred the adjacent wall pooling crimson in the rainwater beneath.

Focus, he told himself. *Remember the layout. Antivenom.* "Medical storage," he indicated a dark opening in the main structure of the center tower. "Through that door. Up the stairs. They'll have ransacked the med-ward. Storage is our best hope."

Raindrops pelted the cobbles. The *rifs* scurried out of the gatehouse and through the door, illuminating a wide corridor with an iron chandelier askew on the floor. Pushing her wet hair out of her eyes, she aimed for the stairwell, situated in a peaked opening at their right. Addis and Jinsen illuminated the spiral, throwing spooky shadows. *Stairs.* He grimaced.

Panting with the effort of the climb, Thom clutched the wood railing. Hauling him up each step, her breath came in hoarse gasps. The stairwell ended, opening up to a large mess room with a wood floor and beamed ceiling. The smell of blood tinged the moist air. *Where are the bodies?* He scanned the room. *This isn't right.*

The *rifs* illuminated the space as Thom scanned it.

"Here?" Poppy looked around. "Are the supplies here?"

Spying marks across the floor, he halted. "Wait." He motioned for her to stay near the stairs. "I need to see something."

Clutching a chair for support, he stumbled across the wood planks, scanning for clues. The *rifs* followed him, their flames stiff and edgy. He scrutinized a dark stain on the floor, half-hidden by a trestle table. Bloody paw prints the size of dinner plates faded as they crossed the room to the stairwell. Alongside, ragged stains marred the planks, as though something heavy had been dragged. *Not good.*

"Where are the bodies? Of the humans?" Poppy's brow lowered. "Do the elementals take them?"

Thom shook his head, doubled over with nausea, and vomited. Pain spiked his collarbone, and his vision went dark at the edges.

Rushing to his side, she thrust her shoulder under his arm. *Don't let her see.* Staggering, he knocked over the table and shoved a chair to the floor, covering the stains. Sparking with agitation, Addis darted out of the way.

"Come on." She maneuvered him toward the stairs. "Antivenom."

Thunder echoed up and down the stairwell, disorientating. Pausing to catch her breath, she adjusted her arm across his back. Thom clung to the railing, swaying, his knuckles white. By the time they reached the top his legs shook with strain.

They passed a broken window with banging shutters. Wet gusts of wind buffeted the interior. The *rifs* scuttled aside as she shielded her face. Below, curtains of rain pummeled the moors.

"There." Thom motioned to a door straight on from the windows, marked with a white Swiss cross.

She jiggled the latch. "It's locked. That's good, right?"

The discovery strengthened him. He kicked the wood near the lock. The casing splintered as the door banged open. White stars cluttered his vision, and he swayed against the stone wall as nausea renewed its assault. Poppy murmured something, but he couldn't make it out. Her arms circled him like she was about to attempt to carry him the rest of the way. *Come on, Magnusson. A few more steps.*

Addis and Jinsen entered first, lighting the room like moving lamps. A jumble of curtained beds cluttered the room, along with walls of cabinets, some metal, all undisturbed. Leaded windows punctuated the outer stone wall, glittering with the *rifs'* light.

Dropping the pack, she lowered him into a chair near the entrance. Turning away, he retched and vomited, mostly water and bile, bitter and burning in his throat.

"Addis. Jinsen," she said. "Warm him up."

They fluttered on either side of him and warm currents bubbled through the room. Eyes shut, he leaned against the wall for a moment, fighting to stay conscious, breathing in short pants. Pain needling every movement, he shrugged out of his coat. "The vials we need will be labeled Ettar AV, and AS-serum." Blearily, he studied the cabinets and indicated a metal one. "Look in there."

Poppy threw open the cabinet doors and rifled through the vials. She appeared in front of him, and it took him a moment to realize she'd found them. His chest rose and fell, and he deliberately plucked one from her, squinting at the label. He shut his eyes and leaned back against the wall.

"We need syringes, tape, IV needles, caphs," he said. "There are IV bags in the cold cabinet. And towels, bandages, cording. We'll need those too. Wash. First."

Time bled and faded as she scurried around the room. Her hands on his face, gripping his biceps, brought him back to consciousness. Eyes wide, she looked between an IV bag and a caph.

"Addis or Jinsen will need to warm that." Moving slowly, he peeled his sweater off, his stomach roiling at the putrid tang of the venom.

Addis took the IV bag from her and cradled it. Eyebrows low with concentration, Poppy pushed his hands away from the buttons of his shirt and undid them. Underneath, the bandage had soaked through; it fell away as she removed the shirt. Her face went white, but she set her jaw, turning back to the sink.

Tying her hair back, she washed again, and doused his hands with antiseptic. Swallowing hard, he picked up a syringe and the vial of antivenom, and squinted at it, his eyes shifting to Poppy's shaking hands. *No time to teach her.*

"Clean my arm." He motioned to the inside bend of his elbow. "And tie the cording at the bicep."

She did as he asked. Goosebumps rose up and down his flesh as the veins popped out in his forearm underneath the tattooed landscape. His hands shaking, he pushed the needle into the vial. Habit taking over, he made a fist, pressed on a vein, and inserted the needle, nodding at the tourniquet. "Loosen it."

Using his other arm, they repeated the procedure with the AS-serum vial. His arm bent against a bandage, he leaned back against the wall, his eyes shut, his chest heaving. Blood oozed from the wound in his collarbone, and she pressed fresh packing against it.

The bed creaked as she sunk onto it. "Did we make it? In time?"

His eyes still closed, he nodded. The benchmark for ettar venom mortality was usually pre-coma injection, and he was conscious enough to have injected himself.

"So, you're going to be okay?"

A hint of a grin pulled at his lips. "Considering what we faced at this time yesterday, I'm better than okay. I'm still trying to work out what happened."

"I've a lot to tell you." Her freckles stood out, even in the dim light.

The room began to move around him. "I think I need to lie down."

She helped him stumble-crawl-roll onto the bed next to the chair, adjusting a pillow under his head and taking off his boots. Feeling the warmth of her hip against his thigh, he shut his eyes and breathed for a time. The wound at his collarbone began to ooze into the packing again, and he grimaced. *Need to get that stitched up.*

Hearing sniffling, he nudged Poppy. Wiping her face with the back of her hands, she faced him, her eyes red, her nose running.

"Hey." Tugging her down next to him, he squeezed her in a one-armed hug. "It's okay. We're going to be okay." Tears streaming down her face, she huddled against him. "You saved the day, you know that? Cry all you want, but know that."

He cradled her until her tears subsided, his lips brushing her cheek. Outside, night fell in a deep black curtain, dimming the room so he could barely see the freckles on her cheeks. Wiping her face and nose, she sat up. Without her close, he shivered.

"Think you can help me with the IV?" He squinted, trying to ascertain how much of his shoulder he could see. *Not enough.* "We can save the hard part for last." He looked around for the *rifs*. "We'll need some light."

"The hard part?" She fetched the IV bag from Addis, who flared with a bright bloom of flame.

"How good are you with a needle and thread?"

"That's all?" She grinned. "I guess we'll find out."

Chapter Forty

Much later, Thom lay still, blankets up to his chin, listening to the water in the sink as Poppy scrubbed her hands. Despite the throb and prickle at his collarbone, he kept drifting off.

Under the circumstances, her stitching wasn't too shabby. When he told her so, she joked that he was just being nice. Or the meds were talking. Or both. Regardless, when he examined the stitching in the reflection of a metal tray, he was satisfied. Her handiwork served its purpose; he wouldn't lose any more blood.

Their warmth heating the room comfortably, Addis and Jinsen diminished into resting states. Rubbing her neck, Poppy wobbled across the room to the window. Through the thick wavy panes of glass, tar-black darkness shrouded the watery moors. *Night.* His brain jolted with memory.

"Poppy…"

Her expression wrinkling with concern, she approached.

"Prop a chair against the door handle," he said. "It'll give us a warning if…" he tried to keep his face unconcerned but did a bad job.

"If what?" She secured a chair under the door latch.

"It's probably nothing. Just a precaution." He studied the *rifs*, huddled together against the wall. "Jinsen, Addis. If you could be as dim as possible, that would keep us safer. We don't want anyone to know we're here."

They murmured in low crackles, their flames waning to a faint purple.

"Does this have anything to do with the gigantic animal tracks downstairs?" she asked, watching his reaction.

He grimaced at the half-truth he'd decided to go with. "Wolfhounds are pretty common here. A few large tracks aren't bad. It's just a precaution, so we can sleep." Scooting over, he flipped the blanket up. "You're exhausted. Lie down with me."

Scrutinizing her grubby sweater, she hesitated.

"Come on. You'll keep me warm."

She shrugged out of the damp sweater and hung it on a chair. Fussing with the crumpled garment underneath, she kicked off her boots and sidled under the blanket, her warmth pleasant next to his body. He wrapped an arm around her waist, nestling her against him, weariness mixing with vestiges of his pain.

"Thom?"

"Hmm?"

"Are you really going to be okay now?" Her voice cracked.

"Yes. I could probably sleep for a week straight, but yes."

Her chest rose and fell.

"I always knew you were unique." He spoke softly in her ear. "That description doesn't do justice to what I witnessed today, but it's still true."

"I don't know what happened." She half-shrugged. "I just–I thought I was going to lose you, and I was determined not to."

He rested for a moment, feeling the shudder of grief through her body. "You're going to have to fill me in. I'm still pretty confused about some other things." He eyed the slumbering *rifs*. "We still have our little jailers tagging along."

"That's because *Ryn*ess, that was my nickname for him, as a child, he ordered them to help us."

Sleepiness and curiosity fought, but he said, "Tell me."

Contemplating, her brow wrinkled. "The Firekind are different to what you told me. Different than Caelithian folklore. And *Ryn*ess, I'm one of his descendants. Back a few generations. And my father has aether blood, so, yeah." She broke off, uncertain how to proceed.

"Well, that explains a lot." He chuckled. "I don't think I've ever been happier to be wrong in my life."

Relaxing in his arms, her body sunk deeper into the mattress, and she began to recount the story *Ryn*ess had told her, followed by what she'd discovered; the Firekind's rescue and care of her mother, the real threat to Caelith and their strategy to fight the *nephyl*, and then how she'd pressed him to come to Caldys's aid. Circumstances he thought would end tragically had shaken out miraculously, beyond anything he could've ever guessed might happen.

"Poppy, what you did, for Caldys I–I–" He shook his head. "I don't know what to say."

"I was thinking of you, and what you would've done. And what I would've wanted someone to do. If I'd been at Caldys. All those people, elementals." She swallowed hard. "I hope they're okay. But honestly, it's *Ryness* you should thank. He said they were taking a very great risk."

"He said he would find you?"

She nodded, and he felt her ribcage rise and fall, relaxing into him. He kissed her neck behind her ear and her jawline. Her skin felt both velvety and electric.

"Mmm." She rotated so their lips could meet.

Tucking her hair behind her ear, he cradled her cheek, and kissed her – the kind of kiss made of spring and rainbows and mountains. Momentarily, he forgot where they were, forgot that they smelled like blood and gym clothes and antiseptic. The pain behind them, the pain before them, bowed to the beauty, the goodness, of the present moment. An alive sort of gratefulness coalesced inside of him, and a contentment he hadn't experienced in years settled in his bones. Everything was going to be okay.

Chapter Forty-One

The sky was black as oil when Poppy awoke with a jolt, a ringing in her ears. Nearby, Addis and Jinsen's flames wavered red-violet, subdued with rest. Thom's warmth cradled her back, and she would've returned to the bliss of sleeping next to him, if her heart hadn't been racing with apprehension.

Unable to recall the fleeting noise, or if there had been a noise at all, she lifted her head, listening through her heart-beat. The windows along the eastern wall were solid with stormy darkness, dotted with rain. Surely the night only seemed oppressive because she was accustomed to streetlamps and light pollution?

Lightning flickered across the sky and thunder bounced around the moors. She let her head fall to the pillow again.

Maybe it had just been the clamor of the storm. Or a weird species of nightmare that resisted recall. Her eyes grew heavy.

A howl reverberated across the moors, startling her. An answering bay ended in a yipping snarl, followed by a cascade of wails, drawing closer. Throwing the blanket aside, she stumbled to the window. Beyond the cold panes, the darkened landscape fell silent.

"Poppy?" Thom's voice, sleepy.

Her eyes wide, she motioned out the window. "Listen."

A stab of lightning lit up the moors, revealing a writhing darkness the size of a house, hovering at ground level. It was thicker than the night, like an earth-bound black hole. A knot of dark shapes, moving fast and low to the ground, ringed the cloud, tethered to it as though to an enormous ball of black yarn. As she watched, they broke away, tearing toward the outpost. A strangled noise escaped her throat.

"What did you see?" Yanking the IV tubing from the catheter, Thom staggered to the window.

"A weird cloud of darkness, and animals running toward the outpost!"

Another howl, nearer this time, followed by a noisy squabble.

"Djöfullinn." He grimaced.

"What?" She remembered the bloody paw print.

"Djöfull hunda. Devilhounds of the nephyl. His hunters."

He ripped out the cath and wrapped his hand in a bandage. Without bothering to button his shirt, he yanked his sweater over it, tossing Poppy hers. Her limbs seized up with fear.

The *rifs* flickered next to her, concerned. *'They smell us.'*

'This is bad.'

'Danger. Great danger.'

Lightning illuminated the moors again. The hounds had disappeared below. The dreadful black cloud lingered, bulging with anticipation. Horror slithered in her veins. *We're trapped.*

Thom thrust on his boots and tossed hers across the floor, where they tottered at her feet. "Get your coat. Hurry."

Baying ricocheted off the stone walls far below, followed by echoing snarls, drifting up the stairwells like ghouls. The snarls morphed into cackles, stiffening the hair on her arms. Shoving on her boots, she flew into her coat.

Wrenching open the door, Thom marched to the stairwell and halted in front, listening. Below, the rustle of paws mingled with slavering, harsh breaths. As she joined him, a sharp, musky smell invaded her nostrils.

Pivoting, he slid the storage room door off its hinges and wedged it into the stairwell opening, striking it with his *cydern*. The wood groaned, flexed, and stiffened, blocking the opening, splintering at the edges with the tension.

His knuckles whitening around his *cydern*, Thom scoured the room and the stairwell leading to the floors above, before whirling on the *rifs*. "Can you engulf this level of the outpost? Trap them with fire? Quick enough so they can't escape?"

Addis and Jinsen surveyed the plank floor and the interior walls, glanced at each other, and then at her. *'If Poppy helps us. We can.'*

Through her trepidation, she sensed a stirring in her chest cavity, a sensation that intensified as the *rifs* brightened with flames, the center of their chests sparking a vivid blue. Opening her hands, she hissed in surprise; her palms glowed with a similar energy, trickling off her fingertips in wisps of smoke. This was different than earlier, more Firekind energy than aether. *How?*

The door blocking the stairwell rattled with a jarring thud. Claws screeched against wood and iron and the planks groaned with the strain, vibrating with bone-chilling snarls.

She knelt before the *rifs*. "What do I need to do?"

Together, they held out their hands, fingers spread, their forms glowing specters of multi-colored flame. '*Lend us your strength. Your astrettur.*'

Reaching out, she let herself sink into the vein of energy she'd experienced earlier, suspending thought. Thom paced in front of the door, *cydern* tight in his fist. As she connected with the *rifs*, a sizzle went through her, and she yelped, more with surprise than pain. The sensation felt sharp, burgeoning with dynamic power – similar to the power of magma roving beneath the surface of the earth.

Gracefully, a membrane of translucent flame surrounded her, and the *rifs* flames billowed toward the ceiling, brilliant and beautiful and terrifying. The room darkened in the corners, swirling with smoke. Heat kissed her, enough that sweat beaded on her forehead, and suddenly afraid, her concentration wavered.

The *rifs'* remained solemn and tranquil. *'Command the fire, Poppy. Tell it what you want it to do. Speak its tongue.'*

Speak its tongue. Gripping their tingling hands, she shut her eyes, sensing, connecting. Letting instinct take over. Letting herself meld into the warm currents around her, like sinking into tropical waters. The waves of flames vibrated with a rhythm, complex and unpredictable, but personable – like a curious cat, rubbing at her ankles. Pain brushed at her skin. *Not too close,* she warned. The rhythm thrummed inside of her now. *Yes,* she told it, *you're majestic and beautiful. But don't embrace me or Thom. If you do, we'll burn and die.*

As if from a great distance, Thom shouted. "Hurry! They're breaking through!"

Crackles resonated around them, like minuscule staccatos of thunder. Along with the *rifs,* her hands found the planks at her feet, and they answered in kind. From their touch, veins of fire crawled and popped in the floorboards, like tiny rivers of spreading lava. She felt as though she saw the room with a hawk's eye, from miles away, as if it was a barren geothermic landscape, ribboned with fiery cracks, about to unleash the energy contained within.

Smoke billowed across the ceiling, respecting the barrier surrounding her and Thom. More percussions of sound, and suddenly, she felt herself thrust away as the *rifs* withdrew their connection, their forms merging into one body of fire, spreading in the room like the branches of a fiery tree. Thom landed next to her, returning to his feet in an instant. With a cry, she sprang to her knees.

'Poppy! Go!'

A glimmering membrane of fading translucent flame separated them from the *rifs*, now burning with the intensity of a wildfire. Behind them, the door splintered, clattering to the floor. Slavering hounds the size of tigers exploded into the room, their eyes reflecting the flames, their yellow teeth as long as her fingers.

'Go! Go now!' Addis and Jinsen roared, billowing with flames.

His grip like iron on her bicep, Thom dragged her up the other stairwell – a spiral tucked away in a corner. He seemed to be shouting, but she couldn't understand him, couldn't take her eyes from the *rifs*.

Why aren't they following?

Addis and Jinsen's flames shuddered and expanded, engulfing the room like a backdraft, snatching each of the hounds in arms of flames and smoke.

Pain, hollow pain in her chest.

His arm around her waist, Thom dragged her up the stairwell, into the darkness. The steps twisted and grew steep. Choking on her protest, she fought against him, to go back to the *rifs*. Halting, he grabbed her shoulders and shook her, mouthing her name. She blinked at him.

"Poppy!" His voice exploded in her ears. "We have to move!"

Blankly, she let him haul her up the stairs, her body numb. An arm of flame sprinted up the ceiling behind them, roaring. Smoke filled her lungs and she retched. They reached the next floor, Thom herding her through smoky shadows toward another stairwell.

Windows lined the next level on three sides, the panes blackened with night. A fork of lightning illuminated a ladder propped in a hatch in the ceiling.

Thom's breathing came ragged. "Up the ladder."

Addis and Jinsen. "But—"

"Quickly!"

They'll follow? Surely, they'll follow!

She flew up the rungs with him at her heels. Crouching on his knees, he shoved the ladder out of the opening where it clattered on the floor. He swung the trap door shut and thick, cold darkness surrounded them, punctuated by a strange glow. With a start, she realized the glow came from her skin, her hands. It faded as she watched, leaving them blind. Rain pattered on the roof, inches above their heads. The smell of dusty, ancient wood and smoke surrounded them. *But Addis and Jinsen? How will they escape?*

Distant thudding echoed from below. The tower trembled with an explosion, rattling her chest with its potency. Grief washed over her, pricking the elemental space near her heart. She hadn't comprehended the depth of connection she'd felt with the *rifs* until that moment, when their life flames vanished, like water consumed by desert heat.

Another explosion shook the outpost and the timbers around them creaked. Thom's hand traveled down her arm and wrapped around her fingers. "We're in the roof of the watchtower. I'm going to find a way out. We need to be quick."

"Okay." Her voice shook with suppressed tears.

"Stay on your knees."

Crawling, she ducked her head, the wood cold and rough on her palms. A flash of lightning lit up a thin space where the roof met the floor at an angle. He stopped and felt around near the edges, his gloves rasping on the timbers.

The clamor below intensified. Smoke tickled her nose and the floor vibrated under her knees. Wood creaked and Thom forced a square hatch in the roof to fly open, letting in a cold spitting rain. As he peered out, a faint orange glow reflected off his hair. Lightning veined the sky.

He drew his head back into the tower. "There's about a ten-foot drop. The ground angles against the tower where it meets the cliffside. I'll go and then you follow. The footing will be tricky, but I'll help you land."

She nodded. His body facing the tower, he swung out his feet, his breath coming in a sharp gasp. Lowering himself, he let go, landing with a thud. Rocks scattered, rolling down the incline next to the tower and disappearing off the adjoining cliff face.

Trembling, she crawled to the opening, peering out through the darkness. The sky exploded with a flash of lightning and a colossal boom of thunder. In the light from the flash, the drop looked a lot longer than ten feet.

"Poppy! Hurry!" Thom's voice sounded far away.

The floor shuddered. From outside, the roar of flame and crash of debris filled the night. Trembling, she edged out of the hatch, clutching the wooden ledge. Splinters bit into her palms. Fiery light splayed in the darkness and glass shattered. Smoke rose thick into her face, filling the attic of the watchtower.

Holding her breath, she grappled at the edge, her feet looking for purchase on the mossy stones of the tower. It felt like she was fifty feet in the air and blind.

"It's okay! Just let go!"

Her feet skidded and she lost her hold.

He broke her fall, but the momentum sent them tumbling. Thom managed to stop himself, but she careened down the incline bordering the circular tower, scrabbling for traction. Lunging, he caught hold of her coat, bringing her to a jarring stop right above the rocky drop-off next to the tower. Choking on fear and smoke, she clutched his forearm.

Wrenching her away from the drop-off, he hoisted her to her feet, and propelled her up the incline. Below them, the fire ravaged the outpost, sending brilliant flames into the night sky. The radiant heat warmed her back, her cheeks. As her heartbeat slowed, sorrow tightened her chest, choking her as much as the smoke.

Catching their breath, they stopped at a level area on the forested cliff, about even with the point of the turreted watchtower. Smoke poured from the hatch they'd escaped through, billowing into the sky, joining a plume as big as the outpost itself. The acrid smell thickened in the rainy air. From their viewpoint, the moors crawled dark and gloomy, glowing subtly in the flames.

"What about," she asked, "the shadow, with the hounds?"

"It'll have fled. Shadow-beasts fear fire."

They retreated from the cliff's edge, sheltering in the trees. The rain dropped cold on her head. Wheezing, she drew in great gulps of air. Beside her, Thom's breathing slowed. The fire's heat made strange company in the chilly night.

As her adrenaline jitters subsided, the pain burrowing in her spirit sharpened, replaying visions of the *rifs*, what they'd done. They'd known it would be too much for them, but they'd done it anyway, sacrificed themselves, so she and Thom could escape. The guilt, the feeling that she could've saved them somehow, sharpened inside her.

Thom's hand wrapped around hers, compelling her away from the fiery scene before them. "Let's find shelter."

Chapter Forty-Two

U nder an overhang of the granite cliff-face, they discovered a spot sheltered from the wind and rain. Though wet, the rock reflected the heat of the fire, making their shelter as cozy as if they had a campfire. But Poppy couldn't stop seeing the *rifs* as the flames billowed around them. Pulling her knees to her chest, she hugged them, tensing under an onslaught of sorrow, holding her breath against blubbering.

"I'm so sorry." Thom's arm slid around her shoulders, pulling her close.

Holding her breath, she dropped her face to her knees.

"They were bound by their word to *Ryn*." His voice rumbled, so gentle she barely heard it over the wind. "Even if you'd ordered them to follow, they wouldn't have listened. They just wanted to protect you."

She shook her head.

"If anyone's to blame, it's me. I just wanted to get you out of there."

"What am I going to tell *Ryness*?" She wiped her nose on her coat sleeve.

"You won't have to tell him. He'll know."

"They've been with me. Since I first awoke here, in Caelith. And even before. They...I didn't realize..." Tears crammed her throat, strangling her words.

"There's no shame in grief." The deliberate gentleness of his voice uncorked her sorrow. Her shoulders shaking, she wept silently, until her head ached from it. He said nothing, but the comforting weight of his arm was enough.

After a while, he rummaged in the pack and slid a cloth into her hand. Mopping up her face, she blew her nose. Her grief exhausted, they sat in intimate silence, watching the dance of the fire and the sparks as the wind whisked them into the sky. Muted crashes echoed from the outpost. The patter of the rain ceased, and the sky grew patchy and dappled as the clouds dissolved.

Her mind ticked over what they'd witnessed and she shuddered at the memory of the sinister darkness – at its impersonal hunger to crush and consume and corrupt life and light and goodness. When *Ryn*ess had described the shadow-beast – the *nephyl* – which had taken her foremother, she'd known it was awful, but only in the way you think you know a root canal is awful, when you haven't had one. Experiencing it, being in its presence, even from a distance, was a level of dreadful she was unprepared for, changing the urgency she felt for Caelith and the lasting survival of its inhabitants. The thoughts she'd entertained of figuring everything out so she could return to Riverston weakened every second, especially with Thom at her side. "So, that was a *nephyl*. That's what we're up against."

A grunt vibrated deep in his chest, as if he had similar thoughts.

Poppy wasn't sure she could bear to continue talking about the shadow. "*Ryn*ess said they could use someone like you. *We* have a place with them." In the dark, as well as she could, she tried to find his eyes, to discern his thoughts, his response.

He faced her. "Are you going to fight alongside me?"

"Only if you don't mind an occasional avalanche."

He grinned. "Is that a promise? Because I want to be on the side of the badass girl with the avalanche skills."

"I'm just glad to be on the side of the guy who took the seven truckers against one bracket."

"You're not going to let me forget that, are you?"

"Not a chance."

Warming her hands, she slid them into her coat pockets. Her fingers poked something substantial and smooth, and she withdrew it, remembering. The glimmer of the blue stone, glittering like the milky way, edged in fire. It gave her a peaceful feeling, like a heavy blanket over her shoulders.

She understood now; the stone closed the distance between her and *Ryn*ess, enabling a connection, even over great distances. Having a legendary *lostaja* for a relative would take some getting used to, and she had a feeling the blue stone would help with that adjustment. Gratefulness swam inside of her, remembering the expression on *Ryness*'s face as he disappeared. Her eyes went to the horizon. Would Thom even be alive if it hadn't been for him? And Deidre, where would she be?

She pocketed the stone. "They're trying to find Ayden. They have *feys* searching for him."

He nodded. "Good."

"Do you think he's still alive?"

"I do. They can use him to bargain with. If the *feys* haven't found him yet, the Grens probably have him hidden. That's my best guess."

Thoughts of her father troubled her, but she shoved them aside, remembering how he'd chosen to do the same. Perhaps now she understood why. Perhaps it meant she could approach him with the same detachment, helping her with the question of what to do next. But that could wait…for now.

The clouds continued to scuttle away on a fresh, brisk wind that pulled and twirled the flames ravaging the outpost. They'd sheltered leeside of the cliff, so they were spared all but the worst of the gusts. In the south, eerie red flashes spread across the sky. At first, Poppy thought it was just retina imprints, leftover from the brightness of the outpost blaze, but after a particularly bright glint followed a distant rumble, Thom pointed. "That's from Caldys. Our Firekind friends are putting on a show."

"I hope they're okay."

"Me too." He swallowed hard and cleared his throat. "I'm in their debt."

Watching, she relaxed against the rise and fall of his chest. Leaning back, he adjusted his shoulder and hissed, a sharp intake of breath.

"You popped your stitches, didn't you?" she asked.

"Probably. I've had worse, though." He chuckled. "We've been through a lot together, haven't we?" His voice resonated like the string of a bass, relaxing into his Icelandic accent.

She sighed, letting her head drop against his neck. "And it's only been, like, a week." His beard scraped her forehead. "That can't be right."

His face wrinkled with concentration. "Yeah, about a week."

"Sometimes I wonder about us." She traced his fingers, laced over hers. "I mean, I don't even remember how you like your coffee. I don't know what you would do for fun, on a Sunday afternoon. There's so much, we don't know about each other." She tried to find his eyes in the dark. *I don't know if I can handle any more loss right now.*

"You forget we've known each other a lot longer than Target. Now that you're here, I think you'll start to remember." He kissed the top of her head. "But regardless of what comes next, I know enough to know that I love you." Pulling back, he cupped her face. "Everything else might change, but that never will."

Relishing the warmth of his hands, she breathed in his words, as memories of him, new and old, gave shape to the ardor between them, the mysterious bond that had knitted them together.

"I suppose that's more than enough to go on." As well as she could in the dark, she met his eyes. "And I love you the same."

He cocked his head, and when he spoke, she could hear the grin in his voice. "I'm surprised you can't guess what I would do on a Sunday afternoon."

Heat rushed into her cheeks, making her glad of the dark.

"Take you to see the Maris volcano, of course."

She laughed. "You *do* love me!"

From the outpost, a burst of flame illuminated the grin lines around his eyes. Tracing them with her fingers, she leaned in and kissed him.

Much later, wrapped in each other's arms, they watched their first romantic sunrise together.

Acknowledgements

I used to think novels were birthed in glorious isolation fueled by tortured creativity and gallons of coffee. The writing process *is* sometimes like this, especially in the beginning stages.

But the truth is, success in this field doesn't happen alone. I would've given up a long time ago without the lovely humans I'm about to mention. I'm so grateful to have you in my life!

A heartfelt thanks to my agent, Stephanie Hansen. Thank you for championing Poppy's story and for partnering with me in this journey. You have a heart of gold and a will of iron!

Jess K. Hardy: I'm so glad you tweeted about "shit sand-wiches." Back then, I had an inkling that you were something special – a brilliant, witty writer and a brave woman (probably too cool for me). But you became the greatest of unexpected soul-friends. When I responded to that tweet I found a treasure beyond a critique partner, and I feel so lucky. If I could have a drink with anyone in the world, it would be you. Thank you will have to suffice until I can visit Montana. Much love!

Tommi Clark: speaking of soul-friends, you're in a class of your own, both as a beautiful human and a creative. Thank you for all the hours you've spent talking me down from metaphorical cliffs, encouraging me, and reading my stories. My life is more colorful, thoughtful, wise, and joyful because of you. I love you forever!

Sandy Holliday: You were the first person to really believe in me and be enthusiastic about my work. I wouldn't have persevered beyond beginner without you. Love and thanks!

Brittany Churchill and Rachel Lewis-Niemeier: both dear friends and powerful women, you read my work in early stages and cheered me on. Much love!

These wonderful folks deserve mentions: Sara Pantos, Greg & Shannon Benne, Kat Mancos, Suzanne Leder-Burmeister, and Meg LaTorre.

To the team at Cayelle, thank you for giving my story-children a home. I appreciate the chance to share this world with readers!

To Mom and Dad, who taught me to be open-minded and kind to others. You valued education and creativity and gave me a safe place to grow and learn. I'm grateful for canoeing, art lessons, and a big backyard for star gazing. I love you!

To Jeremy and Will: I love you forever and always, to the moon three thousand and back, infinity times infinity, through the fires of Mordor, and all the Wars of the Stars. I'm thankful for the cosplay, difficult hikes, neighborhood walks, volcano gawking, pizza nights, untiring hope, and generous patience. I wouldn't be who I am, or have gotten this far, without my beautifully imperfect family. I love that we have eternity.

FIREKIND TERMS

Aetherkind - One of the five elementalkind, the rarest and least understood. Born of spirit or dark matter. (others: air, fire, water, earth)

Astrettur – The spirit of Cael-Astrett, the purest form of love.

Asys – Mountains on the border of Caldys and Greya.

Borderland – A passage between Caelith and the contemporary world, wide-open spaces with borders that shift based on natural phenomena like the aurora borealis, volcanic activity, storms. Often located in ecologically significant areas. Rare.

Cael-Astrett – The father of elementalkind and the creator of Caelith.

Caelith – The realm of elementalkind.

Caldys – One of the five regions of Caelith, also the name of the haven city in that region.

Comfreyi – Firekind medicine

Crims – Lesser elemental of ash, born of fire and earth.

Cydern – a polymorphic weapon of elemental bone.

Cym – Elemental of light waves. Born of aether and air.

Dew – An addictive drug of waterkind secretions.

Eirians – Mountain range in northern Caelith and Huldra.

Enkka – One of the five regions of Caelith.

Ettar – A large arachnid species originating in Caelith.

Fey – Elemental of wildfire, born of fire.

Fyn – Lesser elemental of sparks, born of fire.

Glu – Lesser elemental of swamps, born of water.

Gren/Grens – Elemental of Obsidian, born of earth.

Also: An extreme elemental sect led by Sava (Obsidian earth-kind). Bent on purifying Caelith of unnusti, uthers, and the elementals who support them.

Greya – One of the five regions of Caelith

Grimsvoht – Elemental of mountains (many clans, related by rock composition). Born of earth.

Haven city – The largest city in each region of Caelith where humans and elementals could shelter if threatened by the Grens.

Havenlands – A descriptive term sometimes used for Caelith.

Huldra – One of the five regions of Caelith.

Kairyn Passage – a passage through the Eirian mountains, guarded by an outpost.

Kesili – Elemental of deserts (many clans, related by sand composition), born of earth.

Kysim – a shackle made of lesser earthkind minerals.

Lostaja – The de facto leaders of each of the five elemental-kind. They led elementals into Caelith from the Uther-Erai.

Lyls – a valley in the Eirian mountains

Mesian – Elemental of volcanos, born of fire and earth.

Michawe – Elemental of freshwater rivers, born of water.

Muiras – Lesser elemental of mists, born of air and water.

Nephyl – Sometimes called the shadowbeasts. The manifestation of evil that passed from Uther-Erai into Caelith that works to corrupt and ruin all life.

Norsen – a river in northern Caldys

Nors/Norsi – Elemental of frost and snow, born of water and air.

Offysfyn – the coalition of humans and elementalkind that defend and protect Caelith. Led by a governing council of both humans and elementals.

Orys/Orysi – elemental of wind, born of air.

Rif – Elemental of flame, born of fire.

Slagere – an indentured servant.

Slagerei – a death-bound slave.

Soldati – Offysfyn soldiers.

Steward/Utherling-Steward – The ranking human on the Offysfyn council (Felix Paquin)

Symsara – One of the five regions of Caelith

Trias – Elemental of seas (many clans), born of water.

Twin – The river in Poppy's hometown of Riverston.

Ulli/Ullis – Elemental of basalt, born of earth.

Unnusti – The hybrid offspring of a human and an elemental.

Uther/utherling – A human.

Uther-Erai – The contemporary world, separate from Caelith.

Well – The numerous and small passages into Caelith from the contemporary world. Stationary and common. Often dangerous and need elemental/unnusti assistance to pass through.

Wyster/Wysterwilds – A remote, forested region of Huldra

Xust – An addictive drug of ground elemental scales, skin, or hair.

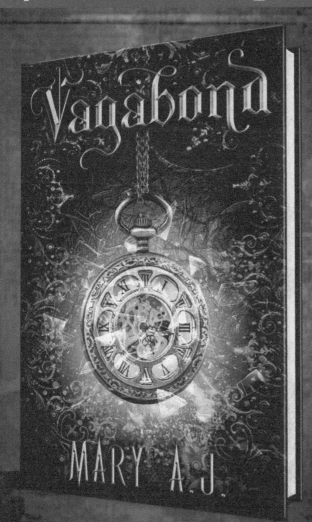

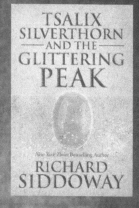